For Ian and Rohan

Ten Reasons
Not to Fall
in Love

Linda Green

Quercus

First published in Great Britain in 2009 by Headline Review,
an imprint of Headline Publishing Group

This edition published in 2019 by

Quercus Editions Ltd
Carmelite House
50 Victoria Embankment
London EC4Y 0DZ

An Hachette UK company

A CIP catalogue record for this book is available
from the British Library

PB ISBN 978 1 78648 710 0
EBOOK ISBN 978 1 78648 709 4

Printe p.A.

One

My hand reached out sleepily across the bed to touch the man who wasn't there. Who hadn't been there for a year now. Time, it turned out, was actually a lousy healer with fake qualifications and dodgy references.

On realising the date, my eyelids refused to open. I heard a canal boat chugging past outside my bedroom window. A car door slamming in the cobbled side street below. Nina's dog barking next door. Familiar sounds, reassuring me that although 25 November had indeed come around again, life was continuing as normal outside the four walls of our home.

I rolled over to the other side of the bed. To Alfie. Feeling his chest rising and falling next to mine. Instinctively, I pulled him closer. Buried my head in his hair and breathed him in. Any second now he would wake. And from that point on I would have a smile on my face. Do everything I could to make his special day a memorable one – for the right reasons this year. These were my last moments to myself. A time for quiet reflection and contemplation.

Bastard. Fucking bastard.

There is no such thing as a good time to be left but I had to hand it to Richard. Walking out on me and Alfie on the night of our son's first birthday had demonstrated exquisitely bad timing. It also suggested that he'd been waiting to do it for some time but had wanted to ease his conscience by saying at least he'd given it a year. So that if people ever asked how old his son had been when he'd left he could say 'one', rather than eleven months, which somehow sounded less brutal. And there was the present thing as well, of course. Richard's warped rationale being that the arrival of a Wheelybug, a push-along truck and assorted things to bang, rattle and shake would somehow compensate for his disappearance.

Alfie stirred and snuggled closer to me. I'd brought him into our bed the night after Richard had left. Not, as my mother had later suggested, as a substitute for Richard, but to give him some sense of security. So that he could hear my breathing as he slept, feel the warmth of my body and see the second he woke that I was still there. That I had not deserted him in the night too.

Alfie hauled open his enormous blue eyes and smiled.

'Bob,' he said. 'Mummy' would have given my ego a much needed boost but I had become used to the fact that I appeared to rank just behind Bob the Builder in his affections, though mercifully slightly ahead of Wendy. Although if he was anything like his father he would be unable to resist the lure of a capable blonde with a girlish giggle for long.

'Watch Bob later,' I said. 'Happy Birthday, sweetheart. How old's Alfie today?'

'Two,' he replied, his head bobbing up from the warmth of my armpit, his grin threatening to outdo the sunshine which had just crept through the muslin curtains on to the floorboards in the corner of the room. The pilot light inside me roared into life. It was the one thing I hadn't expected. To love him this much. Alfie wasn't a planned, longed-for baby. He was an accident. A split condom. An 'oh fuck' moment swiftly followed by a 'don't worry, I'm sure it'll be OK' reassurance that had turned out to be untrue. My main concern during the resulting pregnancy, apart from wondering if I would ever stop feeling sick, was whether I'd love my baby enough. Whether I'd be one of those mums who didn't bond and would feel absolutely nothing. But no, the moment he arrived I was awash with love for him. And even later, after all those endorphins had drifted away and I was sore and exhausted, I still felt it. The strongest love I have ever felt for anyone in my entire life. Maybe Richard resented that. Maybe that was why our relationship careered downhill from that point onwards. Although the sleepless nights fuelled by colic and then teething clearly hadn't helped.

'Presents,' said Alfie, kneeling up in bed.

'Yes,' I laughed, ruffling his silky blond hair which had been pressed flat against his head by sleep. 'You've got presents.'

Just from me this year. Hard as I'd tried to resist the competitive parent thing, I'd spent far more than we had between us last year. The main present was a wooden cooker, sink and washing machine in one. The sort of thing which had made me think they should do a grown-up version of it for people like me with a tiny kitchen. But the other present, the thing he'd really love, was a toy vacuum cleaner. Garishly coloured and the sort of plastic fantastic battery-operated monstrosity that Richard had once vowed we'd never have in our house, but Alfie would love it. And anyway, Richard wasn't here to complain.

Alfie started using my tummy as a bouncy castle. It was particularly suited to this purpose, given that my post-baby bulge had remained with me longer than the father. I sometimes wondered if that was why Richard had left. Though as much as I hated what he had done, I didn't want to believe he was that shallow.

'Come on, then,' I said, unzipping Alfie's sleeping bag to reveal his Bob the Builder pyjamas. At two you could get away with it. At thirty-four I had no such excuse, lying there as I was in an Eeyore nightshirt which doubled as a comfort blanket for Alfie. Richard had never seen it, of course. It wasn't as if I'd tried to drive him away. But now he'd gone, well, it really didn't matter if I had the sexual allure of an ageing Tweenie in bed. No one was going to complain.

'Let's go and open some presents.' The smile was on my face. Nothing was going to spoil his day this time.

Rachel arrived early for the party to help. Seriously help. Not just offer to put some serviettes out and tell me the sandwiches would have looked better with the crusts cut off, which was the sort of help my mother always gave.

'Hi, Jo. How are you?' she said as she squeezed through the kitchen door with Poppy in her arms and her floral changing bag slung over one shoulder.

'We're fine, thanks,' I said, hugging the bag and Poppy and a little bit of Rachel's left arm.

'No,' said Rachel, bending down to deposit Poppy on the floor before fixing me with one of her concerned looks, 'I asked how you are.'

'Oh, you know,' I said with a shrug. 'Hanging on in there.'

Rachel gave my shoulder a reassuring squeeze as Alfie ran into the kitchen.

'Hey, Happy Birthday,' said Rachel, giving him a hug. 'Why don't you show Poppy your presents while I help Mummy with your birthday tea?' Alfie took Poppy's hand and they disappeared into the living room together. Rachel and I had already decided that they should marry. It would make a fantastic story for the wedding speeches, the fact that they had met while still in the womb when their mothers had sat next to each other at a National Child-birth Trust ante-natal class.

'I'll put the kettle on and you can tell me what needs doing,' said Rachel, donning an apron. If Rachel was ever sawn in half by a magician, I swear she would have the word 'capable' running right through her middle. On several occasions during the past year when she'd seen I was close to breaking point she had calmly taken Alfie home to play with Poppy and brought him back a couple of hours later changed, fed and watered and with his changing bag restocked with everything that was missing out of it. Rachel had motherhood licked. I was still taking notes.

'Er, you'd better have a look at the cake,' I said. 'It's not exactly a Jane Asher.'

It was my third attempt at creating something which would pass as a train. The first had ended up in the bin, the second had at least graduated to being edible duck food, the third had emerged from the cake tin in one piece but appeared to bear little resemblance to a train. I deposited it on the kitchen table where Rachel examined it from a distance, as if it was road kill and she was a bit squeamish.

'You don't know what it's supposed to be, do you?' I said.

Rachel poured us two mugs of tea before turning to me.

'Some kind of construction vehicle?' she suggested hopefully.

'A train,' I said. 'It's supposed to be a steam engine. I haven't decorated it because I haven't got an icing bag and, besides, I'd only mess it up even more. Oh God, what am I going to do?'

Rachel stared at the cake for a moment. 'Fruit,' she said. 'Have you got any fruit?'

Five minutes later I was the proud owner of a steam engine cake with kiwi wheels, puffing banana slice steam from a pineapple chunk funnel. I gazed at it in utter admiration.

'Why didn't I think of that?'

'Because you're a frazzled single mum with more important things to do than read cake decorating articles in patronising parenting magazines,' said Rachel.

She was being kind, I knew that.

'So, any word from Richard?'

When Richard had left, it was Rachel who'd been the human blotting paper for my tears, who'd finally drawn back the curtains after I'd sobbed for a week and told me I had to face the outside world, who'd sat through more of my rants about what a bastard he was for abandoning his son than I cared to remember, yet she was still good enough to risk another. Knowing that sometimes I was desperate for a chance to unload.

'He sent a card for Alfie.'

'And is he still seeing him tomorrow?' Richard was supposed to be taking Alfie out somewhere as a birthday treat. I had no idea where though I suspected it would be the local soft play centre where he took Alfie for their monthly contact meetings. I'd gone along with them the first few times. And even on Saturday mornings when the place was full of estranged dads, Richard had been conspicuous by the self-conscious expression on his face as he'd jumped into the ball pool with Alfie. Richard didn't actually like children. Certainly not other people's. Maybe not even his own, it was hard to tell. He'd told me not long after Alfie was born that he was looking forward to him being old enough to play squash with.

'Apparently so,' I said. 'Though as you know, Richard's word counts for very little.' Richard was notorious for cancelling at the last minute. Alfie seemed to rank somewhere behind work, girlfriend, Manchester United and squash fixtures in Richard's order of priority. And that hurt me. Because it hurt Alfie.

Rachel nodded sympathetically as she spread cream cheese on a pile of rice cakes and made smiley faces on them with raisins. She'd never really warmed to Richard though she'd been far too nice to tell me so. It was just the way she'd looked at him at the ante-natal classes when he'd said that he thought two weeks' paternity leave was a bit excessive.

'And how are you feeling about Monday?' asked Rachel.

I'd been so busy dreading the anniversary of Richard's departure I hadn't had time to dread anything else. But Monday was going to be as bad, if not worse. Because the complicated bit, the incredibly annoying, embarrassingly complicated bit was that I was finally returning to work on Monday. And my new boss was one Richard Billington. The same one who'd walked out on us. That's what could happen to you if you were stupid enough to sleep with someone you worked with. Richard hadn't been my boss at the time. That would have been seriously stupid. He'd been promoted while I was on maternity leave. We'd laughed about it at the time, how weird it would be when I went back to work for him. But that was before he'd left me.

'You think I'm mad going back there, don't you?' I said.

'I think you're making things unnecessarily hard for yourself.'

'I love my job,' I said with a shrug. 'And I don't see why I should leave because of him. He's done enough damage to our lives. He's not taking my career away as well.' Even as I said it I wasn't sure that I actually had a career any more. Two years on maternity leave was a long time. I'd been planning to go back after a year but Richard going AWOL had put paid to that. As desperate as I'd been to return to the newsroom, I couldn't desert Alfie when his dad had just left him.

'But there must be other TV reporter jobs going,' said Rachel.

'Not for part-timers like me. Anyway, I don't want to move, you know that. You and Pops have kept us going this past year. We couldn't do without you.'

Rachel smiled and gave me a hug. Although I could tell from the expression on her face that she still didn't get it. But then her life seemed decidedly straightforward by comparison. She'd been with her husband Matt since they were teenagers and they were still blissfully happy. She worked two days a week at the Willow Garden florists while Matt, who was a reflexologist, looked after Poppy. They were a living, breathing example of a perfect life/work balance. And very Hebden Bridge with it, as I often pointed out. That was another thing Rachel didn't get. To her, Hebden Bridge wasn't the alternative capital of the north or the second funkiest town in Europe, or the little town for great little shops or any of the other accolades bestowed on it. It was simply home. The place where she had grown up. To me, an outsider who had moved here from deepest darkest Rochdale, only a few miles down the road but half a world away in terms of character, it still seemed like something out of a *Little Britain* sketch. I loved it but Richard hadn't been so keen. He used to joke that he was the only heterosexual, meat-eating, suit-wearing, car-owning person in the village. He'd found the unwritten politically correct constitution a bit of a minefield and had never really taken to the place or its eclectic inhabitants. I'd tried to sell it to him as the Didsbury of West Yorkshire but the truth was you didn't get people dressed in Alpaca wool ponchos asking for goat's milk in their tea and gluten-free hemp and poppy seed muffins in Didsbury, or anywhere else in Manchester for that matter. Sometimes I'd tried to kid myself that it was Hebden Bridge Richard had walked out on, not me and Alfie. But that was unfair to Hebden Bridge.

'Anything else I can do?' said Rachel, looking up from the plate of edible spiders with tomato bodies and carrot stick legs she'd just created.

'Er, just Postman Pat's van made out of spaghetti hoops, please,' I said.

Rachel looked perplexed for a second before she realised and grinned at me, her freckles catching the afternoon sunshine in the kitchen.

'Thank you,' I said, giving her a hug. 'You are a complete star and have saved my life.'

Rachel took off the apron and brushed a strand of her long reddish-brown hair from her face. We had been mistaken for sisters on more than one occasion due to us having such similar hair. Mine tended to flop in front of my face if it was not tucked back safely behind my ears. Rachel's was tied back loosely behind her neck. We were both on the tall side as well but Rachel's face was much softer than mine, her features more delicate. Richard had once said that my face demanded attention. I think it was his way of saying that my mouth and nose were on the large side.

We were on our way into the living room when there was a knock at the door, one of those rat-a-tat-tat knocks that people only do in sitcoms like *Terry and June*.

'Cooeee, anyone in?'

'Come in,' I called.

Mum entered the kitchen in a cloud of Yardley, dressed in grey nylon slacks, a padded cerise jacket and matching handbag, the type which only she and the Queen still carried. Following a few steps behind, in true Duke of Edinburgh style, was my stepfather Derek, who was wearing his trade-mark checked jacket and clutching a huge present.

'Where's the birthday boy, then?' Mum said, acknow-ledging my existence with only the faintest peck on the cheek. She still held me responsible for sullying the family's name by getting pregnant out of wedlock and ending up as a single mum, although at least she didn't hold it against Alfie.

'He's in the living room, playing with Poppy,' I said. 'You remember Rachel, don't you?'

Mum flashed her a toothy smile. Rachel said Mum looked like me when she smiled, which was true but not something I liked to be reminded of.

'Yes, of course. Lovely to see you again, dear.' She liked Rachel because she was one of my few friends who was married and had a nice job. Derek smiled and nodded a greeting to both me and Rachel. He'd only kissed me once, on the day he'd married Mum six years ago, when I'd been an embarrassed over-age bridesmaid in a ridiculously girl-ish dress. He was one of those men of a certain generation and upbringing who felt awkward socialising with younger women. I liked him, though. He'd made Mum happy. Or as close to happy as she'd allow herself to be.

We went through to the living room where Alfie was busy trying to dismantle the vacuum cleaner.

'Nanna,' said Alfie, swiftly followed by, 'Present,' as his gaze settled on the large parcel Derek was holding.

'Let's have a kiss from the birthday boy, then,' Mum said, bending down to allow Alfie to stretch up and plant a sloppy kiss on her chin. She wasn't one of those hands-on grandmas, crawling around on the floor playing rough and tumble. She preferred not to get her trousers creased. 'Here you are,' she said, taking the present from Derek and handing it to Alfie. I braced myself for what was inside as he started ripping the paper. I'd tried to offer some present suggestions but Mum had insisted she knew just the thing to get. Alfie pulled out the box and stared at the picture. He had no idea what it was. 'Radio-controlled combat battle tank,' it said in bold camouflage letters.

Rachel let out an audible gasp before clapping her hand over her mouth.

'I know, it's fantastic, isn't it?' said Mum. 'Open the box for him, Derek. Show him how it works.'

While I was still rooted to the spot in shock, Derek pulled the tank from the box, picked up the remote control and began military manoeuvres across the floorboards.

'It's even got real smoke and sound,' he said, pulling a lever which unleashed a plume of smoke from the gun to a deafening crescendo of artillery. Alfie clung to my legs and stared in awe as Poppy ran screaming from the room, pursued by Rachel.

'Can you turn it off, please?' I shouted over the din. Derek put the controls down and looked up at me.

'What's the matter?' he said. 'Did she want to have a go herself?'

'No,' I said, trying hard to sound diplomatic. 'I think the noise and smoke just came as a bit of a shock.'

'Sensitive little soul, isn't she?' said Mum. 'At least Alfie likes it.' I looked down at Alfie who was still clinging to my trousers, his face pale and his eyes wide and staring.

Shell-shocked would perhaps have been a more accurate description of his current state. I tried to phrase my objections without reopening hostilities.

'Thank you. Perhaps next time you could check with me first? It's just he's a little young for it.'

'Your brother had a tank to play with when he was Alfie's age,' said Mum. 'It never did him any harm.'

That was a matter of contention. My older brother Adam was a computer programmer who went paint-balling at the weekends, had married a real life Barbie doll and was a hands-off father to his two children.

Derek stared out of the window, obviously keen to keep out of it. Rachel and Poppy were still cowering in the safe enclave of the kitchen. I bent down and picked up the box the tank had come in.

'Look,' I said, pointing at the corner of the box. 'It says not suitable for children under six.'

'Oh, it says that on all the toys these days, it's those silly European directives.'

If she was in danger of losing an argument my mother often resorted to quoting from the *Daily Mail*.

'Well, I'll probably put it away for a few years, just to be on the safe side, if that's all right with you.'

'Please yourself,' said Mum, pulling a disapproving face. 'But I think he'd rather play with a tank than something like this,' she said, pointing to Alfie's all-in-one kitchen. 'I mean it's hardly suitable for a boy, is it? You'll be dressing him in pink next.'

I walked out of the room before I said something I might regret.

Rachel was watching Poppy pull the carrot-stick legs off one of the tomato spiders. I hoped she wasn't suffering from post-traumatic stress disorder.

'Sorry about that,' I said to Rachel. 'Is she OK?'

'Yes, she's calming down now. What about you?'

I shook my head and lowered my voice.

'I can't believe I'm leaving Alfie with them on Monday. I'll probably come back to find him reenacting the Gulf War.' My mother's offer of childcare for the two days a week I was working had been gratefully received at the time. But as the moment when I had to hand Alfie over drew nearer, I couldn't help worrying I'd made a big mistake.

'I'm sure Matt wouldn't mind looking after Alfie as well, you know,' said Rachel. As much as the idea appealed to me I couldn't possibly accept; it was too much to ask and I knew I'd start a huge family row if I told Mum her services were no longer needed.

'No, honestly. It'll be fine, I'm probably overreacting,' I said. 'You know how she winds me up.'

'A cup of tea would be nice, dear,' Mum called from the living room. I flicked the switch on the kettle up, opened the fridge and sighed.

'Great,' I said. 'We're out of milk.'

'Haven't you got any longlife stuff in a cupboard somewhere?' asked Rachel.

'I'm hardly the sensible cupboard type, am I? The only thing I stock up on is Alfie's formula.' An idea floated into my head. I walked over to the cupboard and took out a bottle of ready-made vanilla-flavoured growing-up milk.

'You can't use that,' said Rachel, giggling.

'The recommended age is for ten months and over, there's nothing about an upper age limit,' I said, reading the label before pouring a little into two teacups. 'Let's pray that she doesn't notice.'

There was a knock on the door. One of Alfie's other party guests had arrived early.

'You go and let them in,' said Rachel. 'I'll take the teas in and make sure the army has retreated.'

'Thanks,' I said, taking a deep breath before I opened the door.

It wasn't one of Alfie's guests, though. It was Richard. Standing there with his jacket zipped up high around his neck, his eyes still unable to decide whether to be an appealing blue or a steely grey.

'What are you doing here?' I said.

'I can't make tomorrow. Something's come up.'

'But I've told Alfie you're taking him out.'

'Well, I'm afraid you'll have to tell him there's been a change of plan.'

'But what's more important than your son's birthday?' I said.

'It's a work thing. Something I can't get out of.'

'On a Sunday?' I stared at him hard, trying to work out whether he was lying to me. Daring him to blink first. He didn't.

'Anyway, I just popped round to give him this.' Richard lifted up the Old Treehouse bag he was holding, which I hadn't noticed until then. It was Richard all over. Screw things up then try to make amends with presents when what Alfie really wanted was time with his father.

'We're in the middle of a party,' I said. 'I'm afraid it's not convenient.'

Richard looked hurt, stung. He had a great knack of making me feel like the baddie in this. I hesitated, hovering on the doorstep, while I tried to decide what would be least upsetting for Alfie. The hesitation proved fatal.

'Daddy.' Alfie came running out of the living room at full pelt. He must have heard his voice. Richard bent to greet him.

'Hey, Happy Birthday.' Alfie hugged his legs before his attention switched to the bag.

'Present,' said Alfie, whose materialistic tendencies were becoming rather concerning. I looked at Richard, waiting for him to apologise to Alfie about tomorrow. He said nothing.

'Alfie,' I said, crouching down to his height. 'Daddy's sorry but he won't be able to take you out tomorrow. He's got to work. So he's just popped round to give you your present.' Alfie nodded solemnly. I had no idea if he'd understood any of the words apart from 'present'. Richard looked at me.

'Can I come in?' he said. 'Just for a minute to see him open it. I won't interrupt the party.'

I sighed and held the door open.

'Stay in the kitchen, then. Mum and Derek are in the lounge.' I knew full well he would want to avoid a confrontation as much as I did. Richard handed the present to Alfie who appeared a little reluctant to open it, perhaps fearing another round of artillery.

'You might need to give him a hand,' I said.

Richard crouched down on the quarry tiles and peeled off the Sellotape. I'd forgotten what a tidy present opener he was. Alfie's face lit up.

'Train,' he said. It was a wooden train set. A really good one with a station and turntable. I couldn't say anything. Not even about the fact that I'd been saving up to get him one for Christmas. Alfie was happy. That was all that mattered.

'Thanks,' I said. Richard shrugged and stood up. An awkward silence descended on the kitchen. A kitchen we used to cook meals in together. Where my pregnancy scan was still stuck on the front of the fridge. Exactly where Richard had put it.

'Anyway, I'd better be off,' he said, shuffling towards the door.

'Daddy's going now, Alfie,' I said. 'Say bye-bye.'

Alfie burst into tears, mumbling something incomprehensible to anyone but me. Richard looked at me for a translation.

'He wants you to stay for his party,' I said. Richard appeared suitably uncomfortable. I picked Alfie up, each fresh sob pricking at my conscience.

'Look, if you want to stay . . .' I started.

'I can't actually,' said Richard. 'I've made arrangements.'

I nodded, hackles rising. I had a good idea who the arrangements involved.

'Right, well, you'd better go quickly, then. No point in upsetting him any further.'

'Fine,' said Richard. 'Bye, Alfie.' He turned and left, slamming the kitchen door behind him. I looked down at

Alfie, his eyes red and puffy. He'd only had two birthdays and Richard had now accomplished the considerable feat of spoiling both of them. 'If You're Happy and You Know It' was blaring out from the living room where Rachel was doing her best to get a party going.

'Hey, listen, your favourite song. Let's go and join in.'

Alfie obligingly clapped his hands as we went back into the room where Richard's card was jostling for position with mine on the mantelpiece. Reminding everyone that it shouldn't be like this. 'Happy Birthday, Son' cards were not supposed to come in pairs.

Two

My mum's teddy bears in aprons 'Home from Home B&B'
sign swung back and forth in the breeze as I pulled up outside the house. Personally it would be enough to send me
scuttling back to the Hollingworth Lake tourist information centre to find somewhere else to stay but on most
weekends and most weekdays during the school holidays,
'No Vacancies' was slotted on to the bottom of the B&B
sign. At twenty pounds per night it wasn't exactly lucrative
but it kept Mum happy and allowed her to occupy her
time searching for individual sachets of obscure condi-
ments to put on the breakfast table.

I stepped out of the car and went round to the other side
to get Alfie. It was only as I fumbled with the buckle on
his seat harness that I realised my hands were shaking. I
had never previously left Alfie with anyone other than
Rachel and even then it was only for a few hours, not an
entire day. The umbilical cord was finally about to be cut.
Part of me was desperate to be released from my duties,
freed to reclaim what I had left of a career. But another
part of me was wracked with guilt.

'Let's go and see Nanna,' I said in the brightest tone I
could muster. I slung his changing bag over my shoulder

and picked up the holdall of toys I had packed before staggering up the pastel paving-stoned path and pressing the bell which responded with an out-of-tune rendition of 'Greensleeves'.

'Hello, sweetheart, come to Nanna,' said Mum as she opened the door, grabbing Alfie from me and whisking him off down the hall. I shuffled along behind with the bags, trying not to knock any of my mother's ornaments from the various occasional tables and decorative shelves which lined the hall.

'Here we are,' she said, putting Alfie down on the plush fuchsia-pink carpet in the lounge.

'His changing bag and some snacks are in here,' I said, 'and the other bag's full of toys and books.'

'Oh, we'll be fine, won't we, Alfie?' she said. Alfie beamed up at her.

'Right, I'll just get his buggy from the car, in case you fancy a walk,' I said.

When I returned to the lounge a few minutes later my mother was reading Alfie a faded *Listen with Mother* Ladybird book.

'Where did that come from?' I asked.

'Oh, Derek got a few bits and pieces down from the loft for me. These are so much nicer than those modern books you get him, all those garish pictures and having to read the stories in funny voices.'

'Right,' I said, wondering if there was any aspect of my parenting which my mother actually approved of. 'You have a nice time with Nanna, Alfie. Mummy will see you later, OK?' Alfie's face crumpled and he began to cry.

Huge anguished sobs with hot tears rolling down his cheeks and plopping on to the carpet. If Bob the Builder had been sawing through my heart I couldn't have felt any worse.

'You go,' said Mum. 'He'll stop in a few minutes. They always do.' I looked at her doubtfully before bending down to Alfie and giving him a huge hug, gulping back the lump in my throat.

'Call me if he doesn't stop crying straight away, won't you? I'll come back. It doesn't matter.'

'He'll be fine,' said Mum. 'Now, off you go or you'll be late.'

I felt like a child again, being packed off to school without a goodbye kiss or a reassuring hug. I'd learnt not to expect any outward show of affection from her after a while. But that didn't mean to say that it had hurt any less. I swallowed hard, turned and started walking. Past the gilt-framed print of the Victorian girl clutching a white kitten to her chest. Past the plastic cuckoo clock made in Taiwan, through the white UPVC porch which smelled of air freshener, where I had left Alfie's buggy, out into the biting wind and finally to my car. I got in, glanced behind me at Alfie's empty car seat and promptly burst into tears. When I did eventually compose myself enough to drive, I got as far as the motorway before I realised that the *Teletubbies* CD was still playing.

I'd forgotten how bad the Manchester rush-hour traffic was. Or maybe I hadn't forgotten, maybe it had genuinely got worse in the two years since I last did the commute. So much had changed since then, it felt like an entirely different lifetime. I wasn't the same person who left to go on maternity leave. I no longer had the bump which had caused me to be filmed top half only during the last few months of my pregnancy (Big Denise, the editor-in-chief, had decided that viewers might be offended by the sight of my enormous bump). Instead I had a little boy whose excited babble I was already missing but whose arrival had seemingly turned most of my brain cells to jelly. I no longer had the confidence I used to possess either. Or the energy, for that matter. Indeed, as I walked across the car park to the drab, low-rise studios, I wasn't even sure if I would be any good as a reporter any more.

I walked through the revolving doors, somehow managing to miss my exit and having to go round another time before I arrived in the foyer. The woman on reception was new. She managed to stifle her laughter before glancing up to greet me with a plastic smile.

'Hi, I'm Jo Gilroy. I'm returning to work today,' I said in as confident a voice as I could muster. 'I'm one of the journalists.' She looked at me suspiciously, seemingly unsure whether I was joking or simply deluded. Out of the corner of my eye I noticed a certificate on the wall behind her. Presented to the North West TV Reporter of the Year 2004. I wondered about pointing it out to her to prove I wasn't a fake. That I did exist in a previous life. But I didn't want to sound like some sad, fading star rattling on about a long-forgotten success.

'I'll need to give you a visitor's pass until you get your staff one sorted out,' she said, still sounding rather doubtful. 'How do you spell your surname?'

'G for gate,' I started, before I realised I was doing it phonetically, like I did the alphabet with Alfie. The receptionist looked at me pityingly, as if I suffered from some rare syndrome she'd seen a documentary about.

'Sorry, g, i, l, r, o, y, just as it sounds.'

She slipped the pass into a plastic wallet and handed it to me, the smile getting fainter by the second.

'Second floor, first door on your right,' she said.

I nodded. Knowing exactly where it was but reluctant to actually step over the precipice.

I glanced at my reflection in the mirror in the lift. The slick of lipstick glaringly unfamiliar, my chunky suede jacket pulling across the middle button. I should have bought a new one, a whole new wardrobe, for that matter. I'd realised that this morning when I'd had to put on a longer shirt to hide the fact that the top button on my trousers wouldn't do up. But it was too late now.

The double swing doors were in front of me. Richard would be lurking behind them. A different Richard to the one I used to work with. And to the one I'd loved and the one who'd left me.

Bracing myself, I pushed the doors and strode through into the huge, open-plan office, feeling every inch the new girl, with my visitor's pass snapped attractively on to my lapel. Heads looked up from desks. Some familiar faces amongst them, some new, wondering who the hell the woman in the jacket which was one size too small for her and at least three seasons old was. Several people called out greetings or waved to me. I felt like a guest on a chat show, walking down the steps through the audience, acknowledging their welcome while trying not to trip up and wondering desperately what to say when I reached the stage where the host was waiting for me. Not that Richard was standing there smiling with an outstretched hand, ready to kiss me on both cheeks and tell me how lovely it was to see me. Far from it. He was scrolling through the lunchtime running order on his computer screen, seemingly oblivious to my arrival.

I looked across to my old desk. Someone else was sitting at it. A young man I didn't recognise from behind, lounging in the swivel chair with the phone tucked under his chin. I glanced around for Laura but she, too, was on the phone, deep in conversation with her head down. I was on my own. I hovered behind Richard's chair, realising I was going to have to ask where to sit. I was twelve years old again, though trapped in the rounded, sagging-at-the-middle body of a 34-year-old single mum. I stood there wringing my hands, my face flushed, hoping Richard might surprise me by saying something to put me at ease.

'You're late,' he said, not even bothering to look up from his computer screen. I glanced up at the clock, it was nine thirty-six.

'I suspect you'd have been a lot more than six minutes late if you'd had to feed and dress your son, change his nappy twice, deposit him at his grandmother's house and leave him bawling his eyes out on your way to work this morning.'

For a second I hoped that I hadn't actually said it out loud or that if I had, Richard hadn't heard me. But the look on his face as he turned round confirmed my worst fears.

'I'm glad you've decided to be professional about this,' he said, his eyes flashing grey steel. 'It's going to make things so much easier.'

'Richard, I'm stressed, upset and rather anxious this morning,' I said. 'I've been trying to settle our little boy and if you could excuse me being six minutes late, I promise to make the time up later.'

It was only as I finished speaking that I realised the newsroom was eerily quiet and my voice louder than I had realised. I groaned inwardly. Rachel was right. This was a terrible idea. For a moment I considered turning and walking straight back out of the door, running to the car park and driving like crazy back to my mum's house to pick Alfie up. But then I remembered that I had been waiting for this moment for two years. The point where I could pick up the pieces of my career again. Return to a job I loved and was good at. A job I'd always wanted to do. I was going to stand my ground.

I managed to drag a smile on to my face. I could see the veins in Richard's neck bulging, a sure sign that he was close to boiling point. It was the only visible indication. An untrained eye would think he was at a low simmer. Richard lowered his voice to a barely audible hiss.

'If you think I'm going to make allowances for you because you're the mother of my child, you're wrong. I run a tight ship here, I don't expect anyone to bring their personal problems into work and that includes you. You get here on time like everyone else and I'm not interested in excuses.'

I stared at him, unable to believe that he was the father

of my child. I prayed that Alfie hadn't inherited too many of his genes.

'Where do you want me to sit?' I asked. Richard glanced across at the reporters.

'Andy's off today so you can have his seat at the end,' he said, pointing to the second of the main desks. 'Get one of the others to run through the new computer system with you. I haven't got time this morning.'

I slunk away to my appointed seat. I'd never met Andy although I had of course seen him onscreen. I had that advantage over all my new colleagues. I knew their names and what they all looked like from watching them on *Spotlight North West*. And I'd had character assessments, or in some cases assassinations, emailed to me by Laura to ease my transition back to the workplace. I hung my jacket up and sat down. The chair felt wrong, but it wasn't mine to alter. I pushed Andy's things to one side of the desk; the photo of Kate Moss stuck to his hard drive I would have to live with. This was how it was going to be from now on. I felt more like a work-experience girl than a permanent member of staff. I was the part-timer, the one without her own desk who flitted from chair to chair, depending on who was off that day. It wasn't how it used to be and that unnerved me.

Laura finally looked up from her phone call, waved frantically at me and mouthed 'Hi' before doing the wobbly thing she did with her head which made her mousy shoulder-length hair fly around and indicated that the person at the other end of the phone was difficult to get rid of.

'Hey, it's good to have you back,' she said when she put

the phone down. She leapt up and ran round the desk to greet me.

'Thanks,' I said, standing up to hug her. It was only as I squeezed her bony shoulders that I remembered how slight she was. The Kylie of the newsroom, Richard used to call her, though never to her face, of course. Despite having recently turned thirty she still looked about twenty-one, dressed head to toe in Top Shop. The nearest I had got to high-street fashion lately was the Blooming Marvellous maternity shop in Manchester.

'So, how are things?' I said.

'Oh, you know,' replied Laura, the brilliance of her smile dimming a little. 'Same as ever.' They weren't, I knew that already. Going away and coming back again allowed you to notice how much they'd changed. 'And how's Alfie?' Laura asked. I pictured him sitting in my mother's living room, tears still streaming down his face. I hesitated for several seconds before I was confident my voice wouldn't come out squeaky.

'He's fine, thanks. Growing up fast.'

'You'll have to email me an up-to-date photo,' said Laura. I had a photo in my bag but I wasn't sure about fishing it out as it seemed a decidedly mumsy thing to do. Besides, Laura was not a children person. Maybe that explained why she hadn't seen Alfie since the required new baby visit which all friends feel obliged to go through, and why Alfie had been nearly six months old before even that had happened. A similar drifting apart had happened with other friends who didn't have children, though Laura's absence from my post-Alfie life had been the most difficult to come to terms with. Probably because I'd always regarded her as such a close friend. We'd emailed of course. Her more than me simply because she had more time and seemed to enjoy writing her gossip column-style reports of life at *Spotlight North West*, whereas I had nothing juicy to report. And we'd talked on the phone occasionally. Like when she'd rung to break the news about Richard and Tricia going out together, knowing that unwelcome news, if not able to be delivered in person, was best given over the phone rather than in an email with a 'never mind, cheer up' smiley face at the end of it.

'I'll send you one of his birthday party photos.' I grinned, deciding it was a better option than to risk producing the one from my bag. I didn't want anyone to spot it in case it ended up being passed around the office. Alfie was the only *Spotlight North West* baby in living memory. People were naturally curious. And for some reason I didn't want people remarking that he looked more like Richard than me.

'Oh, shit. I missed his birthday,' said Laura. 'Sorry, I should have sent a card or something.'

I shrugged. I hadn't meant to make her feel bad.

'Don't worry, he's got enough *Bob the Builder* cards to last a lifetime,' I said. 'But what you can do is show me how this bloody new computer system works so I can get started.'

Laura's elegant slim fingers tapped away on the keyboard as she ran through the logging-on procedure, which seemed designed to occupy most of the morning. I chose Alfie as my password. Another mumsy thing to do but one that would at least remain secret. I drew the line at having an Alfie screensaver.

'Thanks,' I said, when I was eventually up and running. 'Maybe we can catch up properly at lunchtime if you're not too busy?'

'Great,' said Laura. 'That'll get me through the morning.' She returned to her desk. Not that anyone seemed to have anything to do. The newsroom was quiet. The buzz which preceded the evening bulletin generally didn't start until after lunch and there was a Monday morning 'not much going on in our patch' feel about the place. The only other reporter not out on a job was the one sitting at my old desk. I recognised him now I could see his face. Simon Hough his name was. Laura reckoned he was even more irritating in the flesh than he was onscreen but having watched him on TV I didn't think that could be possible.

'Hi,' I said, poking my head above the computer screens between us. 'I'm Jo Gilroy. You must be Simon.'

He looked at me as if I'd just announced I had syphilis.

'Oh, yes. The *part-time* reporter. Richard did mention you.' He allowed a hint of a smile to slip out the corner of his mouth before he went back to whatever he was pretending to be doing. Clearly the man famed for declaring that he was 'the next Jeremy Paxman' felt I wasn't worth bothering with.

Something flashed on my screen to tell me I had an email. I opened it up. It was from Richard who had obviously decided it was safer to communicate electronically with me.

SUBJECT: assignment
What: Penguin that doesn't like the cold so keepers
have given it a fleece body warmer.
When: 12 noon
Where: Chester Zoo
Cameraman: Arthur (will meet you in reception 11 am)
Contact: Alan Peebles (keeper)
Brief: Light and fluffy 'And Finally' slot for 6pm
bulletin
Length of package: 1min 45secs

I printed the assignment slip out. My lunch plans had just
gone out the window. A couple of years ago I wouldn't
have minded. Gossipy lunch breaks had been easy to come
by then and an afternoon at the zoo would have made a
change from covering murder trials and motorway pile-
ups. But now alarm bells were already sounding in my
head. I still hadn't worked out why Big Denise (she was on
the large size, but the 'big' actually referred to her hair,
handbag, salary, office and ego) had allowed me to come
back part time. And the choice of first assignment had done
nothing to allay my suspicions that somewhere against my
name in a secret file on her computer was written 'The
And Finally Girl'.

It was cold in the penguin enclosure. Foggy, the penguin
in question, had turned camera shy and was hiding in a
little hole in the rocks, making a loud squawking noise.
Our cameraman Arthur perched himself emperor penguin style on a large rock as if resigned to a long wait.

'So, are you glad to be back?' he asked, running his fingers through the shock of wavy grey hair which showed no sign of thinning despite the fact that he was fast approaching retirement age.

'I was,' I said, rubbing my hands together to try to keep warm. 'Until I had a run-in with my new boss.'

Arthur smiled warmly.

'I think it's very gutsy of you,' he said. 'Coming back here after what he did to you.'

'I'm OK.' I shrugged. 'Can't avoid the newsroom for ever.'

'And how's the little nipper?' he asked.

I tried to block out the latest image in my head of Derek playing tank games with Alfie on the pink carpet.

'He's great,' I said, a smile spreading across my face. 'Good fun to be with if you like mini tornadoes and never sitting still for more than thirty seconds.'

'It's funny,' said Arthur, scratching the bristles on his beard, 'I always thought you were one of those career women. Never had you down as the maternal type, not in a million years. Just shows how wrong you can be.'

I smiled, trying not to feel offended. Arthur was simply of a generation that believed a woman's place was in the home once she'd had children.

'And how unpredictable life is,' I said.

'Wouldn't change it for the world, though, would you?'

I thought of Alfie poking me on the nose to wake me up that morning. And the grin on his face when I'd opened my eyes.

'Nope,' I said. 'Only the choice of father.'

Arthur laughed. 'I used to think he was all right, you know, before he became editor. I guess it's that old power corrupts thing. He was trying to tell me how to do my bloody job yesterday, where to stand to get the best pictures of Tricia.'

It took a moment before his words penetrated through to the functioning part of my brain.

'What was he doing with Tricia yesterday?'

Arthur appeared taken aback by the ferocity of my question.

'Some charity fashion show organised by that Coleen girl, you know, Wayne Rooney's wife. Tricia was one of the models, our very own celebrity weather girl.'

'So what was Richard doing there?'

'Just hobnobbing with Rooney, from what I could make out. And holding Tricia's drink while she did her bit on the catwalk.'

I took a sharp intake of breath and was about to let fly with a stream of expletives when I was interrupted by a loud squawk and a shout from Foggy's keeper.

'Quick, he's coming out. I've bribed him with some fish. You've only got a few minutes before he eats them and goes back in again.'

A few seconds later I was crouching down next to a bucket of sardines, feeding Foggy by hand as I described his designer wardrobe to camera.

'This striking-looking emperor has indeed got new clothes. Because although we might think the north-west is milder than the Antarctic, poor Foggy here still finds it a bit too chilly for his liking.'

Foggy looked up at me, squawked loudly and promptly crapped all over my suede boots. I shrugged and managed a weak smile for the camera. It wasn't Foggy I was mad at, it was Richard. Because his idea of work did not equate with mine. And as a reason for letting Alfie down, it stank. Even more than the sardines.

I marched back into the newsroom. No nerves this time, because they'd been replaced by pure fury.

'I'd like a word please,' I said as I reached Richard's desk. He turned round, knowing me well enough to recognise the pent-up rage in my voice.

'What's the matter?' he said.

'I think it's best discussed in private.'

'I'm busy,' he said.

'And I'm hopping mad. I can say my piece here if you'd rather.'

Richard sighed and stood up.

'Five minutes,' he said, 'in the guest room if it's empty.' He led me along the corridor, the polite tap of his shiny shoes on the polished floor, the irritated squeak of my boots following behind. He opened the door to reveal an expanse of blue easy chairs on tubular steel frames, arranged in neat clusters around the room. Cold and unwelcoming. Richard shut the door behind us and turned to face me.

'Is this about the penguin job?' he said.

I rolled my eyes at him. 'I don't give a toss about being sent to the zoo but pissing Alfie about is an entirely different matter.'

'What are you on about?' he said.

'Yesterday. Working, were you? While you applauded Tricia's little jaunt down the catwalk?'

Richard looked up at the ceiling and sighed. 'I'm the editor of the programme now. I have to put in an appearance at these things, it's all part of the job.'

'Bollocks. You only went because Tricia was invited and you wanted to meet Wayne Rooney.'

'That's what Arthur told you, is it?' He was rattled now, I could see it in his eyes, the guilt jockeying for position with his pride.

'Don't blame Arthur. The fact is you let your son down in order to keep your girlfriend happy and to meet Wayne bloody Rooney. Alfie cried yesterday, you know. He couldn't understand why you weren't coming.'

'But I told him on Saturday, when I gave him the present.'

'Correction, I told him because you didn't have the balls. And I'd also told him the day before that you were taking him out. Funnily enough, the boy was a little bit confused about being mucked around like that.'

Richard walked across to the other side of the room. I wasn't sure if it was because I still smelt of fish or he was simply playing for time.

'Look, I'm sorry if he was upset,' he said, turning back to me. 'Maybe next time don't mention it to him until the day I'm due to come.'

'Just in case you get a better offer in the meantime, you mean?'

Richard shook his head. 'You're twisting things now, Jo.'

'I don't need to. They're pretty twisted as they are. But at least I know where Alfie comes on your priority list.'

'That's out of order. I told you, I need to be seen at these things.'

'Yeah. And I'm telling you your son should come first.' I lowered the finger that was jabbing violently at him and grabbed at the door handle. I started to walk back down the corridor, taking deep breaths to try to calm myself down. After a second I heard Richard's footsteps following a few paces behind. The doors at the other end of the corridor swung open and someone started walking towards us. I recognised her instantly from the weather reports. Although I had to admit she looked even more stunning in real life. Sashaying along like she was on the catwalk, her trendy wide trousers flapping around her boots, the bangles on her elegant wrists jangling together, a toss of her head as she swished her perfect blond hair back from her face. She ignored me, presumably having no idea who I was, and having eyes only for Richard.

'Hi, gorgeous,' she called out.

I couldn't see him but I suspected from the confused look on Tricia's face that he was shaking his head and gesturing in my direction. I stopped as I drew level with her.

'I think what he's trying to tell you,' I said, 'is not to call him that in front of me because I'm Jo, Alfie's mum. Pleased to meet you,' I said, sticking my hand out.

Tricia smiled weakly and reached out to shake my hand as if fearing she might catch something from me. I heard Richard groaning behind me.

'Do say hi to Coleen and Wayne for me, next time you see them,' I added. 'Such a lovely couple.'

I strode off down the corridor, leaving Richard to do the awkward explanations for once, determined to hide the hot tears streaming down my face.

Three

I picked Alfie up from his high chair (where he'd been squashing baked beans into the cracks of our once-pristine wooden table), put his jacket on and got him into the buggy before he had a chance to realise what had happened. It was one of those three-wheeler all-terrain buggies that had cost half as much as the first car I'd bought. Richard wouldn't have been seen with anything else and had justifiably pointed out it would be useful to negotiate the canal tow-paths and all the cobbles in Hebden Bridge. The fact that it would be a bugger to fold up and lug about on my own if he ever left me had not been on our list of purchasing considerations at the time.

I grabbed my coat, opened the kitchen door and bumped the buggy down the step on to the muddy towpath.

'Nee-nah,' said Alfie, pointing down the towpath as he demonstrated his uncanny ability of being able to spot anyone he knew from a good five hundred yards away. Though it had to be said that it wasn't too difficult with our next-door neighbour Nina. She had the 'When I am an Old Woman I Shall Wear Purple' poem by Jenny Joseph stuck to her fridge and took great delight in interpreting it to the letter. Hence today she was sporting her trademark purple coat, topped off with a red hat. She carried the whole thing off with such aplomb that you couldn't help but admire her for it. She walked with a bit of a limp, a problem with her left hip which she could have an operation for but had decided against it as she couldn't think of anything worse than being laid up in hospital for ages. Besides which she had Dougal, the cocker spaniel trotting eagerly at her heels, to look after.

'Nee-nah,' Alfie said again as we finally drew level.

'Hello, sweetheart.' Nina beamed as she bent down to greet him, her long white hair sticking out from under the hat, her face powder lounging contentedly in her wrinkles. 'And where are you off to?'

'Train,' said Alfie. 'Reeka.' Nina looked at me for the translation.

'We're catching a train to Eureka, the children's museum in Halifax.'

'How lovely,' said Nina as she tried to stop Dougal from licking Alfie's face off. 'I've seen pictures in the paper. It looks grand.'

'Alfie loves it,' I said. 'They're having a Christmas party today for members. Santa's going to be there.'

'Goodness, what fun. My first Christmas party isn't for another two weeks yet.'

I smiled at Nina, not wanting to admit that this was currently the only festive event in my social calendar.

'Bought anything nice?' I asked Nina, gesturing at the small white paper bag she was clutching.

'Well, as a matter of fact, I have,' she said. 'I had some birthday money, you see, from my son. He told me to get something special with it. Something I wouldn't normally be able to afford with my pension.'

'So, what is it?' I asked.

Nina glanced over both shoulders before delving into the carrier bag and producing a scarlet thong.

'There,' she said with a twinkle in her eye as I roared with laughter. 'My first thong. That's shocked you, hasn't it?'

'Nothing you do shocks me, Nina,' I said. 'You give me hope for the future.'

'I didn't even know they did them in my size,' she said. 'The lady in the shop asked if I wanted it gift-wrapped. She must have thought I'd bought it as a present for someone else. I don't suppose they get many septuagenarians in there.'

'Well, good for you,' I said. 'Where are you going to wear it to?'

'Oh, just about town and to the Co-Op. Maybe to my poetry class. It will give me a bit of a thrill, knowing what I've got on under my thermals. And I'm sure it will give my Gordon a chuckle up there.' Nina gestured heavenwards. Gordon had died ten years ago. Though you wouldn't have thought it the way she talked about him, as if he'd just popped out for a pint of milk. Every detail of him was clearly still fresh in her mind. I thought that was wonderful. The idea that it might be possible to love someone so much they would be imprinted on your memory for ever.

'Well, have fun and don't go flashing them to anyone you shouldn't do.'

'The bit I'm looking forward to most is hanging them up on my washing line.' She grinned. 'Can you imagine people's faces? I'll have to pretend they're yours if anyone asks.'

I laughed, not wanting to admit that my thongs were buried firmly at the back of my wardrobe.

'We'd best be off,' I said, with a grin. 'Don't want to miss the train.'

'Well, you have a lovely time, Alfie dear,' she said. 'And come and tell me all about it tomorrow, won't you?' Alfie nodded and attempted to kiss Dougal goodbye.

We hurried on up the towpath towards the station, Alfie providing the train noises, me wondering how I'd got to the point where my 74-year-old neighbour wore sexier underwear than me.

I pushed the buggy up the yellow brick road towards the sprawling glass-fronted museum, my coat buttoned up to my chin, wishing I'd remembered to bring my hat as well as Alfie's. At the entrance I turned round and leant against the big glass door. It was the only toning exercise my bum got these days, pushing doors open. I dragged the buggy inside. It was unusually quiet in the foyer, so quiet I wondered if I'd got the right day. We zig-zagged our way along the empty queuing barriers. It was only as I got to the end that I noticed the one person in front of us. He was sitting on one of those little clown bikes, moving backwards and forwards ever so slightly to retain his balance. For a second I thought he was a dwarf, it was only when I followed his legs down to the end of his green and black striped trousers that I realised he was a fully grown man and it was just the size of the bike that made him look small. He had his back to us, all I saw was a crop of black hair poking out from under a crumpled top hat and a bulging satchel slung across a green waistcoat.

'Bike,' said Alfie, pointing frantically. The man turned round, revealing eyes so dark that you couldn't see where his irises ended and his pupils began, and a face which managed to smile broadly even though his mouth remained shut. He looked at Alfie, glanced quickly up at me and then back to Alfie.

'Hello,' he said. 'Are you here for the party too?'

Alfie nodded.

'I like your chariot,' he continued. 'I saw one like that in *Ben Hur* once.'

Alfie looked up at me with a quizzical expression on his face.

'The man says he likes your buggy, Alfie,' I said.

'Is she your sister?' asked the man. 'She's very tall for her age, isn't she?'

I smiled at him but he immediately averted his eyes back to Alfie. We were interrupted by a whirring sound followed by a loud splash as the huge sculpture of Archimedes suspended above the foyer went crashing down into his bath.

'Eureka,' shouted Alfie. It was the first time he'd ever said it properly. The man started laughing at exactly the same moment as me. A deep, throaty laugh.

'Wow, you didn't tell me you were into Greek mathematicians,' he said to Alfie. 'Do you like philosophy too?'

'No,' Alfie replied firmly. 'Like Hoovers.'

The man laughed again, his dark eyebrows lifting, the creases around his mouth deepening. He had a foreign look about him, although he spoke with a distinct Manchester accent. He was, without doubt, incredibly attractive. Although as soon as my brain registered this fact, the logical, sensible part of it sounded the alarm bell ringing. I was sworn off men for life. And anyway, he was well out of my league.

A woman in a yellow polo shirt behind the admissions desk beckoned him over.

'Oh, looks like they're ready for me. I'll see you at the party,' he said, manoeuvring towards the entrance gate on his bike.

'Santa,' said Alfie.

The man turned round. 'He's coming later. I'm afraid I'm only the warm-up act. Never mind, I'll make something special for you.' He winked at Alfie, waved an acknowledgement to the woman behind the counter and cycled through the gate as it swung open. Alfie looked up at me, his eyes full of disappointment at the disappearance of his new friend.

'It's OK,' I said. 'You'll see him later.' I hoped the man had meant it when he'd said he was going to make something special for him. Alfie never forgot anything anyone promised him.

I walked up to the desk.

'Hello, we're here for the party,' I said, handing her our membership card.

'You're a little bit early,' the woman replied. 'It doesn't start until three.'

I'd got the time wrong, it was only half past two.

'You're welcome to go through,' the woman said. 'But

I'm afraid the entertainment won't start for another half an hour.'

'That's OK,' I said. 'We'll have a wander round.'

She stamped a dinosaur print on both my and Alfie's hands and pushed a button to open the gate for us. As soon as Alfie was freed from the buggy he ran off towards the town square. I trailed after him, rummaging in my bag for a tissue to wipe his runny nose. I rounded the corner to find him standing transfixed as he watched the man we'd met in the foyer blow slowly into a long red balloon. Now he was standing up, I could see he was actually fairly tall, his frame lean and sinewy. He was wearing glasses, small, round, dark-rimmed ones. They suited him. I didn't think he'd had them on before or maybe I hadn't noticed.

'Hey, Alfie, he's blowing up balloons. Shall we watch?' Alfie clearly had no intention of doing anything else.

'You don't mind, do you?' I asked the man. He shook his head and kept on blowing, one balloon after another, long thin ones, followed by some shorter ones in a variety of different colours. He tied each one and put it into what looked like a large laundry bag he had next to him.

'I'm surprised you don't use a pump,' I said. 'Wouldn't it make your job easier?'

He looked at me as he took another balloon from his satchel and stretched it a little with his thumb and forefinger.

'It would,' he said, 'but they'd have nothing but air in them. This way they have my breath trapped inside to give them life.' I smiled at him.

'Ah,' I said. 'We have a purist in our midst.' He smiled back with his eyes as he kept on blowing.

'Right, young man,' he said, turning back to Alfie. 'I believe I promised to make you something special.' He took a silver balloon out and held it to his lips. I watched his face as he blew, his eyes fixed on the tip of the balloon, his cheeks flat and firm. He tied it and put a small twist in near one end, before reaching for a purple balloon he'd already blown up. His hands worked deftly as he twisted this way and that with a rhythmic squeaking noise. I squatted down next to Alfie, providing a step-by-step commentary for him. I lost count of how many balloons he used, how many twists he put in along the way. It took me a minute or so to realise what he was making; it wasn't until the clear balloons had been twisted into a cylinder shape that I allowed a smile to spread across my face. At last he stopped and held the finished article out to Alfie.

'Here you are,' he said. 'That's the first one of those I've ever made. You might want to keep it in case it's worth something one day after I'm gone.'

Alfie took the balloon model and gazed at it in wonder before looking up at me.

'Hoover,' he said, practically shaking with excitement.

'Yes, it's fantastic, isn't it? Thank you very much,' I said, turning to the balloon man. 'You've made his day.'

It was only at that point I realised we had been joined by some other early arrivals. An older girl of four or five, dressed from head to toe in pink, and her baby brother and parents. The girl looked at the balloon man expectantly. He took a long pink balloon from his bag.

'I'm going to make you something in your favourite colour,' he said.

'How did you know what it was?' she gasped.

'Aahh, I have magic powers,' he said, with a wink to her parents. He started twisting again, other people began to gather around, the children jostling for position at the front, keen to be next in line. With a final flourish of his hands he presented the girl with a stunning pink and white windmill. She squealed in delight.

'Thank you,' said her mum, visibly impressed. 'It actually looks like the thing it's supposed to be. Usually when you see these balloon sculptures they all look kind of the same.'

The balloon man smiled, the merest hint of a blush on his cheeks.

'I chose to do something everyone else was rubbish at in the hope that I would shine,' he said. The corners of my mouth crept up again. His quotes were so good I wished I was interviewing him.

'Do you want to go and have a look at something else now, Alfie?' I said.

'No,' said Alfie, shaking his head. 'Stay.'

So we stayed. While the balloon man created a penguin, fairy wings, a lion, a dinosaur, a sailing boat and a tractor. All of them perfectly formed but none as special as the first Hoover. The balloon man kept up the banter, all of it directed through the children, though much of it aimed at the adults. Alfie was hooked, his eyes following every twist of the hand as if he was making mental notes so he could try it at home later. Every now and then there was an announcement on the Tannoy about a new activity due to start somewhere in the museum, but Alfie wouldn't move. It was only the arrival of a stout white-bearded man dressed in red and white on the balcony above the square much later in the afternoon that finally prompted Alfie to take his gaze off the balloon man.

'Santa,' he shouted. There followed a wild scramble as a couple of hundred children surged forward, clustering around the two elves who were going to be leading Santa's festive sing-song. Santa descended the stairs and took his place at the front. I realised that unlike the other children, we hadn't actually moved from our spot. And nor had the balloon man who was still standing beside us.

'Hey, Alfie. Is that the guy you were waiting for?' he said.

Alfie nodded.

'And what are you hoping he'll bring you for Christmas?'

Alfie hesitated. 'Hoover,' he said. The balloon man smiled.

'You've already got a toy one at home, Alfie,' I said. 'And a new balloon one now. Think of something else. Something you haven't got that you'd really like.'

Alfie thought for a moment.

'Daddy,' he said.

I winced and turned my face so Alfie wouldn't see my smile shatter into pieces. I glanced across at the balloon man, aware that for the first time that afternoon there hadn't been an instant comeback. A witty wisecrack or some words of wisdom. He was standing silently, staring out of the huge glass windows. Perhaps as embarrassed as I was. The deep creases around his mouth no longer visible.

'Rudolph, the red-nosed reindeer, had a very shiny nose.' Santa and the elves began the singsong with gusto. I looked down at Alfie who was clapping along, seemingly oblivious to the impact of his reply. I knew I ought to say something to him. Reassure him that he did have a daddy. It was just that he didn't live with us. But right now he was happy watching Santa.

We stayed until the very end. The point where the elves finally managed to escort Santa through the crowds and out of the building. Alfie's face crumpled as the town square emptied.

'It's OK, Alfie. You'll see Santa again soon.'

Alfie shook his head. 'Balloon man,' he said.

I looked around. He must have slipped away quietly without us noticing during the mêlée which had surrounded Santa's departure.

'I think he's gone, sweetheart. Never mind. You've got that lovely Hoover he made you to take home.' I picked Alfie up and hurried towards the buggy park, keen to get away before he started crying. A few minutes later we were heading back down the yellow brick road, me singing 'Dingle Dangle Scarecrow' at the top of my voice to try to take Alfie's mind off our departure. 'When all the cows were sleeping and the moon had gone to bed . . .'

'Up jumped the scarecrow and this is what he said.' The deep voice which had cut in was familiar. I spun round to see the balloon man cycling behind us, his hat pressed firmly down on his head. Alfie jumped up and down excitedly in the buggy. The balloon man grinned and gestured as if introducing me on stage. I realised he was wanting a duet and it was my line.

'I'm a dingle dangle scarecrow with a flippy, floppy hat,' I sang, my cheeks reddening as I realised other people were watching.

'I can shake my arms like this and shake my legs like that,' finished the balloon man, managing to somehow stay on the bike while doing the actions and attracting a round of applause from passers-by and a squeal of delight from Alfie. I joined in with the applause.

'Thank you,' said the balloon man, taking his hat off and bowing to me. 'You were a pleasure to work with.'

I grinned back at him. Trying not to show how much I'd enjoyed it.

'Again,' said Alfie.

The balloon man laughed. 'I'm afraid I have to go now. Have a magical Christmas, Alfie. I hope Santa brings everything you wish for. And for your mum too.' He glanced up long enough for me to glimpse the light burning deep within his eyes. And with a wave he was gone, leaving only a plume of breath hanging in the icy air.

We walked on silently. My step unusually light. Alfie with a smile restored to his face, clutching his Hoover, the balloon man's breath warming him from inside.

Dan

Saturday, 11 June 1977

I am playing a game with Daddy. I am hiding behind the sofa in my orange pants. Mummy said it was too hot to wear clothes indoors today. She said she wished she could go to work in her underwear. She didn't though. She had a blue skirt and white top on. I watched her go.

I have to keep as quiet as a mouse. That's what Daddy says. It can be a bit boring. Sometimes I have to wait for a long time but I think that is part of the game. I do a thing with my finger on the pattern of the carpet. It makes a noise but only a really little one that he can't hear. He is watching the television, there are some horses racing and a man talking very fast. You are not supposed to talk that fast because people can't understand what you are saying. Grandma told me that once. I know the name of a race-horse. He is called Red Rum and he wears a noseband but Daddy says he is not running today because there are no fences and it is the wrong time of the year and I am not to ask any more questions.

I am hungry but Daddy says I have to wait until Mummy gets home from work then she will get me something to eat. If I am good she might put some fish paste in my sandwich. Daddy has cheese and pickle in his sandwiches. Mummy says little boys don't like tastes like that. I don't know if little girls like it. I haven't got any sisters. I haven't got any brothers either. Or any pets. Which isn't fair because my friend Philip has got a brother and a sister and a cat that scratched me on the nose once.

I have finished my milk. I am allowed one glass in the morning but none at teatime because the cow only makes enough to fill one bottle and it has got to last until bedtime when Daddy has some in his tea. I am too young to drink tea. I am too young to do a lot of things. Like ride a skateboard or have a big boy's bike or go to the park on my own. I can play out in front of the house as long as I don't go off anywhere with Philip who lives across the road. Philip has got a skateboard but Mummy says that is their business and something about jumping off a cliff and him being older than me. Philip is seven and a half. I was only six last week. Philip came to my birthday party. And Sean and Ian and Lisa. They all live in our road. I don't play with Lisa much but Mummy says she invited me to her party and it would be rude not to ask her. Picking your nose is rude too. And not saying please and thank you. We had paste sandwiches and Hula Hoops at my party. I ate the Hula Hoops off my fingers, they taste better like that. For pudding we had red jelly and one slice of ice cream. It was only a little slice because one block had to do for everyone.

My finger is getting a bit warm and tingly from going round the pattern on the carpet. It is brown with orange swirly bits on. Orange is my favourite colour. Mummy says brown carpets are good because they don't show the dirt. Auntie Susan has a cream carpet but she hasn't got any children. We all have to take our shoes off when we go there. Auntie Susan doesn't live in Fairfield, she lives in a different bit of Manchester called Stalybridge. You have to get a bus to go there.

Daddy is getting excited. He is jumping up and down on the sofa and shouting 'Go on' in a loud voice. The man on the television is getting very excited too. He is talking really quickly and lots of people are cheering.

When all the noise stops I hear Daddy scrunch the can. That is my signal to go. I jump up on my feet as the can flies over the top of the sofa. As soon as it lands on the carpet I run to the fridge. Faster than Stevie Heighway on the wing, Daddy says I have to be. He is a footballer. He wears a red shirt and plays for Liverpool and sometimes he wears a green shirt and plays for another team. Daddy likes him. He says he is the best footballer to have come out of Ireland. I have never been there but Daddy was born there and says he will take me one day. Daddy said that about the fair too but we never went because he forgot and we played the can game instead. The next day the fair had gone and I cried. Mummy gave me a kiss and said she would take me next time it comes. She was a bit upset too. I think she wanted to go as well.

When I get to the fridge I open the door and get another one of the cans out. They are black with a bit of white and he keeps them at the bottom so I can reach them easily. It's very cold. Daddy says it tastes best like that. I don't know what it tastes like because I am too young to drink it. I drink orange squash and I'm allowed one can of pop on special occasions, like my birthday. Pop costs a lot of pennies. I shut the fridge door and run back into the room. I have to go the long way round the sofa so I don't get in the way of the television. I give the can to Daddy. This is the best bit of the game. He says, 'That's my boy,' winks at me and pats me on the head. His hands are big and warm. His breath smells warm and fuzzy. His eyes are all twinkly. Mummy likes Daddy's twinkly eyes. She told me that once. I stay next to him, hoping he'll lift me up on to his knee like he sometimes does and give me a Red Rum ride. But he doesn't do that today.

'Finish the job then, son,' he says. Daddy nods his head towards the backyard. I run back round the sofa, pick up the empty can and take it outside. The concrete is warm on my feet. Like sand on the beach. I have only been to the beach once. There were lots of people and a big tower and I had a donkey ride and went into the sea and cut my big toe on something sharp in the water. We don't know what it was. I didn't realise until I came out and there was loads of red stuff. I didn't cry or anything. I want to go to the beach again but Mummy says we'll have to see, which I think means I haven't been good enough.

I put my hand on the dustbin lid, it feels hot. You are not supposed to touch hot things without an oven glove but I have to put the can in here to hide it from Mummy. It is all part of the game. I lift the lid up, it is heavy but Daddy says I am a strong boy. It is all pongy inside, the same smell the bin men have. I drop the can in quickly and put the lid down again. It makes a clattering noise, I hope Daddy isn't going to be cross. I shake my hand a bit and blow on it. I can hear some noises in the street, people talking and banging and things. I run back into the house and climb up on to the chair in the living room to look out of the window. There are three tables in the middle of the road with big paper cloths over them. One is red and one is white and one is blue. Philip's daddy and another man are putting some chairs out round the tables. Ian and Lisa's mummies are putting little flags out, with the same pattern on as the ones hanging from the lamp post. I think they are getting ready for the party Mummy told me about. It is not anyone's birthday, it is a silver jubilee party for the Queen. They are having them all over the country, we learnt about it at school. It is because she has been on the throne for twenty-five years. I don't think it is the same throne Daddy talks about. Nobody could sit on the toilet that long. Not without fidgeting. The Queen is not coming to our party because she is very busy. My mummy has the same name as the Queen. Daddy calls her Lizzie but her real name is Elizabeth. Grandma always calls Mummy by her real name. Like she always calls me Daniel even though everyone else calls me Dan. And she calls Grandad Victor even though Daddy calls him Vic. Grandma says I am the spitting image of Grandad when he was younger. Which is funny because spitting is rude and Grandma doesn't like rude things. Grandad comes from Romania which is a long way away and has lots of mountains. He was a refugee which means it wasn't very nice there and he doesn't want to go back.

The grown-ups are bringing food out now and putting it on the table. I can see sausages on sticks and paste sandwiches and big bags of crisps. They are yellow and green so they must be cheese and onion flavour. My tummy is rumbling. I climb down and run over to Daddy.

'Can I go to the party now?' I say.

He carries on watching the television and drinking from his can. I ask again and say please this time because sometimes when you say please you get what you want.

'I'm a bit busy right now, son,' says Daddy. He doesn't look at me or smile or anything. I don't know if that means I can go or not.

'They've got paste sandwiches and I'm hungry and Mummy isn't home yet.'

Daddy is still looking at the television. There are lots of horses being led round a big field. He is wearing his red T-shirt. Red is his favourite colour because he supports Liverpool. Liverpool are the best team in the world. They have just won a big cup to prove it. Daddy was very happy. He picked Mummy up and kissed her. Mummy likes it when Liverpool win. She says it keeps Daddy sweet.

'You'll have to wait for your mother, she'll be home soon.'

I stand there a bit longer but he doesn't say anything else. I climb on to the chair to look out again. The grown-ups are putting more food on the table. There are sausage rolls and Twiglets and everything. Someone has put the radio on. They are playing 'Dancing Queen' by Abba. I know it is Abba because Mummy likes this one. She turns the radio up loud when it comes on unless Daddy is in the house. He doesn't like the radio loud. Only the TV.

Philip comes out of his house and sees me through the

window. He has got his school plimsolls on and a red T-shirt and blue shorts. He waves at me to come over. Daddy is still busy. I don't think he will notice if I go. I will just have a paste sandwich and come back again.

I climb down and creep out of the room and through the kitchen. I open the door very quietly this time and slip outside. The air is all kind of wavy. I open the back gate and run up the alleyway on to our street. Philip gives me a funny look.

'Why haven't you got dressed?' he says.

'It's too hot.'

'My mam says everyone's got to wear something red, white or blue,' says Philip. 'Else you can't go to the party.'

I run back down the alleyway, creep back into the house and put my blue shoes on and come out again. All the grown-ups are busy doing things. I don't think they will mind if I take a sandwich. I reach up and grab the nearest one to me.

'Oi, Daniel Brady, put that back.' Ian's mummy is shouting at me. She's mean and scary. She's got hairs growing on her chin and short hair. My mummy is pretty and smiley and has long hair. Everyone is looking at me. I don't know what to do. I don't want to cry because Philip will see me and he says big boys don't cry. I look up and see Mummy coming round the corner. I run over to her, much faster than Stevie Heighway on the wing. So fast that I run straight into her legs. I bury my head in her skirt and hold on to her leg with one hand. I've still got the paste sandwich in my other hand.

'Hello, sweetheart. What's the matter?'

'Ian's mummy shouted at me and I only took a sandwich because I was hungry. They've got loads of them and the Queen isn't coming and you did say I could go to the party.'

Mummy picks me up in her arms and brushes my fringe out of my eyes. She wants to cut it again but I don't like having my hair cut.

'The party hasn't started yet, love. You need to wait until everyone sits down. Why are you out here in your pants? Why isn't Daddy with you? Why hasn't he got you dressed?'

There are a lot of questions I don't know the answer to.

'Daddy's busy watching the horses. I put my blue shoes on.'

Mummy looks cross. I must have put the wrong shoes on. She is taking me back down the alleyway into our house. I have still got the paste sandwich but people aren't staring at me any more. My hands are warm and sticky. Mummy's are too. She pushes the back door open and carries me through the kitchen into the living room. Daddy is still watching the horses. He has got a can in his hand. The one I gave him. He looks surprised to see us.

'I found him in the street, Michael. In his pants. Taking a sandwich off the table he was that hungry.'

'The boy can look after himself. He's come to no harm.'

'He's six years old, Michael. How much have you had to drink?'

'For fuck's sake, Lizzie. I've been working hard all week. Can a man not have one wee drink on a Saturday afternoon?'

Daddy sounds cross. He said a naughty word. Mummy puts me down on the floor.

'Go upstairs and put some clothes on, sweetheart. Your T-shirt and shorts are on the bed.' I look down at my paste sandwich. 'You can take that with you and eat it in your room.'

I go upstairs. I have made Mummy and Daddy cross. I can hear them shouting downstairs. I can't hear what they are saying but they sound angry. I should not have taken the sandwich. I eat it quickly. When I have finished it I get dressed and sit down cross-legged on the floor to wait until the shouting stops. I hear the back door bang. I wait quite a bit longer then Mummy comes up the stairs and into my room. She has got a red mark on her cheek, a bit like clowns have but only on one side. She looks upset. More upset than I have ever seen her before.

'I'm sorry I took the sandwich,' I say.

Mummy starts to cry. She picks me up and cuddles me.

'I'm not cross about the sandwich.'

'Can I go to the party now, then?' I ask.

She laughs and cries some more. It is like she doesn't know whether to be happy or sad.

'Of course you can,' she says. 'You wait here a minute while Mummy puts her face on.'

She goes into the bathroom. I hear the taps running. I think she is washing her face and putting her powder and lipstick on. When she comes back she looks pretty and I can't see the red mark so much.

'Is Daddy coming too?' I ask as we go downstairs.

'No,' she says. 'He's gone out.' She doesn't say where.

'I'm glad the Queen isn't coming,' I say. 'It means I'll get more Twiglets.'

Mummy laughs as she opens the door. I like it when Mummy is smiley instead of sad. We go outside together, she holds my hand very tight and finds a special space for me to sit at the table. Right next to the paste sandwiches.

Four

'Do they always do that?' I asked Laura, gesturing to the far corner of the canteen where Richard and Tricia were sitting in splendid isolation.

'Afraid so,' said Laura. 'Bloody ridiculous, isn't it? I guess the rest of us are not worthy of their company.'

I cast my mind back to when Richard and I had started going out together. We rarely sat together at lunchtimes and certainly not away from everyone else. Richard had wanted to keep everything very professional at work. Now, it seemed, the rules of engagement had changed.

'So, does everyone hate him?' I asked. I tried to position myself so that I could eat my jacket potato without having to look at them.

'Not everyone,' said Laura. 'He and Stuart are in a mutual appreciation society. Simon reckons he's a good boss but that's probably because he gives him the best stories. Pamela seems to be one of the few people he hasn't rubbed up the wrong way, and of course Big Denise thinks the sun shines out of his pert little arse.'

Laura didn't need to mention that she loathed him, the tone in her voice gave it away. Though to be fair, she'd resisted the temptation to say 'I told you so' after he walked out on me. She would have been quite entitled to do so; she had warned me off him from the start. She'd never understood what I'd seen in him and didn't buy the 'opposites attract' line. But then she'd never known the Richard I knew. The one who'd been surprisingly tender once I'd got beneath the super-cool journo exterior. Who whisked me off on surprise romantic weekends, who massaged my swollen ankles every night during my pregnancy. The one who I thought was going to be a great father. Until Alfie had arrived.

'And what about Tricia?' I asked.

'She's rather aloof. Doesn't really lower herself to talking to the likes of us. Most of the women are pretty cool on her – apart from Big Denise who has big plans for her. Stuart is obviously smitten, you've seen his pathetic attempts to flirt with her onscreen, Simon seems to have decided she's someone worth being pleasant to, Toby appears to be scared of her, Andy and Rafiq's tongues hang out when they see her but they know she's completely out of their league, and Arthur can't stand her but then again he's probably the only one too old to get a stirring in his trousers when she walks past.'

I nodded slowly. It was only my second week back at work and I still hadn't got my head around the idea that the Richard and Tricia show now seemed to dominate proceedings. Before I'd gone off on maternity leave, most of the gossip had centred around our two warring newsreaders, Moira and Stuart (it was, of course, the biggest in-house joke going. How *Spotlight North West* hadn't been able to afford the real Moira Stuart but had decided to go for a cheap imitation in the hope some people might be duped into tuning in) and how long they could keep up their pretence of getting on together famously onscreen whilst despising each other off it. But since my departure the Jo-Richard-Tricia saga had obviously been the main topic of conversation. I imagined the headline of my dumping on the cover of one of the trashy women's magazines: 'You Are My Sunshine: Richard ditches dowdy mum Jo for temptress Tricia'. He still insisted he'd left me because he 'needed space' but I suspected he'd had it all planned out. He may have left it a respectable three months before taking up with Tricia publicly but I only had his word that nothing had been going on beforehand. And as I'd learnt to my cost, his word counted for very little. I opened my mouth to say something about Tricia and shut it again. I realised I was in danger of sounding bitter. And I was so determined not to go there.

'So, how are things with David?' I asked, deciding to steer the conversation away from my disaster of a personal life.

'Oh, fine,' said Laura. 'Same as ever, really.' This was Laura's way of saying they were still happy together (she was far too practical to use words like 'love'). I suspected she was also being kind to me, not wanting to wax lyrical about how wonderful David was while I was watching my ex gaze lovingly into the eyes of his new girlfriend. And trying very hard not to mind.

'So what are you going to say when he asks you again to marry him this Christmas?'

'You know what I'll say,' said Laura, chasing some stray

tuna around her plate. Laura's aversion to commitment was on a par with Richard's. She joked that having his and hers flats with hefty mortgages was a small price to pay for not having to wash his socks but I suspected there was something deeper to it than that.

'Aren't you worried he'll get fed up asking one day?' I asked.

Laura licked her lips and sighed. 'What I'm hoping is that he'll surprise me by not asking. By finally accepting that this big domestic bliss lark is overrated and that there's no point spoiling things when we're perfectly happy as we are.'

I shrugged and took a slurp of my coffee. Not being in a position to give relationship advice.

Richard and Tricia rose from their table simultaneously and walked out of the canteen, their steps perfectly synchronised.

'Look at them,' said Laura, 'like bloody Torvill and Dean.'

'I'll ask them to put "Bolero" on the Tannoy when they leave tomorrow,' I said.

Laura smiled mischievously. 'I've got just the thing for you,' she said, reaching into her bag. 'I bought it this morning, thought it might help you to get through the first few weeks.' She handed me a brown paper bag. I opened it and pulled out a pair of Barbie and Ken dolls, complete with a little box of pins. I laughed out loud.

'So now, whenever they do something to wind you up, you just stick a pin in,' she said.

'Thank you.' I grinned. 'I'm sure they will come in very useful.'

★

The newsroom was quiet when I got back from lunch. Laura went straight off to interview a mother about her anti-gun campaign and Toby and Andy were out all day on big court cases. The sort of big court cases I used to cover in a previous life. I busied myself as best I could updating my contacts book, seeing who had moved on and letting those who remained know I was back – though only on Mondays and Wednesdays. It was good when people remembered me; said they'd be sure to put some stories my way. It made me think I could do this. Be a good reporter again. I phoned the Manchester police media line, one of the few numbers I still knew off by heart. They'd just updated it with an announcement about a press conference an hour later. I scribbled furiously in my notebook and dashed round to Richard's desk.

'They've found a woman's body in Wythenshawe,' I said. 'Hasn't been identified yet but there's a press conference at two o'clock.'

Richard looked up from the screen. For the first time since my return I appeared to have said something of interest to him.

'Right, thanks, Jo,' he said. I waited for him to tell me to get ready, to let Arthur or Rafiq know. He didn't though. He turned back to his computer screen.

I returned to my desk. Or rather Pamela's desk, which I was sitting at until she came in for the late shift. I saw Richard pick up the phone and press one of the speed-dial numbers and listen, as if he didn't trust my ears or my shorthand. Two minutes later he came over to talk to Simon. He spoke quietly, too quietly for me to hear, but it was obvious by the way Simon jumped up and put his trench coat on where he was going.

I caught Richard's eye as he looked up. For a second I thought I detected a hint of embarrassment. But if I did, it soon disappeared.

'I've sent you details about a job at two thirty, Jo,' he said as he breezed past. 'A pregnant woman with a craving for eating newspapers. Should make a funny piece.'

'Great,' I said. 'That's right up my street.'

Richard scowled at me, opened his mouth to say something and shut it again, having presumably realised there was nothing he could say. I wondered if he had actually forgotten that I was a decent reporter. If all he saw now was the woman who had carried his child. Not the woman who'd been in line to get the chief reporter's job a few years ago. Until the line on the pregnancy testing kit had gone blue.

An hour later I was standing in a chip shop, interviewing a heavily pregnant woman called Debbie about why she liked eating the newspaper wrapping rather than the fish and chips. All the dreams I'd had of getting into the BBC, maybe moving on to a national network, even becoming one of Jeremy Paxman's awkward brigade of interrogators on *Newsnight*. And here I was, in the Battered Friar in Stalybridge.

'So, Debbie,' I said. 'When did you first develop a taste for eating the news rather than reading it?'

'It was when I gave up smoking because of the morning sickness,' she said, 'I went right off cigarettes but I needed something to do with my hands and something to put in my mouth. I tore off a piece of the *Sun* one day and started to chew it. By the time my boyfriend got home that night there was hardly anything left of the newspaper. Just the sports section and the page three girl that I'd saved for him to look at.'

I glanced up and caught Rafiq the cameraman smirking behind the lens. No doubt realising that I would be trying desperately not to laugh, groan out loud or slap the woman round the face with a wet fish.

'So are you a bit peckish at the moment, Debbie?' I asked.

'I'm starving.'

'Great,' I said, passing her a newspaper. 'Front or back page?'

'I'd forgotten how good you are at stuff like that,' Rafiq said afterwards as we got into his car.

'What do you mean?' I asked, unaccustomed to receiving any compliments, even back-handed ones.

'Talking to ordinary people, getting them to say the right things. Simon can only interview people in suits. Put him with someone like that and he hasn't got a clue. He'd never have got her to put the salt and vinegar on the newspaper like you did.'

I smiled weakly. Maybe I'd found my forte in life. Interviewing people in chip shops.

The local news bulletin came on the radio as Rafiq started the engine: 'Police have launched a murder hunt following the discovery of a young woman's brutally beaten body in Wythenshawe.'

'That's the lead for tonight sorted,' I said.

'Yeah, but at least our piece will send them away with a smile on their face at the end,' said Rafiq. 'And that, remember, is what Big Denise wants.'

We gathered around the newsroom TV monitors as the evening bulletin was about to begin. It was weird if you thought about it. What other job allowed you to watch a video diary of your colleagues' work at the end of the day? It was, of course, accompanied by much piss-taking of ourselves and back-stabbing of those in the studio and gallery who couldn't hear us.

Strangely enough it was how I first fell for Richard. His acerbic wit during our not-so-gentle banter always used to make me leave the newsroom with a big smile on my face. And make me wonder what else lay beneath the ice-cool exterior. But that was in the days when he was still one of us. Before he'd been promoted and gone over to the other side.

'Tonight, police hunt the murderer who bludgeoned a young nurse to death in her own home,' Stuart's voice boomed out the main headline. He was so desperate for a job on Sky it was embarrassing at times. Particularly when he resorted to topping up his already permanent tan in the middle of winter.

'Perhaps he could sound just a little bit compassionate for once,' I said. 'Instead of being so full of himself.'

'Look at the colour of him,' said Andy, splurting out a mouthful of tea as Stuart came on screen. 'They'll all be reaching for the controls to turn the brightness down.'

It was a relief when Moira, with her altogether more

subtle Scottish tones and pale complexion, did a rundown of the other headlines before handing back to Stuart and doing that 'look at the camera while glancing occasionally at your co-anchor while he's talking' thing that producers seem to like.

'She's still smiling,' said Simon, shaking his head as he emerged from the editing suite. 'It's a fucking murder story and she's still got that inane grin on her face.' Moira wasn't actually smiling, she simply had one of those faces which looked permanently jolly even when it was supposed to be set on neutral. It was one of the reasons she'd gone down so well on Breakfast TV. Until they'd traded her in for a younger, sleeker model, that is. Moira's star was undoubtedly on the way down, as she cheerfully admitted herself. But she was still the nicest person at *Spotlight North West* and I wasn't going to let some Oxbridge upstart start slagging her off behind her back.

'Maybe when you've got fifteen years' experience on national TV under your belt you'll be qualified to criticise her,' I said.

Simon appeared taken aback.

'I'm the best fucking reporter in this city, actually,' he said. 'And when I move on to national television I certainly won't ever come back to this dump.'

Laura, Andy and Toby did at least attempt to stifle their laughter. I threw back my head and roared. A reaction which seemed to irritate Simon even more. He stalked off to the other side of the newsroom. The rest of us were still sniggering when the ad break came on.

'Maybe we can do a viewer vote,' said Laura. 'Who's the

best fucking reporter in this city? Text "arsehole" for Simon.' The really worrying thing was that if she suggested it to Big Denise she'd probably go for it. We'd already done a viewer vote on whether they liked viewer votes, that was how low we had sunk.

We dutifully sat through the rest of the programme. My newspaper-munching woman was explaining how it all started when I glanced over at the studio monitor where Tricia was slipping her shoes off. I nudged Laura.

'What's she playing at?' I asked.

'Oh, I forgot to tell you that. She does the weather in bare feet. That's what all the guys get off on.'

I looked around; sure enough Andy and Rafiq were visibly salivating at the mere sight of Tricia's freshly pedicured toes. I didn't get it. Zola Budd had never had this effect on the male population.

A hush descended over the newsroom as we watched Tricia's toned arms swirling gracefully across the screen as she indicated where the cold fronts were coming from. Her green eyes sparkled, her full (possibly collagen-enhanced) lips pouted, the little arrows at the corners of her mouth smiled suggestively without the need for her to open her mouth. At the end of her performance she handed back to Stuart who said 'Thank you' to her as if she had just given him a blow job, not read the weather report. It was at that point I realised I had no idea whether I needed to wrap up warm or bring a brolly the next day. I suspected half the population of Manchester (the male half) regularly got caught out in this way. She oozed sex. From her 'come to bed' eyes down to her manicured toes. There was no way I could have ever competed with that.

I heard Tricia's girlish giggle before she emerged into the newsroom. Richard was walking a few paces behind her – whether it was something he'd said which had prompted the laughter I couldn't be sure. But what was clear was the way Richard was looking at her. The tooth-paste advert smile lighting up his face. His eyes decidedly blue now and unable to focus on anyone but her. A way I liked to think he'd looked at me once. But couldn't be sure he ever had. I turned away. Not wanting either of them to see how much that hurt.

We filed into Big Denise's leather-clad office for the debriefing. It was similar to being lined up before a firing squad, though probably more brutal. The sole point of the exercise appeared to be mass public humiliation – quite which management guru had espoused such an approach I wasn't sure.

Big Denise had learnt to do that little praise sandwich thing, so there was always a good word for someone at the beginning and at the end, but unfortunately the sandwich was made of wafer thin slices of Nimble bread with a huge 'eat as much as you can' style filling of abuse in between.

Simon received the opening plaudit for his murder report, before Big Denise pushed her dark-rimmed glasses further up the bridge of her nose and launched into a sting-ing attack on Roger, one of the producers, about some supposed cock-up with the regional round-up which I hadn't even noticed. We had all learnt to our cost that there was no point arguing with her. The best strategy was simply to nod and look rueful. That way we would at least stand a chance of getting out of the office before seven. And right now that was all I wanted to do. To rescue Alfie from my mother's attempts to fatten him up on fondant fancies and get him home to bed. I wasn't even listening, to be honest, which was why Laura had to elbow me a few minutes later. I looked up. Big Denise was talking to me. I braced myself for the barrage of abuse which was about to come my way.

'Making something out of nothing like that is a real skill, Jo. And you looked as if you were enjoying it. The rest of you please take note.' It took a few seconds for the words to sink in. It was only as everyone else started drifting away that it dawned on me that I had just received a compliment from her. I started smiling. Big Denise strode up to me and slapped me on the back manfully.

'Good to have you back, Jo. How's the little one?' I opened my mouth to reply but Big Denise carried straight on.

'When are we going to see you back full time? Not long, I hope?'

'Er, well, I'll have to see how it goes.'

'Don't leave it too long. It doesn't pay to get left behind when there are all these bright young things snapping at your heels.' Big Denise didn't have any children. And she'd just made it perfectly clear that I was going to be stuck on 'And Finally' stories until I went back full time.

'Right. Thanks,' I said. There was an awkward silence. Big Denise never seemed to close a conversation so you ended up having to do it yourself and hoping you didn't seem rude in the process.

'See you next week, then,' I said. She nodded and returned to her desk.

'Bloody hell,' said Laura, when I finally emerged from the office. 'Looks like you're flavour of the month.'

'You can't beat a good chip story,' I said. 'We'll be asking viewers to text "salt" or "vinegar" tomorrow.'

'So, what did she say to you?'

'Oh, just that I'll be doing a lot more chip shop stories unless I come back full time.'

'So it was the build you up to knock you straight back down again thing.'

'Yep, 'fraid so.' I shrugged and pulled my coat on, picked up my bag and was about to head for the door when I was aware of a dark shadowy presence behind me. I turned round to find Richard hovering uncomfortably, trying to remember how to smile at me.

'Can I have a quick word? It's about Christmas,' he said. Somehow I knew he was not about to suggest a festive get-together and sing-along.

'Oh. What about it?'

'We were wondering if Alfie could sleep over on Boxing Day.'

This was not what I expected. Richard had never asked to have more contact with Alfie than the one morning a month he had suggested after the split. The Boxing Day arrangement had been my suggestion, mainly because I had always got on well with Richard's parents and wanted Alfie to have some sort of relationship with his paternal grandparents. For a moment I was pleased, for Alfie's sake, that Richard was at least showing some interest in his son.

'Oh, I didn't think your parents were staying over.'

'Er, no. They're not. But it would be nice if we could relax and have a drink and not worry about having to drive him home.' I realised from the way he looked down at his feet who the 'we' actually referred to.

'You didn't say *she* was going to be there.'

'I thought it would be obvious.'

'So, let me get this right. You're asking if it's OK if the son you walked out on can stay over at your place so you can have a drink and some extra shagging time with your girlfriend?' I was aware my voice had taken on a slightly hysterical tone but I couldn't shake the image of the three of them together from my head. Richard looked around the newsroom, where the others were taking an extraordinarily long time getting their coats on, and lowered his voice, presumably expecting me to do the same.

'That is not what it's about, Jo. Tricia's an important part of my life and she's keen to meet Alfie.'

'So where are you proposing he sleeps?'

'Haven't you got one of those travel cots?'

'I meant which room.'

'In with us, I guess. You know I've only got one bedroom.'

'And how do you think Alfie would take to spending his first night away from his mother in a room where his father is sharing a bed with some woman he's never met before?'

'I don't know why you're making it sound like such a big deal, Jo.'

'Because it is a big deal for a two year old who still doesn't understand why Daddy doesn't live with him any more.'

'I think you're being over-protective.'

'And I think you haven't got a fucking clue! You bring him back by seven thirty as we agreed. And it's just you and your parents. No Tricia. End of story.'

I stormed out of the newsroom, the momentum taking me straight past Laura who'd been loitering in the corridor outside.

'Hey, slow down. What was all that about?'

'Him, wanting to play happy families with Alfie and Tricia,' I said, trying not to show how upset I was.

'I'd have thought you'd have been glad of the break.'

I shook my head. 'If he had Alfie's best interests at heart I wouldn't mind but as usual he's just being a selfish bastard.'

'Why don't we go for a drink somewhere? It sounds like you need to unwind.'

I smiled gratefully and was about to agree when I remembered it didn't work like that any more. I had Alfie.

'Sorry, I can't. Alfie will be tired. I need to get him home to bed.' I smiled again at Laura, appreciating her concern before I dashed off, wishing I'd had time to stick a pin in my voodoo Ken and Barbie.

Five

'So, are things getting any easier at work?' asked Rachel as we hurried along the road, bumping Alfie and Poppy over the cobbles in their buggies.

'No. You were right,' I said. 'Watching Richard and Tricia together is like putting myself through a mangle every day.'

'So hand in your notice and look for something else. I can ask at the florists if they've got any part-time work over Christmas.'

I smiled at Rachel. 'Can you see me arranging a bunch of azaleas?'

'Azaleas are pot plants, they don't come in bunches.'

'There you go, my point exactly. I don't know the first thing about flowers and I can't even tie a bow on a Christmas present, let alone a bouquet.'

'So what are you going to do?'

'Learn to live with it, I guess. Maybe I could develop masochistic tendencies so I could appreciate my work more fully.'

'You don't have to put yourself through this, Jo.' Rachel frowned, still not understanding.

'I'm a TV news reporter. It's what I've always wanted to

do and he's not going to stop me doing it,' I said. 'Anyway, it's probably good for me. When you don't see your ex you do the rose-tinted spectacles thing and only remember the good things about them. When you have to work with them every day you see all the annoying, irritating things that used to wind you up. It could become the new therapy of choice for getting over a break-up, working with your ex and his new girlfriend.'

Rachel smiled and gave me one of her 'I love you dearly but I don't understand you' looks as we crossed over the road and hauled the buggies up the steps of the church hall. To be honest, it wasn't seeing Richard and Tricia together which had been the worst thing these past few weeks. The thing I couldn't get my head around was how I could have been so wrong about someone in the first place. Even allowing for the fact that Richard had changed in the past two years, and that good-looking guys can get away with the odd personality defect, it still didn't let my judgement off the hook. I'd fallen for the wrong guy. For someone who I didn't even like any more.

'Alfie, how lovely to see you. And Poppy. What a beautiful hat.' Hermione always managed to sound genuinely enthusiastic when she welcomed the members of the Little Acorns group, her grey-streaked ponytail swinging gaily behind her. She was, according to the flyer, an experienced music and drama teacher who delighted in 'awakening the senses and taking your little ones on a magical journey which stimulates their minds and bodies'. Which, translated into mum-speak, meant, 'They get to run around, make a lot of noise and pretend to be fruit bats.' Rachel had persuaded me to come a few months after Richard had left. She thought it would be good for us to get out of the house and meet other parents and children. I suspected she had the ulterior motive of trying to set me up with Brendan, the group's token single father (his partner had run off with a woman, which even in Hebden Bridge was a tad unusual) who, although I felt sorry for him, was the person least likely to cheer anyone up or take their mind off a broken heart.

'Hi, Brendan,' said Rachel as she joined the circle of two on the floor. 'How's Reuben?'

'He's not himself. I think he's coming down with something.'

I looked at Reuben, who was happily singing a little song to himself and appeared to be in the peak of good health. I knew I worried too much about Alfie sometimes but Brendan made me feel positively laidback in comparison.

Rachel nodded in an impressively sympathetic fashion as Poppy sat down next to her. Alfie, not being a 'sitting quietly in a circle' type of child, continued to career around the hall at breakneck speed, occasionally stopping to see if the pile of chairs at the side would topple over if he tried to pull the bottom one out.

The door jerked open again and little Zach steamed in, followed by a breathless Nicole.

'Hi, sorry we're late. Earth Elves overran again,' said Nicole. She wasn't actually late, Nicole simply laboured under the impression that she was permanently running late because she spent her life rushing between various toddler classes with Zach. We'd tried Earth Elves once but neither I nor Alfie were keen. It involved the chanting of New Age-style mantras and a lot of tree-hugging and sermons on compulsory recycling by a guy who made David Icke look positively mainstream. I hadn't yet worked out whether Nicole was one of those reluctant career-woman mums who had to keep busy because she couldn't bear the thought of being at home with her child or whether she genuinely believed in hot-housing from a young age. Either way, Zach appeared suitably dazed and confused by his packed schedule. Once when I'd asked him how he was he'd sighed with an air of resignation and said, 'Always late.'

Suzanne was next to arrive with Darcy (who was two and undeniably cute) and Elouise (who was Satan cunningly disguised as a four year old festooned in pink frills). While Suzanne was taking Darcy's shoes and coat off, Elouise sauntered up to Reuben and, with the casualness of a seasoned football hooligan, whacked him over the head with the plastic fairy wand she was carrying. Reuben's howl alerted Suzanne to the crime and Elouise's proximity and the 'it wasn't me, I didn't do it' expression gave the game away.

'Elouise, look, you've hurt Reuben. What do you say to him?'

'Sorry,' said Elouise, grinning and clearly not meaning it.

'Brendan, I am so sorry. Is he OK?' asked Suzanne.

Brendan pulled an emergency first-aid kit from his rucksack and began applying arnica cream to Reuben's scalp.

'I don't know. There's a nasty bump coming and he seems a bit dazed.' He bent down to examine Reuben more closely and as he did so his rucksack swung down off his shoulder and bashed Reuben on the other side of his head. I looked hard at the floor, trying desperately not to laugh. Rachel's shoulders were shaking. Even Reuben, who was clearly fine, seemed to find it amusing although Brendan looked as if he might burst into tears at any moment.

Hermione did what only she could do, clapped her hands and said, 'OK, everyone, let's sing the welcome song.'

The children dutifully curled up on the floor as we started singing, 'Tiny little acorns planted in the ground, feel the sun, hear the rain, jump up and run around.'

I did, of course, regularly question what had become of my life while attending Little Acorns classes. Three years ago I would have laughed myself silly if anyone had suggested that this was how I would spend my Thursday afternoons. But then three years ago I had no desire to have children and believed that unplanned pregnancies didn't happen to women like me. I sometimes imagined a parallel life, the one I would have lived if I hadn't got pregnant. Where I'd still be covering the top stories or maybe even working for one of the national networks. The pictures I saw in my head were fuzzy around the edges but I was there all right. I had a waist and an expensive-looking coat and no bags under my eyes when I talked into the camera. I looked like a serious journalist. Someone who was going places. Who was making a name for herself.

'Boo.' Alfie hurtled into me with an unfeasibly large grin on his face, bringing me back to reality and reminding me that I couldn't and wouldn't want to imagine life without him now. But as I stretched up and pretended to be an oak tree swaying in the breeze, I couldn't help wondering what story Laura was working on. And whether I'd ever get a sniff of a big exclusive again.

We walked back along the canal afterwards, Alfie and Poppy quacking loudly every time they saw a duck and attracting smiles and comments from elderly ladies shuffling along the muddy towpath in totally unsuitable beige court shoes. It was a bit like having a dog, being the parent of a toddler. It gave people a reason to engage in conversation, although they tended to talk to Alfie, not me. Suddenly Alfie pointed and jiggled about in his buggy shouting, 'Balloon man, balloon man.' I followed the direction of his finger to the red and yellow harlequin-patterned canal boat which was moored up alongside the pumping station. Standing on the back of the boat was a tall man wearing frayed jeans with a hole in one knee, black boots and a black beanie hat pulled down over his hair. It was the dark eyebrows and glittering eyes beneath that I remembered. We stared at each other for a second. I realised that I was smiling and that I was almost as pleased to see him as Alfie was.

'Balloon man,' Alfie shouted again.

'Hello again, Alfie,' he said. I was surprised he remembered Alfie's name, he must meet an awful lot of kids in his line of work. I glanced across at Rachel who was looking at me expectantly, waiting for an introduction. I turned back to the boat.

'Hi,' I said. 'Sorry, I don't know your name. We only know you as the balloon man.'

He smiled. 'Dan,' he said. 'But Alfie can stick with the balloon man if he wants.'

'I'm Jo, Alfie's mum.' This was, of course, blindingly obvious. I was unexpectedly floundering. 'And this is my friend Rachel and her daughter Poppy,' I added quickly.

Dan took off his hat, exposing his dark thatch of hair, and bowed to them theatrically.

'Delighted to meet you,' he said. 'Alfie and I are old friends.'

'Dan provided the entertainment at the Eureka Christmas party,' I explained to Rachel.

'Hoover,' said Alfie.

'He's still got it,' I said, turning back to Dan. 'Plays with it every day, it hasn't gone down at all yet.'

'Hoover,' said Alfie again, this time pointing to a large pipe from the pumping station which disappeared into the cabin of Dan's boat, from where a noisy whirring sound was emanating.

'Aahh, I see where you're coming from,' said Dan. 'It's actually a giant hosepipe, Alfie. I'm pumping out the contents of my toilet. I'm sure you and me could have a good conversation about domestic waste matters.'

'Noo-noo,' said Alfie.

Dan laughed before proceeding to put his arm up and make a loud sucking sound as he gave a very good impression of Noo-noo from the Teletubbies. Alfie and Poppy rocked with laughter in their buggies. Rachel turned to me and smiled, clearly impressed.

'See pump,' said Alfie, who had no qualms about inviting himself anywhere he wanted to go.

'Oh, Dan's busy, Alfie,' I said. 'We'd better let him get on.'

'It's OK,' said Dan. 'I'll be here for another hour or so yet. You're welcome to come aboard and have a look, although it's not very fragrant down there.'

Alfie nodded enthusiastically and tried to edge his buggy closer to the boat. I put the brake on and looked across at Rachel.

'I can't, I'm afraid,' she said. 'I need to get some shopping in for tea. But you go.'

We were having alphabet spaghetti out of a tin for tea. I had no ready-made excuse. Other than that my mother had always told me not to accept invitations on to strange men's boats, of course.

'On boat,' said Alfie.

'Er, well, if you're sure it's OK?'

'Be my guest,' said Dan. 'Here, let me help you with the buggy.' He jumped down off the boat while I took Alfie out, watched carefully as I showed him how it collapsed then carried it on to the boat.

'Say goodbye to Rachel and Poppy, Alfie.'

'Bye-bye,' said Alfie without so much as a backwards glance.

'See you soon, have fun,' said Rachel. She was looking at me when she said it. I knew exactly what she was thinking and attempted to give a discreet visual rebuttal before she carried on up the towpath.

'Would you like me to take Alfie?' asked Dan.

'It's OK, thanks,' I said, bending to pick him up and hovering uncertainly on the towpath.

'Here, let me help,' said Dan holding out his hand to

me. The boat bobbed down as I stepped aboard on to the welcome mat, clutching Alfie to me. I felt Dan's hand grip mine as I stumbled before steadying myself.

'It's OK,' I said to Alfie. 'Mummy's legs went a bit wobbly there.'

Dan pretended to lose his balance too, staggering exaggeratedly from one side of the boat to the other, Alfie started laughing.

'He likes you,' I said.

'Probably because I'm a big kid at heart. We're on the same wavelength. It's usually the parents who think I'm a bit odd.'

I smiled, not wanting to admit that the last thought which had gone through my head was, 'I hope he's not a paedophile.' I told my inner journalist to shut up. That not every man who chose to work with kids had questionable motives.

'So you're strictly a children's entertainer, are you?' I asked.

'I do adult functions every now and again,' said Dan. 'But they invariably involve people getting drunk and asking me to make rude things with balloons and it all gets rather boring after a while.' I suspected he had a point. That actually it was those who spent their time creating a succession of outsized male members and Jordanesque boobs who were the ones to worry about.

Alfie was tugging on my hand, desperate to go down into the living quarters.

'Sorry, Alfie, you were wanting to see where that pipe goes, weren't you?' said Dan.

'Yes,' said Alfie, nodding firmly.

'Let's go then. Mind your heads as you come down.' Dan pulled open the double doors which led down a small flight of wooden steps. I followed his example and walked down backwards, holding Alfie's hand as he negotiated the steps.

'Well, this is it,' said Dan.

I gazed around me at the Shaker-style wood panelling and the burnt-orange walls which were dotted with clip-framed black-and-white photographs of sunrises and sunsets over canals. A black cat was curled up on one of the two easy chairs and a small coal-burning stove was giving off an impressively warm glow. I had expected it to look more bohemian, more like Dan, perhaps. But this was positively homely.

'This is great,' I said. 'Are they yours?' I asked, pointing to the photographs.

'Oh, I dabble a little.'

'They're really good.'

'Thanks,' he said. The cat yowled and jumped off the chair as Alfie gave it an unceremonious waking.

'Alfie,' I said, dragging him away. 'We don't pull tails, you know that.'

'It's OK,' said Dan. 'Sinbad's not very sociable at the best of times. He's a bit of a loner.'

I looked around. There was only one chair at the tiny table. One plate and set of cutlery on the kitchen drainer. No evidence of another person's presence.

'How long have you lived here?' I asked. I was slipping into reporter mode again; what I always did when I was unsure of what to say.

'Nearly eight years,' said Dan, rubbing the stubble on his chin.

'Wow. I'd always thought living on a boat was something people probably did for a year or so until the novelty wore off and they got fed up with all the hard work.'

Dan shrugged. 'I guess I'm not most people.'

'But don't you ever want to put down roots?'

'My roots are in the water,' he said, pausing a second to look out of the window. 'Anyway,' he continued more brightly, 'if I got a mortgage I'd have to get a proper job and I love doing what I do too much to give it up.'

I nodded. Understanding entirely.

'So where do you store all your work stuff?' I hadn't noticed the bike on my way in.

'I have a shed, up at Mayroyd where I'm moored.'

'It's not one of those sheds with net curtains and carpet inside, is it?' I asked with a grin.

'No,' said Dan, laughing. 'Although it does provide a very nice home for a family of spiders.'

'Music,' said Alfie, pointing at a car radio which was embedded in the wooden panelling.

'That's right. I need little versions of everything on my boat, you see, Alfie. Things that don't use much power. Apart from the toasted sandwich maker which is my one luxury item. Have you ever had a toasted cheese sandwich?' Alfie shook his head. 'Well, I must make you one sometime. I do paste sandwiches too. Children have all the best sandwiches.'

'Noo, noo,' said Alfie, pointing in the direction of the pumping noise.

'I'm sorry, there's me wittering on and you're desperate to check out the plumbing arrangements. Let's go and have a look and I'll tell you how it all works.'

Alfie grabbed Dan's hand and led him off to the far end of the boat. I smiled. An aching sort of smile, for all the times Alfie would have taken Richard's hand but he wasn't there. I followed them down, past Dan's bed, which had a porthole window to one side and a multicoloured throw over the top. I found myself checking to see if there were two pillows – there weren't – then stopped myself. What on earth was I thinking of? I was supposed to have quit men. And here I was checking out his availability, like some sad teetotaller gazing longingly behind the bar.

When I reached the bathroom, Dan was crouched down explaining the finer points of sanitation to a fascinated Alfie.

'Sorry,' said Dan, glancing up at me. 'I'm not a very good host, am I? I'm entertaining you in the toilet and I haven't offered you a drink or anything.'

'It's OK. Alfie invited himself onboard, remember. Anyway, we should be going soon. I'm sure you've got things to do.'

The expression on Dan's face suggested he hadn't and that he was disappointed.

'Juice,' said Alfie, who didn't miss a word and was obviously keen to prolong our stay. Dan smiled.

'Sorry, we haven't mastered manners yet,' I said.

'It's OK. Manners are overrated. The Queen's polite but I wouldn't want her to tea. She might bring the corgis with her. Or Prince Philip.'

I smiled as he stood up. I couldn't help it.

'One orange juice coming up, Alfie. What do you think your mummy would like to drink?'

'Tea,' said Alfie.

Dan turned to look at me for confirmation.

'No, honestly. I'm fine, thanks. We really do need to be heading back soon.'

We followed Dan back into the living area. As soon as Sinbad saw Alfie approaching he jumped up and squeezed through the cat flap at the end of the boat, no doubt fearing another unwarranted assault. Alfie craned his neck up to the window, trying to see where he'd gone.

'Sinbad splash?' he enquired.

Dan grinned as he took a carton of juice from the fridge. 'No, Sinbad doesn't like swimming. Look, he's on the ledge, see.' Alfie followed Dan's finger to where Sinbad was perched outside one of the windows, washing himself in the sunshine.

'Has he ever fallen in?' I asked.

'Let's just say he's only got six lives left.'

'You'll have to get him a little cat life jacket. Or his own lifeboat.'

Dan smiled and handed a full glass of orange juice to Alfie. I knelt down to hold it for him as he sloshed some down his jacket.

'Sorry, I've put too much in, haven't I?' said Dan.

'It's OK,' I said. 'But yes, about a third of that would do next time.' I felt my cheeks redden. Of course there wouldn't be a next time. Alfie had invited himself on to a balloon man's boat to have a look at the toilet being pumped out. That was it. End of story. I let Alfie take a few more sips and as soon as he started trying to blow bubbles, removed the glass and placed it back on the kitchen counter.

'Right, well, we'd better be off. Thanks ever so much for showing us around. Say goodbye to Dan, Alfie.'

Alfie screwed up his face and started to howl. Dan looked at me in alarm.

'Hey, it's OK, Alfie,' I said. 'Maybe we'll see Dan's boat from the towpath one day. We'll have to keep a lookout, won't we?'

Alfie shook his head. 'Boat ride,' he wailed.

I looked up at the ceiling and sighed, annoyed at myself that I hadn't realised what he'd been expecting. I opened my mouth to begin to explain but Dan got in first.

'I'm really sorry, Alfie,' said Dan. 'I haven't got time today. And I'm flat out with work from tomorrow until Christmas, then I expect you'll be busy opening all your presents and seeing your folks.'

Alfie's bottom lip trembled, his eyes watched Dan intently, hanging on his every word. It was only a temporary cessation of the tears, I knew that. Dan was going to have to pull something out of the hat in the next few seconds.

'So ...' Dan glanced up at me. I wasn't sure if he was looking for inspiration or confirmation that he was doing OK. I nodded, although I had no idea what I was agreeing to.

'I'm inviting you on a New Year's Eve boat ride. A few days after Father Christmas has been. We'll go through locks and tunnels, the whole works. What do you say?'

I waited with Dan. The dam wall held. A glimmer of a

smile even. And then Alfie nodded. Clearly he had no comprehension of how far away New Year's Eve was and I suspected I would have to spend the next three weeks telling Alfie that no, it wasn't today. But he was happy.

'Thank you,' I said to Dan as Alfie busied himself trying to pull the tassels off a rug on the far side of the room. 'You really didn't have to do that, you know.'

'I did. I couldn't have slept tonight, otherwise. Did you see his face?'

I smiled, surprised and touched by his concern.

'He would have got over it with the promise of a *Bob the Builder* DVD later, but thank you for saving me from the bribe.'

'It is OK with you, isn't it?' asked Dan. 'I hope I haven't messed up any plans you'd made.'

I wasn't about to admit to Dan how the only events in my diary were for under-threes.

'Not at all. It's great. Give him something special to look forward to after Christmas.'

Dan nodded. I shuffled my feet. Dan looked as if he was about to say something then looked down at the floor.

'Right. Well, we'll see you then,' I said. 'Where shall we meet you?'

'Along here's good for me, as long as that's OK with you?'

'Great, we're only in Eton Street, a few minutes that way,' I said, pointing down the canal.

'About tennish suit you?'

'That sounds fine. Do you want my mobile number?' I groaned inwardly as I said it, aware that it must have sounded like a sad come-on from a desperate single mum. 'In case anything comes up, I mean,' I added quickly. 'And you can't make it. Or maybe I should take yours in case Alfie's ill or there's an emergency or anything.' I suspected by the amused look on Dan's face that I should shut up before I made it any worse.

'I'll be there,' said Dan. 'And I'm sure Alfie will be too. There's no way we're going to let each other down, is there, Alfie?'

Alfie turned and grinned at Dan. The two of them clearly had it all worked out.

Dan

Wednesday, 10 May 1978

Philip is being Luke Skywalker. He has a proper light sabre and he is fighting evil in space. I am R2D2 who is a kind of robot who can only talk in robot language which I am not very good at. I am helping Luke but I do not have a lightsaber and I don't know what I am supposed to do because I haven't seen *Star Wars*. I have asked for a lightsaber for my birthday but Mummy says we will have to see, which I think means I won't get one. She tried to make me one out of kitchen roll holders but it kept breaking and Philip said I wasn't allowed to use it any more and that R2D2 doesn't have a lightsaber anyway.

The baddies' spaceship is called *Death Star*. It is a big sheet on Philip's mum's washing line. Philip is hitting it with his lightsaber. His mum bangs on the window. She looks cross and she is shouting something at him.

'We've killed the baddies now,' says Philip, putting his lightsaber down.

'Oh,' I say.

Philip goes and sits down on the kerb and I sit down next to him.

'Got anything to eat?' he says. I put my hand in my pocket and pull out a little bit I have left of the Curly Wurly Grandma gave me last week.

'Only this,' I say.

'Can I have a bit?' says Philip. 'I did save you from evil.'

I shrug and let him have a bite. He takes a very big one. There is only a tiny bit left. I eat it quickly.

'Your lot are gonna lose tonight,' says Philip.

Liverpool are playing in the European Cup Final. Daddy says our name is written on the cup. I don't know how they will get it off if we lose.

'No we're not,' I say. 'We're the best team in the world.'

'Not as good as Man United.'

'Yes we are.'

'Who says?'

'My dad.'

Philip's mum is banging on the window again.

'I've got to go in for my tea now,' he says.

'See you,' I say. I go back inside too. Mummy is in the kitchen getting our tea ready. She is wearing her flappy red trousers and a red top under her flowery apron. The kitchen smells of Sundays.

'Hello, did you have fun with Philip, love?' she says.

'Yeah, we killed all the baddies. What are we having for tea?'

'Chicken and potatoes. I saved some from Sunday. So it's special for Daddy.' Mummy is smiling and her voice is sing-songy. I think she is excited about the match too.

'Please can I stay up and watch it?'

Mummy puts the big spoon down and wipes her hands

on the front of her apron. 'I'm sorry, love. You know what your father said.'

'Philip says we're gonna lose,' I say, scuffing my toe against the table leg and trying not to cry. Mummy walks over and bends down to hug me.

'Well, let's hope Philip's wrong,' she says. She holds on to me for a little bit after the hug is finished, smiles at me and brushes my fringe back out of my eyes. 'Now, run upstairs and get your hands clean. Let's be all ready for tea when Daddy gets home. Give him a nice surprise.'

I go up to the bathroom. The soap has fallen into the sink and is squishy underneath. I wash my hands and put it back near the taps because Daddy doesn't like waste or mess. Daddy doesn't like a lot of things. I go back downstairs to the kitchen and climb up on my chair at the table. Mummy is singing the Matchstalk Men song. It is about a man who drew pictures of cats and dogs a bit like the pictures I draw. I smile and join in when she gets to the bit I know. Mummy does a funny dance as she spoons the potatoes out. I like it when she makes me laugh. Usually she has her thinking face on while she is making tea. Like she is concentrating really hard.

Daddy comes home just as she is finishing the gravy. I run up to him and give his legs a hug. He bends down and ruffles my hair. His jeans and boots are all dirty as usual. Daddy is a grave digger. It means he digs holes in the ground for people to be put in when they die. I don't think he puts the dead people in, he just digs the holes. I asked Mummy once how he knows how many holes to dig but she said it didn't matter, they would all get used in the end.

'Hey, what's all this, then?' Daddy says, taking his boots off and putting them on the kitchen mat. He is sniffing the air like the boy does in the gravy advert on TV.

'Special roast tea for the big match. We thought we'd surprise you.' Mummy is smiling as she says it.

'Lizzie Brady, you're a star. Bob Paisley should have you doing the pre-match meals for the team,' he says, grabbing her around the waist and kissing her neck. Mummy's cheeks go a bit pink.

'I'll keep it warm for you until you've got changed,' she says.

Daddy ruffles my hair again on his way past.

'Come on, you Reds,' he says, smiling at me. I swing my legs under the table.

'Philip says we're gonna lose. We won't lose, will we, Daddy?'

He stops at the doorway and looks back at me. 'What, with King Kenny in the team? Of course not.'

Kenny Dalglish has scored twenty-nine goals this season. Daddy says he is the best striker in the world. We bought him after we sold Kevin Keegan last season. Daddy said he was the best striker in the world too.

Daddy goes upstairs to change his trousers. He says he spends all his time at work dirty so he likes things to be clean at home. Mummy puts his tea on the table as soon as he comes back down and pours the gravy for him. Then she brings mine over, I've got chicken and potatoes too but no gravy because I don't like it. I like tomato sauce but Mummy says you can't have it with everything. Mummy sits down with her tea and smiles at me. I swing my legs a bit more. I look up at Daddy but he has stopped smiling. He is staring at his plate. I look at Mummy, she has stopped smiling too. Her face has gone all pale.

'How many roast potatoes do I always have, Lizzie?'

'I'm sorry, Michael . . .'

'How many, Lizzie?'

'S-six.' It is Emlyn Hughes' shirt number. I think that's why Daddy always has six. Everything has to be the same before a big match. Otherwise he says it is bad luck and Liverpool will lose.

'How many have I got on my plate?' Mummy doesn't answer. I count them up, my teacher at school says I am good at counting.

'Five,' I say.

'That's right, Danny boy. You tell your mother. She can't count, you see, she's so stupid. Tell her she's stupid, Dan.' I look down at my plate and don't say anything. 'What's up? Cat got your tongue, boy?'

'It's all right, Dan. You can say it,' says Mummy quietly. 'Daddy's only playing a game.'

I don't like the game. Mummy always says not to call people nasty names.

'What is she?' he says again.

'Stupid,' I whisper.

'Louder,' says Daddy. 'Say it louder so she can hear you.'

I don't want to. It is my fault because Mummy was singing the Matchstalk Men song to me instead of counting the potatoes. I start to cry.

'Leave him, please, Michael,' says Mummy. Her voice is

shaky. Daddy turns to look at her, his eyes are dark and flashing. He's got little spots of water on the top of his lip.

'Here, have one of mine,' she says, sticking her fork into a potato and holding it out over his plate. Daddy swings his arm and knocks the fork out of her hand. It makes a clattering noise as it falls in the gravy dish. The gravy splashes all over the tablecloth. I would have been told off if I'd done that.

'Please, Michael. Don't spoil it,' she says.

'Me, spoil it?' Daddy shouts. 'It'll be your fault, you know. If they fucking lose.' Daddy stands up and throws Mum's plate on the floor. It smashes into bits on the lino.

'Go upstairs, Dan,' says Mummy. Her hands are shaking. I do not want to go. I want to give my potato to Daddy. I want it all to stop. To go back to how it was before.

'Upstairs, now,' she is shouting at me.

I get down from the table and run upstairs as fast as I can. I am not quick enough, though. I shut my bedroom door but it is no good. I can still hear Daddy shouting and smashing things. I want the noise to stop. I look around my room. The wardrobe. I can hide in my wardrobe. I open the door and climb inside. There isn't much room, it is full of my clothes and loads of old toys and stuff. I shuffle into the corner and squeeze sideways between some jumpers, they are soft and warm on my face. It is better but I can still hear the shouting. I pull the wardrobe door shut behind me. I don't like the dark. But not as much as I don't like the shouting. I press the jumpers against my ears, after a while they start to go soggy where I am crying. I stay in there for ages. My tummy is rumbling, I never got to eat my chicken and potatoes. And I've got pins and needles in my leg. But I'm scared that if I open the door it will all start up again.

After a long while I open it a crack. There is no shouting, only the noise of the television on downstairs. I climb out of the wardrobe. I squint a bit, it is still light outside. It's like I have been to bed and woken up again on a different day. My leg is funny to walk on because of the pins and needles. I creep out on to the landing. I can hear the television louder now. I don't think the match has started yet, I think the people on TV are just talking about it. I am not bothered about the talking. I can hear Mummy clearing up in the kitchen. I want to go downstairs and get something to eat but I don't know if Daddy is still cross at me for having his potato on my plate. I go for a wee and run back to the bedroom and sit on my bed.

A few minutes later Mummy comes into my room. Her eyes are all red and puffy. Her lip is puffy too. She has got a different top on, a black one. I don't know why she took her red one off, she said it was her lucky one for the match.

'I've brought you up a special picnic,' she says, trying to smile. She holds out a plate with triangle sandwiches on and some Hula Hoops.

'What's in the sandwiches?' I ask.

'Paste,' she says. I wonder what happened to the chicken but I don't want to ask in case it makes her upset.

'Can I eat them in bed?' I ask.

'Of course you can, sweetheart.' She walks over to the bed, sits down next to me and holds out the plate. Her hand is still shaking. I take it quickly.

'I'm sorry I called you stupid,' I say.

Mummy starts to cry. I lean over and give her a hug. She holds me very tightly. It is a long time before she stops crying. When she does she looks down at me and brushes my fringe out of my eyes.

'I know,' she says. 'It wasn't your fault.'

'Why does Daddy get cross like that?' I ask.

Mummy sighs. 'I don't know,' she says. 'Daddy doesn't know either. I guess he's just very superstitious.'

I nod although I don't know what that is because I have never had it. I don't even know if you can take medicine for it.

'Can I watch the first half?' I ask.

Mummy does a little smile. 'Better not,' she says, stroking my head. 'Daddy wants to watch it in peace.'

Mummy draws the bedroom curtains and switches my bedside lamp on. 'You have your tea, now,' she says. 'And then pop your pyjamas on and brush your teeth and I'll come up and tell you the score when you're tucked up in bed.' She kisses me on the forehead and walks quietly out of the room.

It is still nil–nil when Mummy comes in to kiss me goodnight. I lie awake for a long time afterwards. I hear the taps running in the bathroom. I think Mummy is having a bath. Not long after she turns the taps off I hear a big cheer from downstairs. And a big sigh from the bathroom. I shut my eyes and go to sleep.

As soon as I wake up I can feel that something is wrong. My pyjama bottoms are stuck to me and there is a funny smell. I put my hand down and feel under the sheets. It is all wet. I have peed my pants. I haven't done that since before I started school. I don't understand because I don't remember doing it. Or even wanting to go for a wee. I try to rub it a bit with my hand but the wet won't go away.

Mummy comes into the room. Her eyes are still puffy. And her lip too. She is smiling, though.

'They won one nil,' she says. 'King Kenny scored the goal.' I smile as I lie there. I don't want to get up. I don't want her to see what I have done. 'Up you get, then. Let's get ready for school,' she says, pulling back the covers. She stops and looks at the wet patch on my pyjamas and back at me. She shuts her eyes and looks up at the ceiling. She was happy when she came in and now I have made her sad again.

'Sorry,' I say. 'I didn't mean to.' She sits down on the bed and pulls me close to her and hugs me.

'It's OK, sweetheart,' she says. 'It's not your fault.' It is though. I know that. Nobody else did it.

'You go and take your wet things off,' she says. 'I'll just whip these sheets off and put some clean ones on.' I swing my legs out of bed, it feels cold where the pyjamas are sticking to me.

'You won't tell Daddy, will you?' I say as I stand up.

'No,' she says. 'Not if you don't want me to.'

I nod and go into the bathroom and peel my pyjama bottoms off. When I go back in carrying the wet pyjamas, she is sitting on the bed with her eyes shut again.

'I'm so sorry, sweetheart,' she says.

I go over and give her a hug. Though I have no idea what she is sorry for.

'Can I wear my Liverpool scarf to school?' I ask. She does a little smile behind the tears. If her face was the sky, there would be a rainbow now.

'Of course you can, love,' she says.

Six

'Lights, lights,' squealed Alfie as we drew up outside the 'Home from Home' B&B. My mother's Christmas lights were the sort which flashed on and off, complete with a neon Merry Christmas sign and a giant Santa on the roof who intermittently appeared to descend the chimney. All the scene lacked was the guiding star of Bethlehem hovering above the shed. I'd been dreading *Spotlight North West*'s annual 'Light Up Your Street' competition in case someone nominated my mum's house. Fortunately I'd got away with it this year but it was only a matter of time.

The only redeeming factor about the whole thing was that Alfie loved it (the optimum age to appreciate my mum's taste being between two and five). If she'd done it for her grandchildren's benefit it would have been sweet. But sadly the annual display was designed simply to outdo Mrs Burke across the road.

'Nanna will turn the lights on later,' I said, 'when it gets dark.' Alfie could barely contain himself. He was already in an overly excited state due to the arrival of a sack of toys and a ride-on fire engine at the foot of the bed this morning. It was the first Christmas he'd had some idea of what was going on. I'd have liked to spend the entire day with him at home, playing with his new toys, just the two of us. But attendance at my mum's Christmas Day lunch was compulsory for all family members. I'd only missed it once, when I'd been in Papua New Guinea on a round-the-world gap-year trip. And even then she hadn't understood why I couldn't have 'popped home' for a bit of Christmas pudding. Most years blurred into each other in my memory as one long, uncomfortable family get-together. But last year's did stand out on its own as being particularly awful. To have three generations of your own family say words to the effect of 'What a silly girl you've been, getting yourself up the duff and ending up as a single mum' had really made my Christmas.

I stepped out of the car. The persistent drizzle coated my hair within seconds. My brother's Rover was parked in front of us. I noticed the 'Little Princess on Board' sign in the rear window which I presumed referred to Jemima, and made a mental note never to buy any sign relating to Alfie's presence in my car.

I got Alfie out of his car seat, put his hood up and carried him up the path as quickly as I could, deciding I'd go back for the present bag later. I rang the doorbell. 'Greensleeves' had been forsaken for 'Jingle Bells'. I prayed my mother never decided to buy a mobile phone. I could just imagine her selection of ring tones.

'Happy Christmas, Alfie,' Mum said as she opened the door in a festive snowman apron. She planted a bright pink lipstick smudge on his left cheek. 'Did Father Christmas come and visit you last night?'

'Yes,' said Alfie. 'Carrots.' My mother looked at me as if I'd committed some act of child cruelty.

'Doesn't he give chocolate buttons any more?' she asked.

'He's talking about the carrots he left for Rudolph,' I explained.

'Well, we've got lots of chocolate pennies for you on the tree here,' she said, ignoring my explanation. 'You come in and choose one.'

I followed them down the hallway, Alfie staring up in wonder at the fairy lights and sea of foil decorations which made the Santa's grotto he'd visited at the local toy shop look decidedly minimalist.

'Derek's gone to get your nan,' said Mum over her shoulder. My 79-year-old grandmother Vera lived in a sheltered housing complex in Rochdale, having refused Mum's offer to move in on the entirely reasonable grounds that she didn't want to be told off all the time. 'But your brother's here,' she added.

Adam was ensconced in an armchair from where he was tutoring my thirteen-year-old nephew Luke on the finer points of succeeding in whatever game he was playing on his PSP. He'd been just the same when we were growing up, always telling me I was doing things the wrong way. Now Luke was a teenager I was looking forward to the day, surely not far away, when he would turn round and tell his dad to fuck off and get one of his own if he was so bloody good at it.

Adam had, unusually for his generation, warmly embraced middle age at thirty-nine. His hair was already thinning (which I accept he couldn't help) but he also wore grandad-style glasses, carpet slippers and M&S trousers with a crease down the front. I didn't understand how fashionable Marie let him go out dressed like that. When Richard had met him for the first time, when I'd been pregnant with Alfie, he had given me an 'I don't want to become a dad if that's what it does to you' look. I'd had to reassure him when we got home that fatherhood did not do that to all men. That it was simply Adam's way of assuming his role as patriarch.

'Hi, sis. Happy Christmas,' Adam said, scratching his belly through his jumper and not moving from the armchair.

'And to you,' I replied, bending down to give him a peck on the cheek.

'Happy Christmas, Luke,' I added, not expecting a reply and knowing that he was of an age where kisses from female relatives were not welcome. 'And you, Jemima.' Jemima continued prancing around the room in her ballerina costume, oblivious to everything going on around her. I turned to offer festive greetings to Adam's wife Marie. She was sitting primly on the edge of the sofa, her neat platinum blond bob enveloping her heavily made-up features, her eyes transfixed by Alfie who was attempting to dismantle the Christmas tree to reach another chocolate penny.

'He's gorgeous,' she said, clearly not being able to believe that her large-nosed, size seven-footed sister-in-law could be capable of producing a child who was so pleasing on the eye.

'Takes after his mother,' I said.

'Yes. Yes, of course,' said Marie who had never understood my sense of humour. 'I could speak to Jane at the agency if you like,' she said. 'Show her a photo. I'm sure she'd be interested. He's exceptionally fine boned for a boy.' Luke had been on the books of a child modelling agency from toddler-hood right up until his recent ungainly lurch into adolescence which had resulted in a 'growth time-out' as Marie had put it. In the meantime she was concentrating all her efforts on six-year-old Jemima. Her first catalogue appearance had been at the ripe old age of seven months (Marie had confided that she'd shown her pregnancy scan to the agency boss) and she had narrowly missed out on being Miss Pears last year, amidst allegations that the judges must have been bribed by the winner's parents.

'Er, no thanks,' I said. 'He doesn't sit still long enough for a photo, to tell you the truth.'

'Oh, what a shame. I'd have thought you'd have been keen to earn some extra cash. I'm always hearing single mums saying how tough it is.'

I smiled politely and was saved from any further references to my lowly financial and social status by Jemima's squeal as Alfie pulled her ponytail.

'Sorry,' I said as I removed his vice-like grip on Jemima's pink ribbon. 'Cats' tails have the same effect on him. I think it's a boy thing.'

'Luke never did it,' said Marie.

I smiled again through gritted teeth.

Mum came into the room from the kitchen, took another chocolate penny from the Christmas tree and handed it to

Alfie, who was already showing signs of being in a chocolate-hyper state.

'Poor little thing doesn't get any at home,' she said to Marie as if I wasn't within earshot.

'Need any help?' I asked.

Mum shook her head firmly. 'No, thanks, all in hand.' She disappeared back into the kitchen. Her confidence wasn't due to Delia Smith eat-your-heart-out culinary talents. It was simply that virtually everything on the menu had been bought ready-cooked, chopped, peeled or grated in a plastic bag from M&S.

Seconds later the front door opened and a shrill voice entered the fray.

'I'm not staying, you know. I'm going back home tonight.' Nan had arrived in the hallway and already felt the need to make good her escape. I understood how she felt.

'That's fine, Vera,' I heard Derek say. 'Come and see the family.' Nan shuffled in wearing her red pom-pom carpet slippers and a gold-patterned headscarf over her rollers. Alfie wandered up to her, chocolate smeared all over his hands and face and poked her feet as if he wasn't quite sure whether she was real or a toy to play with.

'Hello, sweetheart,' said Nan.

Alfie grinned and did a Teletubbies style 'Eh-oh' back.

'Happy Christmas, Nan,' I said, stooping to give her a big hug. She may have been a curl or two short of a full perm and have the diplomacy skills of a sledgehammer but she was still my favourite member of the family. When I was little I'd always thought she must be my father's mum, because she was so full of fun. When I'd found out she'd actually given birth to my mother, it had come as quite a shock.

Nan looked around the room.

'And where's your young man?' she asked. The ghost of Christmas past hung over the room.

'We're not together any more. Do you remember, Nan? I explained it all last Christmas.'

'Oh yes. He went off with that weather girl on TV, didn't he? Pretty little thing she is too, although a bit bony for my liking. Your grandad would have told her to put some meat on. She needs plumping up to your sort of size.'

I managed a faint smile.

'Happy Christmas, Jo,' said Derek, trying his best to jolly things along. 'I expect Alfie was up early this morning.'

'Oh, about six thirty, much the same as usual really.'

'Look at me. Aren't I pretty?' said Jemima, as she pirouetted in front of Nan.

'Very nice, dear,' said Nan. 'Is she coming to lunch?'

'Who?' said Derek.

'The weather girl.' Derek shook his head.

'Happy Christmas, Nan,' said Adam, prising himself from the armchair to give her a peck on the cheek. Marie followed on behind him, being careful not to actually touch Nan with her air kisses, then beckoned Luke to come forward.

'No,' he hissed from the floor. 'She's too smelly.'

'It's all right,' said Nan, who possessed the selective hearing ability much favoured by elderly people. 'I don't fancy getting too close to his spots, to tell you the truth. Can't you do something about them, Marie? You must have creams and things.'

Marie, who had her own beauty salon in Cheadle Hulme, scowled. Luke shrank back into the carpet, hiding his disparaged features behind the PSP.

Mum opened the serving hatch at the far end of the room.

'OK, everyone. If you can take your places, lunch is about to be served,' she called.

We trooped obediently to the dining table at the end of the through room. There were no place names on the table but we all knew exactly where to sit: Mum and Derek at either end, my brother and his family on one side, and me, Nan and Alfie, strapped into his booster seat, on the other, the spare chair next to me a stark reminder that I had buggered up the seating plans again. Derek carried the turkey in as Mum hastily rearranged the table to try to create some space amongst the plethora of plastic holly leaf garlands, crackers and boiled-to-death vegetables. We sat in silence as Derek poured the wine (the same bottle of Blue Nun we had every year) and then stood to say a few words.

'It's lovely to be here all together again. Before we eat this wonderful meal which Pauline has prepared, let's pause to remember absent family members' – Derek's two grown-up sons were 'doing their own thing' – 'and those dearly departed.' His voice faltered as he referred to my father Bob, my grandfather William and to his own late wife Sylvia.

I stroked Alfie's hair. It always saddened me to think that he would never know his grandfather. That all I could do was tell him about my own fond memories. The image which stuck in my head was one from my childhood, of

Dad in his postman's uniform, smiling at me as I ran out to greet him at the school gates. He'd been the only father there in those days, the perk of having a dad who started work at seven in the morning. It had made me feel special, walking home holding his hand, chattering to him about my day.

I couldn't seem to recall him ageing, although he obviously had done. He was fifty-one when he'd died. I'd been away at university at the time. Enjoying the independence, having made the big break from home. The phone call from my mother was still etched in my head.

'I've got some bad news, love. Your father's had a heart attack. He's dead.' The words ricocheting around the room. Refusing to enter my head. It hadn't felt real somehow. Coming home, going to my father's funeral and travelling straight back to university. More like a walk-on part in my old life. It hadn't really hit me until the following Christmas when I'd come home to a house devoid of fun. And a family who had lost its starring member. Mum had coped remarkably well in the very British sense that she hadn't broken down and wailed at the funeral, just dabbed at the corners of her eyes with a neatly pressed hankie then busied herself passing sandwiches round and thanking everyone for coming. When the last guests had left, and she was finally alone with me and Adam, all she said was that she was having the real fire taken out and a new gas one put in in its place. That's when I'd known. I was on my own from that point. I think Adam knew it too. He proposed to Marie a few weeks later.

My mother rarely spoke about Dad afterwards. And

when she did he was always referred to as 'your father', as if he'd had nothing to do with her. There were no photographs of him in the house, which was in marked contrast to Derek who still kept a wedding photograph of himself and Sylvia on a corner shelf in the room. Something which clearly rankled with Mum judging by the number of times a vase of flowers was strategically placed in front of it. I wondered if she ever thought of my dad at all, or whether she was still bitter at him for leaving her so suddenly.

'So,' said Derek, composing himself and raising his glass. 'A Happy Christmas to one and all.' There were murmured Happy Christmases from around the table and the compulsory clinking of glasses. Derek carved the turkey while Mum started fussing over everyone with gravy and stuffing. As hard as I tried not to, all I could think of was the other Christmas lunch. The one involving Richard and Tricia in their Manchester love nest. Although of course it wouldn't have started yet as they'd probably still be in bed together. I had distant memories of a very long Buck's Fizz and cream cheese and smoked salmon bagels Christmas morning brunch in bed back in that pre-Alfie life I once lived. I had no idea at the time that the next year I would be sitting bleary eyed in bed in the early hours of Christmas morning trying to latch a screaming baby on to my cracked nipple so Richard could get back to sleep.

Nan patted my knee under the table.

'You never stop missing them, do you?' she whispered. 'The men you used to love.'

I smiled at her and squeezed her hand.

'Crackers,' said Alfie, tugging at my sleeve.

'Oh, yes. Do you want to pull one with Mummy?' I said. Alfie jumped as it went bang and a yellow paper hat, a plastic ring and the obligatory joke fell out.

'Come on, let's hear it,' said Derek, who was a stickler for cracker humour.

Trying to get into the spirit, I unfurled the paper and read it out loud in a forced jolly tone.

'Why are chocolate buttons rude? Because they are Smarties in the nude.'

Derek started chortling. Mum looked at my blank face.

'Oh dear, was that one racist?' she said.

'Why did you think it was racialist?' asked Nan.

'Because chocolate buttons are brown, like, you know . . .' Mum replied.

'You can get white ones too,' chipped in Luke.

'Would that be OK, then, Jo? If it was about white ones?'

I sighed as I put the hat on Alfie. Sometimes, it was difficult to know where to begin.

'Let's do yours then, Luke,' said Derek, reaching over to pull his with him. Luke discarded the hat and dutifully read out the joke.

'Why do women have orgasms? It gives them something else to moan about.' His voice trailed off into a mumble as he realised what he had said. The table fell silent.

'Where did you get these, Derek?' asked Mum.

'At the market,' he replied. 'They said they were good quality.'

'Well, you can take them back next week and ask for your money back. I should have got some at M&S. You can't trust these foreign ones.'

'Was that one racialist as well?' asked Nan.

Marie shook her head. 'Just a bit rude.'

'Why was it rude?' asked Jemima.

Marie fiddled with the ribbon on her blouse. Adam took a huge mouthful of turkey.

'Help yourself to sprouts, everyone,' said Mum, passing the dish round.

Jemima picked up her cracker. Marie pulled it with her quickly, handed her the plastic car and discreetly removed the joke and slid it under her table mat. We carried on eating in silence.

'Would anyone like some more sprouts or stuffing?' asked Mum as we neared the end of the meal. 'It's a shame for it to go to waste.'

'Maybe you could invite them next year,' said Nan.

'Who?' asked Mum.

'Alfie's dad and the weather girl,' said Nan.

Derek got up and turned the television on. Introducing me to the entirely new phenomenon of being relieved to see the Queen.

'So did you have fun yesterday?' asked Richard when he arrived to pick Alfie up the next morning. I was about to explain how the only high point of the day had been finding Derek secretly reading Marie's hidden cracker joke after the meal, when I realised he was talking to Alfie.

'Father Christmas treated you very well, didn't he?' I said. Alfie nodded and ran off to fetch his fire engine.

'That's for your parents from Alfie,' I said, handing Richard a carrier bag with a hastily wrapped present in it.

'Oh, thanks,' he said. I wondered for a moment if he was going to offer to call a festive truce. Like that Christmas Day football match with the Germans during the First World War. 'They can't wait to see him. Though of course they're disappointed that Tricia isn't being allowed to stay.' Richard had clearly decided to go back to the trenches to resume hostilities.

'Here's his changing bag,' I said as Alfie returned, riding his fire engine. 'Any problems just give me a ring. I'll be at home all day.'

Richard nodded. I suspected he had visions of me lounging around watching television and eating chocolates, having no idea about the pile of hand washing which had lain festering in my laundry basket since he had left or all the odd jobs about the house which needed doing.

I put Alfie's jacket on and whizzed him outside minus the fire engine. After a few minutes of watching Richard struggle with the car seat I intervened.

'I'll do it,' I said. 'It'll be quicker.'

Richard held Alfie while I leant inside. I could smell her perfume straight away. I was tempted to check in the boot in case he'd smuggled her along and she would jump out the moment I turned my back. I took Alfie from Richard and strapped him in the seat, trying to keep a comforting smile on my face as I did so.

'You have a lovely time,' I said, kissing him on the forehead. 'Mummy will see you later.'

'OK,' said Richard. 'See you at seven.'

I waved at Alfie and went back inside, sure it was smoked salmon I'd smelt on Richard's breath.

Seven

'Enjoy your date,' said Rachel. Although she was on the other end of the phone I could see the expression on her face very clearly.

'May I remind you again that it's a boat trip organised purely for Alfie's pleasure.'

'At the invitation of a particularly attractive skipper,' said Rachel.

'Who is of no interest to me, bearing in mind that I am officially off men for life.'

'Oh, come on, only lovesick teenagers say that.'

'OK. Let's go through my Ten Reasons Not to Fall in Love list again, shall we?' She'd listened to this before but I wanted to remind myself again. 'I'd have to start shaving my legs again – even in the winter; I could no longer get away with wearing maternity knickers two years after the birth and would have to spend a fortune on new underwear; neither would I be able to get away with doing a tin of spaghetti hoops for tea; I'd have to introduce him to my mother; my boss is my ex and no man would accept that; there's no point because single mums are about as attractive to men as syphilis; it would be going against the lyrics of "I'll Never Fall In Love Again" which I have adopted as my theme tune; in common with the aforementioned Bobbie Gentry, I have a nasty habit of falling for guys with an exceptionally large pin with which to burst my bubble; I can't imagine ever trusting another man again; and, still at number one, I'm not going to risk anything which could end up hurting Alfie again.'

Rachel fell silent for a moment. I realised I'd depressed us both. But I'd wanted to remind her that 'moving on' wasn't an option for me.

'Well, anyway,' she said eventually. 'I wish you all a pleasurable trip.'

'Thank you,' I said. 'Now, if you'll excuse me, we have a boat to catch.'

Dan was waiting for us at the pumping station, standing on the back of his boat with his beanie hat pulled down over his ears and his fleece jacket collar turned up against the wind. Unfortunately he was one of those men who looked good in anything. Which was not making it easy for me. Alfie spotted him as soon as we rounded the bend and could barely contain his excitement.

'Balloon man,' he called out.

'Alfie, so glad you could make it,' said Dan. 'And your delightful escort, of course,' he added, glancing up at me with a smile. I looked straight down at my feet.

The boat looked cleaner than I remembered it and for the first time I noticed its name, painted in bold black letters along the side.

'Elizabeth,' I said out loud. 'Not named after our esteemed sovereign, I take it?'

'Er, no,' said Dan. 'It's, um, Elizabeth Taylor, actually.' For a second he looked a little uncomfortable, maybe even embarrassed. 'I was brought up watching *Lassie Come Home* and *National Velvet*,' he explained. 'Although I'm more of a *Cat on a Hot Tin Roof* man myself,' he said, slipping into a Deep South drawl.

I laughed and shook my head. Despite my best efforts it was hard not to enjoy his presence.

'Now, if you'd like to come aboard, your exclusive cruise will begin in five minutes.'

I lifted Alfie out of the buggy and went to fold it up.

'Please, do leave the chariot for me to take care of,' said Dan.

I smiled and took his outstretched hand as I stepped down on to the boat. To my surprise I didn't wobble at all this time.

'I do believe your mother has found her sea legs,' Dan said. Alfie started laughing. I suspected Dan could tell him to give all his toys away and Alfie would still find it amusing. Dan folded the buggy up without me having to remind him how to do it and secured it under some straps on the top of the boat. 'Right, please bear with me during the official safety announcement.' Dan clapped his hands to gain Alfie's attention, pointed at the water and shivered before wagging his finger and handing Alfie a picture of a little boy swimming with a big red cross through it.

'What I didn't tell you is that I'm the British Waterways public cruises health and safety inspector,' I said.

Dan laughed. 'Not textbook, I know, but I think he understood. And just in case . . .' Dan disappeared round the side of the boat and came back holding a tiny life jacket. 'I hope it fits,' he said. 'I borrowed it from somebody with a three year old.'

'Thank you. I'm sure it'll be fine,' I said, putting it over an obliging Alfie.

'I've got an adult size if you want one,' Dan offered.

'I'm fine, thanks.'

'Living on the edge, are you?'

'Something like that,' I said.

'Well, if the worst happens, it's shallow enough to stand up in there anyway. Just watch out for the shopping trolleys. Now, if you'd both like to follow me downstairs, refreshments will be served before we set off.'

The two chairs inside had been turned round to face the window with a couple of plump cushions sitting on one of them and a pair of binoculars on the other. I picked up a piece of paper on the chair which read, 'Cruise Itinerary: welcome, refreshments, lock and tunnel excursion with full commentary, return leg with musical accompaniment by Rachmaninov, Radiohead and the Teletubbies, lunch of toasted cheese sandwiches and paste sandwiches.'

'Is everything to your liking?' asked Dan, his eyes beckoning me in, doing their best to lead me astray. Everything was to my liking. That was the problem. And I suspected from the playful expression on his face that he knew it.

'Absolutely,' I said. 'I'm particularly looking forward to hearing how you've segued "Rhapsody on a theme of Paganini" into "Creep" and "No Surprises" into "Eh-Oh, Here Come the Teletubbies".'

'Well, I thought I'd cater for all tastes in the hope of

finding something you both liked. And personally I always find that I need a bit of Teletubbies to lift me back up again after a Radiohead CD.'

I was beginning to ache from trying so hard not to like him. And all the time he kept on looking at me in that way. As if I might be in some way interesting. I hadn't had anyone look at me like that in a long time. I averted my gaze again.

'Now, Alfie, tell me about your Christmas,' said Dan, crouching down beside him. 'Did you have the most magical, fantastical time ever?'

'Jingle bells, jingle bells,' Alfie started singing, jumping up and down.

'He's been having a bit of a post–Christmas low,' I said. 'He doesn't want to let it go.'

'And why should he? I'm with Roy Wood on that one. And what was your favourite present, Alfie?'

Alfie pondered for a moment before replying.

'Tool kit.'

I tried not to let it show that I was disappointed.

'Is that what Father Christmas got you?' asked Dan.

'His daddy, actually. Father Christmas got him a fire engine.'

'Wow. How lucky are you? And if I ever have a fire or need something mending, I know who to call.' Alfie nodded. 'Now, we have a range of beverages available and I am licensed to serve alcohol,' said Dan, turning back to me.

'It's a bit early for me. Tea would be great. Just a spot of milk and no sugar, please.'

'One tea coming up.' Dan walked over to the kitchen

area and filled an old-fashioned tin kettle with water and put it on the stove. 'Is this OK for Alfie?' he asked, holding out a little carton of organic orange juice and a fruit chewy bar which he'd obviously got in specially.

'That's great. Thanks very much,' I said, taking it from him carefully so that my fingers didn't brush against his. I pierced the silver foil with the straw and handed it to Alfie.

'So how was your Christmas?' I asked as we waited for the kettle to boil. It would have been rude not to enquire. And despite my best efforts I was curious about him. Desperate to know more.

'Pretty quiet, really,' Dan said.

'No big family knees-up then?'

'No, just me and my gran at her house.'

I nodded, wondering why his parents hadn't figured in the festivities. Whether they were divorced or he'd fallen out with them, or they'd gone abroad even. The journalist in me wanted to find out but there was something about the tone in Dan's voice which suggested he wasn't comfortable on this subject. Besides, I knew the potential pitfalls of such questions. People asked me where my dad was sometimes. And although I never let it show, it still hurt.

'What about you?' he asked after a moment's silence. 'Were you at home?'

'Oh, me and Alfie were at my mum's, along with my stepdad, brother, sister-in-law, niece and nephew and grandmother.'

'Not exactly a barrel of laughs, I take it?'

'It may have been entertaining if it had been someone

else's family but unfortunately they're mine. I suspect I may have been swapped at birth but I haven't been able to prove it yet.'

Dan nodded, although the smile seemed slightly strained this time.

'Hat off,' said Alfie, pointing at Dan, who was still sporting his beanie.

'Sorry,' I said. 'That's what I always tell Alfie when we go indoors.'

'Happy to oblige,' laughed Dan, removing his hat and placing it on the kitchen counter. I'd forgotten how dark his hair was, practically black. It looked as if it was the sort of hair which did its own thing, regardless of its owner's wishes. Even his dark stubble gave the impression it would stubbornly resist any attempts to remove it. Alfie jumped as the kettle started whistling.

'It's OK, love,' I said, hugging him to me. 'It's only the kettle singing.'

When I looked up, Dan was staring at me as if trying to remember where he'd seen me before.

'What is it?' I asked.

'Nothing,' he said, his eyes still searching, probing, for a way past my defences. 'You just reminded me of something my gran used to say.'

Alfie peeked out from under my arm as Dan picked up the kettle then put it down again quickly with a loud clang, shaking his hand.

'Oven glove,' said Alfie, running up to Dan and offering him one of his huge padded mittens. Dan smiled and looked at me for permission. I nodded.

'Go ahead,' I said. 'I did tell my mother he was small for his age before she got them but she never listens to me.'

'Thanks, Alfie,' said Dan, holding the glove round the handle as he poured the boiling water into the teapot. He gave it a stir and put the lid on.

'Tea cosy,' said Alfie, pointing to Dan's hat on the counter. Dan's smile broadened into a grin as he dutifully placed his beanie on the teapot.

'I can see your mum's got you well trained,' said Dan. 'You must be a real help around the house.'

Alfie nodded. 'Hoover.'

'Yes, and you vacuum as well. Does your mother hire you out? She ought to, you know.'

'You'll have me sending him up the chimneys next.'

'Well, it never did them any harm, did it?' said Dan with a grin.

'I suppose it's the one thing Hebden Bridge lacks,' I said. 'Some good old-fashioned child labour.'

'Exactly. Five aromatherapists per head of population but you can't find a chimney sweep for love or money.'

I laughed.

'Boat ride,' said Alfie, having demolished his chewy bar and drunk his juice with indecent haste. He was clearly impatient to get going.

'Let's go then,' said Dan, handing me my mug.

'Please sit down,' he said, gesturing to the chairs, 'and fasten your seat belts as the cruise is about to begin. Are you all right with the door open?'

'Yeah, fine.'

'Good. Only my budget didn't stretch to a Tannoy

system for the commentary.' Dan retrieved his hat from the teapot and bounded up the steps. I pulled Alfie up on to my lap, not trusting him to sit still on the cushions, and seconds later I heard the engine start up and a gentle vibration from the back of the boat.

'We'll head up towards Mytholmroyd,' he called out. 'The first lock's up ahead.' There was barely time for me to show Alfie how the binoculars worked before the boat slowed down as Dan edged it carefully in towards the bank.

'Do you need a hand?' I called out to him.

'Alfie could throw me the other rope if he likes. Just go through to the front inside the boat.' I held Alfie's hand as he toddled beside me. Sinbad, who had been asleep on Dan's bed, jumped up when he heard us coming and sought sanctuary underneath. Alfie picked up a tube of Nivea hand and nail cream which was lying on Dan's bed.

'Let's put that back, it doesn't belong to us,' I said. I wasn't sure who it belonged to. But what I was surprised to discover was that it bothered me. It was only as I turned back that I noticed a small pot of clear nail varnish on the shelf above the bed. Obviously Dan had female company. The sort of female company who was familiar enough to leave her personal belongings lying around. I considered going into the bathroom to check for a second toothbrush but Dan was waiting. I pushed open the two small doors at the far end and helped Alfie up the steps out to the front of the boat. Dan leapt across on to the towpath, tied his rope through the mooring ring and ran up to us. He was still smiling. Only now I was wondering if he was smiling because of what he may have been up to last night. And feeling stupid for even thinking he may be in the slightest bit interested in me.

'Your turn, Alfie,' Dan called. Alfie took the end of the rope from me and flung it in the direction of the banking. Unfortunately it didn't quite make it and slithered down into the canal.

'Good try,' said Dan, kneeling down to fish it out. 'It takes a lot of practice to do this, Alfie.'

'It must be hard on your own,' I said. 'Without anyone else to help you with the locks, I mean,' I added quickly, trying to make it sound as if I wasn't fishing.

Dan shrugged. 'I guess I'm used to it. I just take twice as long as other people to get anywhere. But as I'm not usually in a hurry, it doesn't matter. Now', Dan continued, turning his attention back to Alfie, 'you see that lock? Let me show you one I made earlier.' He leapt back on to the boat, disappeared inside and returned a moment later with a model of a canal lock made out of cereal packets and washing up liquid bottles.

'Wow,' I said, suitably impressed.

'I watched *Blue Peter* a lot as a kid,' he said, by way of explanation. 'And this is your chance to be Lesley Judd, or Valerie Singleton if you prefer, although they were both pretty straight and I've got you down as more of a John Noakes, flying by the seat of your pants type,' he said, handing me the model.

'Thank you,' I said, unsure if it was a compliment or not.

'Now, Alfie,' said Dan. 'Your mum's going to explain how locks work on the model while I get the gates open.'

He hurried off over the other side of the canal, leaving me to do the science bit to a perplexed-looking Alfie.

'Right, all set,' said Dan when he returned a couple of minutes later. 'You two can stay there if you like. Just keep all little fingers inside the boat, please.' He untied the boat, jumped back on board and started up the engine again. With Alfie standing safely between my legs, I leant forward with outstretched arms and head back, Kate Winslet-style, as we sailed into the lock. Dan smiled and shook his head.

'Remember, if we hit anything it will be the lock gate, not an iceberg,' he shouted from the back.

I laughed. I hadn't felt this relaxed with a man for ages. Maybe never. A middle-aged couple stopped on the tow-path to watch as Dan climbed up the ladder to get out, closed the gates behind us and opened the paddles to send the water gushing in. Every move was deft and assured. He appeared to expend the minimum effort needed to accomplish the task. The woman said something I couldn't hear to Dan and smiled down at Alfie. I realised she was probably thinking he was Dan's son. That we were a family on a New Year's boating trip. I smiled back at her. Not wanting to correct her assumption. As the water level rose, Dan leant against the lock gate, circling his head as he stretched out each leg in turn and finally standing tall and stretching up towards the sky, allowing a glimpse of tanned, washboard-flat stomach beneath his fleece. It still troubled me. The nail polish thing.

'Did you enjoy that, Alfie?' Dan called as he jumped back on board afterwards, having closed the lock gates behind us. Alfie nodded enthusiastically. 'Well, the good news is we're going to do it all over again on the way back. Meanwhile, I've got a job for you. I want you to look out for crocodiles and shout when you see one. OK?'

Alfie sat with his eyes peeled as we glided slowly along past the other boats moored along the canal.

'Croc, croc,' he squealed, as he spotted the mock crocodile head poking up through the water. Dan started to sing.

'Row, row, row your boat, gently up the stream, if you see a crocodile, don't forget to scream.'

Alfie dutifully obliged, louder than I had expected and directly into my left ear. I winced. When I glanced up, Dan had a broad grin on his face.

'Is it yours?' I asked.

'Yep, guilty as charged. Thought it would make people smile.'

I nodded, remembering all the times I had walked past it along the towpath while trying to get Alfie to sleep when he was a baby. It was weird, knowing now that it was Dan's. That even before I'd known him he'd been capable of putting a smile on my face.

'If you look over there you'll see my big red shed,' said Dan, pointing. 'I suspect I'm the subject of some considerable shed envy amongst my neighbours.'

I followed the direction of Dan's finger. It was indeed a large shed, standing a couple of feet taller and wider than any of the others along the crowded stretch of boats nestling bow to stern. And just to the right of it was a boat's-length gap.

'Look, Alfie. That's where Dan lives.'

'Balloon man's house,' said Alfie, pointing at the shed. I laughed and shook my head. Clearly I hadn't explained it very well. We carried on past the last boat on the mooring towards the point where the canal disappeared under the Halifax Road.

'We're going into the tunnel, Alfie,' called Dan. 'It'll be dark in there, OK?'

Alfie's little fingers dug into the palm of my hand. As we moved deeper inside, he let out a tiny whimper. Immediately Dan switched the boat light on and a huge beam lit up the tunnel. Alfie gazed up in wonder and laughed as a drop of water dripped on his head.

'Thanks. That's a neat little torch you've got there,' I called back to Dan.

'It's great for attracting moths at night,' said Dan. 'I'll have to show you some time.' His words echoed around us, refusing to go away. Leaving me wondering if he had meant it or if it had merely been a casual, throwaway line.

We emerged from the tunnel, and just past the next bend Dan performed an impressive three-point turn and headed for home. I took Alfie downstairs into the warmth of the cabin and sat with him on my lap as we glided back through the tunnel.

'Press play on the hi-fi,' Dan called out. I reached up to the shelf above me. Something classical which I vaguely recognised came on.

'This really is terribly civilised, you know,' I said, as the music echoed around us through the tunnel and Alfie stared out at the shadows the light was casting on the brick-work. 'You should start up a little sideline in boat trips.'

'No thanks,' said Dan. 'It would mean dealing with members of the public.'

'So what are we, then?'

'You're my guests. It's entirely different. I couldn't choose who my passengers were if they were paying for the privilege. Plus I'd be spending all my time at the sanitary station. It takes two hours to pump that toilet out, you know.'

'So I've done the right thing not to use your onboard facilities?'

'Absolutely,' laughed Dan. 'People who live on boats never go on anyone else's. Well, only for a wee if they're desperate. Never anything else. It would be quite rude. It happened to me once, you know. A clown friend of mine and his wife came to visit with their two children. School-age kids. They were only here an hour or so but all four of them used the loo and let's just say all of them were gone for some time. What are the odds on that? That four people in the same family would need to poo within an hour of each other in the middle of the afternoon? Needless to say I didn't invite them back.' He kept a straight face as he said it so I couldn't be sure whether he was joking or not.

'Well, you'll be pleased to know Alfie's self-contained in his nappy,' I said.

'Fantastic. You're the perfect boat guests,' said Dan. 'Very low maintenance. You'll be on my invite list again.'

'Again, again.' Alfie had a disconcerting ability to pretend he wasn't listening while all the time being fully aware of what was being discussed.

'Oh, not for a while, sweetheart,' I said. 'Dan's too busy with work to give us boat rides all the time.'

'See shed,' said Alfie.

'You'll see it again later when we go past,' I said, although I knew that wasn't what he meant.

'Are you wanting to come back another time and visit my shed?' Dan called out from above, having obviously been listening. Alfie squealed with delight that someone had finally understood. 'Why, of course. I'd be delighted to show you inside. I'll introduce you to the spiders if you like. It'll have to be next year, of course.' My heart sank for a second until I remembered it was New Year's Eve.

'Are you sure?' I said, picking Alfie up and carrying him up the steps to where Dan was steering the boat.

'Of course,' said Dan, letting Alfie hold the rudder as the Teletubbies blasted out from below. 'This is the most fun I've had in ages.'

'Good,' I said. I took a deep breath and gazed out across the canal to the hills beyond, trying not to let him see how pleased I was about that. And trying not to think about the nail polish.

'Gosh, someone's been busy,' said Nina, picking up Alfie's canal lock model as she settled herself on the sofa later that night.

'Oh, er, yeah. A friend of Alfie's made it for him. We went for a ride on his canal boat today,' I said, handing her a glass of red wine. It was getting to be something of a tradition now, us seeing in the New Year together. It was, as she'd pointed out last year, silly both of us sitting there on our own on different sides of the same wall.

'How lovely. What's his name?' asked Nina. 'This friend of Alfie's.'

'Dan,' I said. 'Although Alfie calls him the balloon man. That's what he does, you see. Balloon modelling.' I tried to busy myself tidying up some of Alfie's toys but I could still see the mischievous twinkle in Nina's eyes.

'And will Alfie be seeing Dan again?' she said, placing the model back down on the floor.

'Er, yes. Next week, actually. He's going to visit his shed up on Mayroyd moorings.'

'I wondered what had put that warm glow in your cheeks.'

'It's the wine,' I said quickly, pointing to the half-empty bottle. 'I've had a few glasses already.'

'Ah, but alcohol doesn't put a lightness in your step, does it now? I saw you pushing Alfie back down the towpath today. Floating on air, you were.'

I put Alfie's wooden xylophone down and turned to look at her. 'I had a really nice day. Dan may be gorgeous, charming, funny and a huge hit with Alfie, but that doesn't mean to say there's anything going on between us.'

'Well, it sounds like there should be,' said Nina. 'Men like that are hard to come by.'

'And would probably stick around for all of five minutes,' I said.

Nina put her glass down on the coaster on the coffee table.

'Before I met Gordon,' she said, 'I was engaged, you know. A young man called Peter he was. Such a polite fellow. Proper manners he had, as my mother used to say.

We'd got as far as booking the church and arranging the flowers. The only blessing was that my mother hadn't got round to sending out the invitations when we found out.'

'Found out what?' I said, perching on the edge of the sofa.

'He was married,' said Nina, her eyes misting over for a moment. 'Technically separated on the grounds that he hadn't lived with her for a couple of years. He'd left her behind in Newcastle when he'd come up to Scotland to find work. Silly sod thought he could get away with it. Marrying someone else in a different country. And going back to her for a bit of how's your father whenever he fancied it, no doubt.' Nina brushed a strand of her snow-white hair back behind her ears. Her lips pursed in indignation.

'Oh, Nina,' I said. 'You poor thing.'

'I felt such a fool,' she said. 'I told people we'd called it off because I'd decided I was too young but everyone knew the real reason. News like that soon got round in a little village like ours.' She picked up her wine and took a large gulp before continuing.

'The reason I'm telling you,' she said, 'is that when Gordon came along a couple of years later, I thought he was too good to be true. And I told him I couldn't start courting him because I didn't want to make a fool of myself again.'

'So how come you ended up marrying him?' I said.

'My mother told me that one bad apple didn't spoil the cart. It just meant you had to grab the good ones before someone else did.' She looked up at me and smiled as she reached over and patted my hand.

'The thing is,' I said, 'it's not just me. I've got Alfie to think of. I couldn't bear it if he got hurt all over again. He's been messed about enough.'

'Maybe Alfie would think it's worth the risk,' Nina said. 'To see his mum as happy as you looked today.'

I smiled at Nina and turned the television on. Graham Norton was presiding over some sort of New Year's Eve party.

'Oh, I do like him,' said Nina. 'He's ever so saucy. Now, any chance of a top-up? I need to get tiddly before Big Ben.'

Dan

Thursday, 22 January 1979

Daddy is going on strike today. He has stopped digging holes for dead people because they don't pay him enough and he is going to stand in a line with some other men instead. I am watching him put his boots and jacket on in the kitchen.

'Won't you get cold?' I say. 'Just standing still all day.'

'I expect we'll light a little fire to keep us warm,' he says.

'Can I come and see it?' I ask.

'Don't bother your father, Dan,' says Mummy, who is standing at the sink washing up the breakfast things. She is not going to work today either but she is not on strike, it is just her day off.

'But I don't have to go to school today.' Mr Greenwood our caretaker is going to be on strike as well. And the dinner ladies. They don't get paid enough either.

'We'll find something for you to do,' says Mummy. 'Picket lines aren't places for children to be.'

'And make sure you don't go crossing any,' says Daddy. 'No son of mine is going to be a scab.' He is laughing as he says it. I don't know why. I had a scab on my knee last summer but

131

it is gone now. I got it from falling off my bike and it hurt. It wasn't funny at all. Mummy looks at me and smiles.

'It's OK, Dan. Your father's only teasing you,' she says. I still don't know what about.

Daddy opens one of the kitchen cupboards and gets a little glass bottle out and slips it inside his jacket.

'What's that for?' I ask.

'Just a wee something to help keep me and the lads warm,' he says, winking at me. 'I'll see you both later.' He gives Mummy a kiss and goes out the door.

I sit down on the chair while Mummy finishes the washing up.

'What if someone dies and there's no one to dig a hole for them?' I ask.

'I'm sure they'll have dug some spare ones just in case,' she says. She takes her washing-up gloves off and hangs them over the taps before picking up the blue and white tube of cream. I go over to her as she puts some on. I like the smell of it on her hands.

'Right, let's get ready,' she says.

'Where are we going?' I ask.

'Can you keep a secret?'

'I nod my head.

'We're going to visit Grandma and Grandad.' She seems excited about it. I am too. We haven't seen them for ages. They don't come to our house any more. Not since Mummy and Daddy did some shouting about it. I asked Mummy why they didn't come any more and she said something about Grandad finding it difficult to get about. But they only live a few roads away.

'Why is it a secret?' I ask.

'Because it's our special little outing while Daddy's out. You mustn't tell him about it when he comes home. Just say you've been playing with Philip, OK?'

'I nod my head although I still don't understand why.

'Good. Come upstairs with me then and we'll get ready.'

Mummy goes into the bathroom while I get dressed. She has put my best blue jumper out to wear. She spends a long time in the bathroom putting her face on. When she comes out, her hair is a bit different too. She has brushed it over her face a bit. I can't see the bruise on her forehead any more.

'Don't you look smart?' she says and bends down to kiss me. 'Grandma will be so pleased to see you.'

It is cold outside. I have my gloves and hat on and I have to walk fast to keep up with Mummy but my nose is still cold. I need a little fire like Daddy's to keep warm. I keep a lookout for picket lines on the way. I am worried I might cross one by accident because I don't really know what they look like.

Grandma and Grandad's house is right next to the canal, you can see it from their backyard. I open the gate and stand there staring. The little building with the toilet in it has gone. There is a new building stuck on the end of the house instead. Mummy smiles.

'Grandma's got a new bathroom,' she says.

I run up the path and reach up to knock on the door. I hear footsteps coming and then Grandma opens it. I give her legs a hug and she starts crying. I look round and

Mummy is crying too. It is the funny crying that ladies do because they are both smiling at the same time.

'Oh, Daniel. What a lovely surprise,' says Grandma. She picks me up and gives me a big kiss, her face is warm and soft and smells of soap. Her hair is curly because she uses rollers. Sometimes she leaves one in by mistake. She hasn't today though, I check. She puts me down and hugs Mummy.

'How are you, love?' she says.

'Fine,' says Mummy. 'Really, I'm fine.'

Grandma takes my hand and leads me inside the house. There are cracks in the lino in the kitchen and the kettle on the top of the oven isn't as shiny as ours. I remember it does a good whistle, though. Grandma says it sings instead of whistling. The wireless is on in the kitchen, Grandma calls all their radios wirelesses. She has a lot of them, one in nearly every room. I don't know why she needs that many. We go down the hallway, past the photograph of Elizabeth Taylor on the wall. She is Grandma's favourite film star and Mummy was named after her and everyone says Mummy looks like she did when she was younger except she hasn't got violet eyes. I don't know anyone with violet eyes. We go into the front room where Grandad is sitting in the arm-chair. He is much older than Grandma, his hair is white. It used to be very dark brown like mine, though. There are photos of him with dark hair and big, bushy, dark eyebrows on the mantelpiece. His eyebrows are white now too.

'Hello, Daniel. Come and say hello to your grandad,' he says, smiling at me.

I walk over to him. The sunshine is coming through the

window, I can see lots of specks of dust in the air. Grandad smells of old. He holds his hand out to me, his fingers are bony and wrinkled. I let him take hold of my hand and he gives it a squeeze.

'My, you're growing into a fine boy, Daniel. A fine boy, indeed.'

I want to ask him where he keeps his marbles because Mummy says he's still got all of them though I have never seen him playing with them. I don't ask though, in case he has them hidden in a secret place like Philip does. Some people aren't very good at sharing.

'How's school going, Daniel?' asks Grandma. 'Are you still enjoying your numbers?'

'Yes, I can do adding now.'

'Good for you,' she says.

'He likes painting too, don't you, Dan?' says Mummy. I nod my head.

'That's nice. What's your favourite colour?'

'Red,' I say. 'Like Liverpool.'

Grandma smiles. I follow her into the kitchen as she goes to put the kettle on. The water whooshes in with a rattling noise.

'And how are things at home, Daniel?' she says quietly. 'Is Daddy looking after you and Mummy?'

'No.' The kettle falls with a clatter on to the hob. Grandma looks at me, she is not smiling any more. It looks like she is waiting for me to say something. 'Not today, he's on a picket line,' I say. 'Have you ever been on a picket line, Grandma?'

Grandma sighs and shakes her head. 'No, Daniel. Your

grandfather has, though. Many years ago when he worked in the cotton mills.' She crouches down next to me and takes hold of both my hands. 'You know you can talk to me about anything, don't you, Daniel? If anything at home is troubling you, if you are worried about anything, you can always come and tell me. Will you promise to do that?' She is looking very serious. I don't know what I am supposed to say so I just nod. She nods back and taps her nose. I think that means it is supposed to be our little secret. There are so many little secrets going on it is hard to remember who they are all secret from.

The kettle does its lovely singing whistle, Grandma pours the boiling water into a brown teapot, puts a woolly tea cosy on it, gets me a glass of Ribena and lets me carry it back into the room on my own. I don't spill any of it. Grandad starts talking about the old days in Romania, he always talks about that. His voice is different from other people's. Mummy says it's because he was born in Romania and we were born in Manchester. I like listening to his voice, it makes me feel a bit sleepy. They all talk about the strikes and what the Prime Minister is going to do about it. I don't know what his name is but he lives in a big house in London with number 10 on the door. I have seen it on the telly. Mr Benn lives at 52 Festival Road. I have seen that on the telly too.

Grandma pours the tea and brings her biscuit barrel in. It is a magic barrel, whenever you pull the lid off there are always biscuits there, lots of different sorts and a few chocolate ones. However many you eat, they never seem to run out, there are always more in the barrel the next time you come.

Grandma takes the lid off and passes it to me. I take a chocolate finger, they are the best ones in there. She passes it round and everyone else takes a biscuit and puts it on their saucer. Grandad dunks his in his tea. He says it tastes better like that. My chocolate finger has all gone. I am looking at the biscuit barrel.

'It's OK, you can have another,' Grandma says, smiling. 'A growing boy like you needs lots of energy.'

I take a long time choosing because I know that once you pick one up you're not allowed to put it back. In the end I go for one of the pink wafers because there are no chocolate ones left.

'I need a wee,' I say. 'Can I go in your new bathroom?'

'Of course you can, sweetheart. That's what it's for,' says Grandma, smiling. She leads me through the kitchen to the new bit of the house. 'There you are, love.'

I push the door, there is a blue toilet in front of me and a blue bath with shiny taps too. I am careful not to splash anything while I am weeing. I wonder what has happened to the woolly toilet seat cover Grandma knitted for the outside loo. I peed on it once by accident when I forgot to put the seat up but I didn't tell her.

When I am all done, Mummy and Grandma come in. Mummy says 'ooh' and 'lovely' a lot. Grandma shows me the knitted lady toilet roll cover she has made. She can knit anything you ask her to.

'Where's the woolly toilet seat cover?' I ask Grandma.

'Oh, I took it off and washed it. It's in a bag somewhere,' says Grandma. 'Nobody seems to need one these days.'

'Can I have it please?'

'What on earth do you want it for?' asks Grandma.

'I want to make a den for creepy crawlies. There were always lots of creepy crawlies in your outside toilet.'

Grandma laughs and looks at Mummy who shrugs and nods.

'I'll pop upstairs and dig it out for you,' says Grandma. 'Why don't you go and ask Grandad to play shove-ha'penny with you?' she says.

I get the board out from the cupboard under the stairs. Grandad is very good at shove-ha'penny, Grandma says he's a rotten loser and sometimes she gives him a special look and I can usually win the next game.

'Will you stay for lunch, Elizabeth?' asks Grandma a bit later, when we have finished playing. 'We've got plenty of bread in for some extra sandwiches.' I want to stay. They are nice, Grandma's sandwiches. She uses bread called Mother's Pride and always cuts the crusts off for me.

'We'd better not,' Mummy says. 'I'm not sure what time Michael will be home.'

Grandma looks disappointed. 'Oh, maybe another time, then,' she says.

'Yes,' says Mummy. 'That would be nice.'

Mummy gets our coats. I do not want to go. Grandma's eyes start to glisten. She bends down to give me a hug.

'Come and visit me again soon,' she says.

I go over to Grandad's armchair. He reaches out his hand and ruffles my hair, a bit like Daddy does but gentler.

'Be a good boy for your mother, now,' he says.

I nod and start walking towards the door. Grandma and

Mummy are having a hug, they are both doing the crying thing again.

'If the strike carries on and you need a hand with the rent . . .'

'We'll be fine,' Mummy says, patting her hand. She picks up her handbag and follows me to the door. Grandma opens it.

'Oh, don't forget this,' she says, hurrying back inside before handing me the woolly toilet seat cover. 'And remember what I said, Daniel.'

I nod as I step outside. Grandma stands there waving as I walk down the path.

'What did Grandma say to you?' asks Mummy as we get to the gate. I think for a moment before answering. Picturing Grandma tapping her nose.

'To be good,' I say.

'And remember what I said,' she says, walking on over the bridge. 'Not a word to Daddy about where we've been.'

I nod. I am losing count of all the things I've got to remember.

We could have stayed at Grandma's for lunch because Daddy doesn't get home until it's nearly dark. His cheeks are all rosy when he walks through the door and he calls out hello in a loud cheery voice.

'Have you put your little fire out?' I ask.

'Yes, all done for the night. We'll be back there again tomorrow, mind.'

Mummy looks up from the sink where she is washing

up and sighs. Her hair is back like it was before. She did it as soon as we got home. And she made me change out of my best clothes.

'What about the dead people, won't they need some more holes?' I ask.

'They'll have to wait till strike's over, whenever that is. Don't suppose they'll kick up much of a fuss. Deathly quiet, most of them.'

'Michael,' says Mummy.

He laughs and starts taking his boots off. His breath smells sweet and warm. I watch as he takes his jacket off but I can't see the little bottle he took with him.

'So, what've you been up to today?' he asks. Mummy looks at me hard.

'Nothing much. Just playing out with Philip,' I say.

Mummy smiles and goes back to the washing up. Daddy goes upstairs to get changed. When he comes back down a few minutes later he comes into the kitchen and stands there. He's never usually home at this time, when Mummy is getting tea ready. It's like he doesn't know what to do. I don't know what to do either.

I look across at Mummy. She is frowning at something on the floor. She makes a little sound like a dog does if you tread on its tail. I see it at exactly the same time. Grandma's woolly toilet seat cover. Lying underneath the table. Right where Daddy sits. My tummy feels funny. Like there is a lift inside it going up and down. I look at Mummy. Her face is all pale. If he sees the toilet seat cover he will know where we've been. And we both know what will happen then.

'The pie's in the oven,' says Mummy, brushing the flour off her apron. 'Why don't you play a game with your father until it's ready?' Her voice is shaky. I don't know why she has said it. We don't play games very often. I only have two, Operation and Buckaroo. Daddy has one called chess but I'm not old enough to play that yet. They are kept in the cupboard behind the kitchen table.

'Eh, that's a good idea,' says Daddy. 'But don't think I'm going to let you win, son,' he says, rubbing his hands. 'I'm going all out for victory tonight.'

Mummy walks towards the table. When she gets there she tries to kick the woolly toilet seat cover out of the way. But she is not very good at kicking. She kicks the table leg instead. Daddy looks round, Mummy's face goes even paler. I know I need to do something to make Daddy look at me. I pick up the satsumas in the bowl on the table.

'Look, Daddy. I've been practising,' I say. 'I can juggle three now.' I keep them up in the air for a little bit until I drop one. Daddy is smiling and clapping.

'Nice one, Danny boy. I'll make a showman of you yet.'

I pick the satsuma up off the floor. I look under the table. The woolly toilet seat cover has gone.

'Come on then, you two,' says Mummy, putting Operation down on the table. Her voice is still a bit wobbly. And the smile on her face is not a real smile. I notice the bulge in her apron pocket. She is trying to cover it with her hands. Daddy lets me have first go. My hand is shaking too much though. The buzzer goes off straight away. Daddy rubs his hands together.

'Right,' he says. 'Let me show you how it's done.'

Mummy checks the pie and waits until Daddy is concentrating really hard before she leaves the kitchen. I hear her footsteps go upstairs. When she comes back into the kitchen a few minutes later the bulge in her apron has gone. My hands are still too wobbly to play. The buzzer sounds again. Daddy lifts his arms in the air.

'Never mind, love,' says Mummy, smiling at me. 'You did really well.' It is a proper smile this time. With a big sigh at the end of it.

Eight

'Hi, Jo.' Tricia stood smiling intently at me, the fine lines which made little arrows just past the corners of her mouth pointed up towards her ears. If she smiled any harder the arrows would scissor all the way round her head and the bottom half of her face would fall off. Tricia had ditched her cool and aloof thing and was being nice to me. Perhaps it was a New Year's resolution. Perhaps some cynical ploy to get me to agree to her seeing Alfie. But whatever the reason, she had lowered herself to speak to me, one of the proletariat, and the other people filing into the conference room were watching me, waiting to see how I'd respond.

'Hi,' I said. Feeling compelled to reply.

'I like your boots,' said Tricia. 'Were they a Christmas present?' The being nice thing was difficult enough to cope with. Entering the realms of conversation, particularly gossiping about fashion, was taking it just that little bit too far.

'Er, yes, from Richard, three years ago. They don't really fit now because my feet grew a half size during pregnancy but I can't afford to splash out on any new ones.' It was a suitable conversation stopper. Tricia nodded, the smile on her face shrinking back into her mouth, and walked over to the other side of the conference room. I felt a twinge of guilt. Perhaps I should have lied to spare her feelings. But then I remembered that neither she nor Richard had done anything to spare mine. I went to stand next to Laura who was looking at me with a raised eyebrow.

'Your new best friend, is she?' she whispered.

'She could have been but I think I've blown it,' I replied.

We stood in silence until everyone else had squeezed into the room. It was standing room only. The annual 'Moving Forward Together' meeting was not something I had missed during my absence from *Spotlight North West*. It was delivered by Mark Redfern, the head of regional news at our parent company in London, and consisted of a résumé of our successes (usually brief), followed by a detailed analysis of where we were going wrong and the results of some expensively commissioned research which had established the sure-fire route to improved ratings. (Strangely enough he never addressed the fact that the previous year's research findings had obviously been bollocks, otherwise ratings would have gone through the roof and we would merely be gathered together each year for a well-deserved pat on the back.) Attendance was compulsory – even for part-timers – and people had been known to be summoned from their sickbeds and ordered to phone in from their holidays to be put on conference call so they could listen while on the beach.

At five to ten Big Denise strode in, her hair wilting slightly under the weight of the hair gel, her make-up ending highly visibly along her jawline.

She was accompanied by Richard, who had once dismissed these meetings as 'a power kick for Redfern and a waste of fucking time for the rest of us' but was now of course 'on message' as Denise's second-in-command, although looking slightly uncomfortable in the role.

'Happy New Year to those of you I haven't seen yet,' said Denise (this was actually everyone, as Denise always gave herself January the second off as well in order to complete her New Year sales shopping schedule).

'We'll go straight over to London where Mark's ready to give us a new mission statement for the programme.' Although we had all presumably thought we'd groaned inwardly, the cumulative effect was actually audible. 'Jake, could you do the honours please.' A young, spiky-haired guy from IT fiddled with a laptop and Mark Redfern popped up on the huge television screen, sitting casually on the corner of a desk, American news-anchor style.

I think it was at the point where he spoke about 'breaking the depressing news habit in editorial' and 'giving the viewers plenty of fun, fizz and flirting between the facts' that I accidentally laughed out loud. Richard shot me a warning look and I managed to disguise the rest of the laugh as a coughing fit. At this point Tricia sat down cross-legged on the office floor. I stared at her open mouthed. Unable to imagine having so much confidence that you could sit down on the floor like that in an important meeting in front of all your colleagues. She'd be taking her shoes off next and asking Richard for a foot massage.

'So,' said Big Denise as Mark at last faded from view, 'let's have some ideas about how we can meet the challenge of appealing to the younger demographic and making our bulletins fizz.'

'It seems to me,' said Richard, 'that we need to get away from the tired, frumpy, daytime TV sofa feel of the programme and make our presentation style more hip and happening.' The snipe was so obviously aimed at Moira that it appeared to have left a red mark on her cheek where it had slapped her.

'I will endeavour to fizz more on screen but I'm afraid I draw the line at flirting,' said Moira, trying hard to retain the smile on her face. Stuart looked down his nose at her, obviously taking the comment as a personal slight.

'The chemistry has to be right for anything to fizz,' said Stuart. 'Perhaps Tricia could have a bigger role in the programme. There's no need to keep our greatest asset confined to the weather slot.' I hadn't felt such a need to vomit since I'd been confined to bed with morning sickness. Tricia, who was still sitting on the floor, raised her head to offer the sweetest of smiles to Stuart.

'What do you think, Tricia?' asked Big Denise.

'Well, I'd love the chance to get out and about on location. Other channels have done that successfully with their weather presenters. It would give me more creative opportunities and give the viewers a greater awareness of their natural environment.' I had visions of Tricia skipping barefoot through a meadow in a re-creation of the Timotei shampoo advert.

'Perhaps we could go to Tricia before the break for a piece about wherever she is that day,' said Richard. 'Then return later for the weather report.'

'Tricia's Travels, we could call it,' said Big Denise.

'Maybe in summer she could report from some of the region's holiday hotspots,' added Stuart, no doubt hoping for some lingering bikini shots.

I looked across at Moira. She shrugged. Clearly, they'd all lost the plot.

'And what about our news coverage?' I said.

Big Denise looked at me as if I'd said a rude word. 'You heard what Mark said. The viewers don't want a diet of depressing dirge. Anything too heavy will have them reaching for the remote control.'

'But we have an obligation to cover hard news as well,' chipped in Laura.

'And we will do. Especially if it involves a celebrity. But some low-life on the Miles Platting estate complaining about the crackheads next door is no longer going to be part of our remit. We'll leave that to the Beeb. We want fun, frothy headlines that reel the viewers in, like the cover lines from the women's mags.'

'What, like "I gave birth on the bog" and "My sex-change grandad stole my husband",' I joked.

'Exactly,' said Big Denise, pointing enthusiastically at me. 'Jo's got the idea.'

The weak laugh which emanated from my mouth slid out and immediately crashed on to the floor.

'Perhaps we could expand the "And Finally" pieces from Jo,' chirped Tricia. 'They're always such good fun.'

Laura nudged me, trying not to smirk.

'Absolutely,' said Denise. 'We need to entertain as well as inform our audience. Now, any more questions?'

'Where does this leave our political and business coverage?' asked Simon, in a clear plea for a voice of reason in all this. Richard looked at Denise before answering.

'Viewers who want business and politics have got the BBC2 button on their remotes. We can't beat *Newsnight* so why try to be a poor imitation of it? From now on we're concentrating on our strengths.'

I shared a rare moment of empathy with Simon before Big Denise issued a final rallying cry which reminded me of something Bob the Builder said to his machines before embarking on a big job. We filed out of the conference room in silence.

'How much did you sell out for?' I asked Richard, as we found ourselves walking side by side back to the newsroom.

'I don't know what you're talking about.'

'Yes you do. I know you, remember. And I know how much you hate all that management bullshit.'

'You have to adapt to survive in this game,' he said, his steely grey eyes staring straight ahead, refusing to look at me.

'And that's what you were trying to tell Moira in that oh so subtle way of yours, was it?'

'If it was up to me we'd have got rid of her long ago. She's wrong for our image.'

'I'm glad the heart by-pass op went well,' I said. 'Enjoy humiliating your staff, do you?'

'Go and find me a good funny for tonight's programme,' said Richard. 'We pay you for your productivity not your opinions.'

I shook my head and walked slowly back to my desk, got out the Ken doll and stuck a pin in. Right where it would hurt.

The office copy of *Broadcast* magazine was already being passed around, folded over to the jobs section. Even the coffee machine seem depressed as it slowly emptied some brown sludge into the polystyrene cup.

'Are you OK?' I asked Moira as I turned to find her standing mournfully behind me.

'He sure knows how to make a woman feel good, doesn't he?'

'Take no notice. He's no longer a member of the human race as far as I'm concerned.'

'He's only saying what everyone else is thinking, though,' she said as she held her cup under and pressed the button. 'I'm on borrowed time until they find a younger model to replace me.'

'Hey, come on. The viewers love you and Denise brought you here in the first place, remember.'

'Yeah, but Richard's got her ear. And if he tells her enough times that I'm bad for viewing figures, she'll believe him in the end.' The tone in her voice was one of resignation, even her wavy red hair appeared limp and lifeless today. I noticed her moist eyes.

'Hey, are you all right?' I said, putting an arm round her.

'I'm sorry,' she said. 'It's all getting too much.'

'What is?'

'Trying to keep all the balls in the air at the same time. I'm never at home in the evenings when the kids need me and Rob's getting frazzled trying to make sure they're doing their homework instead of playing computer games and by the time I get home we're both exhausted and that's putting a strain on our marriage and then I come in here and get told I'm a frumpy old has-been in front of everyone and I just don't know if it's worth it any more.'

I took Moira's arm as the first tear fell and led her out into the corridor, away from all the prying eyes in the newsroom.

'It sounds like you need some time off,' I said. 'When did you last have a holiday?'

Moira shrugged. 'But if Pamela stands in for me for a week, I'll probably be out on my ear. You now how good she is.'

'And would that be the end of the world? You heard what they said in there. The direction we're going. I used to live and breathe this place, you know that. Remember me ringing you all up for the office gossip while I was waiting for Alfie to arrive?'

Moira nodded, no doubt recalling giving me a running commentary on Stuart's battle to get a bigger desk than hers.

'And I was desperate to come back, to feel like a proper journalist again. But now I'm here, I sit there and listen to that pile of crap and I see straight through it. All those sad, pathetic people desperate to further their careers by toeing the company line. No one cares about *real* news. It's all so shallow and pitiful.'

Moira smiled. 'I'm glad you feel like that too,' she said. 'I thought I was the only one.'

I shook my head. 'Maybe it's having kids that does it to you,' I said. 'Makes you realise that there are more

important things in life to get worked up about than viewing figures.'

'Wise words for one so young,' smiled Moira. 'It should
be me telling you this.'

'You did. I still remember the text you sent me when
Alfie was born.'

Moira smiled. 'Enjoy the reason for existing,' she said.

'Exactly. Maybe you need to listen to your own wise
words. You slog your guts out for this lot but they could
get rid of you tomorrow if they wanted to. Your husband
and your children are the ones who need you most.'

Moira sighed. 'I know you're right. I'm just not sure what
to do about it. It's hard when you work full time. You get
sucked into this whole "thou shalt not have a life outside
work" thing.'

'Well, if it's any consolation, you won't be the only one
plotting your escape after listening to that nonsense. And at
least with a CV like yours you'll have no shortage of offers.'

Moira gave me a 'thank you' smile and walked off, gazing into her hot chocolate.

When I got back to my desk there was an email from
Richard to all the editorial staff.

SUBJECT: Mission Statement
Please note it is not a case of choosing to accept
the contents of this mission statement. You either
embrace it wholeheartedly or you bugger off to work
for some obscure cable news channel that no one
watches. Alternatively, if you want an easy life and
aren't prepared to adapt to meet the needs of an

ever-changing news agenda, you could always open your own florists in Alderley Edge.
Brgds
RB

At that precise moment in time, the florists option looked rather appealing (Rachel would no doubt be appalled at Richard's slight on her profession). I decided a reply was called for.

SUBJECT: RE: Mission Statement
Dear RB
Working here is going to be fun, fun, fun from now on! I've spent my entire career as a journalist waiting for the moment when someone would tell me to slap anything that looks like a hard news story in the face and concentrate on fluffy stories while fizzing happily along like a sherbet dip. You're so hip and happening I'd like to flirt with you but unfortunately you've got your head stuck so far up Redfern's arse that I can no longer make eye contact with you.
Your ever fizzing funster
Jo
X

Much as I wanted to send it to Richard, the immediate need to keep a roof over Alfie's head prevented me from adding him to the list of recipients. Although judging by the smirks on Laura and Moira's faces a few moments later, I at least succeeded in cheering them up.

★

'So who do you reckon will get their resignation in first?' I asked Laura over lunch.

'Probably Simon. I know he's got some good contacts at the Beeb. I can't see him hanging around here much longer.'

'What about you? Any irons in the fire?'

Laura took a mouthful of spaghetti and wiped the sauce from her chin before answering.

'There's an assistant producer's job going at Sky. I don't think I've got enough experience so I wasn't going to apply for it but now, well, what have I got to lose?'

'Good for you. The only trouble is I'm going to be skint with all these leaving collections to put in to.'

'So get out yourself.'

'I've only just come back. Anyway, when was the last time you saw a part-time reporter's job advertised? I'll have to stick it out here, at least until Alfie goes to school.'

'But that's years away,' said Laura. 'This place will have gone to the dogs by then.'

'Before I came back,' I said, trying to explain, 'I really thought I could make a go of it, get my career back on track. But that's never going to happen while I'm part time. So I need to think of it differently. Like a job that normal people have. Where you simply go to work, do your thing and go home again.'

'But why would you want to do that?' asked Laura.

'Because of Alfie,' I said, breaking off some bread and scooping up the last of the soup from my bowl. 'I have to do what's best for him. And the way this industry's going,

I'm beginning to think that looking after Alfie three days a week is a damn sight more stimulating for my brain than working here.'

Laura laughed. 'You're probably right,' she said. 'I'm off to interview the Bishop of Burnley later for this report on last summer's race riots. Richard's told me he wants ten seconds max from him on how to resolve racial tension in the city.'

'Pah, he should be able to explain how to bring about world peace and prove God exists in that time as well.'

'I'm too bloody embarrassed to tell him how long he's going to get,' said Laura. 'I'll have to let him talk for ten minutes or so and then ask him to recap the main points so I can edit them out later.'

'Well, just make sure you don't let it overrun,' I said. 'Because I need my full ninety seconds tonight.'

'What for?' asked Laura.

'Moira and I have got something up our sleeves. You'll have to wait and see,' I said.

We gathered around the television screen at six o'clock that evening, a rare sense of camaraderie amongst the usually bickering reporters. Even Moira and Stuart appeared fractionally less frosty towards each other – although they were still a very long way from flirting. Moira ran through the headlines as a clip of each report came on, until my face appeared on the screen.

'And I'll be reporting on the mum who's going into rehab to break her addiction to sherbet dips.'

Moira was grinning as the camera came back to her.

'There you are,' she said. 'Plenty of fizz to look forward to on the show tonight.'

The others were still laughing when Big Denise and Richard emerged from the gallery at the end of the show.

'Loved it, Jo,' said Big Denise. 'More of the same please.'

A stony-faced Richard beckoned me over. 'You might fool her,' he whispered, 'but not me. You were taking the piss.'

'Not at all,' I said. 'Simply embracing the new mission statement wholeheartedly.' I turned and walked away quickly so he couldn't see the smile on my face.

Nine

'Hi, Brendan. Did you have a good Christmas?' asked Rachel. We'd met him on the way to Little Acorns and while I understood Rachel's desire to be friendly, I wished she had remembered that such polite enquiries were generally met with a tale of unfettered woe.

'Not really,' he said. 'Reuben wasn't well. I think it was the combination of all the excitement and an out-of-date mince pie he ate. He threw up in bed on Christmas Eve.'

'Oh dear,' said Rachel, as we pushed the buggies in single file along the narrow cobbled street. 'Poor thing.'

'Yeah,' said Brendan, lowering his voice as he turned round to Rachel. 'The trouble was I'd already left the stocking for Santa at the end of his bed and it got covered in projectile vomit so I had to put his presents in a Co-op carrier bag instead. I felt bad about it because of this plastic bag ban we're supposed to be doing in Hebden. I know Santa should have set him a better example but it was one in the morning and it was all I could find. The trouble is, Reuben asked a lot of questions about Santa the next morning and I'm worried he's worked it out. About Father Christmas not being real, I mean. He's already been through so much and I don't want him to be traumatised any further.' The last bit was said in a barely audible whisper. As Brendan finally paused for breath, I nodded in what I hoped was an understanding fashion and Rachel made suitably sympathetic clucking noises. I kept telling her she should volunteer for the Samaritans in order to make full use of her listening skills.

It was a relief to arrive at Little Acorns where Hermione was busy turning up the gas fires and fussing over whether Darcy and Elouise were warm enough.

'Do come in,' she said. 'I'm afraid the caretaker forgot to put the heating on this morning. I was just asking Suzanne whether she thought we should carry on or postpone the session.'

'It is very cold. I wouldn't want Reuben to go down with anything,' said Brendan.

'Let's carry on,' I said quickly. 'The children will warm up as soon as they start running around.'

'That's a good point. Is that OK with everyone?' asked Hermione.

Rachel and Suzanne nodded. Brendan shrugged but Hermione was obviously learning to ignore him.

'Oh good. I've got a new child starting today as well and I don't want to let them down.'

I turned round to see Alfie trying to poke his finger through the guard around one of the fires.

'Alfie, no. That's hot. We don't touch. Come and sit down now,' I said, hauling him away. I loved him dearly but the idea of having one of those little girls who sat still and didn't do anything was occasionally very appealing.

The door opened and an elegant woman dressed stylishly

in a purple wool coat and suede boots walked in, smiling broadly at everyone. The little girl who followed her in was wearing a cream poncho which looked stunning against her black skin.

'Hello, you must be Angela,' said Hermione, rushing to greet her. She bent down to talk to the little girl who was hiding behind her mum's legs. 'And who have we here?'

'Say hello, Carmel,' said Angela.

Carmel peeped out and smiled, displaying two exceedingly cute dimples.

'What an adorable little girl,' said Hermione. 'I am sorry about the cold, by the way. You may want to keep your coats on for a moment until it warms up. Now, come over and meet the rest of the class.' Hermione ushered Angela over and introduced her to everyone in turn. Just at the point when she got to me and Alfie, Carmel pulled down the hood of her poncho to reveal her beautifully braided hair. Alfie stared for a moment and then pointed excitedly as if she was a new exhibit in a zoo which he hadn't come across before.

'Golliwog,' he said.

The silence which followed may have lasted for only a second or two in real time but it seemed more like a fortnight in Holloway prison to me. I felt shocked, embarrassed, appalled, saddened and angry, all within those few seconds of silence as my brain struggled to take in what it had heard and work out where, or rather who, Alfie would have picked up that word from.

'I am so sorry,' was what I eventually said. Utterly pathetic and inadequate but mentioning that I was a former member of the anti-apartheid movement and had cried more than anyone else in the cinema when I'd been to watch *Biko* also seemed entirely pathetic, and insulting to boot.

'It's OK, children say these things.' Angela was being nice. Children didn't say these things. Certainly not in Hebden Bridge. And if they did they were cast out from their social circle pretty swiftly. I glanced around. Hermione's mouth was still gaping open, Rachel was staring in disbelief, Brendan had pulled Reuben protectively to him and Suzanne was busying herself with removing some imaginary speck on Darcy's left cheek.

'My mother looks after him sometimes. She's got some very old Enid Blyton books she reads to him,' I said. People nodded and smiled politely while no doubt mentally crossing Alfie off their child's birthday party invitation list. Just to make matters worse, Carmel, who of course had no idea what a golliwog was, appeared to be quite taken with Alfie and was now leading him by the hand around the room.

The door burst open and Nicole blew in, out of breath as usual and dragging a weary-looking Zach behind her.

'Sorry we're late,' she started then stopped as she noticed Alfie and Carmel hand in hand. 'Oh, who's your new friend, Alfie?'

'Golliwog,' he said again.

'Oh, God,' I groaned, as we sat down in Organic House an hour later. 'How can I possibly face her again next week? We'll have to leave Little Acorns. Leave Hebden

Bridge for that matter.' Alfie banged his beaker on the café table, as if seconding my view.

'Come on. It could have been worse,' said Rachel as she lifted Poppy into the other high chair and gave her a pot of grapes to munch on.

'Only if he'd been caught goose-stepping up and down Market Street shouting "*Sieg Heil*",' I said.

'At least Angela seemed very understanding.'

I decided to ignore Rachel's attempts to always look on the bright side. I was reminded instead of an article I'd read in the *Guardian* when I was pregnant about lefty/liberal people whose children had turned into fascists (as if you don't have enough things to worry about going wrong when you're pregnant). I knew I needed to tackle the root cause of the problem before things got any worse.

'I shall be having words with my mother.'

'Are you sure he picked it up from her?'

'Alfie said he'd seen one in a book at Nanna's house. I'm not surprised, she's probably got a whole collection of golliwog memorabilia. I still remember her cutting out and sending off those Robertson's jam labels when I was a kid.'

'Perhaps you could explain to her that times have changed.'

I laughed and shook my head. Rachel kept forgetting that my mother had never made it out of the 1950s.

'The fact is, if a childminder had her views, I wouldn't leave Alfie alone with her for a minute. But it's difficult to sack your own mother.'

A dread-locked waiter came over and put a large cafetière, two cups and a milk jug on the table.

'Thanks, Jordan,' said Rachel. She came here a lot, because it was organic and they had nice art on the walls. I hadn't confessed that when Alfie and I were on our own we sometimes went to the café opposite the park instead. Because it was cheap and they did chips.

'You could always try to find a decent childminder,' said Rachel. She said it half-heartedly, being well aware that it could sound rich coming from someone who had been able to avoid childminders because she had a childcare-sharing new man of a husband. The truth was I couldn't bear the thought of leaving Alfie with a stranger. He had already been deserted by one parent and I didn't want him to feel I was now deserting him.

'Better the devil you know, I guess. Anyway, even if I sacked her as a childminder she'd still be his grandmother.'

I sighed and gazed out of the window. Our table looking out on the traffic lights before the bridge was one of the best vantage points in Hebden Bridge for human traffic. It was impossible to sit here for ten minutes without seeing some-one you knew. Rachel had once seen one of those naked rambler guys walk past and claimed no one else had batted an eyelid. That was the kind of place it was. A middle-aged woman with burgundy highlights in her hair and pulling the latest in designer shopping trolleys strolled past, followed by two little boys who looked as if they had walked straight out of a Dickensian tale. And a tall man in his thirties wear-ing chunky boots, frayed jeans with a hole in the knee, a black fleece and a black beanie hat pulled down over his ears. I had that feeling inside me again. The one I used to get when I was thirteen and my jaw-droppingly gorgeous

English teacher walked in the room. But being thirty-four I also had the sense to know that I was best off out of it. I put my head down and pretended not to have noticed. Alfie, of course, had other ideas.

'Balloon man,' he shouted, showering chewed-up rice cake from his mouth across the table as he pointed and waved frantically through the window. The commotion was enough to make Dan look in. He waved and smiled as he recognised Alfie, and again, although more subtly, as he saw me. He was still waving as he disappeared out of view. Alfie banged his beaker on the table in protest. But a second later Dan reappeared, doing a comedy backwards walk past the window. Alfie and Poppy shrieked with laughter as he reversed through the door and pretended to jump as the bell dinged.

'Sometimes,' he said, arriving at our table, 'it takes a while for my legs to catch up with what my head is telling them to do. I'm not sure if I have the early onset of some kind of degenerative disease or it's just because I'm tall.'

I smiled up at him. I wasn't even aware how big the smile was until I caught sight of Rachel's raised eyebrow out of the corner of my eye.

'Hi, Dan. Do you remember Rachel?'

'I do indeed. And Alfie's young friend Poppy here. Are they courting?'

'The only thing Alfie courts is trouble,' I replied with a grin.

'Oh, what's he been up to?'

'Just putting race relations in Hebden Bridge back thirty

years. It wasn't his fault, though. My mother's been feeding him a diet of Enid Blyton.'

'Oh dear,' he said. 'I never trusted the folk of the faraway tree. All very sinister if you ask me.'

Dan looked down at the empty seat next to us. I realised that this was the point where I was supposed to invite him to join us. But something stopped me from doing it. So it was Rachel's voice I heard asking if he wanted a coffee.

'We've got plenty for three,' she said.

'Thank you but I'm on my way to pick up some supplies for my act. I need to get to the shop before they shut.'

'See shed,' said Alfie.

'Yes,' I said. 'That's next week. If it's still OK with Dan.'

'Absolutely. I'm going to tidy it up especially for you, Alfie,' said Dan. 'You'll be the first official visitor it's ever had.'

Alfie looked suitably chuffed.

'See you then,' said Dan, turning to me. 'Do you remember where to come?'

'Yep, got it all written down. Through the rickety green gate and down the wiggly path to the big twisty tree.'

'Sounds like an Enid Blyton book,' said Rachel.

'Just watch out for the boat goblin,' smiled Dan.

'I will,' I said. 'I've got his card marked already.'

Dan grinned, took off his hat to bid us farewell and walked backwards out of the door and back past the window.

'Why didn't you mention your shed date with the gorgeous Dan?' said Rachel when he had disappeared from view.

'Because it's not a date. Alfie wanted to visit his shed. He saw it from the canal when we went for the boat ride.'

'How long do you think you can get away with it?'

'What?' I said, refilling Alfie's rice cake pot from my emergency supply packet.

'Pretending it's Alfie and not you who's seeing him.'

I pushed the plunger on the cafetière and slowly poured two cups of coffee. Anything to give me a bit more time.

'Alfie adores him,' I said.

'And so do you. That's why you didn't ask him to join us.' Rachel was more perceptive than I sometimes gave her credit for. I put my cup down in the saucer and lowered my voice.

'OK,' I said. 'I admit it. If I was on my own I'd probably be jogging past his boat every day to try to get his attention. But I'm not. I've got Alfie to think about. I don't want him getting hurt again.'

'Why are you starting from the assumption that it will all go horribly wrong?'

'Because unlike Enid Blyton, I no longer believe in happy endings. Anyway, why are you assuming that he'd be interested?'

'He seemed pretty keen to me.'

'He's just being friendly because of Alfie, he's not interested in me. Remember what my old hairdresser Paul said about single mums? I think the quote was, "If the father of their child doesn't want to sleep with them any more, why on earth do they think any other man would?"'

'Yes, and he also thought that hanging should be brought

back and that there should be compulsory national service for fourteen year olds.'

'Well, anyway,' I said, lunging forward to prevent Alfie from emptying the entire contents of the salt pot over the table. 'It doesn't matter because I think Dan's seeing someone.'

'What makes you say that?'

'There was a pot of nail varnish and some hand and nail cream on the shelf above his bed.'

'Well,' said Rachel, who was never one to admit defeat. 'There could be all sorts of innocent explanations for that.'

'Like what?'

'I don't know,' said Rachel, 'you're the journalist. Ask him when you go to see his shed.'

'See shed?' said Alfie, looking up expectantly from his pot of rice cakes.

'Next week,' I said. 'Five big sleeps to go.'

'Not that you're counting,' said Rachel.

'Haven't you finished that coffee yet?' I replied.

It was midway through Friday morning by the time Alfie and I finally made it to my mum's.

'Oh,' she said when she opened the door. 'This is an unexpected surprise.'

I wondered if we'd interrupted a repeat of *Cash in the Attic*.

'Have you come to play with Nanna, Alfie?' she said.

'He has but I need to talk to you as well,' I said, taking my shoes off in the porch and following her into the lounge. Derek was at work which was probably for the best as I knew he would have backed my mum's view, having once declared that he thought the BNP 'only said what everyone else was thinking'. Alfie launched himself head first into the toy box while I rummaged through the pile of old children's books in the corner, keen to secure the evidence before I made the accusation.

'This,' I said, holding up a dog-eared copy of *The Three Golliwogs*, 'has got to go, I'm afraid.'

'But it's Enid Blyton. You and your brother both read that.'

I gestured to Mum to follow me out into the hallway, out of earshot of Alfie.

'I'm not doubting it but yesterday Alfie called a little black girl a golliwog.'

'Aahh. He was only being friendly.'

'Funnily enough I don't think her mother saw it like that.'

'One of these fundamentalists, was she?'

I shook my head. The *Daily Mail* had a lot to answer for.

'No, she was a normal mother who quite rightly didn't expect her daughter to hear such outdated language. Even Robertson's have dropped their golly now, you know.'

'Of course I know, I wrote to them to complain about it but all I got back was a silly letter telling me I'd grow to love the Roald Dahl characters just as much. I switched to Hartley's instead in protest.'

I sighed. My head hurt from banging it against the brick wall so often.

'All I'm asking is that you put the book away and please don't use that word with Alfie, OK?'

'I still think you're making a big fuss over nothing,' said Mum, doing her indignant of Hollingworth Lake impression.

Alfie emerged from the lounge and ran up to Mum.

'Sugar cubes,' he said, holding his hand out. I stared at her, waiting for an explanation, hopefully one that didn't involve Mary Poppins.

'He only has two a day,' she said. 'He likes the noise they make when he crunches them with his teeth.'

I shook my head, not wanting to believe what I was hearing.

'Let's just hope he likes the noise of the dentist's drill as well then, shall we?'

Ten

The rickety green gate was more like a door actually. Wide and solid and higher than my head. I pushed it open and went through, half expecting to enter the magical kingdom of Narnia. In front of us a winding dirt track led down through the trees, the early morning frost still clinging to their otherwise bare branches.

'Ooohh,' said Alfie. I couldn't have put it better myself. If it wasn't for the drone of passing traffic on the main road above, I could have imagined we were deep in the middle of an ancient forest, about to embark on an adventurous trek to the home of some remote hill tribe.

I held Alfie's hand tightly and began edging my way along the slippery track. There was a sheer drop on one side and I was glad I had heeded Dan's advice to wear boots as we negotiated a variety of exposed roots and small gullies on the descent. As the track dropped down towards the canal, we caught our first sight of the boats through the trees. At least the *Elizabeth* would be easy to spot; looking for a red and yellow harlequin painted boat was the waterways equivalent of searching for a bright orange Beetle in a multi-storey car park. As we picked our way carefully along the mooring ropes I noted that when it came to naming their vessels, most boat owners had a worse line in puns than hairdressers did when naming their salons.

'Shed,' called Alfie, pointing up ahead. Sure enough I could see the top of Dan's big red shed poking out above the others.

'Hey, yes. And look,' I said, crouching down to Alfie's height and pointing. 'There's the twisty tree Dan said to look out for.' A second later I spotted the *Elizabeth*, a riot of colour leaping out from the dark water beneath. I smiled as I saw the red carpet laid out along the wooden board-walk and a smaller piece leading up to the shed. There was no sign of Dan on the boat. The curtains on his bedroom window were still drawn. I looked at my watch, we were quarter of an hour early. I hoped he wasn't still in bed.

'Hi,' I called out. No answer. I waited a moment and called again but still no one came. I picked Alfie up and gingerly stepped across on to the boat and knocked on the door. There was a shuffling noise from inside and a second later Dan's head popped out, his hair still wet from the shower, his smile eclipsing anything the sun had to offer.

'Hi, sorry about that. I didn't hear you arrive. You haven't been waiting long, have you?'

'No. just got here.'

'Good. Come on in.' I tried to carry Alfie down the steps myself but he kicked up a fuss and insisted on doing it himself. I went down first, my hands poised, ready to grab him quickly if necessary, but he made it all the way to the bottom on his own.

'Hey, well done, Alfie,' said Dan. 'You did that all by yourself.'

Alfie turned to me triumphantly. I was impressed that Dan had noticed and conscious of how rare it was that I got to share one of Alfie's achievements, however small, with anyone else. It was then I noticed the smell. Such a distinctive one that I knew instantly what it was. I glanced down at Dan's hands. I could just make out the clear sheen on his freshly painted nails.

'Aaah,' he said, following my gaze. 'You're wondering about the nail polish and probably wondering if I also dabble with mascara and lipstick when there's no one around.'

I laughed uncomfortably. 'Hey, this is Hebden Bridge,' I said, throwing out an arm to try to emphasise the casualness of my response. 'Anything goes.'

Dan looked at me, his eyebrows arching and his lips pressed together as he tried not to laugh.

'It's OK,' he said. 'That was an admirable attempt to pretend to be cool about it but you don't have to be. The nail care is strictly for professional reasons.'

'Go on,' I said, still not understanding.

'The powder they put inside modelling balloons to keep them from sticking dries out your hands and can make your nails split. And if you've got split nails you'll end up bursting balloons and making small children cry.'

'And that's why you use hand and nail cream as well,' I said, piecing it all together.

'Yep,' said Dan. 'I know one guy whose fingers all split and he ended up having to wear cotton gloves to bed, it was so bad.'

I started laughing. Not at Dan's friend's misfortune but

my own foolishness. Alfie started laughing too, although he had no idea what was so funny.

'You had me down as a transvestite or something, didn't you?' said Dan, smiling.

'No, no. It's just that I saw them by your bed and didn't know what to think. Whether they belonged to you or someone else.'

'And why did it matter if they did belong to someone else?' said Dan, grinning. He was teasing me now, knowing I'd be too embarrassed to answer. That I'd unwittingly revealed my hand and the next move was up to him.

'It didn't matter at all,' I said, letting my hair fall across my face as I became aware of the colour rapidly filling my cheeks. 'I just wanted to make sure I understood the situation.'

'And is everything clear now?' he said.

'Yes, thank you. As clear as the nail polish,' I replied with a grin, my gaze still unable to free itself from the magnetic pull his eyes exerted.

'Good. At least we managed to clear that up without any embarrassment,' he said, his eyes twinkling with mirth. It was my turn to raise my eyebrows.

'Stop taking the—'

Dan put his finger to his lips. 'Watch your language,' he interrupted, pointing down at Alfie.

I wasn't going to let him get away with teasing me any further. I stepped forward and pretended to playfully box his ears. He flinched, his eyes wide, his hands raised to defend himself before he dropped them quickly. We stood for a moment in silence. The playful atmosphere lying shattered on the floor around us. I was about to ask if he was OK when he jumped back again exaggeratedly, this time with a silly expression on his face. A second later he was bouncing around the boat pretending to be Tigger, sending Alfie into a fit of giggles.

'Tigger thought your mum wanted to be a boxing kangaroo there,' he said.

Alfie laughed, thinking it was all part of the act. Although I wasn't so sure.

'OK, Pooh,' he said to Alfie. 'Would you like Tigger to take you on the shed tour?'

Alfie was back up the steps so fast I had to run to catch him before he got to the top.

'I think you can take that as a yes,' I called over my shoulder. Dan followed us up the steps before jumping on to the towpath.

'Allow me,' he said, helping us across and ushering us on to the red carpet.

'I would have dressed up if I'd known we were going to get the red carpet treatment,' I said, looking down at my tatty combats.

'Some sleek and stylish Ralph Lauren number?' enquired Dan.

I laughed, pleased to have returned to the banter. 'Yeah, right. Which would no doubt have been covered in grubby little hand prints and tomato ketchup stains before I'd even left the house.'

'And your stilettos would have been slightly the worse for wear by the time you'd made it down the path from the gate,' pointed out Dan.

'Exactly. It's a good thing that my dressing-up days are

long gone,' I said. 'Alfie is the only one who gets his clothes from Next and Gap these days. I get most of my stuff from the charity shops of Hebden Bridge.'

'Hey, me too,' said Dan. 'Who needs the Trafford Centre when you've got five charity shops within a few hundred yards?'

'And such great stuff in them,' I said. 'It's why I don't complain about all these bright young things moving up from the south to snap up converted mill apartments. You get to buy their cool cast-offs in Oxfam.' We were interrupted by Alfie who was now tugging the sleeve of my Jigsaw jacket, another Oxfam find, and jumping up and down outside the shed door.

'Here goes then, Alfie. I hope this isn't going to be a let-down for you,' said Dan. 'I'm afraid it really isn't that exciting.' He lifted the latch and pulled open the door.

The contents were split in two halves with a narrow gangway between. On one side the practical boat things: sacks of coal, various tools, a hosepipe, some sort of pump and a cable. On the other side work things: a selection of juggling implements, plastic stacking boxes with what looked like an assortment of costumes and props inside and – the jewel in the crown as far as Alfie was concerned – Dan's clown bike. Alfie toddled up to the bike and reached for the horn, looking round at Dan for permission to touch it. 'Go on then,' he said. 'Just one little hoot.' Alfie pressed the horn and chuckled at the noise that came out before sitting down and starting to spin the raised front wheel around. Something which I suspected would keep him occupied for the next half-hour.

'Wow, I didn't realise you'd have mains electricity here,' I said, pointing at the meter.

'Yep, one of the perks of having a permanent mooring. Along with the lack of gawpers away from the towpath, of course.'

'What gawpers?' I asked.

'Pensioners on day trips, mostly,' said Dan. 'Before I had a permanent mooring, when I used to have to tie up in whatever space I could along the towpath, I used to get them all the time. Peering in at the windows as if I was some kind of museum exhibit. I even had two come on the boat uninvited one morning. It was a bit like *Goldilocks and the Three Bears*. "Oh, that must be his bed," one of them said. And as I turned over and opened my eyes, the other one said, "Oh yes, and look, he's still in it."'

'What a cheek,' I said. 'What did you do?'

'What I wished I'd done afterwards was jump out of bed naked and give them a fright. What I actually did was point out that they were trespassing on private property and politely suggest they go and do their sightseeing elsewhere.'

'So you like your privacy here?' I said.

'I love it,' he said. 'I wouldn't want to live anywhere else.'

I turned and looked out at the view from the shed. The *Elizabeth* bobbing gently in the wake of another boat going past, the sunlight hitting the tops of the hills on the other side of the canal, a couple of ducks waddling along the boardwalk.

'I don't blame you. This is being alive,' I said, breathing in a lungful of fresh, crisp air.

'Juggle,' said Alfie, looking up expectantly at Dan with a skittle in his hand.

'Sorry,' I said. 'Do you perform on demand?'

'Only for a very select few,' said Dan, collecting some more skittles from the tub and moving to a clearing near the shed. 'Stand back, Alfie. Just in case.' Alfie watched mesmerised as Dan juggled three, four then five skittles, his head rolling in a figure of eight as he kept his eyes on each one. I clapped and whistled when he finished.

'Where did you learn to do that?' I said.

'I started at home, when I was a kid, with fruit and stuff. I did a clown workshop when I was a teenager and I was hooked. So when I left school I went to a performing arts college where I learned how to do it properly.'

'And what about the balloons? Did you learn to do that there as well?'

'The basics. From then on most of it was self-taught. Trial and error and lots of clown droppings.'

I looked at him quizzically.

'That's what they call the broken bits of balloons,' he explained.

'And is there a secret to it? I mean, I have so little puff I had to resort to a pump for Alfie's birthday balloons. If the police ever ask me to blow into a bag I don't think I'd be able to manage it.'

'You have to use your diaphragm,' said Dan. 'Come on, I'll show you. This way, Alfie. Balloon show time.' Alfie took Dan's hand and trotted back happily with him to the *Elizabeth*. Dan turned to look at me, obviously checking if I wanted to carry Alfie on board myself.

'It's OK. Go on,' I said.

Dan picked Alfie up and held him so tightly I wondered if he'd be able to breathe. Once aboard he placed him down gently at the top of the steps and went down in front of him, encouraging him all the way.

'Did you have younger brothers or sisters?' I asked as I followed them down inside, intrigued as to why he was so good with Alfie.

Dan shook his head. 'No, just the six children of my own.'

I froze as I realised I had made another rash assumption about him. And then looked at his face and realised he was joking.

'All by different women, I presume,' I said with a grin.

'Of course, and all living at lock-keeper's cottages, funnily enough.'

I laughed and shook my head. 'Do you ever give a straight answer?'

'Do you ever stop asking questions?'

'Sorry, it's my training.' It was Dan's turn to look at me quizzically. 'I'm a journalist,' I explained.

The look on Dan's face suggested I'd just admitted to being a call girl.

'Come on,' I said. 'I know we rank up there with estate agents and traffic wardens but I'm really not that bad.'

He walked across to the other side of the boat and started rummaging in some drawers.

'Who do you work for?' he asked, still with his back to me.

'I'm a local TV news reporter for *Spotlight North West*. It's like the *Calendar* for the Manchester area.'

Dan stopped rummaging. 'I know,' he said. 'I grew up in Manchester.'

'Oh, right. Whereabouts?'

'Fairfield, right on the border with Tameside.'

'And do you still have family there?'

There was a pause from Dan's end as he did some more rummaging.

'Only my grandmother,' he said eventually. I wanted to ask more but I took it from his tone of voice that I'd already asked one question too many.

'It's all right, I'm not one of those Rottweiler reporters. I don't do proper news any more. They've relegated me to being the "And Finally" girl since I went back two days a week. Hamsters that think they're dogs, kids who can play the *Lazy Town* theme tune on their epiglottis, that sort of thing.'

Dan straightened and turned to face me. He managed a proper smile this time.

'Well, that's a relief,' he said. 'For a minute there I thought you might be doing some kind of undercover exposé on balloon sculptors.'

'What have you got to hide, then?' I said.

'The fact that I get paid to blow up balloons, twist them into funny shapes and give them to children to put a smile on their faces. I don't want other people to know what a great life it is in case they all jack in their boring, crappy jobs and start doing it.'

'Put like that, it does sound kind of appealing.'

'Come on then,' said Dan. 'Let's see if you have the makings of a professional.' He bent down and pulled out a box with the words 'Qualatex 260s' on it from the cup-board and delved inside to produce a long, clear balloon.

'The easiest ones to blow up,' he said. 'Don't ask me why. Give them a gentle pull first, they're easier to work with when they're warm. Now,' he said, handing me the balloon. 'Don't think of it as blowing. Think of breathing into it from your diaphragm.'

I put the end of the balloon between my lips and took a deep breath. I barely managed to inflate a centimetre. Dan threw his hands up in the air and shook his head in mock horror. Alfie started laughing.

'You're still puffing up your cheeks and blowing from your mouth,' said Dan. 'Keep them in, otherwise you'll get Dizzy Gillespie cheeks. Here, come and stand behind me and I'll show you.' Dan's eyes beckoned me forward. I moved silently to within a couple of inches of his body, any closer and I feared the magnetic field around him would pull me in and I would stick fast, refusing to give up my grip. I watched Dan's arms reach back and lift off his fleece. Saw his T-shirt underneath ride up to reveal a broad, sinewy back before he tugged it back down again. Told myself to stop thinking what I was thinking.

'Now, place your hands just under my ribs, so you can feel me breathe in.'

My hands did as they were told. Resting lightly against his T-shirt. Obeying the instructions sent urgently from my head to behave themselves. I felt Dan's muscles moving beneath my fingers as he reached over and took another balloon from the box and put it to his lips. My hands rose gently as he inhaled before contracting back with him as he let go of a long, slow breath which slithered all the way up his body and emptied into the balloon, fully inflating it. Alfie clapped. Dan tied the balloon and gave it to Alfie. I realised my hands were still on Dan and quickly pulled them away, immediately missing the warmth beneath my fingertips.

'Well, did you feel anything?' asked Dan, turning round with a wicked grin on his face.

'Oh yes,' I said. 'Something definitely moved.'

'Good. Now it's your turn,' he said, stretching another balloon and handing it to me. 'I want you to do the same thing and make my hands move. OK?'

I nodded and we swapped places. His arms folded around me and one thumb brushed accidentally against my breast as he placed his hands under my ribs.

'Ooops, sorry,' he whispered.

'It's OK,' I said. 'They're on a mission to reach my waist by the time I'm thirty-five.' I couldn't believe I'd said that out loud. I blushed. Dan started chuckling.

'Cuddle Mummy,' said Alfie, running up to hug the front of my legs. I laughed and turned to him, ruffling his hair to cover my embarrassment. I could feel Dan's breath on my neck, knew he was still laughing too. Weirdly, it felt as if Alfie had run into the bedroom while we were having sex. Except of course we were fully clothed. And Dan had a perfectly innocent reason for having his arms around me.

I composed myself, put the balloon to my lips and let my stomach rise into Dan's hands, then pushed the breath out into the balloon and watched it grow. Not all the way to the end but a good third of the way along. Alfie started jumping up and down and clapping. I turned to look up at Dan as he slid his hands from my stomach to take the balloon from me and tie a knot in it.

'How did I do?' I asked.

'I think my search for an assistant is over.'

'Fantastic. I could be the next Debbie McGee.'

'Doth compare me to a small balding man with an irritating nasal voice?' asked Dan.

'Well, now you come to mention it.'

'Oh, cheers,' said Dan. 'On second thoughts, I'm not sure you're up to the rigours of the job.'

'What, blowing up a few balloons and mucking about with kids all day?'

'You may jest but I should get danger money for doing this. I've heard of people inflating their sinuses and having seizures because they've been blowing incorrectly. Quite a few suffer with glaucoma and ear infections. And eye injuries are pretty common from bursting balloons.'

'Is that why you were wearing glasses at Eureka?'

'Yeah, they're clear lenses, just there for protection. Then there's the RSI and carpal tunnel syndrome from all that twisting, and if you survive that, some obnoxious parent will try to sue you for emotional distress because they let their kid sit on the balloon and pop it two seconds after I gave it to them.'

'More balloons,' said Alfie, who was clearly expecting his own personal show.

'And then you get the demanding kids,' I said.

'They're brilliant,' said Dan. 'They're the reason it's all

worth it. Seeing the look on their faces. Right, Alfie, let me make you a souvenir of your visit.' He took a handful of red balloons from the box and started blowing them up. I watched his cheeks, perfectly flat as he blew, and his fingers, expertly separating the air bubbles in the balloon, ready to twist them into place. Alfie worked it out this time, just as Dan was putting the roof on.

'Shed,' he squealed in delight.

'Thank you,' I said. 'Honestly, all this free entertainment you're providing and presents as well. I feel like some sponging single mum.'

'Don't be daft,' said Dan. 'This isn't work. It's pleasure.'

'Well, if there's ever anything we can do to say thank you properly.'

Dan thought for a moment before his eyes lit up.

'Maybe there is,' he said. 'Alfie doesn't happen to have any Thomas the Tank Engine books, does he?'

'Toot, toot,' said Alfie, careering around the boat with his arms and legs pumping in full steam.

'You may have gathered that the answer is yes,' I said. 'Personally I find the stories dull and unimaginative and the engines downright nasty. But for some reason which I can't fathom, Alfie loves them.'

'I expect it's a boy thing,' said Dan.

'Were you into them when you were a kid?' I asked.

'I guess not,' said Dan. 'I can't remember them at all. That's why I'd like to borrow Alfie's.'

I scratched my head, not sure I understood. 'Are you on some sort of nostalgia kick for your lost childhood?'

Dan looked down at his feet and shook his head. 'I've

been booked to entertain the hordes when Thomas the Tank Engine visits the National Railway Museum at York in a couple of weekends' time. I've got to keep the kids happy while they're queuing for rides and I'm expected to be able to create every Thomas character in balloons.'

I started laughing.

'Charming,' said Dan. 'And there was I hoping for some encouragement.'

'Sorry,' I said. 'I've just got this vision of you studying photos of Harold the Helicopter for homework.'

'There's a helicopter?' said Dan, looking aghast.

'I tell you what,' I said. 'Alfie will loan you his Thomas books so you can swot up.'

'Thank you,' said Dan. 'That'll be an enormous help. There's one condition, though.'

'What's that?' I said.

'That you two come with me as my treat.'

It felt as good as being asked on my first proper date when I was fourteen. And then I remembered that I wasn't supposed to feel like that. I was supposed to be a responsible mother now.

'No, you don't have to do that. This was supposed to be us repaying your kindness, remember?'

'Nonsense. I need all the moral support I can get. And Alfie would love it.'

I hesitated. He was right, I knew that. But I also knew that this was veering dangerously into third date territory.

'OK. You're on. But just as a treat for Alfie, you understand.'

'Absolutely,' said Dan. 'I will mark it in my diary as such. Alfie's big day out. Jo coming too.'

'That's fine then. As long as it's understood.'

Dan nodded. Though I sensed he was trying hard to keep a straight face.

'Hey, Alfie. We're going to see Thomas soon,' said Dan.

Alfie beamed, tooted loudly and continued his steam engine impression up and down the boat.

Dan

Monday, 15 December 1980

I walk home from school with Philip. He doesn't say much because he is doing his Rubik's cube. It has lots of different coloured square stickers on it and you have to twist it to try to get all the same colours on the same side. Philip hasn't done his yet. He says he is taking his time as there is no point doing it straight away because it will spoil the game. He let me have a go once but when I gave it back to him he had a go at me and said I'd messed it up. I hadn't though, it was messed up to start with.

'You watching *Grange Hill* tonight?' he says.

'Might do,' I say. I'm not allowed to watch *Grange Hill*. Mummy says it's for older children. Sometimes I pretend I've watched it. I know there's a boy called Tucker in it and a black boy called Benny who's good at football and a fat boy called Alan who says 'Flipping heck, Tucker' a lot. It's easy to pretend you watch it, you just go round the play-ground saying, 'Flipping heck, Tucker.' You don't let the teachers hear, though. It's not as bad as the naughty words Daddy says but you're still not supposed to say it.

It starts raining. I pull my parka hood up. Mummy got

it second-hand off the market. I have worn it every day since. She says she will have to cut it off me in the summer when it gets too hot. We turn the corner into our road.

'See you, then,' I say.

'See ya,' says Philip. He is still doing his Rubik's cube. The colours are still jumbled up, though. I've never seen one that's been done. Apart from on the telly.

I go down the alley and into the kitchen. Mummy is sitting at the table crying.

'Where's Daddy?' I say, looking around. She shakes her head.

'Come and sit down a minute, love. I need to tell you something.'

I sit down on the chair next to her. She strokes my head.

'I'm afraid I've got some bad news,' she says. I wonder if Daddy has run away. If he's not coming back. A girl called Michelle at school hasn't got a daddy any more because he ran away.

'Grandad passed away last night,' says Mummy.

I go all cold inside. Like someone has turned the heating off. I think she means he is dead. It is what grown-ups say when someone dies. I feel a tear rolling down my cheek. Part of me wishes Daddy had run away now, it would have been better than Grandad being dead. Mummy leans over and gives me a hug.

'Was he shot?' I ask. John Lennon was shot dead last week and they have been playing his songs a lot on the radio. Mummy said being shot dead in the street only happens in America.

'No, love, of course not. Grandad died in his sleep. Very peaceful, Grandma said it was.'

'Is Grandma sad too?' I ask.

'She is, love. But only because she loved him so much. Like we all did.'

'Is Daddy sad?'

'He doesn't know yet, love.'

'He won't get mad when he finds out, will he?'

Mummy shuts her eyes for a second and looks down. 'No, sweetheart. He'll just be sad like the rest of us.'

I sit with Mummy for a bit and we have a little cry together and talk about nice things we remember about Grandad, like his bushy eyebrows and the way his face creased up when he laughed.

'Will Daddy have to dig a hole for Grandad now he's dead?' I ask.

Mummy shakes her head. 'Grandad's funeral will be at a different sort of church, because he was Romanian and he believed in different things,' she says as she dabs her eyes with a tissue. 'He's going to be buried in a different part of Manchester.'

'Can I go to the funeral?' I ask.

Mummy hesitates before she answers. 'Funerals aren't very nice places for children. They're a bit gloomy and sad.'

'I want to go. I want to say goodbye to Grandad.'

Mummy strokes my cheek with her finger. 'We'll see what your father says,' she says.

Mummy lets me watch telly for a bit while she gets on with the tea. They are making a space rocket on *Blue Peter*. John, the man who looks after Shep, is finding it tricky to stick the rocket fins on the washing-up bottle. When *Grange Hill* comes on, Mummy comes in and turns it off. The last thing I see is the cartoon bit at the beginning where someone has a sausage on their fork and is sticking it in someone else's face. I think that's the bit Mummy doesn't like.

Daddy comes home not long after it gets dark. I hear him open the door and I run into the kitchen where Mummy is cooking tea. We are having fish fingers and chips today. She says it is a fish fingers kind of day.

'Grandad's dead and I want to go to the funeral,' I say as soon as he steps on to the mat.

Daddy looks at Mummy, she nods and cries some more. He looks a bit sad but he doesn't cry. He goes over to her and raises his hand. I screw my face up and shut my eyes but there is no noise. When I open my eyes, Daddy has pulled Mummy's head on to his chest and is giving it a stroke. I like it when he is like this. I am sad that Grandad has died but at least it has made Daddy be nice to Mummy. Grandad would have been pleased about that.

I wear my grey school trousers and jumper to Grandad's funeral. You are supposed to wear black to funerals but I haven't got anything black and Mummy says it doesn't matter so much for children and grey is the next best thing. I wear my parka too which is navy blue but Mummy says that doesn't matter either and that Grandad wouldn't have wanted us wasting money we haven't got on new clothes. Mummy is wearing a black skirt and coat and Daddy has got a black suit on that I didn't know he had.

We walk round to Grandma's house. Nobody says

anything and Mummy holds my hand very tightly. Grandma opens the door, she's got a black dress on and her lipstick is red like her eyes.

'Hello, sweetheart,' she says to me. Her voice is a bit shaky and so is her hand when she strokes the side of my face. She looks older than last time I saw her. Mummy gives her a big hug. Daddy nods but doesn't say anything.

We follow her inside to the living room. Grandad's armchair is still there. It looks empty without him in it. No one else sits on it. I don't think we are allowed to. Grandma puts the kettle on. I follow her out to the kitchen to hear it singing.

'I miss having Grandad here,' I say.

Grandma bends down and strokes my cheek again. Her eyes are glistening. 'So do I, sweetheart. So do I,' she says.

When we go back in, Auntie Susan and Uncle Roger have arrived. Mummy and Auntie Susan are talking very quietly; they stop when they see us. Auntie Susan gives Grandma a hug too. Uncle Roger gives her a kiss on the cheek. They have forgotten to say hello to me. I don't mind that they haven't kissed me. Auntie Susan always smells of perfume and leaves lipstick marks on my face and then tries to wipe them off with a hankie. And Uncle Roger has a beard and smells of cigarettes. Daddy is standing by the door shuffling his feet and looking out of the window. Everyone has a cup of tea and I have a glass of Ribena. They talk about how cold it is and about John Lennon being shot. Nobody talks about Grandad. There is a knock on the door and everybody starts putting their coats on even though no one has answered it to see who it is. Mummy zips my parka right up and brushes my fringe out of my eyes. She gets a tissue from her handbag and wets it a bit before dabbing at the corners of my mouth. I hate it when she does that.

'I need to get the Ribena off,' she says when I make a face at her.

Uncle Roger opens the front door. There is a man in a big black coat standing on the path and two big black cars parked on the road outside. Grandad's coffin is in one of them. Mummy told me it would be. There are lots of flowers as well. Special ones called wreaths. I went with Mummy to the florists to order ours. It spells out Dad in flowers. I wanted to get a Grandad one but Mummy said best not to and got me a little circle of red and white flowers. She said it was Man United colours. Grandad supported Man United. I am not to tell anyone it is from me, though. Especially not Daddy. But Grandad will know it is from me and Mummy says that is all that matters.

We all get in the big black car behind the one with the coffin in. I sit on Mummy's lap, even though I am a bit old for that now, because there is not much room. No one says anything on the way. I notice Mummy is holding Grandma's hand. We pull up outside a big church and everyone gets out. Mummy carries on holding Grandma's hand as the men in black suits get the coffin out of the back of the car. I feel my lip start to tremble.

'Don't cry now, son,' says Daddy. 'Men don't cry at funerals. Only the women.'

I try very hard not to cry as the coffin comes past me. I look at the faces of the men in black suits. I think they are finding it hard work. The coffin must be very heavy with Grandad in it. I wonder what would happen if they dropped it. Whether Grandad would fall out and whether he has still got his pyjamas on. Because he died in his sleep.

Grandma walks behind the coffin, Mummy and Auntie Susan both have their arms round her, and I walk with Daddy and Uncle Roger behind them. The priest talks to Grandma at the front door, he pats her hands a lot. We start walking again and climb up the steps and go inside. There are a lot of people dressed in black already in there, I don't know any of them, Mummy said there would be some of Grandad's friends here. Some old people who came over from Romania like he did. Mummy looks round and whispers, 'Are you OK?' to me. I nod my head, she gives Daddy a look and he reaches out and holds my hand. I can't remember the last time he did that.

When we get to the end of the aisle I squeeze on to the bench next to Mummy. The men carrying Grandad's coffin put it down at the front of the church and take the lid off. I stretch my neck up to see if I can see Grandad but I can't. A man comes round and hands us all a little white candle. I am not allowed to hold candles at home but Mummy whispers that it is OK to hold this one. There is a long boring bit with lots of singing and talking. Daddy tells me not to keep fidgeting. When it is quiet I can sometimes hear Grandma crying. I try really hard not to cry because Daddy is sitting the other side of me. Mummy whispers that it is nearly finished and that it is our turn to go and say goodbye to Grandad now. She takes my hand

and we walk up to the coffin. I am a bit scared. I have never seen a dead person before. I expect him to look a bit like a ghost or a monster. He doesn't though. He looks just like Grandad. And he has got a suit on. Not pyjamas.

'He looks very peaceful, doesn't he?' says Mummy. I nod. Mummy kisses the cross on the side of the coffin. 'Time to say goodbye now,' she says to me.

'Bye, Grandad,' I whisper. Mummy starts to cry. I give her hand a little squeeze.

After the burial we go back to Grandma's house for a sort of party. I don't know why she is having a party when Grandad has just died but Mummy says it is what grown-ups do. Auntie Susan is making lots of cups of tea in the kitchen and Mummy is handing round some sandwiches. Daddy has got a little bottle of drink all to himself. Lots of people I don't know have come back as well. There isn't much space but still nobody sits in Grandad's chair. It is kind of like Grandad is still there but we can't see him. I go and sit on Grandma's knee.

'Grandad looked like he was having a nice long sleep, didn't he, Grandma?'

She nods and brushes a tear away. 'He would have been proud of you, today, sweetheart,' she says, 'looking after your mummy like that.'

It is quite a while before people start leaving. Most of the sandwiches have gone but there is still some cake left. It is chocolate cake with cream in it. I have had two pieces. The old friends from Romania go first. Some of them say good-bye to me although I don't know who they are. Daddy calls out goodbye to them all as they go. He is standing by the fireplace talking to an old man in a very loud voice. He has another little bottle in his hand, a different one to the one he started with. His cheeks are rosy and he is laughing a lot. Mummy and Grandma are in the kitchen making some more tea. I go out to help them. When we come back in, the old man has gone and Daddy is sitting in Grandad's chair drinking from his bottle. Auntie Susan is staring at him. It all seems to have gone very quiet.

'Michael, will you show some respect,' says Mummy.

'Aah, the old boy's gone now. He won't mind me keeping his seat warm.'

Mummy leans over and tries to snatch the bottle from his hand. He moves it away and grabs hold of her wrist and starts to twist it.

'Don't you dare lay a finger on her.' The voice is angry and loud, it comes from the back of the room. We all look round. It is Grandma. I have never heard her talk like that before.

'And what's it got to do with you?' says Daddy.

'I'm her mother and you're in my house. I don't know what goes on in your house and I dare say I wouldn't like it if I did but you are not so much as touching her here.'

Everyone is looking at Daddy. He lets go of Mummy's hand.

'You're an interfering old cow, Ruby. Always were, always will be. Poor old Vic must have been glad to get shot of you.'

Mummy starts crying. I run over and give her a hug. I want to shout at Daddy to stop. He is saying nasty things.

He is spoiling everything again. I open my mouth to say something but all that comes out is a little squeak. Grandma is standing very still. She doesn't say anything but she doesn't cry either. She just stares at him and shakes her head. Daddy gets up out of the chair and puts the bottle inside his jacket pocket.

'You can have his fucking chair back, we're going home.'

Mummy looks at him and shakes her head. 'I can't go yet. I've got to help tidy away. There's a pile of washing up to do.'

'You're coming home with me now, Lizzie. We're done here.' Daddy walks towards the door. Mummy stands there wringing her hands, looking between Daddy and Grandma. Daddy stops and turns back when he reaches the door.

'Did you hear me, Lizzie? Now I say.'

Mummy shuts her eyes for a second and opens them again. She goes up to Grandma and gives her a hug. They are both crying again.

'Please stay, Elizabeth,' says Grandma.

'I'm sorry,' she says, her voice shaking. She waits while I give Grandma a kiss then takes my hand and leads me out of the front door. Daddy is waiting outside. His face looks like a thunder cloud. I can feel Mummy's hand shaking. She knows what is going to happen when we get home. Just like I do.

Eleven

I had long considered that staff appraisals ranked up there as one of the worst ideas of the late twentieth century (along with wearing hipsters with your thong showing). To be honest, it wasn't the idea itself which was wrong, merely the way it had evolved, or rather mutated. Getting together with your manager to discuss any problems you had and suggest ways to overcome them was an entirely sensible thing to do. However, that was not what happened any more. What happened was that you sat in front of some over-promoted management lackey who informed you that the spurious objectives you'd been set had not been met (because you were too busy getting on with your job) and he therefore had no option but to grade you as under-achieving and sent you on your way knowing that your performance-related pay rise would not be triggered due to your so-called under-performance.

When the management lackey in question happened to be a man who had caused me more heartache in the past year than anyone else walking the planet, it was fair to say that my disposition as I entered Big Denise's office was not a particularly sunny one. Big Denise was of course above the need to fraternise with the proletariat on a one-to-one basis, which is why she had delegated the task of carrying out the appraisals – sorry, performance reviews – to Richard. Quite why he felt the need to hold court in her office I wasn't sure, though I suspected it had more to do with massaging his ego than the need to afford privacy.

'Take a seat, Jo,' he said, with all the warmth of the freezing January weather outside. 'Have you got your form?'

I stared at him, sitting there behind the desk, his tie so tight it was almost a noose, clipboard in his hand, pen poised.

'Morning, Richard,' I said, keen to inject a modicum of civility into the proceedings.

He appeared thrown for a second. 'Oh, yes, morning.'

'Here you are,' I said, handing him the ridiculous four-page form full of objective boxes and testosterone-driven acronyms such as FIRST (Fast, Initiative, Responsibilities, Self-motivated and Teamwork), against which my performance was being measured.

'Let's have a look, then,' he said. He started reading it; a frown appeared on his face as he flicked between the pages.

'You haven't commented on your performance against your previous objectives,' he said.

'Well, as they were set nearly three years ago and I've been back at work less than eight weeks, I didn't really see how I could.'

'Or maybe you didn't want to admit that your dedication and enthusiasm are not what they used to be.' Any notions of being civil went out of the window. Clearly Richard was using this as an opportunity for open warfare.

'That's bang out of order. I work hard and produce good reports. You know that.'

'Yeah, between nine thirty and seven on the two days a week you're here.'

'What's that supposed to mean?'

'Well, you're clearly no longer dedicated to your job. Otherwise you'd have come back full time.'

I shook my head and blew out. Despite everything he'd done to me, Richard still had the ability to take my breath away.

'Has it crossed your mind that I might love to come back full time but am prevented from doing so by caring for our son?'

'You could put him in childcare like everyone else.'

'Yes. That would be great for him, wouldn't it? Seeing the only parent he's got left at weekends and for half an hour in the mornings.'

'Oh, that's right,' said Richard. 'If you're struggling, resort to emotional blackmail.'

I stood up to leave, unwilling to listen to any more of this.

'Where are you going?' he said. 'You can't walk out of a performance review.'

'This isn't a performance review, Richard. It's a bigoted, ignorant swipe at someone who's doing her best to keep all the balls in the air. To do her job properly and look after her child.'

Richard appeared suitably chastened, although he wasn't about to admit it, of course. He stared hard at his clipboard for a moment.

'Come on. Sit down. Let's get this finished.'

I sighed and reluctantly sat back down. Richard turned over to the next page of the form.

'You haven't completed this bit, either,' he said. 'About your goals for next year.'

'Well, it doesn't matter what I put, does it? You're still not going to let me cover any decent stories.'

'I'm afraid every section has to be completed, there are no exceptions.'

'Fine, make something up then.'

He gave me his best disapproving look. 'Do I detect a note of cynicism?' he said.

'Of course you do, I'm a journalist. Anyway, I seem to remember you saying these were a waste of everybody's time too, once.'

'I'd appreciate it if you kept this on a strictly professional level.'

'Richard, this is me. You don't have to put on this pompous management act. Why can't we just be honest about this?'

'I don't know what you mean.'

'Come on. It doesn't matter what I say because you've got the final version typed up already. This is simply a charade we have to go through so the whole thing looks fair and above board.'

'Bollocks. Look, this is a blank piece of paper,' said Richard, turning the clipboard round so I could see. 'Anything you say will be noted down and given proper consideration before I do the finished form.'

'OK,' I said, deciding to seize the opportunity. 'Perhaps you'd like to explain why childbirth has rendered me incapable of covering hard news? Not that we cover much of it anyway.'

Richard appeared taken aback by my directness. His eyes whizzed around the room, searching for anything to focus on other than my face.

'That has nothing to do with the objectives you were set,' he said, his gaze settling on the coat stand behind me. 'We're supposed to be sticking to what's in the boxes.'

'Sorry, I don't fit neatly into boxes any more. But if you don't want to answer the question . . .' I knew I had him now. Richard could never resist a challenge like that. He put the clipboard down on the desk and swivelled in the chair before answering.

'I told you. You need to come back full time if you want to be taken seriously as a journalist.'

'And I've told you why I don't think that's right for Alfie. Besides which, it wouldn't be worth it financially. Not with the cost of childcare.'

'Rubbish. Single mums do all right. You get all those tax credits and you get my CSA money. Can't you use some of that?'

I gave him the look of utter contempt he deserved. 'I think you've been reading too many tabloid newspapers, Richard. But if you'd ever like a look at my bank statements you're very welcome.'

'Fine,' said Richard. 'Now let's get back to the form.'

I started laughing. Richard loosened his tie a fraction and stared hard at me.

'The least I would expect from you,' he said, 'is that you would take this seriously.'

The trickle of laughter became a howl.

'What?' he said.

'You. Toeing the management line like some brown-nosed pen-pusher.'

The veins in Richard's neck bulged. He loosened his tie a little further.

'Maybe you just can't accept that I've moved on while you've gone backwards.'

'You moved out, Richard. While I looked after our little boy. That's the only thing that happened. You put your career first while I put mine on hold. And now you're criticising me for that.'

'You don't seem to have the same ambition, that's all I'm saying.'

I sighed and shook my head. 'Because I've got a little boy to look after who, quite rightly, is my number one priority. And he's also taught me that there is more to life than work. That climbing up the career ladder isn't necessarily the best route to happiness.'

'Is that supposed to be a dig at me?' asked Richard.

'I'm saying that you should try to step back a little. See what a cold, work-obsessed, humourless person you've become. And how many people you've upset along the way. All so that you get another rung up that ladder. They don't put your job title and performance review grade on gravestones, you know. They put that someone was a much-loved husband and father. And one day you just might regret throwing all that away.'

Richard sat there for a moment, as if allowing the dust to settle around him before speaking.

'Thank you, Dr Raj. Perhaps our viewers could call in so you could impart the benefit of your wisdom on their sad and pathetic lives as well.'

'Watch it,' I said, 'you're in danger of regaining a sense of humour. Is there a box for that on the form?'

'Anyway,' said Richard, refusing to break into a smile. 'Moving swiftly on . . .'

I let him carry on, throwing in the occasional grunt, nod or shake of my head as appropriate. It was easier than fighting him all the way. I'd learnt that the hard way, when he'd come home from work complaining that he needed 'space to unwind' when I needed someone to run the bath for Alfie or get tea ready while he fed on me. I looked back on our relationship in two separate halves, the Before Alfie section and the After Alfie part. Life in the year BA had been easy, we worked together, we socialised together, we slept together. It was all straightforward and obvious. Life AA couldn't have been more different. Richard only took a week's paternity leave; not even the 'Tony Blair took longer than that and he was running the country' line made any difference. And once he went back to work, our lives careered in opposite directions. While he was busy being an award-winning chief reporter, covering the top stories and setting his sights on promotion, I was still muddling my way through sleep-deprived nights and foggy brain-dead days saying 'good boy' to the breast pump when it started extracting milk. And here we were two years on. So far apart that I struggled to remember what he'd been like in the previous life sometimes. And what I'd ever seen in him.

'Did you hear that?' said Richard.

'What?' I replied.

'I just said I'm giving you a grade three under the initiative category.'

'Fantastic,' I said. 'Is that it, then? Are we done?'

Richard rolled his eyes. 'I guess so. I just need to ask whether there's anything else you'd like to raise. Anything that's on your mind.'

'Only whether Alfie's ready for potty-training yet and if I should get the mini toilet with the musical flush which is on special offer in the January sales or stick to a bog standard one from Mothercare.'

'Really, Jo,' he said, shaking his head. 'I'm disappointed in your attitude.'

'That's OK,' I said. 'I'm disappointed in yours as well.' I stood up, my linen trouser suit looking decidedly more crumpled than it was supposed to.

'Human resources will be in touch regarding your salary,' he said.

'Great,' I said. 'I guess that means I'll give the musical flushing potty a miss.'

'So, how did it go?' asked Laura, as we queued in the canteen at lunchtime.

'I think it's safe to say I won't be getting a pay rise.'

'Was he a complete bastard to you?'

'No more so than usual,' I said with a shrug, taking a brie and grape baguette through the self-service hatch.

'You seem remarkably calm, considering,' said Laura, opting for a jacket potato.

'What's the point of getting worked up over it? He's

already done the worst thing he could possibly do to me. I'm determined not to let him get to me any more.' My voice tailed off as I looked up to see Tricia joining the queue behind us, looking suitably glamorous in a shift dress and long tailored jacket.

'Hi, ladies,' she said, her teeth auditioning for a part in a toothpaste commercial. 'Gosh, that looks nice, Jo,' she said, eyeing up the baguette. 'Still, better not,' she added, patting her perfectly flat stomach before reaching for a salad. 'I'm still trying to work off the Christmas excess.'

I resisted the temptation to ram the baguette down her throat and forced a weak smile out of the corner of my mouth before picking up my tray and walking briskly towards the till. Trying to blot out the image in my head of Richard lovingly feeding her chocolates in bed. I didn't understand why she got to me so much. After all, it wasn't as if I wanted Richard back. I had done for a long time, longer than was healthy. But not any more. Not even in my weakest moments when I was curled up on the sofa on my own or I spread out an arm in bed to find the space where he used to be. I knew what he was made of now. And somewhere deep inside, buried under the layers of self-doubt, I knew I deserved better than that.

As I sat down at a table in the far corner with Laura, my phone bleeped with a text message. I rummaged around in my bag until I found it and scrolled down as I read.

'OK. Meet you on platform 2 at 7.45 on Sat. Looking forward to it. Dan.'

We'd swapped several texts while arranging the trip to the Thomas day out at York but he still put his name at the end of his message, as if I might not know who it was from. He had no idea, of course. That his was one of only three numbers I'd put in my address book on the phone. And as my mum hadn't learnt to text yet (which was a relief because I could imagine the sort of messages she'd send if she could), and Rachel's number was only in there so I could text her my regular 'running late' message, Dan's texts were about the only ones I received.

'Who was that?' asked Laura as I slid the phone back into my bag.

'Oh, no one,' I said.

'Well, somebody sent it. And as you're smiling and your cheeks have gone a funny shade of pink, I put it to you that it was either a very rude wrong number or somebody you've met that you're not telling me about.'

I flicked my hair back behind my ears. There was no point trying to hide it any longer.

'His name's Dan. He's a balloon sculptor.'

Laura started laughing.

'What?' I said.

'Why does it not surprise me that you'd take up with a balloon sculptor?'

'I haven't taken up with anyone. He's just a friend. Alfie's friend, really.'

'So what was he texting you about?'

'He's performing at a Thomas the Tank Engine event at the railway museum at York on Saturday so I'm taking Alfie along. We lent him some Thomas books so he could learn to make balloon engines.'

A smile spread over Laura's face. 'This is starting to

sound like one of your "And Finally" stories. You ought to do a piece on him. Be a good one for the What's On slot.'

'No thanks. I've had enough of mixing my work and personal life.'

'But he might jump at the chance. Must be a bit quiet for him, this time of year. A plug on TV could get him a lot of new business rolling in.' She had a point. I hadn't thought of that. Maybe there was a way I could repay him.

'I'll ask him,' I said. 'But I don't think he'll go for it.' I texted Dan back: 'Fancy being my And Finally on Fri? Free plug for your business!' I waited a long time for a reply. So long I'd finished my baguette and was draining the last dregs of my cappuccino when it came.

'No thanks. I'm a bit camera shy. Dan.' The usual witty retort was conspicuous by its absence. I hoped he wasn't annoyed at me for asking.

'Well?' said Laura. I shook my head.

'He's not one for the limelight.'

'Bit weird for an entertainer.'

'He's not your average entertainer,' I said. 'He's not your average anything, really.'

'And is that why you like him?' asked Laura. 'Because he's so different to Richard?'

I hadn't thought about it like that. Though now she'd mentioned it, I couldn't think of two people less likely to get on if they met. Or even anywhere they'd be likely to meet, come to that.

'Maybe,' I said, standing up and brushing a few crumbs from my trousers. 'Anyway, it doesn't matter because nothing's going to come of it.'

'Why not?' said Laura, finishing her coffee as she stood up.
'Too many reasons to mention,' I said.

I popped into the Ladies on the way back to the newsroom.
The noise of someone sniffing could be heard from the
middle cubicle. I bent down and peered under the door,
the way Alfie did when we visited public toilets. I recognised Moira's burgundy boots. And noticed that they were
nowhere near the toilet.

'Are you OK?' I whispered. 'It's Jo.' There was a pause
of a few seconds and another sniff before the bolt slid back.

'Sorry,' she said, dabbing at her red-rimmed eyes with a
tissue. 'Just a minor crisis of confidence. I always like to
take my Rescue Remedy in private. I know TV types are
supposed to snort cocaine but I've never made it past Dr
Bach's flower remedies.'

I smiled and shook my head. 'What's brought this on?'

'I've just had my appraisal.'

'Don't tell me. Richard.'

'He said they're going to give Pamela a week's run on
the evening slot in a couple of weeks. He thinks my style
might be more suited to the lunchtime bulletin.'

'He can't do that,' I said. 'I hope you're going to get the
union on to this.'

'I don't know,' she said. 'The whole thing's rather humiliating. Maybe he's right. Maybe I should go gracefully.'

'Don't be ridiculous, he's just on some power kick. He's
probably lining Pamela up as the next one to shag when
he's done with Tricia.'

'Anyway,' said Moira, 'maybe it's a good thing. All the

stuff at home I told you about before, it's not getting any better. Alice is going through a tough time at school at the moment. You know how mean some girls can be at that age. And Angus is still only eight, he misses his mum. At least this'll mean I'll get home early enough to spend some time with them.'

I nodded. Seeing that the maternal guilt was running deep.

'Just make sure you do this on your terms. Don't let him push you into something you don't want. And don't let him make you feel you're no good. You are. And the viewers love you, remember that.'

Moira smiled and dabbed at her eyes with a hankie.

I smiled back and squeezed her hand. 'I'd better go to the loo. My pelvic floor isn't what it used to be. Are you going to be OK?'

'You go on. I'm fine.'

'Good. Make sure you don't overdose on your flower remedy. The papers would have a field day.'

She patted my hand. 'Thanks, Jo. It's a shame your kind words don't come in a bottle. I'd buy in bulk.'

As she opened the door to go out, Tricia breezed in.

'Hi, ladies. Everything all right?'

'Yes, thanks,' said Moira. 'I was just saying to Jo what a pleasure it was to have Richard as a boss.' Moira winked at me and walked out, her head held high. I disappeared into the cubicle and shut the door behind me without saying a word. And smiled as I peed.

Twelve

I careered across the cobbles into the booking office.

'Ticket,' said Alfie, who probably thought being pushed at breakneck speed along the towpath was a requisite part of catching a train.

'No time,' I said as I ran out on to the platform. 'That's our train.' I leant forward as I approached the doors, like a sprinter dipping for the winning line (although sprinters, of course, tend not to be pushing three-wheeled buggies or wearing boots with two-inch heels). I heard the warning beeps at the same time as I saw Dan's boot wedged against the door.

'Cutting it a bit fine, aren't we?' he said as he lifted the other end of the buggy up and bundled me on to the train. The doors slammed shut behind me.

'Oh, I've got it down to a fine art,' I said breathlessly. 'Timed to perfection. No point in sitting around waiting for half an hour.' I turned the buggy round and removed Alfie's hat which had a habit of dropping down over his eyes.

'Balloon man Dan,' he shouted, a huge grin lighting up his porridge-smeared face.

'Glad you could make it, Alfie. I saved you and your

mum a seat, just in case,' he said, gesturing towards a small rucksack on the nearest table.

'Thanks,' I said, unclipping Alfie's harness and lifting him out of the buggy.

'You two sit down,' said Dan, collapsing the buggy. 'I'll put this with my stuff.' I glanced across at the luggage rack opposite where I could see a battered black trunk and a large round case which I presumed contained his folded bike. I shuffled down the aisle and deposited Alfie on the window seat. I took my coat and hat off, unravelled my scarf and wedged them into the overhead luggage compartment before sitting down next to Alfie. Dan returned and sat opposite us. We grinned at each other across the table. I was starting to get used to it now. How good it was to see him.

'Thanks for the loan of your Thomas books, Alfie,' he said. 'They were a real help.'

'Let's test Dan,' I said to Alfie. 'We'll ask him some questions. See if he's done his homework. What colour is Percy?'

'Green,' said Alfie.

'He's good,' said Dan. 'I want him on my team.'

'Let's give Dan a chance to answer this time,' I said, covering Alfie's mouth with my hand.

'OK, what about Gordon?'

'Blue.'

'And Reuben?'

Dan's face froze. 'God, I don't know. Was he in the book?'

'No, I made him up. He's a visiting engine from Hebden Bridge, runs on eco-friendly organic biofuels.'

Dan started laughing. 'Should have known better than to trust a journalist,' he said.

I wasn't sure how to respond. On the surface it was jocular enough but I detected an underlying uncertainty.

'I hope you didn't mind me asking about filming you,' I said, keen to clear the air. 'I thought it might get some extra work for you, that was all.'

Dan nodded. 'I know. But I'm a tad too reclusive for TV. I've heard how these things can escalate. Before I knew it, they'd be putting me on the tourist trail and bringing coach parties down to the moorings.'

I smiled. I still had the sense that he had minded. But that he was trying very hard not to. The train began to fill up. As more people got on at Halifax, I lifted Alfie on to my lap and moved over next to the window. My leg brushed Dan's as I did so.

'Sorry,' he said, drawing it back sharply. 'I'm working on retractable limbs for public transport.'

I looked up to see a couple in their sixties hovering in the aisle.

'Are these seats taken?' the man enquired.

'No, please, feel free,' I said.

'Did you want to sit next to each other?' asked Dan, standing up.

'Oh, thank you, if you're sure,' said the woman.

Dan sat down next to me. Alfie immediately clambered on to his lap.

'Someone's pleased to see Daddy,' the woman chirped.

Alfie looked at her sternly. 'Not Daddy,' he said. The knife inside my stomach twisted again.

'Oh, I am sorry,' she said, settling into the window seat. 'I assumed you were together.'

'We are,' I said. 'Travelling together.'

'Oh, I see,' said the woman, turning back to Alfie. 'So where's Daddy today? Is he working?'

She clearly didn't get it. But I wasn't about to offer a detailed rundown of my failed love life to a stranger on a train.

'Daddy gone,' said Alfie, who obviously had no such qualms. Far from appearing embarrassed, the woman looked at me and Dan disapprovingly, obviously assuming we were the guilty parties.

I stroked Alfie's hair. 'It's OK, sweetheart,' I whispered, trying not to show how indignant I felt.

Dan leaned forward across the table to the woman. 'It's not what you're thinking, madam,' he said. 'I'm the boy's personal entertainer and travel with him to all his social engagements. Nothing's happened between me and his mother, although it's not for the want of trying on my part. But if you'd care to leave your phone number I can make sure you're informed should the relationship develop beyond a platonic one.'

Our inquisitor's face trembled before us, she muttered something which sounded like 'Really' under her breath and hastily produced a copy of *People's Friend* from her bag which she opened high enough to avoid eye contact. Her husband (or partner, or travelling companion, I hadn't thought it polite to enquire) pulled a copy of the *Daily Mail* from his jacket and turned to the sports pages, the hint of a smirk edging up the corners of his mouth. I stared hard out of the window, trying not to let anyone see the smile on my face and feeling I might just float up into the air like the kids in that old Cookeen advert. It was typical, really, that Dan should formally declare his interest in me to a stranger on a train, rather than directly to me. But at least I knew now. Although, of course, that made resistance harder. Because I could no longer kid myself that I was imagining it.

A second later I felt Dan's hand reach out and take hold of mine under the table. My arm tensed, I could hear the blood rushing around in my head. I was so unused to adult physical contact that my body was telling me to take flight. I didn't want to, though. Because this was Dan. I allowed my fingers to close around his. To even give them a little squeeze before Alfie turned round and I pulled my hand away.

The couple got off at Leeds, although not before the man had winked at Dan, who, I was in no doubt, had made his day.

'Thank you for such a fine riposte,' I said, finally allowing Dan to see my smile. 'I have no idea why women of that age are so cheeky.'

'Probably because they usually get away with it,' said Dan.

I nodded. He was still looking at me. Waiting for some kind of response to his public declaration.

'You look after Alfie for a minute,' I said. 'While I go and get some coffees in.'

Alfie had just about exhausted my supply of *Thomas the Tank Engine* magazines by the time we pulled in to York station.

'Well, that was some good last-minute revision,' said Dan, as he helped us off with the buggy then went back for his cases. 'I'm better prepared for this than I was for my O levels.'

'How many did you get?' I asked.

'Four. English, English Literature, Drama and Art. I flunked the rest. Which was good, really, because it got me out of going to uni and into performing arts college.'

'And got your folks off your back, I guess. About knuckling down to your studies and getting a proper job.'

Dan smiled but said nothing. Still not giving anything away.

We walked on, Dan insisting on helping me carry the buggy over the footbridge despite being weighed down with his own luggage.

'Ooohh,' said Alfie as we emerged from the station and he caught sight of the Yorkshire Wheel, which towered over the museum. 'Go on ride.'

'Maybe another time, sweetheart,' I said. 'We're going to see Thomas today.'

We reached the museum entrance. It didn't open for visitors for another twenty minutes. Dan and I stood there looking at each other.

'Are you going to be OK?' he said. 'I feel bad leaving you two out here in the cold.'

'Don't be daft. You go and get set up,' I said. 'Looks like we'll be first in the queue.'

'Good. Make sure you are. The first balloon's got Alfie's name on it.'

★

From the look on Alfie's face when we reached the station hall of the museum, I suspected this was the closest to two-year-old heaven you could get. There were trains of various shapes and sizes as far as the eye could see. Thomas the Tank Engine was waiting to take him for a ride outside and here to entertain him while he waited was his favourite balloon man. I was glad I hadn't started the potty training yet because I was sure the excitement would have proved too much for him.

It was strange, seeing Dan in work mode. Riding his tiny bicycle, his legs up around his ears like some big kid whose parents can't afford to buy a bigger model. The striped waistcoat and jaunty black hat, the dark-rimmed glasses; everything as I remembered from the last time I saw him perform at Eureka. Except that it was different now. I knew that the lenses on his glasses were clear and only for protection, I had visited the shed where the bike was kept, I even knew the reason for the glossy appearance of his neatly trimmed nails. And he was not the balloon man any more. He was Dan. I still could not bring myself to say 'my Dan', but could manage 'our Dan' at least.

He smiled as he saw us approaching and waved to Alfie, who laughed and kicked his legs as he waved back. It was at that point I realised that it was too late. That Alfie was already involved with Dan, even if I was still pretending not to be.

'Wow, Alfie, isn't it great here?' said Dan, getting off his bike as we stopped at the 'Queue here for Thomas rides' sign. 'What can I make for you today? You can have any of the characters, Thomas, James or Percy. Who's it to be?'

Alfie thought long and hard about it.

'Harold the Herricopter,' he said eventually. Dan raised his eyebrows in my direction.

'Hey, don't blame me,' I said. 'I can't help it if he likes the trickiest one.'

'One Harold coming up,' he said to Alfie. He reached into his bag and pulled out a white balloon and began to blow. I watched with a more educated eye this time; noting the flat cheeks, the way he used his fingers to shape the balloon ready for the next twist. People started queuing up behind us, the adults craning their necks to watch, the children mesmerised by Dan's twisting.

'Can you guess what it is yet?' asked Dan in his best Rolf Harris voice.

'Harold,' came the chorus of replies. I suspected that if there was a choice between the Pied Piper of Hamelin and the balloon man of Hebden Bridge, they'd go with Dan. He twisted the helicopter's rotor blades into place then produced a marker pen from his pocket and drew Harold's face on and wrote 'Alfie 1' on the side.

'Here you are,' he said, bending down to present it to Alfie. 'There won't be another one like that all day.'

Alfie looked up at me in a state of unbridled glee. I swallowed hard.

'Thanks,' I said to Dan. 'I think you've just become his best friend for life.'

'Good,' said Dan. 'That's fine by me. Now, what can I do for you, madam?' His eyes were dancing, playing a game of dare with mine.

'Surprise me,' I said.

He smiled and took out a black balloon. A few minutes later I was the proud owner of a particularly large Fat Controller.

'There you are,' he said. 'Someone to keep you company on those long dark winter's nights.'

'Thank you,' I said, laughing. 'I shall keep it and think of you always.' We were interrupted by a voice behind shouting.

'Can I have a Thomas?'

'I'd better go and entertain the masses,' said Dan, mounting his bike. 'You enjoy the ride, Alfie. And you,' he added, turning to me, 'behave yourself with the Fat Controller.'

As we clambered off the troublesome truck ride for the third time that morning, I noticed that the man in his forties about to get on didn't have a child in tow and made a mental note to ensure that Alfie's train fixation didn't last beyond his thirteenth birthday. I was about to suggest to Alfie that we get a bite to eat when my phone beeped.

'Lunch about 2 b served. Meet u in foyer.' Dan hadn't felt the need to sign his name this time. Things were obviously moving on. I scooped Alfie up, deciding it would be quicker to leave the buggy in the buggy park, and wound my way through the crowds back to the entrance where Dan was waiting for us, minus the bike, hat and glasses.

'Hi, Alfie. Having a good time?' he asked. I put Alfie down on the ground and he shuffled around, arms pumping like pistons, doing a selection of his best train noises.

No need to translate that.

'What about you?' I said. 'How's it going?'

'Good, thanks. Although I'm slightly Thomased out and I can't believe how many parents decided to name their sons after a tank engine.'

'I think it's so they can dress them in Thomas clothes and not have to worry about sewing or ironing name tags on,' I said.

'Well, I'm glad you didn't follow the crowd. Alfie's a great name.'

I decided not to tell him that it had been Richard's suggestion. I didn't want to give him any credit, even for his one positive contribution to Alfie's life.

'My mother thinks otherwise. She says it reminds her of the Alfies played by Michael Caine and Shane Ritchie both of whom are "Cockney wide boys who can't speak properly".'

Dan laughed. 'Anyway. Are you guys ready for lunch?'

'Absolutely, the café's back through there,' I said, pointing to the way we'd just come.

'I know, I've already got some provisions,' he said, holding up a brown paper bag. 'But we're not eating there.'

'Oh, so where are we eating?'

'Up there,' said Dan, pointing to the Yorkshire Wheel. I stared at him, a smile creeping over my face as I realised he was serious. 'How about it, Alfie?' he said. 'A picnic in the sky.'

Alfie looked up at him then back at me, seemingly wondering if he'd heard right.

'That would absolutely make his day,' I said.

'Good. Come on, my treat,' said Dan. 'I've only got half an hour, mind, so we'd better get a move on.'

Alfie lifted his arms up to Dan. 'Carry me,' he said.

Dan looked at me. I nodded. Dan lifted him up off the ground and put him on his shoulders.

'OK, hold on tight, we're preparing for take-off.'

I followed them as they wove their way through the crowds, Alfie laughing and whooping as he clung on to Dan's head. I was torn between being thrilled to see him enjoying himself so much and feeling bad that he'd missed out on this sort of male bonding for most of his life. On the rare occasions Richard had picked him up he'd appeared to have no idea what to do with him.

I stopped at the ticket booth by the entrance to the wheel.

'It's all right,' said Dan turning round. 'I've got them already. And I've got special permission to jump the queue.'

We walked up the series of ramps to the boarding platform, Dan lowered Alfie into his arms, handed the attendant our tickets and a VIP visitor pass and held out his hand as a pod stopped in front of us and the doors opened.

'Your dining car awaits,' he said.

I sat down on one of the plush bench seats, Dan passed Alfie to me before producing a small checked tablecloth from his rucksack, spreading it over the seat opposite and laying out a selection of sandwiches, crisps, fruit, muffins and smoothies. Alfie looked up open mouthed as the wheel started to move.

'Lunch is served,' Dan said.

I smiled and shook my head.

'What?' he said.

'You.'

'What about me?'

'Everything,' I said. 'Absolutely everything.' We stared at each other for a long time. Until our pod reached the top and we stopped for a second, swinging gently in the wind.

'Look,' I said, pointing. 'You can see York Minster from here.'

Alfie fell asleep on my lap shortly before Leeds on the train home, the corners of his mouth curling up slightly, one leg stretched out leisurely over Dan.

'Sorry,' I said to Dan as I stroked Alfie's hair. 'Do you want me to move it?'

'Don't be daft, he's fine. He must be wiped out.'

'He is. He's had a great day. Thank you.'

'No problem. My pleasure,' said Dan.

I gazed out at the blackness rushing past the window. I still had moments when Dan seemed too good to be true. When you were a single mum, good-looking men didn't just come along and make it their business to charm you and entertain your child. It simply didn't happen. Maybe I was being naïve beyond belief, not seeing that he had paedophile written all over him because I had been duped into vainly thinking he had some kind of interest in me. When all he was doing was using me to get close to Alfie. I looked down at Alfie, his head nuzzling into my armpit. So peaceful. So precious. My palms started to turn sweaty. I was getting myself in a state. I needed to know. Needed some reassurance that he was for real. That I hadn't made another awful misjudgement.

'Why do you bother with us?' I said.

Dan turned to look at me, his eyebrows almost meeting in a frown.

'What do you mean?'

'Some crazy, size-fourteen single mum who's well past her best before date and has somebody else's child in tow. You could do better than that, surely?'

'Is that how you see yourself?' Dan shook his head. 'Only that's not how I see you. I see an incredibly strong woman who's been kicked in the teeth but has got up, dusted herself down and not only refuses to feel sorry for herself but who positively sparkles with fun. And a little boy who despite everything is the funniest kid I know and a complete credit to his mum. And as for those size-eight super waifs with their plastic smiles and silicone implant boobs, no thank you. I like my women to be real.'

'Thank you,' I said, looking down at Alfie. 'I was worried you just felt sorry for us.'

'You,' he said, 'are the best thing that's happened to me in a long, long time.'

I could smell the honesty on his breath, hear the emotion bubbling in his voice. Coming from somewhere deep inside, somewhere he hadn't opened up to me yet. It occurred to me that he might be the one good man out there. And that if he was, I shouldn't let my experience of the bad ones get in the way.

'So what you said to that woman on the train this morning . . .'

Dan looked across at me as we pulled in to Leeds station.

'About whether you're ever going to let anything happen between us, you mean?' he said with a grin.

I groaned and put my hand over my face. 'Oh God, I'm making a hash of this. Look, what I'm trying to say is—'

I was interrupted by a chorus of chanting as the train doors opened and a dozen or so Leeds United fans surged into our carriage. They were loud and obviously drunk but they did at least appear to be in good spirits. Just as the doors were about to close, a smaller group of Liverpool fans jumped on, to be greeted by a chorus of jeers from the Leeds supporters.

'You're shit, aaahhh.'

'And you're a cheating bunch of tykes,' shouted the largest of the Liverpool fans, who had the name Alonso emblazoned on the back of his shirt. 'Your number nine should get a fucking Oscar for that dive and we should still be in the draw for the fourth round.'

The comment was greeted by further jeers and a selection of hand gestures from the Leeds fans. The hostility in the carriage was palpable.

I glanced across at Dan. He was sitting upright in his seat, his eyes wide and staring, his fist clenched so tight around his rucksack strap that his knuckles were white.

'Are you OK?' I said.

'I'm sorry. I didn't think there'd be any football fans on this train. There's a direct one to Liverpool Lime Street from Leeds.'

'Maybe they're the Rochdale contingent of the supporters' club,' I said. 'Anyway, it doesn't matter, hopefully they'll all pipe down in a minute.'

'Not if they've lost to Leeds,' he said. 'That's a real upset.'

'I didn't know you were into football,' I said.

'I was when I was a kid,' he said. 'But not any more. Causes too many arguments.'

Alonso and his mate, who was wearing a Gerrard shirt, shuffled down the packed train to stand in the aisle a few seats in front of us, swigging back their lagers, burping and swearing loudly about the referee. A few other passengers muttered or tutted. Most simply stared out of the window – not that there was anything to see in the darkness beyond.

'Do you want to move?' Dan asked me, nodding down at Alfie.

'No, it's OK. They're not bothering him. He can sleep through anything,' I said as the Leeds fans broke into song.

'Build a bonfire, build a bonfire, put the Scousers on the top, put the city in the middle and burn the fucking lot.' Alonso screwed up his empty lager can. Dan flinched at the noise. I looked down at his hand which was visibly shaking. Alonso's arm went back behind his head. Dan jumped up out of his seat.

'Here,' he said. 'Give it to me.'

Alonso spun round unsteadily on his feet to see where the voice had come from. The can misfired, hitting an overhead partition and dropping to the floor a few feet behind us and well short of the Leeds fans. Alfie woke up with a start.

'What's your fucking game?' said Alonso, clearly as surprised by the intervention as everyone else.

'I'll shut them up,' said Dan, his voice rougher than

usual. 'Come on, let's have the rest of them. Full ones, please.'

Alonso shrugged and handed over a can of lager. His mates did the same, though somewhat grudgingly.

'OK,' said Dan. 'Stand back, everyone.' He waited until people stepped back and then threw one of the cans up into the air. Then a second and a third, until he was juggling all five above his head. Other passengers on the train started laughing and whistling.

'What the fuck do you think you're doing?' asked Alonso.

'Providing the post-match entertainment,' said Dan.

The train pulled into Bramley station. The doors opened and the Leeds fans spilled out on to the platform, still goading the Liverpool fans. Alonso looked at his mate; Gerrard shook his head.

'Wankers,' shouted Alonso as the train doors were shutting. The Leeds fans surged forwards but they were too late. The doors slammed shut. Something hit the window next to us with a clatter, the contents splattering over the glass. Dan jumped but managed to keep all five cans in the air. There was clapping and whooping from inside the carriage. Alfie was jumping up and down on my knee.

'Thanks, everyone,' said Dan. 'That's the end of the show. A round of applause for my assistants please,' he added, tossing the cans back in quick succession to Alonso and co. The passengers cheered again. Alonso and Gerrard slunk away to the far end of the carriage. Dan sat back down next to me.

'Well done,' I said. 'I thought you'd lost it for a moment there. How did you know that would work?'

'I didn't,' said Dan. 'But it was worth a go.'

'Well, I think the cops should take you on as a one-man anti-hooliganism unit.'

'No thanks,' said Dan, 'I think I'll stick to my day job.'

I smiled and looked down at Dan's hand as it reached out to stroke Alfie's leg. It was still shaking.

Alfie was back asleep by the time we got to Bradford. Dan didn't say much for the rest of the journey. A woman came up and thanked him for intervening before she got off at Halifax but it barely seemed to register. As we approached Hebden Bridge, he got his things together and lifted a still sleeping Alfie into the buggy.

'Why did you react like that?' I asked as we walked down the ramp and through the subway.

'Well, someone had to do something. We would have been in the middle of a riot.'

'No, I mean before that. You were shaking.'

'All part of the act,' grinned Dan, helping me up the stairs with the buggy without being asked. I knew him well enough to know it wasn't. But not well enough to know what it was he was covering up. We carried on out through the station together until we reached the bottom of the lane where the main road met the canal.

'Can I walk you home?' he said.

'No, thanks. We'll be fine. We'll go back through town.'

'There you go again,' he said.

'What do you mean?'

'Pushing me away. Every time I try to take things further.'

'I've had a lovely day, Dan. We both have. Thank you.'

'Good,' he said. 'So have I.' He leant over to kiss me. I shook my head and pulled away.

'I'm sorry,' I said. 'I can't trust someone who's not straight with me. Who hides behind humour all the time. It's like on the boat, when I pretended to box your ears. There's something you're not telling me and I need to know you. The real you. Before I let this go any further.'

Dan opened his mouth to say something but nothing came out. I turned and walked away. Pushing the buggy over the cobbles. Hoping Alfie wouldn't wake up and see the tears in my eyes.

Thirteen

I lay in bed staring at the ceiling, as I had done most of the night. The only difference now was that it was light enough to see what I was staring at. To be able to pick out a particular crack or cobweb to focus on, rather than a general expanse of black. I glanced down at Alfie who was fast asleep in the crook of my left arm, no doubt dreaming of his day out at York and of the further adventures with balloon man Dan to come. Blissfully unaware that the way things looked at the moment, there weren't going to be any.

I didn't regret what I'd said. I'd meant every word. What I regretted was that Dan hadn't been honest with me. I kept going back over it all in my head. Trying to work out why a bunch of drunken Liverpool football fans had engendered such fear in him. I wondered if he was old enough to have been at Heysel for the European Cup Final when all the trouble kicked off. Or at Hillsborough when the Liverpool fans were crushed to death. Whatever it was, he clearly didn't want me to know about it. And that hurt. That and the fact that I couldn't help thinking he wasn't being straight with me about all sorts of things.

Alfie and I were still eating breakfast when there was a

knock on the door. I leapt up but before I got to the door I heard Nina's voice call out.

'Morning, Jo. Only me.'

'Just a second,' I called, hoping the disappointment didn't show in my voice. I left Alfie trying to re-grout the kitchen tiles with the remains of his porridge and opened the door a fraction, conscious that I was still in my pyjamas and any early morning ramblers on the towpath might prefer not to get a fright.

'Hi, Nina,' I said as Dougal wagged his tail so vigorously I feared it may fall off. 'Are you OK?'

'Yes, fine,' she said, a woolly hat pulled down over her ears against the cold and her familiar purple scarf wound around her neck the old-fashioned way. 'You've got a visitor.'

'Er, yes. So I see. Did you want to come in?'

'No, not me. Your friend Dan.' I frowned at Nina, wondering if she'd been on the sherry again. 'Lovely fellow, why didn't you tell me he was so charming? If I was forty years younger I'd have him myself.'

'So where is he?' I asked, scouring the canal for any sign of the *Elizabeth*.

'He's in my kitchen.' I stared at her hard, still not comprehending. 'He caught me as I was coming back from my walk with Dougal,' explained Nina. 'Asked if I knew which house you lived in.'

'So what's he doing in yours?'

'I suggested it. I got the impression that you two need to talk and I thought it would be easier without Alfie. I'll look after him for you while you go next door.' The relief churning around inside me was joined by a measure of adrenalin and a large capful of hope.

'You,' I said, giving her a hug as I let her in, 'are a complete star.' I turned to Alfie. 'Look who's come to play, sweetheart.' Alfie grinned broadly from his high chair as Dougal circled excitedly beneath. 'He's got a clean nappy on,' I told Nina, 'but judging by the look on his face it might not stay that way for very long. You know where everything is, don't you?'

'Yes, me and Alfie will be fine.'

'I won't be too long,' I said.

'Take all the time you need,' said Nina.

'Thanks. Mummy's just popping next door. I'll be back soon, sweetheart,' I said, kissing the top of Alfie's head.

'Jo, love,' said Nina as I hurried towards the door. 'Aren't you going to get dressed first?'

I looked down at my pyjamas and clapped my hand over my forehead.

'Yes, of course. Only testing,' I said as I dashed upstairs, pulled on a pair of jeans and a jumper and ran a brush through my hair.

'Oh and Jo,' said Nina as I headed towards the door a second time. 'Good luck.'

I smiled and pulled the door to behind me.

Dan was sitting at Nina's kitchen table wearing Sunday morning attire of a baggy grey fleece and a pair of jogging bottoms. I suspected from the dark circles under his eyes and slightly dishevelled appearance that he'd had about as much sleep as I had. He was holding a mug of coffee in his hand; another one, presumably for me, was sitting on a coaster on the table.

'Hi,' he said, standing up as I walked in as if I was his school teacher. 'Sorry, only I figured you'd be up early with Alfie.'

'It's not a sorry thing,' I said, sitting down at the table next to him. 'I'm glad you came.'

'Nina seems lovely,' Dan said, sitting back down again.

'She is. She gives me hope about growing old disgracefully.'

Dan managed a smile. 'She made you that,' he said, pointing to the coffee. 'Seemed to know just how you liked it. She knew my name too.'

'She would do,' I said. 'She's more like a mum than my real mum. At least I can talk to her more, anyway.'

We sat there in silence for a moment, both of us knowing we couldn't go on chatting about Nina for ever.

'I'm sorry,' Dan said eventually. 'About yesterday, I mean. I figured I owed you some kind of explanation.'

'You don't owe me anything,' I said. 'But if you're ready to talk I'm listening.'

Dan got up, still holding his coffee mug, and wandered over to the kitchen window.

'I've got issues,' he said. 'Baggage, whatever you want to call it.'

I felt myself tense inside. Convinced he was about to reveal an ex-wife and family I knew nothing about.

'Most people have,' I said, trying to lighten the moment. 'Mine's sitting next door, probably tormenting the hell out of an ageing dog.'

'No,' he said, turning to face me, the darkness almost spilling out of his eyes. 'I'm not talking about someone else or a past love or anything like that. I'm talking about big shit. Things I can't bring myself to think about, let alone talk about.' He took a sip of his coffee. The mug shaking in his hand. I waited, not wanting to break his flow now he was finally talking.

'Most of the time, it doesn't affect me,' he said. 'Not on the surface anyway. I can get away with seeming normal, well my kind of normal which is most people's weird but you know what I mean.'

I nodded again, encouraging him to go on.

'But I guess it's a bit like a volcano,' Dan continued. 'It can only lie dormant for so long. And every so often something triggers it off and up it goes.'

'And that's what happened yesterday, on the train home?'

Dan nodded but said nothing.

'Were you caught up in some sort of football hooliganism?' I asked.

He shook his head. 'My father used to go mad whenever Liverpool lost. Seriously mad. Hitting my mum and stuff. It wasn't just when Liverpool lost. He had a drink problem as well. He used to knock her about when he'd been drinking. It's why I don't talk about my childhood.'

I nodded, feeling awful for even thinking that he might be involved with another woman, and reached out to squeeze his hand.

'This is exactly what I was scared of,' he said, pulling his hand away.

'What?'

'That if I told you you'd start feeling sorry for me. And I don't want that to be the basis for our relationship. I don't want to be poor, troubled Dan. Or for you to try to rescue me.'

'That's fine by me,' I said. 'I was kind of hoping you might like to rescue me, actually.'

Dan managed another smile.

'The trouble is,' he said, 'as soon as I get close to anyone they get pissed off because I won't open up to them.'

I nodded, not wanting to admit that was how I'd been feeling.

'And what happens when you do?' I asked.

Dan hesitated. 'I don't know. I guess I'm about to find out.'

I raised my eyebrows slightly. It was an answer I hadn't expected. I felt flattered and a little nervous.

'When I met you and Alfie,' he went on, 'I thought it could be different. I kidded myself that I was OK now. That I'd somehow got over it and could have a normal relationship.'

'Why?' I said. 'What made you think that?'

'Because I wanted it so much. And because I felt more comfortable with you than I had with anyone in a long, long time.'

I smiled at him and squeezed his hand. 'That's because you said something nice,' I said. 'Not because I felt sorry for you.'

'OK,' said Dan, 'I'll allow that one.'

'And what about now?' I said. 'How do you feel now?'

Dan shrugged. 'Scared, I guess. Because I've obviously

still got stuff to deal with and yet here I am teetering on the edge of a relationship. And the last thing in the world I want to do is screw up our friendship.'

'Oh, hang on,' I said, putting my finger to my ear, 'here comes some breaking news.'

'What?' he said, a hint of a smile on his face.

'I'm scared too. For all the same reasons. The only difference is that I'm not teetering on the edge of anything any more. I've already fallen.'

He stared at me, unblinking. 'Do you mean that? You're really going to give it a go?'

'I can't go on fighting it when it feels so right. But I meant what I said. I need you to be honest with me. I want to get to know the real Dan. The one behind the showman's mask.'

Dan smiled. 'OK,' he said. 'As long as you understand you'll need to be patient. This stuff has been bottled up a long time. It won't come all at once. It'll be a bit like shaking an HP sauce bottle when there's hardly any left – a lot of effort for very little reward.'

'That's fine,' I said. 'I'm in no hurry.'

'Good,' said Dan. We sat and grinned at each other across the table.

'So what happens now then?' I said, after a while.

'I know what I want to happen.'

'Go on.'

'I want to take you out. One of those date things that proper couples do. Just you and me. So we can get to know each other properly, without any distractions.'

'Alfie, you mean.'

Dan grinned. 'He's a great kid,' he said. 'But two-year-old chaperones are not really conducive to adult conversation. Or various other things I can think of.'

I smiled and looked down at my hands.

'Hey,' said Dan stroking my arm. 'I know it's not going to be easy for you either.'

'I haven't been out with anyone else,' I said. 'Not since Alfie's dad left.'

'And when was that?'

'Over a year ago now.'

Dan nodded and looked up at the ceiling. 'I tell you what,' he said. 'Let's not even think of it as a date. We'll just pretend we both fancied going out for a meal and happened to choose the same restaurant. Then if you decide you want to go home at any point, it's no big deal.'

'OK,' I said. 'Put in such a romantic fashion, how can I refuse?'

'Two conditions,' Dan said. 'I'm paying, so just pretend you've forgotten your purse or something.'

'OK,' I said. 'What's the other one?'

'I'm not a big one for dressing up, as you can probably tell. But would you mind not wearing your slippers to the restaurant?'

I looked down at my feet to find they were encased in the fluffy red slippers that my nan had given me for Christmas. I started to laugh. Dan joined in, his eyes too this time.

'Think yourself lucky,' I said. 'I nearly came in my pyjamas.'

Dan shook his head as he got up and took our empty coffee mugs over to the sink and began to wash them up.

'God, you're well trained,' I said.

'Comes from living on a boat. No room to leave things lying around.'

I watched as he rinsed the mugs off and left them on the draining rack.

'Right then.' I said. 'I'd better get back to Alfie before he runs poor Nina ragged. You're welcome to pop round. I'm only next door, you know.'

'Thanks,' said Dan, 'but I've got loads of jobs to do on the boat. Say thank you to her, though. For her hospitality.'

'I will,' I said.

'So when do you think you might happen to fancy going out for this meal?'

'Oh, probably Friday,' I said. 'About eightish. I don't think Nina will take much persuading to babysit.'

'OK,' he said. 'I've heard good things about Relish, that new place in Albert Street.'

'Great. Maybe I'll give it a try.'

'You never know,' said Dan. 'If I'm feeling peckish I might just see you in there.'

I opened the door and stepped outside. Dan followed me, locking the door behind him and handing me the key.

'There is one other thing,' he said.

'Go on.'

'That kiss I was going to give you last night. It is still available if you're interested.'

I smiled and leant towards him. He met me halfway. His

mouth eagerly seeking mine. The smell of him, feel of him, taste of him better than I had dared hope.

'Ah, just as I thought,' he said when our lips finally parted.

'What?' I asked, still so close to his face that my eyes couldn't focus properly.

'Women in slippers make the best kissers.'

I slid down into the bath that night, disturbed more than usual by the fact that my belly insisted on remaining firmly above the water line. I tried to detach myself and view my body as a neutral. It was a bit like studying an Ordnance Survey map; the lines of stretch marks on my thighs grouped so close together they suggested hills which rose even more steeply than those which lined the Calder Valley; my breasts, which not so many years ago could justifiably be described as peaks, now resembled ancient burial mounds; and there in the middle my stomach, a boggy landscape flecked with silvery ravines leading to a deep creek of a belly button which was once no more than a rabbit hole. As for what lay beneath the water line, an official wilderness area had been declared where there was once a well-maintained bikini line. It was so long since the access route had been used, I feared it may have grown over.

'Fuck,' I said out loud. My head might have been ready for another relationship but my body quite clearly was not. It suddenly occurred to me that Richard was the only man who had viewed my post-baby body and he had left me. It was not a comforting thought.

Every other man I'd been out with had seen the pre-Alfie body, which, while not being in the super model league, had been up there fighting for promotion in the girl-next-door division.

I guessed Mother Nature was shrewder than I'd previously given her credit for. Allowing you to snare your chosen prey when you were in your prime and only reducing you to a muffin-middled blob when your lover's genes were there for all to admire in a bright new shiny baby. And yet here I was, foolishly embarking on a new relationship and expecting the unfortunate Dan to have to admire the view without the benefit of soft-focus memories of how I'd looked before.

There were emergency measures possible for Friday: not eating for five days, jogging up and down the canal towpath pushing Alfie in the buggy, purchasing the entire depilatory shelf in Boots and finding the most resilient hold-it-all-in tights which M&S stocked. But it would only be a matter of papering over the cracks. Anyone peeking underneath would see that what was really needed was a substantial renovation project.

I sighed deeply and sank my shoulders further under the water, breathing in the lavender aroma and allowing my eyes to close. It was the scariest thing in the world, putting myself out there again. Even if I could leave the whole Alfie thing aside – which I couldn't – I was still opening myself up to be hurt again when the wound from last time was still raw.

I dried myself quickly and pulled my pyjamas and dressing gown on, sneaking a quick check on Alfie on my way down the landing. It wasn't until I'd sat down at the kitchen table with a coffee and the *Observer* magazine that I noticed the new message on my phone.

'If u r getting cold feet, it's probably because you've been out in your slippers again. Night, X.'

I picked up my mug but had to put it straight down again. Unable to drink for smiling.

Dan

Wednesday, 29 July 1981

I am playing out in the street with Philip. We are on our bikes. Philip has got a Chopper. Mine hasn't got a name, it is just a bike. Mum got it secondhand from someone she knows. It is red. Philip says it is a girl's bike. Mum says to ignore him because he is talking nonsense. She says he talks more nonsense than ever since he started big school. I don't go to big school for another year and a bit yet. Mum says it is just as well if that's what it does to you.

'Watch this,' says Philip. He does a skid down the middle of the road. We can go in the road today because there are not many cars about. All the grown-ups are indoors watching the royal wedding on telly. Prince Charles is marrying Lady Di so all the grown-ups have got the day off. We were on school holidays anyway so it doesn't make any difference to us. Philip says weddings are for girls. That's why he's not watching it. Mum is watching it because it's a piece of history. I like some history, like the Vikings and stuff. But it is not that sort of history.

Dad has gone down the pub. He goes there a lot now that he doesn't go to work. He isn't a grave digger any more. He is on the dole. A lot of people are unemployed. More than two million. I heard them say that on the telly. Dad says it is Maggie Thatcher's fault. She is the Prime Minister. Dad says it shows what happens if you let a woman run the country. Mum pulls a face when he says it, but only if he can't see her. Dad still gets paid for being on the dole but it is not as much as when he was a grave digger. That is why Mum has to work longer hours now. I have to go round Philip's house after school two days a week because Mum says Dad can't be trusted to be back from the pub in time to look after me. I don't mind because Philip's mum has got a sandwich toaster and she makes me toasted cheese sandwiches which are my favourite thing in the world. You have to wait till the cheese cools down a little bit, though, otherwise it burns your tongue.

Since we broke up from school Dad has had to look after me when Mum is working. He played football with me one day. And he helped me with my juggling. But we can only do it in the mornings because the racing is on the telly in the afternoons. I would like Grandma to look after me but Mum says that's a bit tricky at the moment. I've only seen her once since Grandad's funeral. Mum won't say why but I've heard her arguing with Dad about it. And heard him call Grandma horrible names again.

I do a skid like the one Philip did but he is not looking and when I do it again I fall off my bike and graze my knee and Philip laughs. My knee stings but I am not going to cry or make a fuss because he will call me a girl if I do.

Philip's mum shouts that his lunch is ready. I wonder if

he is having a toasted cheese sandwich. I am kind of missing them.

'See ya later,' he says, jumping off his Chopper and leaving it lying on the pavement outside his house with the front wheel still spinning. I would like to have a go on it but he would know, even if I left it in exactly the same place. Philip always knows.

I prop my own bike up against the wall and go back inside. I can hear people cheering on the telly, although not as loud as they do when Liverpool score. It is kind of a gentle cheering. I go into the living room. Mum is curled up on the sofa. Prince Charles and Lady Di are standing on a red carpet outside the cathedral. She has got a big wedding dress on and he is wearing a uniform.

'Why did the people cheer?' I say.

'They've just come outside,' says Mum.

'So are they married now?' I say.

Mum smiles. 'Yes, they're married.'

I watch as they stand there and smile some more.

'They look very happy,' I say.

'They ought to, it is their wedding day.'

'Were you that happy on your wedding day?' I ask. There is a photo of Mum and Dad's wedding on the mantelpiece. Mum has got a little white dress on. Dad is wearing a suit with flappy trousers. They are both smiling.

'Yes,' she says after a while. 'I was the same age as Lady Di, thought I'd found my Prince Charming just like she has.'

I climb on to the sofa next to her.

'So why aren't you and Dad happy any more?' I ask.

Mum looks sad. Maybe I shouldn't have asked.

'I don't know, love. It's just the way it turned out,' she says, stroking my head.

Prince Charles and Lady Di are getting into a carriage, some people are helping her put her dress in because it is very long.

'I wish you could smile like you did on that photo again,' I say, gazing up at the mantelpiece.

'So do I, love,' she says. 'Anyway, I'd better get some lunch ready. Your father will be home soon.' She gets up and goes into the kitchen. I can hear her getting plates and cutlery out. I watch some more smiling and waving on the telly before I get bored and follow her out to the kitchen. She is slicing a big loaf on the bread board.

'What are we having today?' I ask.

'Just sandwiches,' she says. 'And a bit of salad.' I like tomatoes but not the rest of the things in salad.

'Am I having paste in them?' I say.

'You can do, love. Or I've got a bit of ham in specially, too, if you like.'

I go for paste in the end. With some tomatoes and ham instead of salad. Mum does Dad's ham and pickle sandwiches then her own ones with just ham. She puts them on the kitchen table and we wait for a bit. We can still hear the cheering from the telly in the other room. My tummy does a little rumble.

'Do you want to make a start, love?' Mum says. I nod. 'You can eat it in the other room with the telly if you like, just until Dad gets home, mind.'

I carry my plate through and put it on the floor near the telly and get a cushion from the sofa to sit on. Mum comes in and sits on the sofa. She hasn't got her plate with her.

'Aren't you hungry?' I ask.

'I'd better wait for your father,' she says.

They are showing pictures of the crowd on the telly now. Lots of people waving their Union Jack flags. I know how to draw a Union Jack flag, we did it at school. You have to use a ruler.

'Where have Prince Charles and Lady Di gone?' I ask.

'They're inside Buckingham Palace now. Those people are waiting for them to come out on the balcony.'

'What are they doing?'

'They're probably having lots of photos taken.'

'Do you reckon the Queen has got ham in specially too?' I ask. I say it with a big grin on my face. So she knows I am being funny.

'You never know,' says Mum, smiling.

I eat up all my sandwich and my ham and tomato. I hear Mum's tummy rumbling. There is a huge cheer as Prince Charles and Lady Di come out on the balcony. They are smiling and waving again. Prince Charles kisses Lady Di. The crowd do an even bigger cheer, like he had scored a goal or something. And then the TV goes bang. The noise makes me jump. I look round but Dad isn't in the room. I get up from the floor and run over to Mum. There is a funny burning smell.

'It's OK, love,' she says. 'The tube must have gone. I'm surprised the old thing's lasted as long as it has, to be honest.'

'Will we get a new telly?' I ask.

'I don't know, love. They're very expensive. And money's a bit tight at the moment. What with your father being on the dole.'

I nod. I never will get to see *Grange Hill* now.

'We could go and watch the rest of the wedding at Philip's house,' I say. I'm not really bothered about the wedding but I would like a toasted cheese sandwich.

'Your father will be home soon,' she says. He won't be. I know that.

'We could just go for a little bit,' I say. 'Until he gets back. We'll see him walking past, won't we?'

Mum thinks for a minute.

'I suppose we could do,' she says. 'Hang on a sec. I'll just cover up our sandwiches. Stop them going dry.'

We go over the road to Philip's. I reach up and knock on the door. Philip's dad answers. He is big and jolly and bald. I am surprised he's here. I thought all the men had gone to the pub.

'Sorry to bother you, Brian,' says Mum. 'Only our telly's just gone pop. I was wondering if we could watch a bit of the wedding here? Just till Michael comes home.'

'Course you can. The more the merrier,' says Philip's dad. 'We'll have our own little street party in here.' He looks down and smiles at me and ruffles my hair. I follow Mum through into the room. Philip's mum and his sister are sitting in front of the TV with him. He picks up his comic as soon as he sees me. But I know he's been watching it really.

'Barbara, we've got a couple of extra guests,' says Philip's dad. Philip's mum looks up.

'Telly's on the blink,' says Mum.

'Pull up a pew, then,' smiles Philip's mum, pointing to the pouffe. 'What do you think of that dress? Needs a good iron if you ask me.'

'I think it's beautiful,' says Lorraine, Philip's sister. She is a teenager, she has pictures of pop stars in her bedroom. I have seen them on the way past to Philip's room.

I sit on the floor at Mum's feet. Philip carries on looking at his comic. His dad gets Mum a cup of tea and a biscuit. He does it without being asked.

'Thanks,' says Mum, as he hands it to her. It is on a saucer. We don't usually use them. She puts it down on the floor. I don't know why she doesn't eat the biscuit straight away, I can still hear her tummy rumbling. I think I can smell toasted cheese sandwiches. We have missed them, though. They have finished them and I know it is rude to ask.

Prince Charles and Lady Di are still on the balcony. They are still waving. I bet their arms are aching by now. I swing my legs round because I am starting to get pins and needle. I have forgotten all about the cup of tea. It knocks over and all the tea spills on to the carpet. My stomach ties up in knots.

'Oh, Dan,' says Mum. 'I told you to be careful.' I look up at Philip's dad, waiting for him to shout at me. He doesn't, though.

'Never mind, son.' He smiles. 'I'll go and get a cloth.' He goes to the kitchen and comes back with a wet cloth. I move out of the way while he soaks it all up. There is still a mark left when he is finished. He looks at my face.

'It'll go in a while,' he says. 'If not we'll just put the pouffe over it, eh?' He is laughing when he says it. Philip's mum turns round and smiles at me. My tummy unties itself. It is not going to get horrible. It is different here. Nobody shouts. I look at the wedding photo of Philip's mum and dad on the mantelpiece. They are smiling too. Like in the one of my mum and dad. The only difference is they still are.

Fourteen

'I'll leave my mobile on in case Alfie wakes up and wonders where I am. And here's the number of the restaurant in case I can't get a signal, you know what it's like round here.' I handed Nina a scrap of paper with a scribbled number on it.

'Jo,' she said, placing a hand on my shoulder, 'will you stop fretting and go.'

'One last check,' I said.

Nina rolled her eyes, even Dougal flopped down on the floor as if he was in for a long wait. I hurried upstairs and pushed the bedroom door open a crack, enough for the light from the landing to illuminate the far side of the room. Alfie was curled up in his usual place, his head squashed into the corner against the wall.

'Night, sweetie,' I whispered before pulling the door to. I felt disloyal, somehow. Going out and leaving him like this, especially when I was going to be with someone he knew, someone he would have loved to see. I hadn't told him, of course. There was no way I could have got out of the house on my own if I had. And even that felt mean.

'Right,' I said when I arrived back downstairs. 'How do I look?' I'd gone for black, I always did if I was in any doubt. A three-quarter-length-sleeved top, teamed with a floaty layered skirt, knee-length boots and opaque tummy-toner tights over my buttock-lifting control knickers.

'Gorgeous, as ever,' said Nina.

'You're just saying that to make me feel better.'

'I would have if I'd needed to but as it happened I didn't.' I gave Nina a hug. 'Have a wonderful time,' she said, her beady eyes twinkling. 'And if you want to bring Dan back afterwards, I can make myself scarce.'

'You're only saying that because you want to flirt with him,' I said, picking up the hefty changing bag by the door and slinging it over my shoulder.

'Jo,' said Nina, 'I don't think you'll be needing that tonight, love.'

I groaned and ran upstairs to rummage in the back of a cupboard for an old handbag.

'God,' I said as I ran back downstairs and tried to cram my phone, purse, credit cards and various personal belongings inside, 'how do people fit all their stuff in these things?'

Nina shook her head, handed me my jacket and ushered me out of the door.

'Have fun,' she said. 'You are still allowed, you know.'

It felt weird, walking through Hebden Bridge without a buggy. I couldn't remember what to do with my hands and found myself automatically crossing roads at the slopes in the kerb, even when it meant going yards out of my way. I glanced at my reflection in the window of the Book Case as I walked by and saw someone I didn't recognise; a woman called Jo who'd lived here once before she had a baby. Before her identity had been replaced by the word 'mum'. I carried on up Market Street, crossing over before the Old Treehouse to stop myself looking in the window to see if there was anything nice for Alfie in the sale. I wanted to hang on to Jo for a bit longer, now that I'd found her again.

I pushed open the heavy, wooden door of Relish and stepped inside to be greeted by the smell of toasted cumin seeds and fresh ginger coming from the open-plan kitchen to my left. Relish was small enough to be described as intimate without being so small that it was like eating in someone's front room. A quick scan of the tables confirmed that Dan hadn't arrived yet. A waitress was hovering in front of me, smiling warmly.

'Hi, have you booked?' she asked. It suddenly occurred to me that I didn't know what Dan's surname was. I shuffled my feet, starting to feel as if I was on some tawdry blind date.

'Er, yes,' I said, deciding to bluff it. 'Table for two at eight.'

'Brady?' she enquired, scanning a list on the counter.

'That's right,' I said.

She led me over to a table in the corner by the window, took my jacket, handed me a couple of menus and returned a few minutes later with a jug of water and a basket of bread. I sat there tentatively nibbling on a piece of malted poppy seed, wondering what on earth I was going to do if a Mr or Ms Brady who I had never seen before in my life arrived.

Fortunately when the door opened it was Dan who walked in, looking slightly anxious and decidedly suave in a long black coat, the like of which I was surprised he owned. His face lit up as soon as he saw me sitting there. I noticed that the other women in the restaurant were all looking at him. And couldn't hide my delight that it was me he'd come to dine with.

'Mr Brady, I presume?' I said as he walked over.

'Sorry, I only realised as I got here that you wouldn't know.'

'It's OK, this is supposed to be an accidental meeting, remember.'

'So it is. Hang on a minute, let's rewind and start again.' He went back to the door, handed the waitress the bottle of wine he was holding and went outside. A split second later he came back in, feigning surprise as he spotted me at the table.

'Jo,' he said, bounding over to kiss me on the cheek. 'Fancy seeing you here. Mind if I join you?'

'Not at all,' I replied with a grin, extending an arm to the seat opposite. The waitress came up with a bemused look on her face and offered to take his coat. As Dan slipped it off and turned to hand it to her, a large brown Earth Collection tag with £20 crossed out and replaced with £10 swung into view on his charcoal-grey shirt.

'What?' said Dan as he sat down and saw me laughing.

'It's a lovely shirt,' I said, 'but you might want to take the price tag off.' Dan looked down and groaned.

'Never mind.' I smiled as he removed the tag. 'I'm flattered you made such an effort.'

'Yeah, well,' he said, looking me up and down, 'I suppose I should be grateful you've at least ditched the slippers.' I opened my mouth to remonstrate but shut it again when I caught the smile on his face. 'You look fantastic,' he said. 'Radiant, in fact.'

'Thank you,' I said, feeling the colour rise in my cheeks. 'You don't look too bad yourself.' I picked up another piece of bread.

'I take it you're hungry,' said Dan.

'Starving. I've usually had my spaghetti hoops by now.'

'Is that all you ever eat?'

'Oh, no,' I said. 'Alfie has quite varied tastes. Sometimes we have alphabet spaghetti instead.'

Dan laughed. 'I'm afraid you're going to be disappointed tonight,' he said, surveying the menu. 'Not a hoop in sight.'

'Never mind,' I said. 'I guess I'll just have to make do with Penang curry with tofu, griddled pumpkin and Thai herb relish served with jasmine rice.'

'Do you think that comes in a tin?' said Dan.

'I don't know,' I said. 'But if it does I'll have to ask the Co-op to get some in.'

The waitress returned with Dan's bottle of wine and poured us both a glass before taking our order.

'To chance encounters,' I said, raising my glass as she walked away.

'And absent two year olds,' he said. 'Without whom we wouldn't be here.' The smile on my face crumpled as I was reminded of Alfie. And of the reasons I'd told myself not to do this.

'Hey,' said Dan, reaching out a hand to mine. 'I'm sorry, I shouldn't have mentioned him. You've probably been trying to put him out of your mind all evening.'

'It's stupid,' I said. 'I'm so crap at leaving him. Even after all this time.' Dan's hand tightened around mine, his thumb stroking my palm. 'His dad left at night while he was sleeping,' I explained. 'Didn't even have the balls to say goodbye.'

'Why?' said Dan. 'Why would he do that to his own kid?'

'Some bollocks about needing space. About not having to fight his way past the steriliser and baby blender to get to his cappuccino machine.'

Dan blew out and shook his head. 'Guys like that do my head in.'

'I know,' I said. 'I've spent a lot of time over the past year wondering what the hell I was doing with him. That's what makes it so hard.'

'Going out with someone else, you mean?'

I nodded. 'I'm not sure if I can ever trust a man again. Or my judgement in them for that matter.' Dan sat there squeezing my hand, his eyes reaching out to mine. 'This is the bit where you reassure me I can trust you,' I said.

He shook his head. 'No it isn't. Trust is earned. Not promised. That way you know it's for real.'

I smiled. It was either a line out of some book called 'Fifty things to say to get her into bed', or just about the most refreshing thing he could possibly have said.

'But if it helps at all,' he continued, 'I can reassure you that I don't have a cappucino machine in my kitchen, nor do I desire one.'

'Thank you,' I said. 'That's all I needed to hear.'

The waitress arrived with our mezze starter to share. I sat back and relaxed, took another sip of wine. My appetite for something other than spaghetti hoops had returned.

'Coffee?' asked Dan, ten minutes or so after I'd polished off the last spoonful of my Mexican raisin chocolate pot, the effects of which were still buzzing in my head.

'Not for me, thanks. I don't think it's actually physically possible for me to consume anything else, even liquids.' I glanced at his wine glass which was still half full. I couldn't remember him topping it up at any point during the meal. 'Have you got an early start tomorrow?' I said, nodding towards the wine.

'No, just not a big drinker.'

'Because of your father?' I asked. Dan looked a bit taken aback. 'Sorry,' I said. 'I'm asking too many questions again, aren't I?'

Dan looked down, seemingly trying to compose himself.

'He didn't know when to stop. That's why I've never been drunk in my life. I don't want to go there. I've seen the hurt it can cause.'

I nodded, grateful that he'd felt able to confide that much in me.

'What about you?' continued Dan, nodding towards my glass. 'I thought journalists were supposed to be hard drinkers.'

'When I was younger, yeah. But not since I've had Alfie. My resistance levels have plummeted and I need a clear head when he wakes me up at six thirty in the morning.'

Dan smiled. We sat silently for a moment. Both staring at the wine bottle which still had a good third left inside. The meal had come to an end. In a few minutes' time we would be leaving the restaurant. And the question of what we were going to do next was looming overhead. Inviting Dan back to my place for a coffee wasn't an option with Nina there. Despite what she'd said, I knew it would feel like inviting your first boyfriend back to your parents' house. And after what he'd just said, I didn't think a pub or bar was a good suggestion. Maybe the evening would end here. Maybe that was a good thing – even if I didn't want it to.

The waitress came up, still smiling.

'Can I get you anything else?' she said.

I shook my head.

'No thanks,' said Dan. 'You've beaten us. Just the bill please.'

I reached for my purse.

'Oi,' said Dan. 'You were supposed to forget that. I told you, this is my treat.'

'At least let me go halves,' I said. 'You're always treating us.'

'The other stuff was for Alfie,' he said. 'This is for you. Please.'

'OK,' I said, putting my purse back in my bag. 'But I'm paying next time.' I blushed as soon as I said it but when I looked up at Dan, he was grinning at me.

'So where are you taking me next time?'

'I was thinking the new chippy on the corner,' I said. 'Very reasonable, they are.'

'I shall look forward to it,' he said, leaving cash on the saucer with the bill.

We stepped outside on to the pavement, the air prickling with cold.

'Thank you,' I said. 'I've really enjoyed tonight.'

'Good. Me too.' We stood for a moment not saying anything. I wondered if he was going to make his excuses and leave now. If I'd actually been a disappointment.

'It doesn't have to end here, you know,' said Dan. 'I mean I'd understand completely if you want to get straight home but if you'd like to come back to the boat . . .' His voice tailed off.

'You've got some moths to show me,' I said quickly, filling in the gap. 'With your big light. You promised me, ages ago, when we came for the boat ride.' I was aware I was babbling. A combination of nerves and excitement.

'I did, didn't I?' Dan smiled.

'Come on, then,' I said. 'You lead the way.'

He took my hand. Leading me away from home, away from Alfie. I felt a tug, a wrench. But then I was over the worst, and the further away I got, the easier it became.

The green gate rattled as Dan pushed it open. Beyond it, darkness.

'Sorry,' he said, patting his coat pocket. 'I've left my torch in my fleece. Are you going to be OK?'

'I'll be fine,' I said. 'Just don't let go of my hand.'

'I won't. Don't worry, I know my way in the dark. I've done it loads of times. I'll talk you down.'

We started walking, or rather shuffling on my part. Taking tiny footsteps along the track, the earth beneath my feet hard and slippery. Dan's hand remained firm round mine, his wrist tensing at each twist in the path, his other hand occasionally taking my elbow as he guided me across a gulley or down a steep step. I could hear him breathing, feel the comforting mass of him ready to catch me if I stumbled or tripped. He talked me over each exposed root, every mooring rope until at last we saw the glimmer of lights from the boats through the trees. I was almost disappointed to be able to see again.

'Thanks,' I said, still on a high as we reached the boardwalk to the *Elizabeth*. 'If you didn't get your orienteering badge in the Scouts I hereby award it to you.'

Dan smiled. He still had hold of my hand. I wasn't going to be the one to let go.

'Let's see if I can win my moth-spotter badge in the same night then.' He helped me over on to the boat and flicked a switch. A huge yellow lamp blinked open its eye at the front of the boat.

'We can walk along the side of the boat or go through inside, it's up to you.'

I pointed down inside. Dan let go of my hand for a second to open the doors then took it back again. I followed him down the steps, the heat from the stove like stepping off a plane into a tropical climate. He led me through the main room, past his bed. I tried not to think about who he might have entertained here before, and followed him out of the doors at the front of the boat. The cold was even sharper now, the stars chiselled out of the night sky, a sliver of a moon hanging in the stillness, casting its light down on to the water below. The only noises a gentle lapping of the water and the distant drone of traffic above. It was beautiful. As if you could reach out and actually touch the night.

'Look, there,' said Dan, pointing to a mottled brown moth flittering by the light. He stepped forward for a closer look. 'I think it's a pale brindled beauty. We get quite a few of them at this time of year.'

'Do you ever catch them?' I asked.

'No,' he said. 'I just like looking.'

I shivered on the deck. He stepped back over to me and put an arm round my waist. 'Do you want to go back inside?' he asked.

'No, thanks. I like it out here. You just need one of those little patio heaters.'

'Here,' said Dan, unbuttoning his coat and pulling me in next to him. 'Will I do?' His arms folded around me, his face nuzzled my neck. And then he kissed me. His mouth remembered mine instantly. Reacquainting itself and playfully teasing inside. His hand moving around my back, dropping lower on to my hips. Easing me in, as if trying to ensure that not even the moonlight could force its way between us. One hand moved up again, brushing my hair back from my face, pulling at my neck, slipping beneath my jacket to squeeze my shoulder before dropping down to my breast, his fingers stroking, caressing. His breath hot against my face. I couldn't believe this was finally happening. But I was so glad it was. My fingers crept under his shirt on to his bare back. He flinched.

'Your hands are freezing,' he whispered.

'Your back's a good place to warm them then.' He

laughed and slipped off my jacket. I retaliated by removing his coat.

'If you're going to play that game,' he said, 'may I suggest we go inside before we remove any further garments? It's nothing to do with the cold, just that I don't want to embarrass the moths, or for them to get the wrong idea about the sort of joint this is.'

'I understand entirely,' I said. 'The last thing we need are disapproving moths.' Dan kissed me again, before edging along the side of the boat to turn the lamp off at the back and returning along the side in the dark. Looking at me the whole time but never putting a foot out of place.

'After you,' he said, picking up his coat and my jacket and opening the front doors for me. I lowered my head and stepped down inside. Aware of the direction this was going but reluctant to change course, despite the warning broadcasting on a continuous reel in my head.

'Can I get you anything to drink?' asked Dan, closing the doors behind us and hanging the jacket and coat over a chair.

'No thanks,' I said. I guessed he was stalling, having second thoughts. The interior lighting, although dim, was probably not as flattering to me as the moonlight. Or perhaps it was something inside him that was weighing him down. 'Look,' I said. 'It's fine. You're not sure about this, I understand.' Dan stepped closer to me, taking my face in his hands. Running his fingers through my hair.

'I've never been so sure of anything in my life,' he said. 'All I need to know is that you want it too. And if you don't, it's not a problem. I'll wait. For as long as it takes.'

His voice was dry, the emotion wrung out from it. His eyes wide open, moist and raw. The intensity burning into me, melting any lingering doubts from my mind.

'It is what I want,' I whispered. 'But I'm scared. What if it all goes wrong?'

'Nothing will go wrong,' said Dan, stroking my face. 'I won't let it.' He kissed me again. Drawing out the doubts, breathing life into me. His body pressing against mine. His hands stroking and rubbing. Making me ache inside with wanting him so much. He pulled one shoulder of my top down and started kissing my neck, his stubble rough on my skin. My fingers grappled with the buttons on his shirt before it came open, revealing a toned, tanned torso. I tweaked one of his chest hairs.

'Just checking it's real,' I said. 'And you're not going to rip it off halfway through as some sort of joke.'

Dan grinned, his hands inching up my thighs. I panicked as I remembered the impenetrable tights which had seemed like a good idea a few hours ago. I was reluctant to break the moment but it was scientifically impossible to remove them in anything resembling a seductive manner.

'Sorry, I need to pop to the bathroom,' I said. 'It's OK, I'm not going to use your toilet. I need to surgically remove my tights.'

Dan laughed. 'God, you know how to turn a man on,' he joked. He kissed me again on the lips before I disappeared into the bathroom. I fumbled around in the dark, unable to find the light switch. As I bent down to take my boots off, I kicked something hard which clattered to the floor.

'Sorry,' called Dan from outside. 'My shower broke this morning. I was in the middle of a repair job. Here, it might be easier with the light on.' He flicked a switch from outside to reveal a pile of pipes, a plunger and a pump on the floor. I started peeling my tights down, my flesh spilling out in annoyance at having been kept confined for so long. I looked around for somewhere to put the tights and opened the bathroom cabinet. A box of condoms fell down. A pack of twelve. I wondered if they'd been bought especially for me. Or simply left over from the last woman he'd slept with. I hoped not. I picked them up. They were still in the cellophane wrapper. The ribbed variety, as opposed to the extra safe ones I had in my handbag. I wondered if I could get away with asking him if he'd wear both, the ribbed one over the top perhaps. Just to be on the safe side. Before telling myself not to be so paranoid. That the odds on me getting pregnant for a second time while using a condom must surely be long ones. I put the box back in the cabinet, deciding to stuff the tights inside one of my boots instead. I glanced at myself in the tiny crooked mirror above the sink, my face flushed, excited and unsure at the same time. I took a deep breath, sucked my stomach in and opened the bathroom door. Dan was standing there wearing only his boxers and a wicked grin on his face. Instantly I felt at ease.

'Were they huge iron-clad passion killers?' he asked.

'Yep,' I said. 'The worst kind.'

'Damn. And I missed them. Maybe another time, eh?'

'Only if you're good,' I said.

'I will be. Would you like me to close the curtains?'

I gazed at the moonlight outside and shook my head. As much as I wanted to hide my stretch marks, I wasn't going to let them ruin this moment.

'No thanks, I'd like to keep the stars.'

'That's fine,' he said. 'I think they're more broad-minded than the moths. I hope so anyway.' His eyes glinted dangerously. He pulled me to him and lifted my top over my head, easing my bra straps down as he kissed my shoulders then unclasping it and cupping my breasts in his hands, his fingers flicking over my already hard nipples. I gasped. My back arched, my body awakened and pulsing, desperate to connect with his. I tugged my skirt down over my hips. The boat rocked slightly. I grabbed hold of his arm.

'It's OK,' he said. 'I've got you. And I'm not going to let go.'

I smiled. Knowing he meant it. He turned me round so I had my back to him, pulled me in closer and slid his hand down towards my knickers.

We lay on the bed afterwards. Our bodies entwined on top of the duvet. Never having made it underneath. My finger tracing his spine down to the dampness at the small of his back. His hand brushing my hair back as he nuzzled my shoulder. I smiled at him. Not feeling at all self-conscious as I had expected. But more like some Greek goddess, worshipped and adored.

'Happy?' he asked, kissing my neck.

'Very,' I said. 'And relieved too.'

He looked at me quizzically.

'When you got the condom out, I thought for a moment you were going to blow it up and start twisting,' I teased.

'Thanks,' he said, laughing, 'and there was I thinking I was going to get a compliment.'

'You'll learn,' I said. 'What about you? Are you happy?'

He thought for a moment, twiddling a strand of my hair around his finger.

'The happiest I've ever been.' He said it quietly. As if he dare not speak its name. Then kissed me. Once on the mouth before moving down. I groaned as I took hold of his hand.

'I'd love to,' I said. 'But I need to get back. I don't want to keep Nina up too late.'

'Of course,' he said. 'Sorry, I almost forgot for a moment.'

'That I couldn't stay, you mean?'

He nodded, unable to hide his disappointment.

'Maybe one day,' I said, bending to kiss him. He smiled, it was enough. 'I'd better get dressed then,' I said, reluctantly peeling myself away from his skin.

'Me too. I'll walk you home,' he said. 'And I'll bring a torch this time.'

I woke up with a smile on my face. I suspected I had slept that way. I slithered my arm out from underneath Alfie and reached over to the bedside cabinet to check my phone. One message. From Dan. 'Morning. Missing You. See you at nine. X'

I'd invited him round to use our shower. It seemed the decent thing to do while his was out of action. And of course nothing to do with the fact that I was desperate to see him again. My Dan. I could say that now. It felt good. Better than I'd dared hope. Maybe because my eyes were wide open this time. Or simply because he was the right one for me.

I looked down at Alfie, who was making snuffling noises in his sleep. Blissfully unaware that I had deserted him in the night. I still felt a pang of guilt. But it had been almost blotted out by a huge great dollop of hope. Usually I'd make the most of his prolonged slumber, maybe even try to fall back myself. But not today. Today I poked him and tickled his feet until he woke. I was that desperate to share the news with him. About who was coming for breakfast.

Dan tapped twice on the door. Alfie, who was in his high chair eating his egg soldiers (or anti-war protestors as they were known in Hebden Bridge) shouted out a welcome before I could even open it.

'Hello, balloon man Dan.'

'Hello, Thomas-fan Alfie,' came the reply.

I opened the door. Dan stood there, a morning-after-the-night-before glint in his eyes, holding a carton of orange and passion fruit smoothie. I was suddenly nervous to see him. Ridiculous after how he'd seen me a few hours before.

'I would have got you flowers,' he said, 'but there's nowhere open yet. This was the most appetising thing in my fridge. Narrowly beating the hummus which had a film of mould over it.'

'Thank you,' I said, smiling as I took the carton from him. 'I think you made the right call on the hummus.' I pulled the door to behind me for a moment so I could kiss Dan properly on the lips without Alfie seeing then opened it wide to allow him through.

'Wow, what have you got there, Alfie?' he said.

Alfie opened his mouth to reveal some well-chewed eggy toast. He took a lump out and offered it to Dan.

'Er, thanks, Alfie, but I think I'll let you finish that yourself, looks like you're enjoying it.'

'We do have some non-chewed food if you'd prefer,' I said. 'Toast, bagels, cereal, a fry-up.'

'Bagels would be great, thanks. I'm not a big breakfast person.'

'Sure,' I said, pouring two glasses of smoothie for us and diluting some in a plastic cup for Alfie. 'Sit down, make yourself at home.' I realised as I said it that Dan had never been here before. The closest he'd got had been Nina's kitchen. It was odd, considering how comfortable I felt with him, how much a part of our lives he had already become.

'Great place,' said Dan looking round the kitchen with its oak beams, sloping ceiling and crooked walls.

'Small and perfectly ill formed,' I said, putting a cafetière on the table along with cream cheese, butter and jam. Alfie looked at me, across to Dan and back at me. He swung his legs in the high chair, started banging his beaker on the tray and singing a barely intelligible version of 'Bob the Builder'. He was loving this. The three of us having breakfast together. Almost as much as I was. The bagels popped up, I picked them up with my fingertips, dropped them quickly on to a plate and brought them over to the table and sat down.

'Cheers,' said Alfie, holding up his cup of smoothie.

Dan started laughing. 'I didn't know you had champagne breakfasts here.'

'I wish. He's remembered that from Christmas Day. We did it then. I told him it was a special occasion.'

'Well, cheers, Alfie,' said Dan, tapping his smoothie glass against the cup before turning to clink it against mine. 'And a happy special occasion day to you both.'

I smiled at him as I raised my glass. He squeezed my hand under the table.

We munched our way through the bagels, Alfie regaling Dan with various tales of his exploits in the form of four-word sentences.

'Another coffee?' I asked as Dan drained the last dregs from his mug.

'No thanks. If it's OK with you I'd better grab that shower now. I can't stay too long. I've got a job in Halifax this afternoon and I don't want to scare the Brownies away.'

'Of course, you go on up,' I said, trying not to show my disappointment. 'The bathroom's at the end of the landing. I've left a clean towel out for you and help yourself to shampoo and stuff.'

'It's OK, thanks. I've brought all my own things,' Dan said, pulling a towel and toiletry bag out of his rucksack. 'Us boat types don't like to abuse good hospitality.'

'Does that mean you won't be using my toilet then?' I said.

Dan grinned back at me. 'See you in a few minutes, Alfie,' he said.

Alfie looked at me in bemusement as Dan went upstairs.

'He's just having a quick shower,' I said. 'The one on his boat is broken.'

Alfie looked at me in what appeared to be a decidedly suspicious manner. He was on to us. I was sure of it.

I busied myself washing up the breakfast things, trying to make enough noise to drown out the sound of the water splashing above us. It wasn't easy, knowing he was standing there naked and wet in a steaming shower a few feet above my head. I tried to concentrate on my parental responsibilities. I finished the washing up, removed the remnants of egg and jam from Alfie's face under much protest and lifted him out of the high chair. I was about to take him upstairs to get dressed when there was a knock on the door. For a split second I wondered if it might be Nina, offering to look after Alfie while I hot-footed it upstairs to the bathroom. I opened the door. The faint sniff of hope in the air was replaced by the stench of a large bucket of manure suspended precariously above my head.

'Daddy,' shouted Alfie from behind my legs.

'Richard,' I said, somewhat less enthusiastically. 'What are you doing here?'

He sighed and shook his head. 'You haven't checked your emails, have you?' he barked.

'Not for a couple of days, no.'

'I sent one to you on Thursday. Saying I couldn't make it Sunday and that I'd come to take Alfie out today instead. And that if I didn't hear back from you, I'd take it that was OK.' Alfie had squeezed round the front of my legs and was tugging at the laces on Richard's designer trainers. Richard was ignoring him and staring straight at me.

'Why didn't you ask me to reply if it was OK, then you'd know if I'd got it or not?'

'I assumed you'd have checked your emails by now. The common practice is to check them twice a day, you know.' He was looking at me as if I was some sort of relic from a bygone age. I wanted to call him an obnoxious little shit but Alfie ruled that option out. I resorted to adopting that mock pleasant tone of voice parents use when they argue in front of their children.

'Funnily enough I'm lucky if I get the chance to check them twice a week. Something to do with looking after a two year old. I do apologise for not being on Facebook either. I really should get my priorities right.'

It was a cheap jibe but one that I felt was justified on this occasion. Richard pulled one of those irritating mock smiles. I didn't really want to be having this confrontation on the doorstep. However, I was equally aware that I didn't want Richard to step foot inside the kitchen.

'So do you want me to take him or not?' said Richard. It was a horrible *Kramer vs. Kramer* moment. The sort of thing you vow you will never be reduced to when you split up with someone. I didn't want him to take Alfie, but not as much as I didn't want him to meet Dan. Or for Alfie to be caught up in the middle of a big scene.

'You might as well, now you're here. He won't understand what's going on if you leave without him.'

Richard shrugged and continued to stare at me. 'Fine.

Are you going to get him dressed then or am I taking him in his pyjamas?'

'Yes, of course,' I said, having been distracted by what I thought was the bathroom door opening. 'Hang on a minute and I'll go and get his clothes.' I left Richard on the doorstep, knowing I was pushing the boundaries of rudeness, even to an ex-partner, and tried to slip back inside the kitchen to grab some clothes from the airer. But Alfie pulled the door wide open just as Dan arrived at the bottom of the stairs, his hair still wet and smelling of something fruity, holding his towel and toiletry bag.

'Who the hell's this?' asked Richard.

'Balloon man Dan,' shouted Alfie, doing the introduction by running over to Dan and hugging his legs. I looked around for a trapdoor in the floor. There wasn't one. Somehow I was going to have to explain my way out of this.

'Er, this is our friend Dan. He lives on a canal boat and his shower is broken so he's just popped round to use ours.' Although it was entirely true, I couldn't muster the required degree of conviction in my voice. The expression on Richard's face confirmed that it had sounded like something out of *The World's Worst Half-baked Excuses and Downright Lies Compendium*. He didn't say anything, but the words, 'Yeah, right, and I was born yesterday,' appeared in a thought bubble above his head. I turned to Dan who was looking at me, clearly not understanding what was going on.

'Dan, this is Richard, Alfie's father. He's come to take him to Tiny Toes. There's been a bit of a mix-up over days.'

'Hi,' said Dan, his features struggling to form a smile. 'I was just on my way out.'

Richard nodded. Obviously having decided against any exchange of pleasantries. Dan hurriedly put his things into his rucksack and slung it over his shoulder before bending to talk to Alfie.

'Thanks for letting me use your shower. You have a great time at Tiny Toes.'

Alfie tightened his grip around Dan's legs. 'Dan come too,' he said.

I groaned, imagining Richard and Dan having to make small talk on a bouncy castle.

'Dan's got to go to work now, sweetheart. We'll see him again soon.'

Alfie reluctantly relinquished his grip and Dan edged towards the open door.

'Bye,' Dan said to Richard. There was no reply.

I handed Richard some clothes from the airer.

'Perhaps you could start getting Alfie dressed,' I said. I followed Dan outside and pulled the door to behind us.

'Sorry,' said Dan. 'I've made things really awkward for you, haven't I?'

I shrugged. 'They were pretty awkward already, to be honest.'

'Is it all going to turn nasty?' he said, gesturing in towards Richard.

'He won't say much in front of Alfie. He'll probably save it for Monday.'

Dan frowned. I realised he didn't know and I hadn't meant for him to find out like this.

'He's my editor at work,' I said. 'Not an ideal situation but there you go.'

Dan nodded. He appeared troubled by the whole thing. Still reluctant to leave.

'I can wait round the corner for a bit if you like. Just until he goes.'

'Thanks, but I'll be fine, honestly. I can handle the odd sarcastic comment or two. You go, I don't want to make you late for work.' I squeezed his arm, feeling too self-conscious to do anything else with Richard on the other side of the door.

'OK,' he said. 'I'll phone you later. Bye.'

I went back inside and shut the door. Alfie ran up to me, his jumper buttoned up wrongly at the neck. Richard had a smug look on his face. As if pleased he at last had some fresh ammunition to throw at me.

'I understand now,' he said. 'Why you were too busy to read your emails.'

'You can think what you like, but I don't want to hear it in front of Alfie,' I said, resorting to mock pleasant tone again. I bent down to Alfie, smoothing his hair.

'OK, sweetie. Daddy will put your jacket on while I get your bag together.' I hurriedly packed a water beaker, some rice cakes and nappies into his changing bag and handed it to Richard.

'You can get him lunch there if you like. Have him back by two, please. He'll probably need a nap then.'

Richard nodded. I pulled the buggy outside and strapped Alfie in.

'Have a lovely time,' I said, kissing the top of his head. 'Mummy see you later.'

Richard walked off without a word. I went back inside

and banged my head several times against the door, wondering why it was that Richard was so skilled at buggering things up. I decided to phone Rachel; she was always good at accentuating the positive.

After six rings the answer machine picked up. I put the phone down, not knowing where to begin the message. I plumped for more caffeine instead. I took the kettle over to the sink and started to fill it. As I glanced out of the window, I caught sight of Dan, his rucksack slung over one shoulder, walking away down the towpath.

Fifteen

'Hiya. Good weekend?' I asked Laura as I plonked myself down in the seat next to her on Monday morning.

'Yes, thanks. David took me shopping in King Street on his credit card, although he may regret it when he gets his Visa bill. How about you?'

'Great, thanks,' I said, unable to stop a grin from spreading across my face. I could hear the cogs going round in Laura's head, her lower jaw dropping slightly as the possibility entered her head. She swivelled round in her chair to face me.

'You shagged him, didn't you?' she whispered. 'The balloon sculptor guy.'

I turned on my computer and logged in. 'I couldn't possibly comment,' I said.

'You will do,' she said. 'At lunchtime. I want to know everything, right down to whether you made the boat move.' Her voice trailed off as Richard approached my desk, eyes decidedly steel grey today.

'A word please. In the guest room. Now,' he said.

'What's up with him?' Laura whispered as he walked away.

'He knows,' I said, getting up from my chair. 'At least, he thinks he does.'

I followed Richard down the corridor, feeling like a teenager caught in a compromising position by her father. Justine, one of the producers, was in the guest room. She took one look at Richard and got up and left without a word. Quite clearly he meant business. I decided to get a pre-emptive strike in.

'I thought you said you wanted to keep our business and personal lives separate? You've got no right, hauling me in here for something which isn't work related.'

'Your behaviour and the fact that you won't talk in front of Alfie gives me no option,' he said.

'And what is it exactly I've done which is so bad?'

'Do I need to spell it out to you?'

'You think Dan stayed the night, don't you?'

'Given that he came downstairs on a Saturday morning after having a shower in your bathroom, yes. That would be the obvious conclusion.'

'Except that I wouldn't allow that to happen. Have Alfie wake up to find a man sharing his bed.'

'Don't tell me I'm supposed to believe your little story about the shower on his boat being broken.'

'It's true. Whether you believe it or not is up to you. I know it sounded far-fetched but if I was going to make something up, do you really think I'd come up with such a pathetic story?'

Richard hesitated, obviously seeing my point.

'So do you invite many men in for showers? Do you put flyers up around Hebden Bridge advertising the service?'

'Now you're being ridiculous.'

'OK, so how long has his shower been broken?'

'His name's Dan and it only broke on Friday. It was the first time he'd been to the house.'

'So are you seeing him or what?'

'Yes, Richard. I'm seeing him. Although Alfie doesn't know yet. He thinks we're still just friends and I'd like to keep it that way. Now if you don't mind, I've got work to do.'

'Oh no you don't,' said Richard, grabbing hold of my arm as I went past. 'You've got a few more questions to answer yet.'

'Bloody hell, what is this?' I said, pulling his hand off me. 'I didn't give you the third degree over Tricia.'

'No, because she doesn't have access to our son.' The word 'access' rankled with me.

'What are you getting at?'

'Alfie certainly seemed to know him pretty well.'

'They've spent quite a bit of time together, if that's what you mean. Alfie's been on his boat a few times. And seen him perform.'

Richard raised an eyebrow.

'He's a children's entertainer. Makes balloon animals, that sort of thing.'

'Fucking hell,' said Richard, his hands flying up to his head. 'It's one of those police psychological profiles. Single. Lives on his own on a canal boat. Children's entertainer.'

'What are you saying, Richard?'

'That he's a fucking paedophile.'

I snorted a laugh and shook my head. 'You think I'd let Alfie spend time with him if I had any reason to believe that he was?'

'So you've checked him out, have you?'

'He's been police-checked. You have to if you work with kids.'

'That doesn't a mean a thing.'

'So, what would you like me to do?'

'You're a journalist, aren't you? Do a search on the internet. I know a copper who can do proper criminal checks as well. For anything, not just convictions. But you'll need to give me his surname and date and place of birth.'

I started laughing. 'You've got a bloody cheek.'

'What?'

'Since when have you been so bothered about the welfare of your son? You walked out on him, remember? Before you start accusing other people, perhaps you should take a long, hard look at yourself. Because you're the only man who has ever hurt Alfie.' I turned on my heel and strode out of the room, my feet stomping back along the corridor. The steam still hissing from my ears.

Laura had gone on a job when I got back to my desk. I shuffled papers and scrolled down my contact list onscreen, anything to keep my head and hands busy. After a few moments Richard skulked past me back to his desk. I waited until he got up a while later and went into Big Denise's office before going on to Google and entering 'Dan Brady', highlighting pages from the UK and clicking search. Twenty-three thousand entries, headed by an experimental architect, a PS3 game developer and a member of Benfleet Cricket Club. I scrolled down and clicked on next; one, two, maybe five times before eventually returning to the search and trying 'Daniel Brady'. A hundred and seventy-five thousand entries this time. I hadn't made it much past the motorbike racer and the historian on the first page when I heard footsteps approaching my desk. I quit the page quickly, annoyed at myself for doubting Dan, and looked up to find Moira beaming down at me.

'Morning, Jo,' she said.

I looked at her and frowned, surprised to see her in at this time in the morning.

'I thought your stint on the one o'clock news was finished,' I said.

'Nope. You're looking at *Spotlight*'s new lunchtime lass.'

'But I don't understand,' I said, scratching my head. 'Why are you looking so chirpy if they've axed you from the main bulletin?'

'Because they didn't axe me. I asked to be moved. I got to know my family again last week. And I really like them. So much so that I decided I'd rather spend my evenings with them than some grouchy old perma-tanned newsreader.'

I started laughing. Finding Moira's *joie de vivre* infectious. 'Good on you. That's fantastic. It must have been the right decision, you look five years younger already.'

'I know. At this rate I'll look as good as Tricia by the summer.' She laughed again, a Scottish tinkle of a laugh. Other people looked up from their desks. It wasn't normal behaviour on a Monday morning. To be full of the joys of life.

'What did Richard say?' I asked. 'I bet he was gobsmacked.'

'He clearly didn't get it,' said Moira. 'Kept asking if I was sure about it, if there was anything wrong with me. And he's been strangely nice to me since.'

'He probably thinks you've got some kind of terminal illness,' I said. 'He wouldn't be able to think of any other reason why you'd put your family first.'

Moira laughed.

'I bet Stuart was stunned as well.'

'Stunned and delighted, of course, that he's finally got shot of me without the need for bloodshed. I'm thrilled for Pamela, though. She's a lovely lass and she was so good last week. She deserves the break.'

'So everyone's happy,' I said.

'Seems so. What about you? You've got a bit of colour in your cheeks as well this morning.'

I smiled at Moira. Suddenly not caring who knew.

'I'm seeing someone,' I said. 'His name's Dan, he's great with Alfie and he's gorgeous. Far too gorgeous for me but I'm trying not to worry about it.'

'Oh, Jo, that's fantastic. I'm so pleased for you.' Moira whooped and gave me a huge hug. Richard looked up from his desk, having just returned from the morning planning meeting, and scowled in our direction.

'Sorry,' Moira called over. 'Do we need permission for a public whoop?'

Richard rolled his eyes and looked away. I managed to stifle a giggle.

'He knows about Dan,' I whispered. 'And he doesn't approve.'

'Bloody cheek,' said Moira. 'I've a good mind to tell him I don't approve of the way he's treated you and Alfie.'

'I just hope he doesn't try to spoil things.'

'Don't you fret about him,' said Moira. 'You just make the most of being happy. And don't let him put a damper on things.'

An hour later I was standing in a public toilet in Manchester city centre, about to interview a toilet attendant called Doris who had been crowned the 'Bog Lady of Britain'. Richard had, quite clearly, decided to enact his retribution in the most juvenile way possible.

'So, Doris. What's the secret of your gleaming toilet bowls?' I began.

Doris, who was gap toothed and sporting a pair of blue-framed NHS glasses, the like of which I hadn't seen since school, took a deep breath and began.

'You've gotta have eyes in the back of your head and a nose for trouble. You wouldn't believe the mess some of them make, not just the young ones either. Worse than animals, they are. You've got to be quick, mind. Otherwise it sets like pebble-dash and it's a right bugger to get off. Even with a good brush.'

I heard Arthur trying to contain a guffaw of laughter behind his camera and looked down at Doris's slippers while I tried to compose myself.

'Perhaps we can try that again,' I said. 'But maybe with a little less detail, if you don't mind.' Doris stared blankly at me, clearly not understanding. 'It's just that it'll be going out at teatime and we wouldn't want to put people off their food, would we?' I said.

'Right you are, love. Whatever you say. Only it doesn't

bother me because I eat my sandwiches in here. Can't afford not to work through my lunch hour. And if I turned my back for five minutes they'd be crapping in the sinks.'

I nodded at Doris, sensing that this was going to need a serious amount of editing on my return.

By the time I got back to the newsroom I was seriously doubting whether I had a future at *Spotlight North West* and was also seriously in need of the toilet (having decided against going in Doris's loos for fear she had a secret spy hole or would burst in brandishing a giant toilet brush). I went straight to the ladies, let the door slam shut behind me and threw my bag down on the floor.

'Fucking bastard, fucking crappy jobs, fucking *Spotlight* up its arse,' I said, kicking the wall and regretting it instantly as the pain shot through my big toe. I looked up with a start as a cubicle door opened and Big Denise walked out.

'I take it you're having a bad work day,' she said, stony faced.

I smiled weakly. I had two options. To attempt a full retraction or an honest explanation. And I didn't see the point in lying any more.

'Sorry, Denise. I should learn to keep my mouth shut.'

'Well, you're paid to talk. Keep going. I'm listening.' She walked over to the basins and began washing her hands, her large gold bangles rattling together as she did so.

'OK,' I said, taking a deep breath. 'Working for your ex is a bit like having to rub your elbow down a cheese grater every morning and I do take exception to him sending me out on ever crappier jobs.'

Denise shook her hands over the sink and moved across to the hand-dryer.

'The reason he sends you to interview toilet attendants,' she said, speaking loudly above the noise of the machine, 'is because you're the best person for the job. Anyone can do murder stories, they're a piece of piss. But he can't send Simon to interview the Bog Lady of Britain, can he? He wouldn't have a fucking clue. You can interview anyone. And get some real gems out of them. It's a rare skill. It's why I let you come back part time. I couldn't afford to lose a journalist like you.'

She turned to face me as the whirr of the hand-dryer stopped. I tried to bring my eyebrows down from the place on my forehead where they'd shot up to and close my mouth which was gaping open.

'Now what I suggest you do is stop taking it as a personal slight and start feeling flattered. Your piece will be the best report on the programme tonight. And believe me, the others know that. That's why you're one of the most highly regarded journalists at *Spotlight*. Even by Richard. Although he'll never admit it to you, of course.'

I stood rooted to the spot. Having been rendered incapable of speech by Big Denise's candour.

'Now,' she said. 'If you'll excuse me, I'm off for a meeting with the cheese grater on newsdesk.' She turned and walked out. Leaving me standing there with an unexpected grin on my face and a still throbbing toe.

Sixteen

'Are you sure about Sunday? You really don't have to come, you know. It could turn into the most excruciatingly awful afternoon you've ever had.' We were lying on the bed in Dan's boat, in one of the those blissful post-sex states which I had now ruined by mentioning my grandmother's eightieth birthday party. Which was a shame because we only had a few more minutes together before I had to relieve Nina of her toddler-sitting duties.

'Believe me,' said Dan, 'it won't. Anyway, if it's going to be that bad I want to be there for you.' He stroked my hair back and kissed my shoulder. I still wasn't used to it. Three weeks into our relationship I continued to hold my breath, waiting for the bubble to burst. Sure this degree of happiness couldn't last much longer. We'd come through the Richard finding out thing and now we were facing our next big test. Dan was going to meet my family.

'Thank you,' I said, stretching up a hand to stroke his face. 'Just remember that the saying about looking at a woman's mother to find out what she's going to be like in thirty years' time doesn't apply in my case.'

'What's so bad about her?'

I sighed. 'I love her, of course I do. She's my mum. But I

don't actually like her. She's simply not a very nice person. She never stops criticising me. Everything I say and do is wrong. She's been like that for as long as I can remember. She used to have a go at my dad the whole time, too. He could never do anything right. If he used to play with me or my brother in the garden and our clothes got mucky, she'd have a go at him. Even though we'd had a great time.'

'So they weren't happy,' he said, 'your mum and dad?'

'I don't think so. They weren't at each other's throats or anything . . .' My voice trailed off as I saw the expression on Dan's face and realised what I'd said. 'I'm really sorry. Listen to me going on. This is nothing compared with what you must have gone through.'

Dan looked down. 'It's OK,' he said. 'It's still important. It's what happened to you. That's why I want to know about it, not because I'm playing competitive "my childhood was worse than your childhood" games. Anyway, my counsellor says it's good to hear about other people's families. To understand that this idyllic childhood I missed out on doesn't actually exist. That lots of people come from unhappy homes.'

I nodded. Surprised but pleased at the way he'd just opened up to me. 'I didn't know,' I said. 'That you were having counselling. Is it helping?'

Dan shrugged. 'It's hard to say. I've only had a few sessions. I like the guy, though. Which is a good start.'

'What made you decide to go?' I asked.

'You,' he said. I frowned at him. Not understanding. Dan tucked a stray stand of my hair back behind my ear and continued. 'Because I know I've still got issues I need

to deal with and I don't want them to screw our relationship up. I want to do everything I can to make it work.'

I smiled at him, stroking his arm. Unable to believe that
I meant that much to him. And loving the fact that he'd
been able to tell me.

'Thank you,' I said. 'That's a massive thing to do. You've
never been for any kind of help before?'

'No. I guess it wasn't the done thing in those days. And
I always used to think the best way of dealing with it all
was to bury it so deep it couldn't hurt me.'

I nodded. I wanted to know more. I still wasn't sure
what 'it all' actually meant.

'Is that why you never mention your father?' I asked.
'Because of what he did to your mum?'

Dan nodded.

'So I guess you don't see him, or keep in touch or
anything?'

Dan shook his head and stared up at the ceiling. Remaining silent for a moment. I decided it probably wasn't the
right time to ask about his mother. I had pushed things far
enough.

'How old were you?' he said eventually. 'When you lost
your father.'

'Nineteen,' I said. 'I was away at university in Lancaster.
I thought I was all grown-up and independent. And then
I got a phone call to say my dad had died. And I realised
that whatever your age, wherever you are, they're still a
part of you.'

'Were you closer to your father than your mum, then?'

'Yeah. He was more my kind of person. He had a sense

of humour. We used to do fun things together. Building dens, making things, getting dirty. Stuff that my mum never did.'

'But when your dad died, didn't that bring you and your mum closer together?'

I shook my head. 'It drove us further apart, if anything. When Dad died it was like Mum was almost relieved that she didn't have to live with him any more. She got all her best china out. Said she'd never dared use it when he was alive because he was so clumsy he'd have broken something.'

Dan shut his eyes and lay quietly, rhythmically stroking my hair.

'Philip Larkin was right, wasn't he?'

'About them fucking us up, you mean?'

Dan nodded. 'That's another reason why I want to get myself sorted out. If I ever have children of my own, I'm determined not to pass on all my shit to them.'

'I used to say that,' I said. 'And then I ended up as a single mum and gave Alfie a whole load of other issues to deal with.'

'Hey, you're doing a brilliant job. Stop putting yourself down,' said Dan.

'You're right,' I said. 'I should leave that to my mother.'

Dan grinned. 'I'm actually looking forward to meeting them – your family, I mean.'

'I'll remind you of that half an hour after we arrive,' I said.

We stood on the doorstep. Me, Dan and Alfie. My new family – or so it felt. All I could think of was standing here with Richard not so long ago, thinking the very same thing. Not knowing that it was all about to fall apart.

I'd told Mum, of course. That I was bringing someone. Her response had been typically supportive: 'You're not pregnant again, are you?' followed, after my swift rebuttal, by 'Well, I hope he sticks around longer than the last one.' She hadn't asked anything about him. As if she didn't quite believe he existed. Presumably she had decided to wait until she met him in the flesh.

Years ago when I was in my early twenties I used to play this game in my head. The world's worst boyfriend to take home to my mum. All men, dead and alive, were eligible for inclusion. I used to imagine saying, 'Mum, I'd like you to meet Rasputin,' or 'Hi, Mum, this is Swampy.' And I'd delight at imagining the expression on her face. The rebellious teenager in me was looking forward to saying, 'Mum, this is Dan. He's a balloon sculptor and he lives on a canal boat.' But a much bigger part of me, the Alfie's mum part of me, the 'fed up with being the black sheep of the family dumped single parent' part of me wanted her to like him. Wanted her to be surprised that I'd done so well for myself.

I rang the doorbell and turned to look at Dan.

'Remember, if you want to go at any point, simply give me the nod and we'll make a quick exit.'

'It'll be fine,' said Dan, squeezing my hand.

Mum opened the door. She stared hard at Dan, cocking her head to both sides and squinting a little as if he was a painting which she couldn't decide if she liked or not. Finally, without seemingly deciding one way or the other, her gaze fell to Alfie.

'Hello, sweetheart. Come and give Nanna a hug.'

Alfie obliged but broke off quickly and pointed excitedly to Dan.

'Balloon man Dan,' he said.

Mum looked at me.

'Hello, Mum,' I said, determined not to lower myself to her paucity of manners. 'This is Dan. Dan, my mother, Pauline.'

'Pleased to meet you,' said Dan, offering his hand.

Mum took it and seemed to mellow slightly. I knew the soft skin and trimmed nails would be a winner with her.

'Balloon man Dan,' Alfie said again.

'Why does he call him that?' she said, turning to me.

'Dan's a children's entertainer. He makes things out of balloons.'

'Oh, how lovely,' she said, clearly not meaning it, before taking Alfie's hand and walking back down the hall.

'Please don't take it personally,' I said. 'If I'd have turned up with Prince William she'd have said he was too young for me.'

Dan smiled. 'It's OK. I'll play the part of the controversial newcomer. It'll be like being back at theatre school.'

We followed Mum and Alfie through to the lounge where Nan and Derek were sitting on the sofa.

'Happy Birthday, Nan,' I said, bending to kiss her. 'I'd like you to meet my friend Dan.'

Nan took his hand and peered at him over the top of her glasses. 'Have you left the weather girl now then?' she asked.

I took a deep breath and blew out. It was clearly going to be a difficult afternoon.

'No, that was Richard, Nan. He's still with the weather girl. This is Dan, someone completely different. Dan, meet my nan, Vera.'

'Nice soft hands,' said Nan, patting them and seemingly reluctant to let go. 'You're not going to get her pregnant like the last one did, are you?'

Dan turned to look at me, fortunately appearing to see the funny side of it. 'No, we'll just stick to holding hands, I think. It's much nicer.'

'Oh, it is. Who was that pop star chappie? The one who looked like a girl and said he preferred a nice cup of tea to a bit of how's your father.'

'Boy George?' said Dan.

'That's him,' said Nan. 'Is he still alive or did he get that disease all the gay boys get?'

Dan looked at me, a perplexed smile on his face.

'He's still going,' I said. 'Although he was nearly killed by a disco glitterball a few years ago.'

'Shame,' said Derek. 'There would have been one fewer of them, then.'

I groaned inwardly.

'Derek,' I said, keen to move the conversation on, 'I'd like you to meet Dan. Dan, my stepfather Derek.'

'Pleased to meet you,' said Dan, finally sliding his hand away from my nan's grasp.

'And you, Dan,' said Derek, shaking his hand firmly. 'What's your surname?' I knew what he was getting at. Checking out his dark looks, fearing there was a foreign infiltrator in our midst.

'Brady,' said Dan.

'Aah, a good old Irish name. They're the only immigrants that ever did a proper day's work.'

I winced as he said it. Dan had already told me about his European heritage.

'My maternal grandfather was a Romanian refugee, actually,' said Dan. 'He worked pretty hard in the cotton mills in Manchester, from what I've heard.'

'Of course,' said Derek, the smile on his face fading by the second.

'Is Dan one of those asylum seekers?' asked Nan, tugging at my sleeve.

'No, he's from Fairfield,' I said. 'It's in Manchester.'

'So they're not going to deport him?'

'No, Nan. I shouldn't think so.'

'The thing I can't understand,' continued Nan, 'is why no one tells all these foreign nutters that the asylums were all closed down years ago. Then they wouldn't keep coming over here looking for them, would they?'

Dan looked at me, I shook my head, so he knew it wasn't worth trying to explain.

'And what do you do for a living?' asked Derek, turning back to Dan.

'He makes things out of balloons,' Mum said to Derek, in the same apologetic tone Sybil Fawlty used to say of Manuel, 'He's from Barcelona.'

'That's nice. And what's your proper job?'

'That is my proper job,' said Dan.

'How does that pay the mortgage?'

'It doesn't have to. I live on a canal boat.'

Derek frowned and scratched his head, never having been one to understand alternative lifestyles.

'Is he one of those gypsies?' asked Nan. 'They eat hedgehogs, you know. Gypsies.' Fortunately Alfie chose that moment to delve head first into the toy box, providing a welcome distraction.

'If you want to go now, I'd understand,' I whispered to Dan as Mum and Derek went over to Alfie.

He shook his head and smiled at me. 'Not at all. This is good entertainment.'

'Like watching one of those films that are so bad they're unintentionally funny, you mean?'

'As families go,' said Dan, 'they really aren't that bad.'

We were still hovering uncomfortably by the sofa when my brother and his family arrived. Adam didn't even appear to notice that I had someone with me but Marie did a double take, clearly incredulous that a woman in my situation had landed herself such a good catch.

'Where did you find him?' she whispered, sidling up to me once the introductions had been completed.

'Through an escort agency,' I replied. 'They do special rates for single mums. It's part of a government initiative to help us to get out more.'

Marie nodded sympathetically. She watched as Dan played peek-a-boo with Alfie, sending him into fits of giggles. Jemima, who was dressed in a fairy costume this time, went up to them and twirled in front of Dan, no doubt put out that she wasn't the centre of attention.

'Can you do magic with that wand?' asked Dan. Jemima

shook her head. 'Here, let me see if I can.' Dan took the wand and waved it around then pretended Jemima had disappeared. She laughed so much I feared she was going to wet her fairy costume. I glanced across at Marie; I could tell what she was thinking.

'I asked for one who was good with children,' I said.

She nodded. Her eyes not leaving Dan. Her mouth beginning to drool.

'And what's included in his rates. I mean do you get to, er . . .' Her voice trailed off coyly.

'Unfortunately the government scheme doesn't run to that,' I whispered. 'You have to pay extra.'

She looked at me with a mixture of pity and longing in her eyes. I suspected Adam wasn't being attentive enough to his wife's needs.

I heard a car draw up outside, the doors banging several times. A few minutes later the bell rang. I looked at Mum, I didn't think we were expecting anyone else. Derek broke off from his conversation with Adam to go to the front door. Mum closed the lounge door behind him and clapped her hands.

'Now, Mum,' she said, turning to Nan as she adjusted the collar on her lace blouse. 'Derek and I wanted to do something a bit different to mark your birthday. And knowing how much you love music, we thought you'd like a bit of a sing-along.'

'Have you got Leonard Sachs from *The Good Old Days*?' asked Nan.

'I'm afraid not,' said Mum, looking a bit put out. 'But we have got a lovely lady called Shirley who's going to sing some songs from the musicals for you. She's just getting set up now so perhaps if everyone could take a seat.'

I looked at Dan who raised an eyebrow at me. I shrugged as we sat down dutifully at one end of the sofa, Alfie on Dan's lap, Nan and Mum the other side, Adam and Marie in the armchairs, with Luke slumped on the floor and Jemima wriggling on Marie's lap. The lounge door opened; we looked up expectantly but it was only Derek accompanied by a small man wearing an ill-fitting polyester suit and thick bottle-top style glasses.

'Shirley's just getting changed,' Derek said. 'This is Norman, he's going to be doing the music.'

Norman peered out from beneath his Bobby Charlton-style comb-over and nodded in acknowledgement to the room in general before proceeding to plug in an electric organ and take his place behind it. Derek perched beside Mum on the arm of the sofa. I noticed he'd got the video camera in his hand. Not only were we going to have to sit through this live, but we had countless replays to look forward to afterwards. A few seconds later Norman started to play and the door opened to reveal Shirley in all her splendour singing 'Hello Dolly' in a voice which was a blend of Doris Day and Lancastrian karaoke. Shirley proceeded to work the room, smiling and winking at those members of the audience who were brave enough to make eye contact with her as she sashayed around in her full-length gown and blond wig.

'Who's funny lady?' asked Alfie in the slight pause before Norman went into 'Thank Heaven for Little Girls'.

'Her name's Shirley and she's come to sing some songs for Great-Nan,' I told him.

Alfie looked confused although, to be fair, no more confused than Dan.

'Sorry,' I whispered to him as Shirley serenaded Jemima. 'I had no idea you were going to be subjected to this.'

'It's fine,' Dan whispered back. 'If I look perplexed it's because I'm concentrating hard on not laughing.'

Shirley shimmied out of the room with a little wave at the end of the song and we were treated to a brief musical interlude from Norman.

'Are you enjoying it, Vera?' asked Derek.

'She's jolly enough,' said Nan. 'Sounds like a cat being strangled, mind.'

Everyone, including Norman, pretended not to have heard. A moment later Shirley burst back into the room wearing a bowler hat, fishnet tights and a black Liza Minnelli-style waistcoat body as Norman launched into 'Cabaret'. She strutted around the room, followed closely by Derek's camera. He broke off a few times to wipe the lens with a cloth from his pocket. Clearly this was as close as he'd ever come to a *Sex, Lies and Videotape* moment. Shirley put an arm round Derek and hoisted one fishnetted leg on to his thigh. Derek loosened his tie as a rim of moisture formed on his top lip while Mum pursed her lips and looked away disdainfully, no doubt rueing hiring her.

Luke squirmed as Shirley turned her attention to him but still managed to sneak a look down her top as she bent over him before retreating into the hall for another change of costume. She returned much more demurely attired and broke into 'Edelweiss'. All was quiet for a minute or so until Derek sniffed loudly and fled the room. I looked at Mum, who appeared flustered but remained resolutely in her seat. Shirley, of course, carried on like the trouper she was. Someone had to go after him. I figured it was going to have to be me.

'Mummy be back in a minute,' I said to Alfie and slipped out of the room. I found Derek in the kitchen, staring out of the window with tears streaming down his face.

'I'm sorry,' he said, before I had the chance to say anything. 'I wasn't expecting it, that was all. It was Sylvia's favourite, you see.'

I nodded. Understanding at once. And suspecting Mum had known and that was why she hadn't followed him out.

'After Dad died,' I said, 'it was the thing I found hardest. The way everything was swept away as if he'd never existed. You don't stop loving someone simply because they're dead, do you?'

'It's just your mother's way of dealing with things,' said Derek. 'She doesn't like to dwell on the past.'

'Which makes it hard for you,' I said. 'Because you don't want to forget Sylvia.'

He shrugged and dabbed at the corner of his eyes with a neatly pressed handkerchief.

'Your mother's very special to me. I'd do anything for her,' said Derek.

I nodded. 'We all know that. But there's no shame in loving someone's memory. It gives me hope, to be honest. That sometimes love can outlast life. As opposed to lasting a year or two.'

Derek smiled and nodded. 'You're a good girl, Jo,' he said, patting my hand. 'You go back in, I'll be through in a sec.'

I squeezed his hand. Despite the fact that he was a big-oted, narrow-minded dyed-in-the-wool Conservative, he was also a sentimental old thing who was clearly devoted to Mum – and to the memory of his beloved late wife.

When I arrived back in the room, Shirley had gone off for a costume change. Nan was sitting there clutching Dan's hand, clearly having taken a shine to him. Mum glanced up but didn't say anything as Derek came back into the room, still moist eyed. Fortunately Richard's favourite song was 'The Scientist' by Coldplay, which at least meant that I wouldn't be the next one in tears. Shirley reappeared, this time wearing Spandex hot pants, a lurex boob-tube and a long blond wig.

'And now, from *Mamma Mia*, something for all you young ones,' she said, launching into 'Dancing Queen'. She made a beeline for Dan this time, wiggling in front of him. I glanced across at Dan's face. His jaw was set tight, his eyes leaping around the room for something to focus on rather than Shirley's gyrating body. I looked down at his hand, his fingertips digging into his thigh, suggesting he was finding this even more excruciating than the rest of us. For a second I wondered if he was about to flee the room too, before he took Shirley's outstretched hand, jumped up off the sofa and launched into a masterful impression of Benny on the piano, with much leaping around and flying hair, drawing howls of laughter from the previously silent Marie as well as Alfie and Jemima. Even Luke, who had sat glum faced through the previous numbers, managed a smile.

'Are you sure you weren't planted in the audience?' I grinned as he sat back down afterwards to a round of applause. Dan smiled gamely but I could tell it had been an effort. More of an effort than it should have been.

I waited until Shirley had taken her final bow and Alfie was being entertained by Jemima before I followed Dan out to the kitchen, where he'd gone to put the kettle on.

'Who used to sing "Dancing Queen" with you?' I asked.

Dan turned. 'My mother,' he said. 'We used to do a little routine in the kitchen when it came on the radio. If my dad wasn't home, that is.'

'You were close to her, weren't you?'

Dan nodded as he filled the kettle with water.

'So what happened? Where is she now?'

Dan flicked the switch up and turned to look at me, his eyes glistening with tears as Alfie ran into the kitchen with Nan's handbag and threw himself at Dan's legs.

'Big hug,' said Alfie, in his best Tinky Winky voice.

Dan smiled and picked him up. 'Dipsy loves Tinky Winky very much,' he said.

'Laa Laa?' said Alfie, pointing at me.

'Dipsy loves Laa Laa too,' Dan said, his eyes set back to laughing mode. I smiled at him. It was the first time he'd said it and it wasn't exactly in the setting I'd imagined or in Mills & Boon style. But it was real. And I knew he meant it. And that was all that mattered. I leant over and kissed Dan on the lips. Alfie looked up at me and grinned.

'And Laa Laa loves you both very much,' I said.

★

'Funny lady going now,' Alfie said as we went back through the hall where Shirley and Norman were being ushered out of the door. I suspected from the look on Mum's face that they would not be invited back again. And that the video would most definitely not take its place among the family weddings and christenings in the TV cabinet.

We made it through the present-giving and birthday tea without any further upsets and as soon as Alfie had finished his pudding I started gathering our things together.

'Did you enjoy your special day, Nan?' I asked.

'Well, she was a bit brassy for my liking and if they'd done one of those votes like on television I don't think she'd have made it through to the next round. I don't think I'll have her for my ninetieth.'

'Oh,' I said. 'Who would you like then?'

'Your young man will do nicely,' she said with a glint in her eye. 'So you make sure he's still around.'

'I will do,' I said, giving her a hug. 'And you make sure you are too.'

'Nice to have met you, enjoy the rest of your birthday,' Dan said, stooping to kiss Nan's hand.

'You can come again,' she said, patting his hand. 'You're much nicer than the other fellow. So don't you be going off with any weather girls.'

'I won't,' said Dan. 'I don't like their long bony fingers and swirling hands, to be honest. And all those predictions they make. I reckon they might be witches.' Dan winked at Nan before making his way out into the hall to say goodbye to everyone else. Marie sidled up to me when no one was looking.

'You haven't, er, got a card or anything, have you?' she said, nodding in Dan's direction.

'I'll pop one in the post for you,' I said, tapping my nose. 'Discretion assured.'

'Thanks,' she said. 'And here's a little something,' she added, slipping a twenty-pound note into my pocket. 'To put towards any extras you might like. It would be a shame to send him back without trying him out properly.'

I bit my lip to stop myself laughing.

'Thank you,' I said. 'I'm sure he'll be worth every penny.'

Dan

Wednesday, 19 May 1982

'Have a nice day at school, love,' Mum says as she gives me my lunchbox. She always smiles as she says it. Though sometimes I don't think she is feeling very smiley. Today her face is not as bad as yesterday. And yesterday it was better than the day before. That is how it goes now. The bruises fade until her face goes back to being normal for a few days, maybe even a week or so, before he messes it up again. We never talk about what Dad does to her. Not really. I haven't talked about it to anyone else, either. Me and Philip talk about football, bikes and stuff on the telly. Not stuff that is going on at home. The only other sort of thing I can think of that we talk about is the Falklands. It is a war we are fighting over a little island miles away where the penguins live. Philip says we are beating the Argies – they are the army we are fighting. It is a bit like battleships. We sank one of their ships then they sank one of ours. Philip thinks we know where their other ships are. And that we are going to sink them all soon. It is OK talking about things like that. But I couldn't talk to him about Mum and Dad. That is different.

I wonder sometimes about telling Grandma about it. I did promise her. But I think Mum would be mad at me for telling her and I don't want that. I just want her and Dad to be happy. For him to stop hitting her. That is all I want.

I kiss Mum goodbye and pull the door behind me. I walk to school on my own now. Mum has to leave for work soon after me and she goes the other way. And Dad is still in bed. Sometimes I walk with Philip but only if he is late. He leaves before me most days because he goes to the big school.

I kick a stone along the pavement, pretending I am Kenny Dalglish. Liverpool have just won the league again. I wrote 'The Kop Rules' on a wall down our road. Only in chalk, though. It washed off in the rain before Philip saw it and he doesn't believe I did it. I might try Tippex next time. Philip got some on his school jumper and his mum washed it and it still didn't come off.

I get to the playground. Some of the boys are playing football. A group of girls are hanging around the steps, talking about girl stuff. I don't really have a special friend at school. Usually I just join in the football but I don't feel like it today. I have still got the stone, I kick it over towards the wall.

'There he is.' It is Ian's voice, he lives down our road. He runs over to me, some of the other boys follow.

'I know where your mum gets her black eyes from,' he says. I don't know why he has said it. No one talks about our mums at school. I want him to stop. To go back to playing football. I start kicking the stone again. My head down, my fringe hanging over my eyes. Hoping he will go away.

'Your dad does it. He beats up your mum.' The stone

scrapes loudly on the floor as I do a mis–kick. Ian's voice is loud. Too loud. It's like everyone in the playground has heard it. I want to make him go away but I don't know how.

'Liar,' I say.

'Am not. I heard me mam tell me dad.' Ian's mum works at the same factory as mine. Maybe Mum has said something to her. A little crowd of children has gathered around us now. They are all looking at me. I am trying hard not to cry.

'Shut up,' I say. 'Shut up, shut up, shut up.'

He doesn't, though. He goes on saying stuff. Chanting it like a little song. Some of the others join in.

'You dad beats up your mum. Your dad beats up your mum. Your dad beats up your mum.'

I feel my cheeks go red and hot. I am hot all over. I don't like him saying those things. I don't want people to know about what Dad does. I need to make him stop. I clench my fist, swing my right arm and hit him in the face. Hard. Harder than I expected. His nose starts to bleed. He looks shocked but not as shocked as I am. I start to cry. All the children in the playground have come over now. They are standing in a big circle around us. I wonder if he is going to hit me back but he is still standing there looking at the blood on his fingers from where he touched his nose. I look up and see Mrs Roper, our teacher, hurrying across the playground. She goes straight over to Ian and puts her arm around his shoulder.

'Who did this to you?'

He looks down at his feet, a spot of blood drips on to his trousers. He doesn't say anything because he doesn't want to be a grass. The other children are looking at me. I put my hand up.

'It was me, miss,' I say.

Mrs Roper looks surprised. She looks at me from above her glasses.

'Daniel Brady, you should be ashamed of yourself. Go and stand outside the headmaster's office.' She pulls a tissue out from her bag and holds it under Ian's nose.

'Now, let's go inside and get you cleaned up,' she says to Ian as she leads him away.

I walk slowly across the playground. Everyone is looking at me. I feel sick and my legs are wobbly. I can't believe what I've done. I have never hit anyone before in my life. I wish I hadn't done it. I wish he hadn't said those things about Mum and Dad. Most of all I wish they weren't true.

I stand outside the headmaster's office for a long time. Eventually Mrs Roper comes down the corridor and stops in front of me. She doesn't smile at me like she usually does.

'What on earth came over you, Daniel?' she says. 'That's not like you at all.' She is waiting for a reply. I do not know what to say so I just shrug. She shakes her head and goes into the headmaster's office. I hear them talking quietly. I can't work out what they are saying. The door opens and Mrs Roper walks out. She shakes her head at me and walks off down the corridor. Mr Barron the headmaster is standing in the doorway looking at me. He has wavy grey hair and a big red nose. He looks bigger than he does in assemblies. Bigger and crosser. In assemblies he is usually jolly. He sings hymns with us and tells us stories about Jesus and Florence Nightingale and Captain Cook.

'Right, Daniel. You'd better come in,' he says.

I do as I am told. I have never been in his office before. It is small and full of bookshelves and cupboards. He has a wooden desk with lots of things on it and a shiny silver pen in a little case. He sits down at his desk. I stand in front of him. My legs are wobbling again.

'So, what do you have to say for yourself, young man?'

'I'm sorry, sir.' Mum says Dad always says sorry after he has hit her. 'I didn't mean to hit him, sir.'

'Your arm just swung out of its own accord, did it, Daniel?' He is doing that thing grown-ups do when they sound like they're trying to be funny but they're not.

'He was saying nasty things about my mum and dad.'

'That may well be the case but it doesn't give you the right to hit him, does it now?'

'No, sir.'

'We don't solve arguments with our fists. If someone's bothering you, come and tell Mrs Roper or another teacher. You do not take matters into your own hands. Do you understand?'

'Yes, sir.'

He nods his head. I think I know what is coming next. A boy called Peter in my class had it done to him for saying a naughty word to Mrs Roper. It was one of the words Dad says when he gets mad. Mr Barron gets up and walks over to the cupboard in the corner. He opens the door and takes a plimsoll out. I thought it would be a slipper like the ones Mum wears at home but it isn't. It is big and hard. I start to cry.

'I take no pleasure in doing this, Daniel, but your behaviour gives me no option. We do not hit other children and you need to learn that.' Mr Barron points to where I need to stand.

'Take your trousers down and bend over,' he says.

I do as I am told. I clench my fists very tight and shut my eyes. I hear the plimsoll coming through the air before I feel it hit my bottom hard. I step forward to stop myself falling over.

'Keep still, I haven't finished yet,' says Mr Barron. He hits me twice more, hard on the bottom. It stings, my bottom has gone all tingly. I feel hot silent tears running down my face.

'Now, pull your trousers up and don't let me see you in here again. Do you understand?'

'Yes, sir,' I say.

All of Mr Barron's face is red now, not just his nose. He turns to put the plimsoll back in the cupboard. I shuffle out of his office and back down the corridor towards my classroom. When I open the door everyone looks at me, including Mrs Roper. I see Ian sitting there, still holding a tissue to his nose. There are spots of blood on his jumper. I sit down. Very, very carefully.

The walk home takes longer than usual. My bottom has stopped stinging but it is sore and my trousers rub it as I walk. Mum is in the kitchen, she gets home early from work on Thursdays. I know straight away that she knows although I can't work out how. It is the way she is looking at me. The way her eyes look disappointed.

'And what do you have to say for yourself?' she asks, her arms folded across her apron.

'What do you mean?' I say, just in case she doesn't really know and it's something else she is mad about.

'Ian's mum's just been round. Giving me a hard time about what you did to Ian. What on earth got into you?'

I wonder why everyone thinks something got into me. That it wasn't something that was already there.

'He was saying nasty stuff.'

'What sort of nasty stuff?'

I can't tell her that. I can't tell her what he was saying about Dad hitting her. I don't want her to think it is her fault. Or to know what people are saying.

'Just playground stuff.'

'It must have been something bad for you to do that,' she says, crouching down to my level.

I shrug.

'Why did you hit him, Dan?'

'I got mad,' I said. 'Like Dad does.'

Mum looks up at the ceiling and starts to cry. The tears rolling down her face and dripping on to the lino.

'I'm sorry,' I say. 'I didn't mean to do it. It won't happen again.'

She cries some more. I don't know what to say now. Everything I say seems to make it worse. I stand there and let her go on crying until there is a tiny puddle of tears on the lino. She wipes her eyes and reaches over to me, taking hold of both my arms.

'Listen to me, Dan,' she says. 'What your father does is wrong. Very wrong. You're a lovely, gentle boy and I couldn't bear it if you ended up like him. Do you understand?'

I nod. I think I understand a bit of it. Although a much bigger bit doesn't make sense.

'Why do you let him do it?' I say. 'Why don't we just leave and go and live with Grandma?'

Mum sighs deeply and looks up at the ceiling again. 'It's not that simple, Dan.'

'Why not?'

'It just isn't,' she says, throwing her hands up in the air. It isn't a very good answer. It sounds like something I'd say if I didn't know what the real answer was. I pull a bit of a face so she knows.

'Maybe things will get better,' she says. 'When your father gets a proper job again.' Dad does some little bits of work now. Odd jobs for people he knows. Mum says I'm not allowed to tell anyone about it. She wants him to try to find a proper job. One that he goes to at the same time every day like he did before. She says he won't find one at the pub. But he still keeps looking there.

'But what if it doesn't?'

'Let's not think about that,' says Mum, giving me a hug. I wince as she pats me on my bottom.

'What?' she says. I look down at my feet.

'Did you get the slipper?' she asks. I nod. 'Poor, love,' she says. 'I bet that hurt.'

'The worst bit was the waiting,' I say. 'Knowing he was going to hit me and waiting for it to happen. Then once it had, knowing he was going to do it again and again.'

Mum nods slowly and hugs me again. Only she doesn't pat my bottom this time.

Seventeen

'So, Roger, what is it exactly that first attracted you to this trim, good-looking African bird, twenty years your junior?'

We were filming in the purple flock wallpapered front room of a semi-detached in Stalybridge which reeked of stale cigarettes and fry-ups. Roger, an obese, balding man in his late forties, displayed a fine set of yellowing teeth before putting down his cigarette and replying.

'I know people may think I'm going through some kind of mid-life crisis but the fact is I've known Sukhi longer than I've known my wife. And when she told me to make a choice. Well, it was easy really.'

Sukhi, the African grey parrot in question, squawked loudly in agreement and crapped over her bird seed. Clearly they were a match made in heaven. Although I couldn't help doubting Roger's account of his matrimonial split. I suspected the idea of his wife giving him an ultimatum of 'it's me or the bird' and him choosing the latter was something he dreamt up to tell the lads down the pub after the long-suffering woman walked out on him. Still, it made an amusing tale, gave lots of opportunities for parrot puns and would no doubt be the subject of a 'would you rather kick out your wife or a pet?' text vote on tonight's programme.

'So you have an ex-wife now, rather than an ex-parrot?' I continued.

'Yeah, that's about the sum of it,' said Roger, clearly not getting the Python reference.

'And did Sukhi make any comment?' I asked. 'When you told her she was your chosen one?'

'She said she loved Sven-Goran Eriksson,' said Roger. 'My wife taught her to say it when he was the City manager. Just to wind me up, like. Because I support United.'

'And what was your wife's reaction when you told her you'd chosen Sukhi?'

'Sick as a parrot, obviously,' said Roger. I'd teed him up with that one before we started. Not that he'd needed much cajoling.

Rafiq and I spent half an hour trying to get Sukhi on camera saying 'Who's a pretty boy then?' to Roger, before we left the happy couple to their own devices.

'It's another winner,' said Rafiq, climbing into the car. 'Our very own parrot sketch. John Cleese, eat your heart out.'

I smiled and tried to focus on what Big Denise had said. About feeling flattered. Instead of pining for the scoop of the year awards.

'So, what's new?' I asked Laura as we sat down for lunch together in the canteen later.

'Well, I didn't get an interview for the producer's job at Sky.'

'Bastards. They'll regret it someday when you're rich and famous.'

'But I am getting a lodger,' Laura continued, grinning at me over the top of her cappuccino.

'Who?' I asked.

'David.'

I stared at her, waiting for her to tell me it was a wind-up. She said nothing.

'But I thought you were dead against the whole living together thing?'

'Yeah, well. I guess I've mellowed with age.'

'Did he give you an ultimatum?' I asked, thinking of Roger and Sukhi.

'No, but I sensed there was a Valentine's Day proposal coming on. He'd booked a table at a posh restaurant and dropped hints about it being a special night. So I thought I'd pre-empt it by asking him to move in with me.'

I smiled. Laura was the perfect antidote to Valentine's Day.

'So you don't think he'll propose now?'

'No, he knows this is a huge step for me. He won't want to push his luck.'

'Well, congratulations,' I said, leaning over to kiss her on the cheek. 'I'm really pleased for you. Although it's a slippery slope from here, you know. You'll be married with two kids before you know it.'

'Nonsense,' said Laura. 'The only thing about getting married which appeals to me is making you wear a ridiculous pink frilly bridesmaid's dress.'

'In that case,' I said, 'I wish you a long and happy

cohabitation. And I shall buy you his and hers laundry baskets as a moving-in present so you never have to wash his socks.'

'Thank you,' said Laura. 'That would be most appreciated.'

'And are you still going to get the slap-up Valentine's meal?' I said.

'Apparently so. Although it's going to be a moving in together celebration now instead, which is a relief. What about you two lovebirds? Is Dan taking you somewhere nice?'

'No, he doesn't do Valentine's Day.' He'd told me so a week ago. Said he didn't want me to be disappointed or to think it meant he didn't love me because he did. I presumed he considered the whole thing a massive commercial rip-off. Although he hadn't said as much.

'And you don't mind?'

'Not one iota. Richard used to send me a dozen red roses then complain about the cost afterwards. It was hardly romantic.' I glanced across to the far corner of the canteen where Richard and Tricia were deep in conversation at their usual table. Maybe he wouldn't be so grudging about sending her roses. Maybe he thought she was worth it.

'Anyway,' I continued, determined not to dwell on the past, 'if you'd told me a year ago that by next Valentine's Day I'd be with some gorgeous, charming, sexy guy who has a great sense of humour and is best pals with Alfie, I'd have laughed in your face.'

'Jesus,' said Laura. 'You're really gone on him, aren't you?'

I nodded. 'Yep. Hook, line and sinker. All I've got to do now is hang on to him.'

'So when am I going to meet the mysterious Dan?'

'You'll have to wait a bit, I'm afraid. He's only just got over meeting my family, I'm not going to subject him to an evening with you, too. It could be the end of us.'

'Oh, cheers,' laughed Laura, making a face at me. 'I think I'm going to ask Richard to move you away from my desk. I might just get a parrot for company instead.'

The afternoon passed slowly. It was a quiet news day. A time for ringing round old contacts and trying to make something out of nothing. It was beginning to look like they might actually lead with my parrot story. Until the point when Laura picked up the phone. I watched her face drop into serious mode as she scribbled furiously in her notebook.

'There's been a coach crash on the M62 near Warrington,' she called over to Richard as she put the phone down. 'At least two dead. Lots of seriously injured. Pensioners on a day trip from Salford.'

The newsroom lurched instantly into major story gear. Richard barked instructions at each reporter in turn. Laura headed straight for the scene with Arthur. Simon and Rafiq were dispatched to the imminent police press conference in Manchester. Andy was pulled off a court case to head to Warrington Hospital while Toby and I started banging in calls to the emergency services, trying to eke out any extra piece of information that might give us a lead on our rivals. The adrenalin was pumping. People were running across the newsroom. For the first time since my return I felt like a real journalist again. Pamela and Stuart were gathered around the newsdesk, monitoring information as it came in. Only two hours to go until the evening bulletin. Every second mattered.

'It's breaking news on Sky,' Big Denise called out from her office a few minutes later. 'No pictures yet but tell Arthur to get a fucking move on. We need to be there first. We're the local news station, for fuck's sake.'

I could see beads of sweat starting to form on Richard's forehead. It was a big test for him. I knew he'd be relishing it, though. Being at the helm on a national story.

'Pamela, I want you to go out to the scene,' he said. 'We'll go live from there tonight. Stuart, you can anchor from the studio.'

Stuart's face curled up into a scowl. 'I'm the senior presenter. It should be me who goes.'

A momentary hush descended on the newsroom as Richard turned to face him.

'Not in my opinion, Stuart, and unfortunately for you I'm the editor. Pamela, be ready with the rest of the crew downstairs in five minutes.'

Pamela looked somewhat embarrassed to have been chosen so publicly over Stuart. She winced as she walked past me.

'Good luck,' I said. 'You'll be great.' A few seconds later Stuart walked past on his way back to his desk, the scowl getting deeper by the second, muttering something distinctly uncomplimentary about Richard under his breath.

'Well,' whispered Moira who had stayed on to help out. 'Richard's just introduced me to the totally new phenomenon of being on his side.'

'Stuart's not going to take this lying down, is he?' I said.

'No. I imagine that by tomorrow he'll have started a smear campaign claiming that Richard's two-timing Tricia with Pamela,' chuckled Moira.

'Now you come to mention it,' I said, 'I wouldn't put it past him.'

I made another phone call and hit lucky this time. The woman who answered confirmed that it was their coach involved in the crash. I ran to tell Richard.

'Get out there straight away,' he said. 'Take a cameraman with you and see if you can get a line from the boss.'

I hesitated, aware that it would mean I'd be late back for Alfie. That he'd have to go to sleep without me at my mum's house and he'd never done that before. But I was also desperate to go on the job, to be part of the team.

'OK,' I said. I grabbed my notebook and jacket and was halfway down the backstairs when my mobile rang. I fumbled in my bag for a moment before fishing it out. The first thing I heard was Alfie crying in the background.

'Is that you, Jo?' said Mum.

'What's wrong with Alfie?'

'I don't know. That's why I rang you. He's just been sick twice all over my sofa.'

'Never mind the sofa, what about Alfie? How long has he been crying like that?'

'A good hour or so. He keeps saying his tummy hurts.'

'Has he got a temperature?'

'I don't know. He feels hot but I haven't got a thermometer so I—' She was interrupted by the sound of Alfie retching violently in the background. I heard her say, 'Oh Alfie, I told you to use the bucket.'

'Mum, is he OK?'

'It's all over the other cushion this time. You'll have to come and get him, Jo. I've got guests staying, I'll need to get the covers washed and dried by the morning. I can't have everything smelling of sick at breakfast time.'

I gritted my teeth, wondering how on earth she'd coped with me and my brother when we were ill. And then Alfie wailed, 'Mummy,' down the phone. A forlorn, pitiful cry. I stopped in my tracks.

'OK, I'm on my way,' I said. 'Try and get some water down him. I'll be there as soon as I can but it may take a while, there's been a crash on the M62.'

I turned round and headed back up the steps even faster than I'd descended them, cursing under my breath but aware that I had no choice. Alfie was ill and Mum clearly didn't provide childcare for sick grandsons. Only well ones. I reached the newsdesk just as Sky were showing the first pictures from the crash scene.

'I'm really sorry, Richard, Alfie's ill. I've got to go and get him.'

Richard spun round. 'But you're supposed to be on your way to Salford.'

'I know. But he's throwing up everywhere and Mum can't cope. She's asked me to take him home.'

'I don't believe this.'

I was aware that other people were looking at us.

Wondering why we were having a spat in the middle of a major news story. 'I know it's crap timing – I'm sorry.'

'Can't someone else look after him?'

'And who do you suggest. His father perhaps?'

'Stop being facetious.'

'You stop asking stupid questions then. There is no one else, Richard. I've got no choice.'

'Fucking hell,' said Richard, throwing his pen down on the desk. 'This is all I need. You'd better get yourself some proper childcare sorted out. I can't have my reporters disappearing just as the biggest story all year breaks on our patch.'

I shook my head. He had no idea.

'I said I'm sorry, Richard. There's nothing else I can do.' I scrabbled in my bag and tore off a piece of paper from my notebook. 'Here's the phone number and address of the coach firm.' I started to walk away and then turned back. 'Oh, and thanks for your concern about Alfie. I'm sure he'll be fine.'

I listened to the coverage of the crash on *Five Live* on the way to my mum's. Three people had now been confirmed dead. One was in a critical condition in hospital. A lorry had ploughed through the central reservation into the coach. The lorry driver had been arrested. I imagined Laura at the scene. Doing a piece to camera as the emergency services searched through the wreckage in the background. Simon asking the cops for the latest casualty figures, Andy interviewing survivors as ambulances ferried the injured to hospital. And Toby listening to a statement from the boss of the coach firm. I'd let them all down. I knew that. I felt like a footballer who'd messed up that crucial last penalty to the dismay of his teammates. Knowing that however much they said it didn't matter, it did.

The truth was, I was a crap journalist and a crap mum. I wasn't there for work or for Alfie when they needed me. I was sitting in a tailback on the M62. Wondering who'd come up with the bright idea of trying to have it all.

It was nearly six by the time I got to my mum's house. I listened for the sound of crying from within as I rang the doorbell. I couldn't hear anything. I wondered if Alfie had fallen asleep, exhausted from all the retching. A second later Mum opened the door. Alfie tore down the hall and threw himself at my legs with an excited squeal of, 'Mummy.' The same Alfie who'd been wailing pitifully down the phone an hour ago. I scooped him up in my arms and gave him a big hug. He looked a bit peaky and still had vomit caked in his hair but other than that he seemed fine. I turned to look at Mum as Alfie ran back into the lounge.

'That's quite a recovery he's made.'

'Yes, it's a shame the same can't be said for my sofa.'

I decided to ignore the barbed comment. 'So what happened? He just suddenly perked up?'

'Yes. After he was sick again I said he could watch CBeebies and ten minutes later he said his tummy had stopped hurting.'

'And you've no idea what brought it on in the first place? Did he have something unusual to eat for lunch?'

'Not really,' said Mum, fiddling absent-mindedly with the bow on her blouse. 'I suppose he did have rather a lot of chocolate cake but he was enjoying it so much I didn't like to say no. Besides, he needs building up a bit. There's not an ounce of fat on him.'

I nodded at Mum despairingly, deciding to ignore the implication that I wasn't feeding him properly. 'I don't suppose you gave him any fizzy drinks as well, did you?'

'Oh, yes. Now you mention it, I did give him a can of pop when he was running round in the garden after lunch. One of the guests left it behind last week. Red something, I think it was called.'

'Not Red Bull?'

'Yes, that's it.'

'But that's not for children.'

'Well, I didn't know that, did I? It said something about giving you energy on the can. And the way he'd been running round in the garden I thought he could do with it.'

I groaned and shook my head as I followed Mum into the lounge, which was heavy with the scent of forest pine air freshener. The sofa had been stripped bare. I could hear the washing machine whirring in the kitchen. Alfie bounded over and leapt on to my lap as I sat down on the armchair.

'Still, at least he's right as rain again now,' said Mum. 'I don't think the sofa could have withstood another onslaught.' She picked up the remote control and flicked the news on. Pamela was running through the details of the crash as emergency crews were removing debris from the carriageway.

'Terrible business, this,' said Mum, nodding towards the screen. 'I bet you're glad you don't cover that sort of thing any more.'

Eighteen

The knock on the door precipitated a frenzied response from Alfie, involving much whooping, squealing and jumping up and down.

'Hiya,' said Dan, bending down to greet Alfie as he rushed at him the second I opened the door.

'Someone's a tad pleased to see you,' I said. Hyped up was a bit of an understatement to describe Alfie's current state, such was his excitement at being looked after by Dan – even if it was only for an hour or so while I went for a massage. It had been Dan's idea, suggested to relieve the stress of trying to juggle work and Alfie. And he'd been ably assisted by Rachel who had recommended an aroma-therapist who was part of Matt's co-operative.

Dan continued hugging Alfie for a long time.

'Are you OK?' I said, when he finally stood up.

'I'm fine. I'm just very partial to his hugs. And your kisses, if you've got any spare.'

I smiled and kissed him on the lips. A long, slow kiss, which would have led to something else in a different situation.

'Anyway,' said Dan, breaking off eventually. 'There's no time for that. Are you all set?'

'I guess so,' I said, reaching for my chequebook.

'You won't be needing that,' said Dan. 'It's already paid for.'

'I thought you said you didn't do Valentine's Day?'

'I don't. This is nothing to do with the date. I just wanted to treat you to a break. You deserve it. Simple as that.'

'Thank you,' I said. 'I still feel kind of guilty. Leaving you to look after Alfie while I go off to be pampered.'

'Well, don't because we're going to have a whale of a time. I thought we might go and feed the ducks on the canal. I've brought some bread with me,' he said, holding up a small plastic bag.

'Quack, quack,' said Alfie.

'I think that's a yes,' laughed Dan.

'Well, you boys have fun,' I said, bending down to kiss Alfie. 'Mummy be home soon. Love you lots.'

'You go and relax,' said Dan. 'We'll be fine.'

'OK. The spare key's in the pot,' I said, pointing to the kitchen table before putting my coat on. I pulled the door to behind me and walked off up the towpath, turning to wave to Dan and Alfie before I rounded the corner. I was pleasantly surprised at how OK I felt about it. Mainly because I knew Alfie would have a far better time with Dan than he did when my mum looked after him. It was like Rachel had said. Dan was his new best friend. And mine too.

By the time I got to the treatment room above Organic House, the only thing which was bothering me was that I no longer felt stressed enough to justify having a massage.

'And how are you feeling today?' asked Clare, the aromatherapist as she poured me a glass of water.

'Good,' I said, turning my mobile off before taking a sip. 'The best I've felt in ages.'

I was so light headed when I emerged from the treatment room an hour later that I went downstairs, picked up a packet of chocolate chip cookies from the shop and almost walked out without paying for them.

'Sorry,' I said to the assistant as I doubled back from the door and handed her the money. 'I'm not really with it.' She smiled as she gave me my change. I was still in a bit of a daze as I stepped out on the zebra crossing, having to jump back sharply as an ambulance with sirens blaring came screaming past. I felt somehow detached from the world around me, strangely calm and relaxed as I strolled along Market Street, my head still full of the panpipe music from the therapy room and my shirt sticking to the residue of oils on my back. I cut down through Fountain Street and turned right on to the canal towpath, heading for home.

An ambulance was parked as near as it could get to the towpath at Hebble End. I wondered if it was the same one that had gone past me a few minutes earlier. As I walked on I saw a cluster of figures gathered beneath the canal bridge in the distance, two of them wearing uniforms, one with the word paramedic emblazoned across it, another man with a foil blanket round him, all bent over a body on the ground. It was only as I drew nearer that I saw the man with the blanket on was soaking wet, his hair slicked back against his head, water dripping off his clothes. And only when he turned towards me did I realise it was Dan.

My head made the necessary connections in rapid

succession: the anguished expression on Dan's mud-splattered face, the blood on his clothes, the small figure lying motionless on the ground.

'*No!*' The scream ripped through the calmness and hung, reverberating in the sky above me as I started running. Tearing along the towpath, past the bag of duck bread scattered over the cobbles, towards my little boy.

'Are you the mother?' one of the ambulance men said, standing up, holding his arm out to stop me from careering straight into them. I nodded, gasping for breath and unable to speak through the tears, staring down at Alfie who was strapped to some kind of board, a huge collar round his neck, an oxygen mask over his face, his hair matted with blood.

'He's unconscious but his breathing's fine,' said the paramedic. I knelt down to touch him, frowning, searching for words. 'He'd swallowed some water,' he explained. 'But his airways are clear now. It's just the head injuries we're concerned about. We'll get him to hospital as soon as we can.'

I nodded and turned to Dan, my heart pounding, my whole body trembling as I struggled to take it all in.

'What have you done?' I shouted. 'What have you done to my little boy?'

He shook his head and stepped forward to hold me. I pushed him away.

'I'm sorry,' he said, shivering beneath the blanket. His eyes big and scared. 'We were under the bridge. There was a bike coming. We had to jump in. It was the only way. He hit his head on a shopping trolley.' I stared at him blankly. He wasn't making sense. None of it made sense.

I'd only left him for an hour. They were only going to feed the bloody ducks.

'Why didn't you ring me?'

'I did,' he said. 'My phone wouldn't work, the water. The man who rang for the ambulance, I used his phone to ring you. But it was turned off. I tried loads of times. I'm sorry, Jo. I'm so sorry.'

I turned back to Alfie. The ambulance men were lifting the board he was strapped to.

'OK, we're ready now,' the paramedic said. 'Are you both coming with him?'

I looked at Alfie, his tiny body hidden under the blankets, barely any of his face visible beneath the oxygen mask and the dressing taped over his forehead, his eyes closed to the world. I shook my head.

'No, only me,' I said, starting to walk alongside them, searching under the blankets to find Alfie's hand to hold.

'Jo, please,' said Dan, his voice breaking. 'I want to be there, for both of you.'

I carried on walking, quickening my pace to keep up with them. I wasn't listening to him any more. I didn't want to know.

I sat in the back of the ambulance clutching Alfie's hand as we bumped and rattled along the road. Telling him it was OK, Mummy was here, though I had no idea if he could hear me. The paramedic didn't know. He said to keep talking anyway. That it wouldn't do any harm. He did some tests on Alfie. Said it was standard procedure. Alfie pulled his arm back when the man pressed down on his fingernail.

There was a slight moan and his eyelids flickered open for a second before shutting again.

'That's good,' he said. 'He's doing fine.' But he didn't look fine to me. He looked small and fragile and broken. I couldn't believe he was the same boy I had left barely two hours ago. Smiling and laughing and jumping up and down in excitement. I felt bad for leaving him. And awful for switching my phone off. For lying there being pampered while he was lying on the towpath unconscious. I would never forgive myself for that.

The paramedic radioed ahead to the hospital. Told them the boy he was bringing in had a GCS of 9.

'It means his head injuries are classed as moderate,' he told me afterwards.

I nodded, although there seemed nothing moderate about Alfie's condition at all.

'Is it OK to use my mobile?' I asked.

'Sure, go ahead.'

I reached into my bag and pulled out the phone and switched it back on. There were five messages, all from a number I didn't recognise. I listened to the first one which had been sent. Dan's voice urgent and fast.

'Jo, Alfie's had an accident. He's OK but please come straight away. We're on the canal near your place. By the bridge on the bend. The ambulance is on its way. Call me as soon as you can on this number. My phone's not working.' I wiped away the tears as I listened to each message in turn. Dan's voice getting more frantic with each one. 'Jo, it's Dan. Please phone me urgently on this number,' was the last one.

I put the phone down, Dan's voice still ringing in my ears. I tried to drown out the sound. Tell myself he wasn't my problem. He was the one who had got us into this mess. It was Alfie I needed to care for now.

I dialled Richard's mobile. He was his father. Despite everything, he had a right to know. He answered straight away, which threw me. I'd been preparing a message in my head.

'Alfie's had an accident. He's got head injuries and he's unconscious. I'm in the ambulance, we're on our way to the Royal Infirmary in Huddersfield.'

Silence. I wondered for a moment if he was going to tell me he was a bit busy right now. In the middle of a meeting or something and to call back later.

'I'm on my way,' he said, in a voice which I vaguely remembered. A voice which was strong and calm and concerned.

We pulled up sharply outside the hospital. The ambulance driver ran round and opened the doors and together with the paramedic slid Alfie's spinal board on to a big trolley. I clambered out of the ambulance, feeling like an extra in an episode of *Casualty*. Unable to do or say anything useful. My only role to look suitably distraught and anxious. I followed them down the corridor at a half walk, half run, my boots squeaking noisily on the polished floor. We were met by a doctor and a couple of nurses. Everything speeded up a gear. People said things I didn't understand. The doctor shone a torch in Alfie's eyes, asked me what his name was and started calling it. Nothing. I felt my stomach tighten. The nurse fixed him up to some kind of monitor, said it was to check his heart and blood pressure. Alfie grew tinier by the second, dwarfed by all the machines and equipment. Another nurse started cleaning his head wounds; I winced on Alfie's behalf.

'We're going to take him down for some scans as soon as we've got him stitched up,' she said. 'You can't go in there with him but you're welcome to watch through the glass.'

I nodded. Wanting to ask more questions about what they were looking for but afraid of what the answers might be. A few minutes later we set off down a corridor, the coloured lines on the floor blurring into one through my tears.

The porter stopped the trolley outside the scanning unit and looked at me. I realised he was waiting for me to say goodbye.

'You'll be fine, sweetie,' I whispered, kissing Alfie on the one corner of his forehead I could get to, before he was wheeled away and I was ushered into the observation room. I watched through the glass as they lifted Alfie carefully on to a long slab of a table in the centre of the room. He was wearing a hospital gown, child sized but still miles too long for him. A nurse fiddled with various monitors and tubes before retiring from the room, leaving him lying there, tiny and helpless. I put my hand on the glass, reaching out to him in the only way I could. Someone clicked a switch, and the table started sliding slowly towards the tomb-like tunnel at one end. His head disappeared first, then his body slipped away inside. Another switch, a noise this time. Seeming loud even from behind the thick glass. I prayed he wouldn't come to in there, not knowing where he was or what was happening to him. Screaming for me when I couldn't get to him. Alone and afraid.

All I could do then was wait. Scaring myself by thinking of all the things they could find, all the broken bones and internal bleeding, the brain damage, the spinal injuries. I waited for what seemed like an age but was probably about fifteen or twenty minutes. Until the noise stopped and I caught sight of his feet sliding back out to me. I looked down and unclenched my fist, the deep indentation of four fingernails visible in my palm. My hand still shaking. As I looked up again his head came out. His eyes were still shut. A long, deep sigh squeezed out of me.

I sat on a rickety plastic chair next to Alfie's bed in a corner of A&E. Waiting again, this time for the results. Alfie was hooked up to the monitors. The song by Athlete was going round and round in my head. The one about wires going in and out of your skin. I heard footsteps approaching. I looked round expecting to see the doctor. But it wasn't him. It was Dan. He'd got changed into some dry clothes although he still looked somewhat dishevelled and his face was pale and drawn. The part of my body which still hadn't taken on board what had happened felt a surge of love, of relief he was here. My brain had to send it an urgent message; that events had overtaken things and it wasn't to feel like that any more.

'How did you get in?' I asked.

'I told the nurse I was Alfie's dad,' he said, walking up to the bed. 'I'm sorry. I was desperate to see you both.' Alfie's eyelids flickered open for a second before closing again.

Dan looked at me. Perhaps wondering like me if it was his voice Alfie recognised.

'He did that once in the ambulance,' I said with a shrug.

'So what do the doctors say?'

'They don't know yet. I'm waiting for the results of some tests on his head injuries. To see if he's got any permanent damage.'

Dan looked down, his face crushed.

'I'm so sorry, Jo,' he said, his voice breaking.

'I left you with him for one hour,' I said. 'And he ends up like this.' I gestured towards Alfie and shook my head.

'You haven't given me a chance to explain properly,' Dan said.

'I don't care how it happened. The fact is it did. When you were supposed to be looking after him.'

'Jo, please. No one feels worse about this than me.'

'I do,' I said, looking up at him. 'Because I'm his mother.'

Dan went to put his hand on my shoulder. I pushed it away. Not me, Jo. But the angry mother inside, lashing out at anyone who dared to come near her injured offspring.

'I think you should go now,' I said. Before he had a chance to reply the nurse who had taken me down to the scanning room popped her head round the half-drawn curtain. I could hear some kind of commotion further back in the foyer.

'There's a Richard Billington here. Says he's the boy's father.'

I groaned, his timing impeccable as ever.

'If you could ask him to wait a moment,' I said. 'This gentleman's just leaving.'

The nurse looked at me, understandably concerned that I didn't appear to know who the father of my own child was, and shook her head before retreating. Dan stared at me, waiting for me to say something which I wasn't going to say.

'I'll be in the waiting room, then,' said Dan. 'If you need me.' He stepped outside the curtain at the same time as the cause of the commotion arrived.

'What the fuck's he doing here?' said Richard, looking at me.

'I'm sorry,' I said to the out-of-breath nurse who had trailed Richard from the foyer. 'I'll deal with this.'

'As long as you do,' she said. 'Any further disturbance and they'll both be asked to leave.'

I nodded and waited until she was out of earshot.

'Dan's just leaving,' I said.

'I asked what he was doing here in the first place.'

'He was looking after Alfie,' I said, 'when the accident happened.'

Richard looked at Alfie and then back at me.

'I don't believe this,' he said. 'What on earth were you thinking of?'

'Don't have a go at her,' said Dan. 'None of this is Jo's fault.'

'I know exactly whose fucking fault it is,' Richard said, jabbing a finger in the air towards Dan.

'Keep your voice down,' I said to Richard as I stood up. 'Go and sit with Alfie. I need to talk to Dan.' I watched as Richard sat down heavily on the chair, his head in his hands, before I ushered Dan out of the foyer.

'I meant what I said. I want you to go. Before you make things any worse than they already are.'

Dan shook his head, hurt pouring out of his eyes.

'Whatever you may think,' he said, 'I love that little boy a damn sight more than he does.'

'You can't say that. Richard's his father.'

'By name only,' said Dan. 'It doesn't mean a thing. It didn't stop him walking out on you both, did it? If he really loved him, he wouldn't have done that. Couldn't have.'

I shook my head. 'Stop it,' I said. 'I don't want to hear. I want you to go.'

'I'll wait in the café,' Dan said. 'Until he's gone.'

'No, you're not understanding,' I said. 'I want you to leave. And I don't want you to come back.' It scared me as soon as I said it. But I knew it had to be done. I'd let my guard down, dared to trust someone. And Alfie had got hurt again. It didn't matter how I felt about Dan. Alfie had to come first. Dan blew out deeply and shook his head, apparently as stunned by what I'd said as I was.

'I know you're hurting,' he said, 'but please don't do this.'

'I trusted you with my son and he's lying in there unconscious. What am I supposed to do?'

'Let me in to share this with you. Don't push me away like I don't care. I'm hurting too, you know.'

'Not as much as he is,' I said, pointing back towards Alfie's bed. Dan shut his eyes and looked down at the floor.

'So that's it, then. It's over between us. Is that what you're saying?'

I nodded, unable to speak as I blinked back the tears.

'And you think that will help Alfie?'

'Don't make this any harder than it is, Dan.'

'It wasn't my fault. But you don't want to hear that, do you? You want someone to blame, to lash out at.'

'That's not true. I'm his mother. I'm just trying to protect him.'

'What you're doing is punishing yourself because you feel bad for leaving him. You can't protect him twenty-four hours a day for the rest of your life, you know. It's a big, bad world out there. Horrible things happen. And sometimes you can't stop them. However much you love someone.'

'Well, I'm going to try.'

'Even if it means losing everything we have together? You know how much you mean to me.'

'Yeah, and you know how much Alfie means to me.'

'Which was why I tried to stop it. You weren't there, Jo. You don't know. And you obviously don't want to.'

He turned and walked off up the corridor, shaking his head. His footsteps hot and heavy. Like the tears streaming down my face.

Nineteen

I walked back in and sat down on the chair on the opposite side of Alfie's bed to Richard. Knowing that Alfie would hate me for what I had just done. And praying that I'd have the chance, someday, to try to explain. Richard glanced across at me and opened his mouth to say something.

'I've finished with him, OK,' I said, attempting to prevent another onslaught.

'The words "after the horse has bolted" spring to mind,' said Richard.

I shrugged and shook my head. 'It's easy, isn't it?' I said. 'Being wise after the event.'

'I warned you off him before, if you remember.'

'You said you thought he was a paedophile, not that he wasn't capable of keeping Alfie on a canal towpath.'

'Is that what happened? He let Alfie fall in?'

'He said something about a bike coming. That they needed to get out of the way quickly. But why did they have to jump in the water?'

'Fuck knows. Sounds like he's blaming a sodding cyclist for his own incompetence.'

I shrugged again and reached out to hold Alfie's hand.

Battling my instinct to defend Dan. Because he wasn't mine to defend any more.

'But I don't get it,' Richard continued. 'If he only fell in the canal, how did he end up like that?' He nodded down towards Alfie, the bit of him we could see underneath the oxygen mask and tubes. The nurse had cleaned most of the blood off and put a new bandage over his stitches but he still looked a mess.

'He hit his head on a shopping trolley,' I explained. 'Just under the surface, I guess.'

Richard shook his head. We sat in silence for a while. Both staring at Alfie.

'Where were you?' said Richard. 'When it happened, I mean.'

I looked down at my hands, not wanting to tell him but not wanting to lie either. Not where Alfie was concerned.

'I went for a massage,' I said. 'It's the first time I've done it since you left. It was Dan's treat. And before you say anything, I don't envisage ever going for another one and you can't possibly be as angry at me for doing it as I am.' My voice trembled and I started to cry again. Huge silent tears which welled up and slid out of the corner of my eyes, rolling down my cheeks on to my lap. Richard glanced across at me and shifted uncomfortably in his seat. He took after his father as far as public displays of emotions were concerned. Preferred them kept firmly locked inside.

'I'm sorry,' he said eventually. 'I didn't mean to have a go. It all came as a bit of a shock, that's all. One minute I'm going through the running order for tonight's programme, next thing I know I'm on my way to hospital to see my unconscious son.'

'You didn't mind me ringing you, did you?' I said. 'I just thought you should know.'

'Of course not. I'm glad you did. I am still his father, even if I am a particularly crap one.'

I smiled awkwardly, not used to him being so honest and open with me. I wondered if I should say something suitably contradictory but knew it would sound hollow.

'It's OK,' went on Richard. 'Don't be embarrassed on my behalf. I'm well aware of my own failings. Look at him,' he said, gesturing towards Alfie. 'I don't know anything about him. The things he likes doing, what time he goes to bed, what his favourite food is, how to get him to stop crying if he starts.'

'You don't live with him, that's why,' I said, managing to offer something which sounded vaguely supportive.

'Yeah, and when I did live with him I still didn't know, did I? Left it all to you.'

I looked away. There was no point me taking issue with that. Not when I'd been the one who'd complained about it more times than I cared to remember. Although back then he'd always denied it. Claimed he was tired from work rather than uninterested.

'So why admit it now?' I asked.

'Because he's lying there unconscious and I don't know whether I'll ever get the chance to apologise to him when he's older . . .' Richard's voice trailed off. He looked down at his feet.

'He'll be fine,' I said. 'He's a tough cookie. Yorkshire

born and bred, remember. None of this wussy Cheshire nonsense.' The last comment was aimed at lightening the atmosphere. I used to tease him about it. His genteel upbringing in leafy Nantwich. Back in the days when we still did humour.

Richard managed a wry smile. 'You've done a great job with him,' he said.

I was thrown by the compliment. I wasn't used to such things from Richard. We'd been sparring for so long it was difficult to know what to do now that he appeared to have thrown down his sword.

'Thanks,' I said quietly.

'No, I mean it. It can't have been easy on your own.' Part of me wanted to tell him exactly how tough it had been; about trying to change vomit-sodden bedlinen single-handedly while holding a screaming toddler, about never having a minute to yourself, about worrying all the time that he was missing out on having a dad. But I didn't want to succumb to the stereotype and sound like some whingeing single mum. So I decided to ask for an answer instead.

'Why did you leave, Richard?' The question hung in the air. As it had done ever since he'd walked out. Telling me he needed space. Needed some time to himself. I'd been well aware that things between us hadn't been good. But I'd thought it was something all couples with a new baby went through. Not a reason to walk out.

Richard sighed and stared hard at Alfie's heart monitor.

'The truth?' he asked, turning to face me across the bed. I nodded.

'Because I discovered I was a selfish bastard who resented the way Alfie had changed my life and changed you.' I raised my eyebrows. I hadn't expected the truth to be that blunt. 'I know, pathetic, isn't it?' he went on. 'But that's how I felt when I turned on the CD player and Teletubbies came on, when I couldn't walk through the house without falling over some baby clutter, or when I wanted to spend time with you and all I ever got was Alfie's mum.' The last comment was the one which hit me hardest. Everything that had come before was, as Richard acknowledged, pathetic. But the last thing hit a raw nerve. Probably because I knew it was true.

'I didn't have time to be me. I was trying to be the best mum I could possibly be to Alfie.'

'I know. And that's admirable. But I lost you in the process. You were consumed by him. You still are.'

'He's only tiny, Richard. He has to come first.'

'But at what cost? I lost the woman I fell in love with. The fun Jo who made me laugh, the laidback Jo who didn't stress about anything, the sexy Jo who I couldn't get enough of. She disappeared. So I figured I may as well go too.'

I fiddled with my watch strap. Knowing he was right. That somewhere in the mire of new motherhood I'd abandoned myself in the quest to be a better mum to Alfie than my mum had been to me. And by the time I'd realised what I'd done, it was too late. I'd disappeared. And so had Richard.

'What about being a father to Alfie? Didn't that matter to you?'

'Of course it mattered, it still does. But I'm no good at it. I'm too self-centred for children. That's why I never wanted any.'

'So why didn't you tell me to have an abortion? Why did you move in with me, tell me everything was going to be OK?'

'Because I loved you and I thought I should behave decently. And because I desperately wanted it to be OK. Wanted to prove myself wrong. Only it turned out I was right all along.'

'So you don't regret leaving?'

Richard paused for a moment. 'I regret hurting you and Alfie. But I also know I made the right decision. I'm happier now. I've got my life back.' He glanced across at me. Catching the look of indignation on my face. 'See,' he said. 'I told you I was a selfish git.'

The doctor pulled back the curtain.

'Mrs Gilroy?' I didn't bother correcting him about the Mrs. I nodded, desperate to know.

'Well, it appears to be good news,' he said. 'Nothing sinister on the scans. No internal bleeding, no signs of brain damage, no spinal damage. Young Alfie's been very lucky.'

I burst into tears, the dark thoughts which had been cluttering my head oozing out of me with them. I glanced across at Richard. He was looking up at the ceiling, his eyes shut, his cheeks blowing out.

'How long might it be before he comes round?' I asked.

'Hard to tell,' said the doctor. 'Hopefully by the morning but it could be longer. We'll move him to the paediatric ITU as soon as we can. They'll monitor him closely there.'

'He opened his eyes earlier,' I said. 'Only for a second, mind.'

'That's a good sign,' the doctor said. 'It's simply a matter of time now.'

The paediatric ITU was quieter and less frantic than A&E. Too quiet really, for a room full of children. The silence a reminder, as if we needed it, that all was still a long way from being well. A woman sitting at the bed next to Alfie's looked up and gave us a thin, weak, mouth-firmly-shut smile, acknowledging us as fellow members of the parents of desperately sick children club. I glanced around the unit, trying not to compare Alfie's condition with the other children but finding myself counting the number of monitors and wires hooked up to each child all the same.

'When did Alfie open his eyes?' asked Richard as we sat down, again on either side of the bed.

'Just before you arrived.'

'While Dan was here?'

I nodded. Richard rolled his eyes.

'What?' I said.

'Just typical that it would be him.'

'They're very close,' I said.

'Were, you mean,' corrected Richard.

'Yeah. I guess so,' I said. The past tense of our relationship too painful to contemplate at this moment.

'I remember how Alfie was with him,' Richard said. 'When I met him at your place. I was jealous, you know. Another man being more like a father to my son than I am.'

'Yeah, well. You haven't got to worry any more.'

'Is Alfie going to be upset when you tell him?'

'He'll get over it,' I said. 'In time.'

'And what about you?' asked Richard. 'Did you love him?'

I looked away so Richard didn't see me biting my lip, trying to retain some degree of composure.

'Yes,' I said. 'I did.'

A nurse came over to check Alfie. She looked at the monitor, did some of the same tests the paramedic had done earlier.

'How's he doing?' I asked.

'Still no change,' she said, flashing a quick smile before writing something on the board at the end of his bed and moving on to the next patient. I stared out of the window at the far end of the room. It was dark now. It probably had been for ages. I saw Richard glance at his watch and did the same. Six thirty in the evening. Which explained why my stomach was rumbling.

'I need to make a quick phone call,' Richard said, standing up. It was only then I remembered. It was Valentine's night. No doubt he and Tricia had plans.

'Look, if you want to go, that's fine by me.'

Richard shook his head. 'I may be a lousy father,' he said. 'But I'm not that bad.'

He returned fifteen minutes later with a couple of packets of sandwiches and two coffees.

'There wasn't much of a choice, I'm afraid,' he said, holding out a tuna mayonnaise and egg and cress.

'Thanks,' I said, taking the tuna one. Richard passed me the coffee. I opened my bag to get my purse out.

'Don't be daft,' said Richard. 'It's a damn sight cheaper than the meal I was going to pay for tonight.'

I put my purse back in my bag, noticing the packet of chocolate chip cookies as I did so. Bought to share with Dan and Alfie only a few hours ago. I hesitated before offering them to Richard. Neither Dan nor Alfie being in a position to share them now.

'Where had you booked?' I asked.

'A new Italian on Deansgate,' he said, taking two cookies.

'Was Tricia OK about cancelling?'

'Yeah, of course. She was just concerned about Alfie.'

I nodded unconvincingly.

'She's a really nice person, you know. Despite what you might think.'

I shrugged. Not wanting to get drawn into a conversation about Tricia.

'There was nothing going on between us,' said Richard. 'Before I left you, I mean.' His comment surprised me. I had never alleged there was. But obviously he'd realised it would have been a logical conclusion to draw.

'Good. I'll take your word for it.'

'So what's your problem with her?'

'My problem is that a few months after you walked out on me and your son, you and Tricia were canoodling together at work. The phrase "rubbing salt into a wound" springs to mind.'

'I'd hardly call having lunch together canoodling. Anyway, what did you want me to do, take a vow of celibacy?'

'No, but perhaps you could have shown a little more

respect for my feelings instead of immediately taking up with the station's celebrity weather girl.'

He shook his head. 'You make it sound very shallow. She's got a degree in meteorology, you know.'

'Good for her. You'll be telling me it's deep and meaningful next.'

Richard looked down at his feet 'It's pretty serious, actually,' he said. 'We've been talking about moving in together.'

I rolled my eyes. Tricia was supposed to be the early mid-life crisis, on-the-rebound-after-leaving-my-partner-and-son one. Not *the* one.

'So what's stopping you?'

'You, as it happens.'

I frowned at him, not understanding. Richard sighed and lowered his voice even though the woman at the next bed had far more important things on her mind.

'Tricia's a bit insecure. She feels she can't measure up to you.'

I splurted a mouthful of coffee over the floor as I started laughing.

'Are you taking the piss?'

'No, I'm being serious.'

'So you're telling me that the serene, glamorous, blond, size-eight star of *Spotlight North West* feels she doesn't measure up to the scatty, muffin-middled part-timer with split ends and a wardrobe that is two sizes too small for her?'

'It's not about appearances. It's about Alfie.'

I frowned again. Richard sighed and lowered his voice still further.

'Tricia can't have children,' he said.

I shut my eyes and groaned. I felt like such a cow. So embarrassed for still having the voodoo Ken and Barbie dolls in my desk drawer at work. For assuming she wanted for nothing when I had the one thing she wanted but couldn't have.

'I'm really sorry,' I said. 'I had no idea. I take it there's nothing they can do?'

Richard shook his head. 'Some disease of the ovaries that I'd rather not go into. She's pretty cut up about it. Thinks that because she can't give me a child, she can't possibly be what I want.'

'But that's ridiculous. Haven't you told her what you told me earlier? About not being cut out for fatherhood.'

'I have but she thinks I'm just saying it to make her feel better. Insists I'll change my mind when Alfie gets older and I can take him to football matches and stuff.'

'Who said you're taking him anywhere near Old Trafford?'

Richard opened his mouth to say something then realised I was joking. I'd been brought up as a City supporter by my father, although the allegiance was now a weak one.

'Well, whatever,' he said. 'Despite the fact that I walked out on the only child I have, she simply won't accept that I don't want any more children. She loves kids, you see. That's what makes it so hard for her. And she can't get her head around the idea that I don't.'

We were interrupted by Alfie make a moaning sound. The nurse came straight over. His eyelids flickered for a moment, opened then shut again.

'Mummy's here, Alfie,' I said, clutching his hand. 'And Daddy. We're both here with you.'

The eyelids opened again, he appeared to be struggling to focus for a while, then a flicker of recognition on his face.

'Mummy,' he said quietly. His eyes scanned across to the other side of the bed and back again. 'Balloon man Dan gone,' he said.

Dan

Monday, 14 February 1983

'Can you keep a secret?' says Philip. Philip doesn't usually do secrets. We are walking home from school. I am struggling to keep up with him because I have all my books and my PE kit and it weighs a ton.

'Yeah,' I say. 'What is it?'

'I've found Shergar,' says Philip. Shergar is a racehorse who has been kidnapped. Dad says he is the best racehorse in the world and is worth ten million pounds.

'Where?' I say.

Philip leans closer and whispers in my ear. 'In a tin of cat food.' People have been saying Shergar is already dead. And sometimes they put dead horses in cat food.

'How do you know it's him?' I say.

'There was a big bit in it that looked different from all the others. It was hard and smelt a bit different. It was the same colour as Shergar too.'

'So it's just a bit of Shergar. Not all of him.'

'You can't fit all of him in one tin, stupid.' Philip gobs on the pavement. You are not allowed to do it in school or at home so there is a lot of gobbing on the walk between them.

'Is there a reward for finding him?' I ask.

'I should think so. I reckon at least a million.'

It starts raining. Big rain, all of a sudden. I pull the hood of my parka up, feeling the rain lash against the bottom of my legs, sticking my trousers to my skin.

'You'll have to prove it really is Shergar,' I say. 'To get the money.'

'I know. I'm doing some tests on it at the moment, in my bedroom.'

'What kind of tests?'

'Like the ones we do in chemistry. I'm seeing if the Shergar bit goes a different colour from the rest of it.'

'If it does and you get the reward, can I have your bike? You won't need it then. You'll have enough money for a new one.'

'I guess so,' says Philip. 'It is a bit small for me now.' Mum says Philip is having a growth spurt because he's a teenager. It's why he's got greasy hair too, he has to wash it twice a week now. I'm not that bothered about being a teenager if it means washing your hair that much. I think I'll stick at being eleven. We turn the corner into our road.

'When'll you know the results of the tests?' I ask.

'Tomorrow morning,' he says.

'Wait for me before you tell the police, then,' I say.

'OK,' says Philip. 'See ya.' He goes into his house. It is not one of the days I go with him. I asked Mum if we could get a toasted sandwich maker. She said they were too expensive but she makes me cheese on toast now with a sprinkle of Worcestershire sauce. It's OK but not as good as the toasted cheese sandwiches. I don't tell Mum that, though.

I go into the kitchen. Mum is washing the kitchen floor.

'Shoes off, please, love,' she says, squeezing the mop out. She smiles as she says it but only just. There are dark shadows under her eyes which never used to be there. I haven't noticed them before, probably because the bruises are usually in the way. She hasn't got any on her face at the moment. I am glad but I am worried too because usually when that happens it means she is going to get some more soon. I take my shoes off and tiptoe across the floor in giant steps.

'Good day at school?' she says as I go past.

'OK, I guess.' I don't mind school but I wouldn't say it's good.

'I'll do your cheese on toast as soon as the floor dries,' she says with a big sigh, pulling her hair back behind her ears and wiping her forehead with the back of her hand as she stands up straight.

I nod and go upstairs to my bedroom. I know what I can do to cheer her up. I get some paper and my felt-tip pens out and start drawing. It is Valentine's Day today and Mum didn't get a card. Maybe that's why she seems a bit sad. I didn't get one either and it doesn't bother me but I think girls are different. The girls at school all got very excited and went into a little cluster when anyone got given one today. I draw a big red heart on the front. I try drawing a few flowers but I am not very good at flowers so I turn them into little hearts too. I'm not sure how you spell 'Valentine' so I don't write anything on the front. Inside I just put, 'Lots of love from?' That is what you do with Valentine's cards. You don't put your name on them. Mum will know it's from me but it doesn't matter. It's like a little game.

I go back downstairs. Mum is doing some dusting in the living room while she waits for the kitchen floor to dry.

'Shut your eyes,' I say.

'Is this one of your games?'

'Shut your eyes and see.'

She rolls her eyes before shutting them, her long dark lashes flickering slightly.

'Hold your hand out,' I say. I put the card in her hand and run to the other side of the room. 'You can open them now.'

She opens her eyes and sees the card. She looks at me and smiles. The nicest smile she has done for ages.

'I wonder who this can be from?' she says. She opens it and reads the words inside.

'Well, whoever it was,' she says, 'it's made my day and I will treasure it for ever.'

I do a big smile, almost as big as hers. She walks over to stand it up on the mantelpiece. Right in the middle. Like it's really important.

'Is the floor dry yet?' I ask.

'Let's go and have a look,' she says.

It is dry enough. I get the bread out and carry it over to the table. Mum gets the cheese from the fridge. She cuts it very thinly. I would like it chunkier but I don't say anything. I think cheese is expensive.

'Have you got the sauce?' I say. It is always my job to sprinkle the Worcestershire sauce on top. I have to give it a good shake. There is hardly any left and only a tiny bit comes out. It seems to have been like that for ages. We put the bread under the grill and wait until the cheese bubbles.

Mum isn't having any. She says she will have something later when Dad gets home. He is probably at the pub. Usually when he comes home he says he has been working. The secret working that I can't tell anyone about. But he always comes home smelling of beer and cigarette smoke. And Mum says you don't get that from working. Not proper working. Working that brings home the bacon. That is what she calls it.

When it's ready, Mum picks up the cheese on toast with her fingers, drops it quickly on the breadboard and cuts it in half. She passes it to me on a plate and I blow on the cheese to cool it down before taking a bite. Mum sits opposite me. I like this part of the day best, when it is just me and Mum.

I want to tell her about Philip finding Shergar but it is a secret so I can't. Not until he tells the police in the morning.

'Have you ever had a Valentine's card before?' I ask.

Mum smiles. 'I've had a few actually.'

'Who from?'

'Your father, believe it or not. Years ago, before you were born.'

'Have you still got them?' I ask.

'I think so. Put away in a box somewhere.'

'Can you show me?'

'Another time, maybe. When I'm not so busy.'

I think this means she doesn't want me to see them. Mum is always busy. I look down and swing my legs under the table.

'Anyway,' says Mum, 'they weren't anything special. Not like yours.'

I look up at her sharply. Mum claps her hand over her mouth.

'Like the one I got today, I mean,' she says.

I grin at her. I know she knows it is from me but I like playing the pretending game. I suppose I'm a bit old for it now. I wouldn't do it with anyone else, that sort of pretending isn't cool at school. But with Mum it's OK.

The kitchen door flies open. Mum jumps up from her seat as Dad stumbles in. The beer and cigarettes smell comes in with him. I don't think he has done much work today.

'Hello, son,' he says, staggering over and ruffling my hair. I notice the spiky bits on his chin that are not normally there. There are red lines on the whites of his eyes as well, like someone has drawn on them with a felt-tip pen. He goes over to Mum and puts his arm around her shoulder. She does a little smile but it is not a proper one.

'I'm not stopping, Lizzie. Just popped in to borrow a wee something from you to tide me over until pay day.' It is pay day tomorrow. When he gets his dole money. He has to go and sign something to get it and he has to make it last two weeks.

'I'm sorry, Michael. I haven't got anything left,' Mum says. She edges away from him as he leans over her. She is not smiling at all now.

'A tenner will do,' he says.

Mum reaches into her bag and pulls out her purse. She opens it up to show him.

'Look, it's empty. A few coins for my bus fare in the morning. That's all I've got.'

'What've you spent it on?'

Mum laughs, a funny little snort of a laugh. 'Keeping a roof over our heads and food in our bellies.'

Dad pulls away from her. The smile has disappeared from his face. I can see the veins in his neck. His breath smells angry. It all goes quiet. Too quiet. I know what is coming next but the sound of his hand hitting Mum's face still makes me jump.

'Liar,' he says. 'You're a bloody liar. You've got some stashed away somewhere. I know you have. Something for a rainy day.'

Mum's cheek is red. I remember the plimsoll on my bottom. I can almost feel it stinging. I don't understand why she hasn't given him Grandma's teapot. That is where she keeps her rainy day money. She puts something in there every week when Dad's not here.

'Go upstairs, Dan,' says Mum.

I shake my head. I am not going anywhere. Not this time. I am not going to let him hurt her any more.

'Leave her alone,' I say.

Dad looks across at me. 'Only if you tell me where the money is. I bet you bloody know. It's only me she hides it from.' Dad starts opening the cupboards in the kitchen, emptying everything out on to the table. Throwing boxes and packets everywhere.

'Where is it?' says Dad. 'Where's your little emergency pot? The money you save to pay the bills?'

'I told you, Michael. I haven't got one.'

He hits Mum again. With his fist this time. Her head rocks back and her hands go up to her face as she screams. I scream too. When she takes her hands away there is blood on them. Her nose is bleeding. I start crying and run over to her.

'Shut up snivelling and clean your mother's face up before she makes a mess on the floor.'

I look up at him, expecting him to laugh but he doesn't, he means it. I pull some kitchen roll off the holder, give a couple of pieces to Mum and help her hold it over her nose. The blood on it is bright red. I feel a bit sick. I bury my head in Mum's jumper and put my arms round her. I am not sure whether it is my arm or her body which is shaking. Maybe it is both. Dad goes back to emptying the cupboards, kicking or punching the doors when he doesn't find what he is looking for. All around us on the floor are things he has thrown out. Packets of rice, tea bags, paper cake cases and a roll of silver foil. It will take us ages to clear up after this.

Mum lowers her head and whispers to me. 'Run,' she says. 'Go and get help. Now.' It takes me a second to realise what she is asking. I look up at her. She nods as a pile of tins come clattering down from the cupboard. I let go of her and run towards the kitchen door but I slip on a tin and fall to the floor. Before I can get back up again Dad goes to the door, locks it and puts the key in his trouser pocket.

'Going somewhere, were we?' he says. I shake my head. 'Your mother put you up to that, did she?' I shake it again. He turns to Mum and grabs hold of her hair, yanking her head up with it, pulling it so tight I think the skin on her face is about to snap. He drags her over to the kitchen door and smashes her head against it, so hard the door shakes. Mum is screaming, she has her eyes tightly shut.

'The door's locked, see,' he says. 'You're not going anywhere. Neither of you are stepping foot outside this house until you tell me where the money is.' He lets go of Mum's hair and throws her on to the floor. Some blood splatters from her nose on to the lino. The nice clean lino she has only just mopped. I look at Dad. There are still a few strands of Mum's hair in his hand. I hate him right now. Hate him more than I have ever hated him before. I run across to the pots and pans cupboard where Mum keeps the teapot.

'No, Dan,' she says from the floor. I am going to do it, though. It is the only way I can stop him hurting her. I reach behind the pans and slide out the teapot. It is red with little white teacups on. It used to belong to my great-grandma who I never met. She gave it to Grandma who gave it to Mum on her wedding day. Mum never uses it. She says it is special and she would be too upset if it got broken.

'It's in there,' I say, holding it out to Dad. I hear Mum groaning from the floor. She should be happy because I have stopped him hitting her. Maybe she is just groaning because her head hurts. Dad grabs the teapot from me, pulls the lid off and looks inside. I stand there waiting to see the smile come back on his face. To take the money and go back to the pub. He doesn't go anywhere, though. And if anything he looks madder than he was before.

'It's for the gas bill.' Mum's voice is shaky. 'I save it from my wages. I have to hide it otherwise we'd end up being cut off.' Dad's eyes are bulging, his face has gone a strange purple colour. He is boiling over. Any second now he is going to explode. It is like waiting for the plimsoll. Feeling sick in your stomach because you know something horrible is about to happen, knowing it was all my fault. I shut my eyes tight.

'You lying fucking cow,' he shouts at Mum. I open my eyes in time to see him hurl the teapot across the room. It smashes against the wall behind her and a handful of five-pound notes flutter to the floor. There must be fifteen or twenty of them, maybe more. I have never seen so much money before.

Dad lunges forward and grabs Mum, hauling her up off the floor by her hair. He starts smashing her head against the kitchen counter. Over and over again, each time harder than the one before.

I want to help her but I don't know what to do. I know you should dial 999 in an emergency but we haven't got a phone. And now Dad's locked the kitchen door we are trapped. We never use the front door. Mum told me once she wasn't even sure they still had the key.

There is blood on her head now. Bright red blood seeping through her long dark hair. I am screaming at him to stop but he doesn't take any notice. He is going to kill her. I have to stop him. I look around the mess on the floor for something to use. I pick up the rolling pin, for some reason it seems the obvious thing. I walk closer to him. Every time he lifts Mum's head up I see her eyes dull and lifeless, before he smashes her head back down and I hear her

moan, it is more of a moan than a scream. She is not struggling or anything. I don't think she has got the strength
left. I know I need to do it quickly. Because the next time
he smashes her head could be the one that does it. I raise
the rolling pin above my head. I don't have to worry about
Dad seeing. He is too busy trying to kill Mum to notice
me. I need to do it hard, really hard, I know that. Harder
than I have ever hit anything before in my life. I think of
that thing they have at the fairground. Where you whack
the peg with the hammer to try to make the button go up
and ring the bell. I smash the rolling pin against the back
of Dad's head. The cracking noise it makes surprises me.
Dad wobbles for a second before falling to the ground, like
in one of those slow motion action replays on TV. I stand
there unable to believe what I have done. I turn to look at
Mum, hoping she will be pleased but she is not looking.
She is still lying slumped over the kitchen counter, as if she
is waiting for him to start on her again. I run over and try
to lift her up, she is heavy and floppy in my arms. For a
second I think she is dead, that I didn't do it in time. Then
she squeezes my hand. I drag her down on to the floor and
prop her up against the wall. The blood is running down
her neck, soaking her jumper. I grab a tea towel and hold
it tight against her head, trying to stop the blood from
going into her eyes. Dad is still lying on his side on the
floor. He hasn't made a sound. For the first time it crosses
my mind that he could be dead. That I could have killed
him. I look at Mum, she shakes her head.

'Get out of the house, Dan. Quickly, before he comes
round.' She doesn't say what he will do when he comes

round. She doesn't have to. I look up at the kitchen window, I think I could climb out but I couldn't get Mum out, not on my own, and I am not leaving her here with him. Not even for the few seconds it would take to run to Philip's house.

'I'll get the key from his trousers,' I say. I hurry over to where he is lying and edge my hand towards his pocket. It is like playing the Operation game again. Only in this version I must pick up the key without touching the sides. Otherwise the buzzer will go off. And me and Mum will be dead. My fingers are inside his pocket, creeping down his leg. He is facing away from me so I cannot see if his eyelids are flickering, if he might be coming round. I think I hear a noise, feel him move a little. My mouth is dry, my heart racing. My fingers stretch right down inside the bottom of his pocket. The key is not there. It must be in his other pocket, the one under him. There is no way I can get to it.

'Dan. Go. Now.' I hear Mum's urgent hiss before I realise Dad is moving. Trying to haul himself up off the floor.

'Fucking little runt,' he says, turning to face me. His eyes are all over the place. He picks up a kitchen knife from the floor. 'I'm going to kill you,' he says, lunging towards me. I hear Mum scream and I jump to the side just in time, sending him crashing back to the floor with a thud. The knife slips out of his hand and lands at my feet.

'Pick it up,' screams Mum. I stare at it, unable to move. 'Give it to me, Dan. Quickly.' Mum is struggling to claw her way up the chairs and table to a standing position. Dad is hauling himself back to his feet. I don't know what Mum is going to do with the knife. But I know for certain what Dad is going to do with it. I bend down, pick up the knife and pass it to Mum. She stands up and launches herself at Dad as he staggers forward towards me. For a second it looks as if they are dancing, both hanging on to each other to keep themselves from falling over. And then Dad topples backwards and I see the knife in his chest. See that it has gone through his sweatshirt. See the blood seeping slowly out. See his wide eyes bulging before the life drains from his face and he slumps motionless on to the floor. Dead. Dad is dead.

For a second I am relieved. I almost feel like cheering. Then I realise what we have done. I turn to Mum, my bottom lip trembling as I make a whimpering sound. She is hanging on to the table with one hand, the other hand still curled as if she is clutching the knife. The blood is oozing from her head down on to her jumper. She is staring blankly at Dad's body. As if, like me, she can't quite believe what happened. She slides back down to the floor and starts to sob. Screwing her eyes up and shaking her head. I go over to her. She grabs my hand and pulls me down to her, squeezing me tightly. So tightly that I worry I might stop breathing. She starts rocking slowly back and forth. We sit there together like that for ages. Rocking the tears away as the darkness builds around us. The three of us together in the kitchen. Strangely quiet and peaceful.

I hear the police sirens outside. I don't know who called them. Maybe the lady next door. She must have heard all the banging and screaming. I hear footsteps running down the alleyway and someone knocking loudly on the kitchen door. Shouting, asking if we are OK. I half expect Dad to get up. To shout at them. Tell the pigs to fuck off. He doesn't, of course. He carries on being dead. And Mum isn't moving. It's as if she's in some kind of trance. I realise I have got to do it myself. I stand up and walk across to where Dad is lying on the floor. He fell on his back. I can get to the other pocket easily this time. I shut my eyes so I don't have to see him and slip my hand inside. I find the key straight away, take it out, walk over to the kitchen door and unlock it. It is easy now. If only it had been that easy earlier on. When it mattered. When it could have stopped all of this happening.

I open the door. There are two policemen outside, one fat one and one thin one with a moustache. I stand back and they come straight past me into the kitchen, their boots crunching on the broken pieces of Grandma's teapot. The fat one bends straight down and feels Dad's wrist. He shakes his head to the other one and speaks quickly and quietly into his walkie-talkie. I make out the words 'forensics', 'ambulance' and 'coroner'. I do not know what the last one is. The thin policeman goes over to Mum. Her hair is matted with blood. Her eyes are all starey and wide. She looks up at him and nods.

'It was me,' she says. 'I did it.'

I run over to Mum and start crying, proper crying this time. I wish I could go and hide in the wardrobe. I wish I could make it all go away. But I can't. Not this time. Dad is dead. And as much as I hate him and as much as I am glad it is not Mum who is dead, I do not want him to be dead either. The thin policeman gets out some handcuffs and puts them on Mum. He says something about arresting her. On suspicion of murder.

'No,' I scream, holding on to her other hand and pulling.

'Is there someone who can have the boy?' says the thin policeman. 'Someone we can leave him with?'

Mum nods and tells him Grandma's address and phone number. He speaks into his walkie-talkie again. I hear more sirens outside and footsteps down the alley. Some more men come in, they are not wearing uniforms but they do have gloves on. Two ambulance men come in as well. One of them goes over to where Dad's body is and feels his wrist like the policeman did. The other one comes over to Mum.

'Let's have a quick look,' he says. He bends down and examines Mum's head, she winces as he touches it. He turns to the thin policeman.

'We need to get her to casualty. I'll clean her up on the way.'

The thin policeman nods and the ambulance man helps her to her feet. I realise she is going now. They are going to take her away.

'I want to come with you,' I say.

Mum closes her eyes. The thin policeman shakes his head.

'I'm afraid that won't be possible, son,' he says. 'Someone will be here to look after you in a minute.' They start to shuffle towards the door.

'Wait,' I shout. I run into the living room, grab my Valentine's card from the mantelpiece, run back and thrust it into Mum's hand. The one without the handcuffs on. Mum starts to cry. The thin policeman looks down at his feet.

'Grandma will look after you,' she says. 'I'm so sorry, sweetheart.'

Before they get to the door a police lady in uniform arrives. She tells me her name is Maureen. Says she is going to take me to Grandma's, asks if there is anything I need to take with me.

'Pyjamas, toothbrush and a change of clothes,' says Mum quietly. I look down, there is blood all over my jumper and trousers. I hadn't realised before. I go upstairs and get them. The policewoman helps me get changed and puts the other things in a carrier bag for me while Mum watches. 'And you'll need your parka on,' Mum says. 'It'll be cold outside.'

I do as I am told and follow Mum and the thin policeman and the ambulance men out of the kitchen door, round the back and down the alley. The fat policeman and Maureen walk behind us. I can hear lots of voices on his walkie-talkie. All of them talking very fast. When we come out into the street, I see the police cars and the ambulance, their lights still flashing. It is like something from *The Sweeney*. Dad used to like *The Sweeney*. Mum didn't like me watching it. Said it was too violent.

Some of our neighbours are outside too, staring at me and Mum. I hear someone say, 'Poor thing.' I do not know if they are talking about me or Mum. I blink hard, trying to stop the tears from falling. Another policeman is putting orange tape round the front of our house and across the alleyway, telling everyone to stand back. I can see

Philip looking out of his front-room window. He looks upset. I wonder if he thinks I have told them about him finding Shergar. I shake my head. I would never do that. Never tell a secret. The policewoman is holding open the door of a police car. I watch as Mum is helped into the back of an ambulance, the thin policeman still handcuffed to her. She waves to me, still clutching my Valentine's card in her hand. The heart is the same colour as the blood running down her face. I wave back. And watch as they shut the doors and drive her away.

Twenty

'Here we are, Alfie, home at last,' said Rachel as she pulled up outside our house. Alfie clutched my hand tightly in the back of the car, as if sensing the enormity of the occasion. I wondered if he remembered the last time he'd been here. The excitement of going to feed the ducks with Dan. Or whether the accident had wiped it from his memory. In a way, I hoped it had. It would make it easier for him. I wished I could wipe the memories away cleanly and quickly – as if they were etched on one of those children's magic doodle boards, rather than in my head, where they stubbornly refused to shift.

Three days ago I'd walked out of this house for a massage. A warm glow inside me in place of the familiar bitterness and heartache. A growing belief that I'd finally found in Dan a man I could trust. A man I could depend upon. And having no idea that by the time I returned, the warmth, the belief and the man would have gone.

My sigh was overtaken by a yawn. One night without sleep and two nights snoozing fitfully in an armchair in the parents' rest room on the children's ward had left me running on empty. Richard had gone back to work the morning after the accident, although he had at least texted for regular updates on Alfie's progress. As had Laura and Moira, who were no doubt behind the 'Get Well Soon' balloon and card which had been sent for Alfie from work. Mum had visited, of course. Although only to fuss over whether Alfie was eating enough and have a go at me for leaving him with 'some itinerant boat man' in the first place. But fortunately I'd had Rachel who, as I'd always suspected, had been a complete star in a crisis; fetching overnight bags, toys and magazines from home for Alfie and me, lending a sympathetic ear and insisting on bringing us home from hospital.

'You take him in and get him settled,' said Rachel. 'I'll give you a couple of minutes and bring the bags in.'

I nodded and smiled. Amongst all the conflicting emotions, the strongest was relief; I was bringing Alfie home and he was going to be fine. Thinking back to the moment when I'd first seen him lying on the canal towpath, I hadn't thought that would be possible.

I lifted Alfie, who was still clutching his get-well-soon balloon, out of his car seat, carried him round to the kitchen door and wiggled the key in the lock. As I pushed the door open, there was a scraping noise of metal on quarry tiles. I stepped inside and looked behind the door. The spare key lay on the floor along with a couple of get well cards. Dan must have put it through. Some time after the accident. After I had told him it was over. I put Alfie down on the floor and picked the cards and key up. He immediately let go of the balloon and ran to the kitchen table.

'Card for Mummy,' he said, beaming proudly. I followed the direction his finger was pointing. It was standing up on the table. A stiff piece of white card with a big heart coloured in thick red crayon and 'Happy Valentine's Day' written across the top. I walked over and picked it up. 'To the best Mummy in the world, lots of love from?' it read inside. Dan must have made it with him, before they went to feed the ducks. I bent down and folded Alfie into my arms, my eyes screwed up tight, trying to hold myself together.

'Thank you, sweetheart,' I said. 'It's lovely. The best card I've ever had.'

'See balloon man Dan,' Alfie said.

'Not now, love. Why don't you go and play with your hoover? You haven't seen it for a few days.'

Alfie pulled free from me and ran into the lounge to reacquaint himself with his vacuum cleaner. I stood in the kitchen, trying to be grateful for the fact that clearly there was nothing wrong with Alfie's memory. But knowing that meant I was going to have to find some way of telling him that yet another man had disappeared while he was sleeping and wouldn't be coming back. Although this time I'd been the one who had sent him away.

Dan wouldn't be far away though and in some ways that made it worse. Knowing that we'd probably bump into him at some point. Hebden Bridge was a small place, not somewhere you could hide from someone.

'Are you OK?' said Rachel, stepping into the kitchen and immediately putting the bags down on the floor to come over and give me a hug.

'I was,' I said. 'Until I saw the card.'

'That's why I let you come in first,' she said. 'I saw it

when I came to pick up your things. I guessed who he made it with.'

'It's so hard,' I said, wiping the tears away with my fingers. 'Dan did so many lovely things for us. I really thought he was the one.'

'Maybe he was,' said Rachel, handing me a tissue. 'Maybe it was an unavoidable accident that could have happened to me or you or anyone looking after Alfie.'

'You think I was too harsh on him, don't you?'

'I think you were understandably distraught and he was the obvious person to blame.'

'But what if it had been Poppy? Could you forgive someone who let that happen to her?'

Rachel shrugged. 'I don't know. I guess it would depend on how much I trusted them. And whether I thought they could have done anything more to prevent it.'

I sighed as I stared out of the window to the canal beyond. I'd been through it all so many times in my head. Wondering if I'd been right to end it. If I should have given Dan another chance. But always I'd come to the same conclusion. That he'd let me and Alfie down. And I couldn't afford to risk that happening again. Because next time Alfie might not be so lucky.

'Maybe it was because he doesn't have children of his own,' Rachel continued. 'Maybe he simply didn't realise how careful you have to be near water.' She was doing her usual trick of thinking the best of everyone. Giving them the benefit of the doubt. Unfortunately I was a sceptic by trade. Trained to suspect the worst, to go looking for it if necessary.

I shook my head. 'I wish it wasn't his fault,' I said. 'But I'm afraid I can't see how it can be anything but.'

Rachel nodded, although it was her 'I'll support you because you're my friend' nod, rather than her 'I'm in complete agreement with you' one. She took the kettle over to the sink and began to fill it. 'Have you phoned him?' she said. 'Given him a chance to explain properly? Since the day it happened, I mean.'

'I texted him after Alfie came round, just to let him know he was OK. But I didn't hear anything back. So I guess that's it. End of story. Minus the happy ever after bit, of course.'

Rachel walked back over to me and gave me another hug. 'You go and play with Alfie,' she said. 'I'll make the tea.'

I took the Valentine's card from the kitchen table and stood it on the centre of the mantelpiece in the lounge. Alfie grinned up at me. I decided to let him remain in blissful ignorance for a little while longer.

I left it until late Saturday afternoon before venturing out of the house with Alfie. I'd wanted to spend as much quiet time at home with him as possible to allow him to recover from his ordeal. I wondered about walking into town along the canal towpath, past the scene of the accident. It couldn't be avoided for ever and part of me knew it was probably best done as soon as possible, like they recommend getting back behind the wheel immediately after a car crash. But I decided I didn't feel up to it yet and therefore couldn't possibly expect Alfie to be. A trip out was a big enough step for now. Just to the Co-op and back.

I put Alfie in the buggy along with his tooting Thomas the Tank Engine toy and wrapped him up warmly, too warmly really because it was mild for February, but I wasn't taking any chances. Not any more. We turned right out of the house and headed along the pavement and into town along the main road. I chatted to Alfie along the way, pointing out familiar places and objects, trying to give him back some sense of normality. I pulled his hat right down over his dressing and the part of his head which had been shaved for the stitches, so any passers-by wouldn't notice. The last thing I needed was people staring at him, asking me how it had happened. Alfie seemed OK; a bit quiet, fewer toots on Thomas than usual, but that was only to be expected. He perked up a bit when we got to the Co-op, especially when he discovered that the tractor ride was working and I was actually prepared to put money in it, not just let him sit in it and rock backwards and for-wards, simulating movement, like I usually did. I got the few bits of food we needed – which wasn't much as Rachel had already done a big shop for me the previous day – and headed for the checkout.

'Bob,' said Alfie, pointing excitedly at a *Bob the Builder* magazine he'd spotted on the stand opposite.

'You can have a Bob,' I smiled.

Alfie looked up at me with a bemused expression on his face, no doubt wondering why he was being allowed to have all the things I normally said we didn't have enough pennies for or time to do. A grow-your-own-sunflower kit including seeds and measuring chart was taped to the front of the magazine. I decided we'd buy some big plant pots later in the week so Alfie could sow them himself. I needed something bright to focus on for the future. Rather than dwelling on the past.

We set off back along the main road, Alfie gripping the *Bob* magazine tightly and having to be reminded on several occasions that these sunflower seeds weren't for eating. We were five minutes from home when a motorbike roared past us, a small one, not much more than a scooter, the engine revving and exhaust popping as it came by. Alfie screamed. An ear-piercing scream that seemed far louder to me than the motorbike had been. I ran round to the front of the buggy to hold him. He was screaming and crying hysterically, his little heart beating fast against me, his whole body shaking. I had no idea what the matter was, he must have heard motorbikes hundreds of times and they'd never bothered him before.

'It's OK, sweetheart, Mummy's here,' I said, over and over again. Still he went on crying and screaming; people walked past, frowning at him, thinking he was having some kind of tantrum. Eventually the screams turned to sobs and the sobs abated enough for him to finally be able to answer my pleas to tell me what the matter was.

'Noisy bike,' he said.

'It was a bit noisy, sweetheart, but it's OK, it can't hurt you.'

Alfie shook his head, clearly I was not understanding.

'Noisy bike come. Jump in water.'

I stared at him for a second, trying to take in what I'd heard.

'On the canal?'

Alfie nodded, sniffing loudly. 'With balloon man Dan.'

'It was a motorbike on the canal?' Alfie nodded again. 'Not a pedal bike like Rachel rides sometimes?' He shook his head firmly. I had no reason to doubt him. He hadn't learnt to lie yet. And his reaction to the motorbike was too extreme to ignore. The video clip inside my head of what had happened under the bridge rewound rapidly, mangling in the process. New images appeared instead of something entirely different. I'd got it horribly wrong.

I hurried back home in the gathering gloom, reassuring a still shaken Alfie, while berating myself for being such a fool. I'd assumed Dan had had a choice about jumping into the water. Now I could imagine what might have happened if he hadn't.

We arrived back just as Nina returned from her walk with Dougal, her boots splattered with mud, her purple coat undone for the first time this winter. She looked at the unusually silent Alfie, his eyes red and puffy, and bent down to his level.

'Alfie, love. What happened to that lovely smiley face you had for me yesterday?' She'd brought round a little coming home present for him. Which was very sweet considering she'd already given him a get well present in hospital.

'Noisy bike,' said Alfie, frowning as he gripped his *Bob* magazine tightly.

Nina looked up at me. I put the brake on the buggy and opened the magazine up for Alfie to look at before gesturing Nina a few steps away.

'A motorbike went past on the road,' I explained in a

hushed voice. 'He got very upset. Started talking about a noisy bike on the towpath, when he had his accident,' I mouthed the last word, not wanting to upset Alfie any further.

'But I thought you said it was a mountain bike?' said Nina.

'I only remember Dan talking about a bike. I just presumed . . .' My voice trailed off. I'd forgotten the golden rules of journalism. Never assume anything. Always check your facts and get them confirmed from a different source. I looked at Nina for a response but she was staring out towards the canal, her brow furrowed.

'There was a motorbike,' she said at last, turning to me. 'Only a small one, more of a scooter really. Some young lad riding it along the towpath. I remember Dougal barking at it as it came by. Going at quite a speed he was. I would have reported him but he didn't have a number plate, little blighter.'

'On the day of his accident? Are you sure?'

Nina nodded vigorously. 'Yes, I'm certain of it. It was the only day it didn't rain on us last week. I don't know why I didn't think to mention it before. I suppose because you said there'd been a cyclist.'

I groaned and looked up at the sky. Dan's crushed face appearing in front of me.

'Oh, Nina,' I said, the tears pricking again. 'Whatever have I done?'

Twenty-one

'So what's the big emergency?' asked Mum as she breezed into the kitchen the next morning with Derek in tow. I hadn't told her on the phone, mainly because I hadn't wanted another ear-bashing like the one I'd received at the hospital. I'd decided to wait until she got here. So I could explain properly and it would be too late for her to refuse to look after Alfie. I couldn't take him with me. I needed to speak to Dan alone, so we could both say whatever needed to be said.

'Derek, could you go and give Alfie a hand with his new Lego set, please?' I asked.

Derek looked at me blankly for a second. He hadn't come with Mum to visit Alfie in hospital. Derek didn't do hospitals. They reminded him too much of Sylvia. Of watching loved ones slipping away. Although he never said as much, of course.

'Yes. Yes, of course,' he said, the penny finally dropping. 'I used to be a dab hand at Lego with my two.' He disappeared into the lounge. I waited until the door was closed and turned back to Mum.

'I need to go and see Dan,' I said.

Mum rolled her eyes at me and tutted, making me feel about thirteen again.

'I don't believe I'm hearing this. That man almost killed your son. You said you'd finished with him. Don't tell me you've changed your mind.'

'I got it all wrong,' I said. 'It wasn't Dan's fault.'

'And how did you work that one out?'

'Alfie told me.' Mum looked at me as if I'd finally lost it. 'He freaked out in town yesterday when a motorbike came past. Said it was a motorbike on the towpath. One of those scooter-type things teenagers ride. Nina saw it on the day of the accident.'

Mum looked at me warily as she weighed up the fresh information I'd provided.

'He might still have been to blame. You weren't there, you don't know exactly what happened.'

'I know. That's why I want to go and see him. Give him the chance to explain. To fill in the gaps.'

'But he's only going to say what suits him, isn't he? He's not going to admit it was his fault, even if it was.'

'I think he would, actually. That's the kind of man he is.'

Mum rolled her eyes again. 'You've no idea what kind of man he is. You've only known him five minutes. And now you want to go grovelling back to him on your hands and knees, begging him to take you back. Honestly, Jo. Have you no shame?'

I shook my head. I should have known better than to expect her to be able to listen to reasoned argument. Once she formed a view of someone, it was very hard to get her to shift it.

'All I want to do is find out exactly what happened to Alfie. And to apologise to Dan for not giving him the chance to explain before. I think I may owe him a huge debt of thanks.'

Mum snorted a disparaging laugh as she adjusted the silk scarf around her neck.

'I doubt that very much indeed. But I suppose if you think it will help get it all out of your system . . .'

'Thank you,' I said with a sigh. 'I'll be back within a couple of hours, and please, not a word to Alfie about where I've gone. I don't want him upset unnecessarily.'

Mum shrugged and followed me into the living room where Derek had managed to build something which resembled a nuclear power station out of Lego.

'OK, sweetheart,' I said. 'Mummy's just popping out to see a lady from work.'

Alfie looked up from his Lego with what seemed unnervingly like a suspicious expression on his face. He couldn't know, of course. Unless, on some level, he equated me bothering to put make-up on with seeing Dan.

'I want Mummy,' he said, clinging on to my legs. I bent down and kissed him on the good side of his head before unclasping his fingers. Finding it as difficult as he was to part for the first time since the accident.

'Nanna and Derek will look after you. Mummy be back soon.' I stood up and turned to Mum. 'Just stay in the house,' I said. 'And any problems, please phone me.'

'He'll be fine,' said Derek. 'He's just getting into the Lego. You go on.'

I pulled the kitchen door to behind me and checked my mobile was switched on. Trying not to think about the last time I'd left Alfie at home with someone else, but finding it impossible. Because it was still so raw. And I was going to see the someone else in question. I hadn't phoned or texted. I didn't want to give Dan the chance of refusing to see me.

There was the usual Sunday morning traffic along the towpath. Dog-walkers, joggers, the odd cyclist. I wondered if any of them had seen the motorbike on the day in question. Had maybe even witnessed the accident. I resisted the temptation to stop and interrogate them about anything they may have seen or heard. They probably knew no more than anyone else; the brief details contained in the story in the *Hebden Bridge Times* headlined 'Toddler injured in canal fall'. They hadn't named him, of course. And Dan was described simply as a family friend, which is what I guessed he'd told the ambulance men. The mother wasn't mentioned. I wondered if some people had noticed that and tutted before turning the page.

My body tensed as I neared the spot where the accident had happened. The narrow road bridge over the canal loomed in front of me. I found my footsteps quickening. I needed to see it for myself. I walked into the gloom under the bridge and stood there. Looking. Listening. Thinking it through. Nina was right. The towpath was extremely narrow, hardly wide enough for two people to pass, let alone a motorbike. I walked further into the bend under the bridge, turned and looked back the way I had come. I could barely see a few yards down the towpath. The motorbike would have been on top of them by the time

Dan saw it. He would probably have heard it before he'd seen it, although he could easily have thought it was passing above him over the road bridge. And at whatever point he had realised it was heading straight for them, there was clearly only one place they could go. I stared down into the murky depths of the canal. As I did so it occurred to me that the shopping trolley could still be there, lurking unseen beneath the surface. I looked around me, there was no one about. I knelt down, pushed my jacket and jumper sleeves up and dipped my hand into the ice-cold water, reaching down until I was almost up to my elbow. Nothing. It was probably further out – if it was still there, that was. I wondered if there was a special telephone number to report shopping trolleys in canals, the British Waterways equivalent of the traffic cone hotline. And then I realised my fingers were starting to go numb and pulled my arm out, shaking it a couple of times before wiping it dry on my jeans. I knelt there for a moment, my eyes shut, imagining Alfie's face beneath the water, hearing his anguished scream echoing around under the bridge.

'Er, are you OK?'

I opened my eyes to find a middle-aged man staring down at me, his dog's tail wagging against my boot. I hadn't heard him approach, hadn't realised anyone could see me.

'Yes, yes, I'm fine. Really,' I said, knowing I didn't look at all fine.

He nodded and carried on walking, glancing back over his shoulder once or twice. I stood up, attempted to brush the mud off my jeans and walked on up the towpath, knowing for certain I'd made a terrible mistake. And more desperate than ever to try to make up for it.

By the time I got to the green gate, I'd got it all worked out in my head. How I'd tell Dan Alfie was home from hospital first. And then, having delivered the good news, apologise. A great big fat apology, topped with all the reasons why I'd reacted in the way I had and served on a bed of humble contrition. Whether he accepted it was another matter. I realised my begging for forgiveness would sound a bit rich considering I'd told him I could never forgive him. I was well aware there might be no way back from here. That our relationship may well be beyond salvaging. But I had to try.

I made my way down the path towards Dan's boat. The track by now familiar enough for me to be able to navigate it faster than I had before – particularly as I didn't have a two year old in tow. As I neared the canal I craned my neck, hoping to glimpse the *Elizabeth* through the trees. But there were no colours. Only still, grey water. And a gap where the boat was usually tied.

Shit. It hadn't even occurred to me that he might not be here. I kept forgetting that his home was a mobile one. Although as far as I knew the only journeys he usually made were up to the pumping station and back. And I would have seen him if he had been there or on his way. A sense of unease descended upon me. I passed Dan's shed, the rusty padlock rattling against the door in the breeze. I stupidly looked to see if he'd left a note, something along the lines of, 'Jo, just in case you've realised your mistake and popped down to apologise, I've gone to the boat yard, back in twenty minutes.' But there was nothing there, of course. Because as far as Dan was concerned, I was history. Someone from his past who'd made it perfectly clear she wanted nothing more to do with him.

I got out my mobile and rang Dan's number. It went straight to the answering service. I left a garbled message telling him where I was and asking him to call me, before sitting down heavily on the decking, staring out across the water. Wondering if my message would backfire and actually stop him returning home. He could be working, of course. But I knew he rarely went on jobs in the boat. It took too long to get anywhere. I looked up as a woman with a long grey ponytail came out of the next boat along and began busying herself washing down the paintwork. The journalist in me was obviously still half asleep, not to have thought of asking the neighbours.

'Excuse me,' I said, scrambling to my feet and hurrying over to her. The woman put her cloth down. 'I'm looking for Dan. I'm a friend, I've just popped round to see him.'

The smile faded from her face. 'I'm sorry, love. He's gone.'

'What do you mean, gone?'

'He left last week. Wednesday, I think it was.'

My stomach tightened. The day after the accident. The same day he'd probably put the spare key through my letterbox.

'Left for where?'

'I don't know, he didn't say. Just told me he was going away. Asked me to keep an eye on his shed and water his plants for him.'

'Did he say when he was coming back?'

She shook her head. 'I kind of got the feeling he didn't know. That it might be some time.'

Of course she was right. I wasn't thinking. He'd asked her to water his plants.

'Right, thanks,' I said.

'You're the lady with the little boy, aren't you?' she said, looking at me more closely. 'I remember seeing you both here, with Dan. You always seemed to be having such fun.'

'Yes. We did,' I said, managing a weak smile.

'Sorry I couldn't be more helpful,' she said with a shrug.

'How did he seem?' I asked. 'When he told you he was going.'

She paused for a moment.

'Troubled,' she said. 'I'd say he seemed troubled.'

I nodded and went to walk away before turning back.

'Which direction did he go in?' I asked.

She hesitated. I had the feeling she was wondering whether to tell me or not, rather than trying to remember.

'That way,' she said, pointing towards town.

I walked back slowly along the towpath. Keeping an eye out just in case. Although I knew the chances of spotting the *Elizabeth* were remote. When people left suddenly, they usually went far enough not to be found.

By the time I got back to the bridge I'd convinced myself he'd gone for good. Leaving only the memory of him standing there, water dripping from his clothes, hurt pouring from his eyes.

Alfie came running out to greet me as soon as I got home. I scooped him up in my arms and gave him a huge hug, knowing how badly I'd let him down. By driving away the man he adored. The man who had probably saved his life.

Mum looked at me, her eyebrows raised, waiting for an answer. I shook my head and mouthed, 'He's gone.' She nodded.

'Doesn't surprise me,' she said. 'I didn't think he was the type to stick around. Still, it's probably for the best. You're better off without that sort.' She'd said something not dissimilar when Richard had left. Only on that occasion she'd been right.

It was while I was getting Alfie ready for bed that evening that he asked the question.

'Balloon man Dan gone?' he said, a rising intonation in his voice suggesting he knew, that he was only looking for clarification. I readjusted the sticky tabs on his nappy and sat him up on the changing mat. I couldn't avoid answering for ever. And I felt I owed him some kind of explanation.

'Yes, sweetheart, he has,' I said, squatting down to his level so I could look him straight in the eye. 'He's gone for a trip on his boat. Mummy doesn't know if he'll be coming back.'

He nodded solemnly, his eyes big and moist. And kept on nodding as his bottom lip began to tremble. My breath caught as I gathered him to me, it was the first time I'd ever seen him do that. My brave little boy was trying not to cry.

'It's OK,' I said, letting my own tears fall in the hope he would see it was nothing to be ashamed about. 'I know how sad you feel. Mummy loved him too.' We stayed there for ages. Me holding him as we sobbed silently into each other's hair. Before I slipped his pyjamas and sleeping bag on and carried him into our room. I turned out the light and lay on the bed with him until he fell asleep. I kissed him on his forehead, pulled the door to behind me and padded downstairs.

The kitchen was cold and unwelcoming at night, without the morning sunshine bathing it. I put the kettle on and slumped down at the table, my head in my hands. Furious at myself for letting Alfie get hurt again. And wondering what it was with me that, one way or another, I ended up driving men away.

The kettle bubbled noisily before switching itself off. It was only as the noise died down that I heard the tapping on the kitchen door.

'Jo, dear. It's Nina.' Simply the sound of the concern in her voice was enough to start the tears again. I wiped my eyes with the back of my hand and unlocked the door to let her in.

'I wanted to know how you'd got on,' she said, stepping inside and immediately stopping when she saw my face. 'It's not good news, is it?'

'Dan's boat's gone,' I said. 'He left last week, the day after the accident.'

'Oh, Jo. I am sorry.' Nina patted my hand. I felt like a little girl being comforted by her grandma. 'And you've no idea where he's gone to?'

I shook my head as I got a second mug out for Nina and popped a tea bag into it.

'The lady in the next boat said she didn't know. But he did ask her to water his plants.'

'Oh, dear,' said Nina, sitting down at the table.

'He could be anywhere,' I said. 'I don't know where to start.'

'Where are his family?'

'He's got a grandma in Manchester. Fairfield, I think he said it was. That's where he grew up.'

'What about his mother?'

'I don't know,' I said. 'He found it difficult to talk about her. His dad used to knock her about when he was a kid.'

Nina winced and shook her head. 'You need to find out where his mother is,' she said. 'That's where he'll be.'

'What makes you say that?'

'It's what men do when they have a crisis. Go back to their mother. My son Murray did it once, when Karen left him. He hadn't been to see me for almost two years. And yet there he was on the doorstep, suitcase in hand. He knew I wouldn't turn him away, you see. Because unlike a partner, my love is unconditional.'

I managed a weak smile. 'You think it's worth trying to find him? What if I do and he doesn't want to see me?'

'Then at least you'll know. And you'll be able to tell Alfie when he's older that you tried.'

'Thank you,' I said as I handed Nina her tea. 'You're right, as usual.'

'Annoying old bat, aren't I?'

'Yeah,' I smiled.

'So when are you going to start looking?' asked Nina.

'Tomorrow,' I said. 'At work.'

Dan

Tuesday, 29 November 1983

I am waiting outside the courtroom. Grandma is sitting next to me. Every now and then she reaches out and pats or squeezes my knee. I think she thinks I am too old for her to hold my hand. I wouldn't mind if she did, though. Not today.

I am here to give evidence in Mum's trial. My mum. On trial for murdering my dad. She didn't murder him, of course. She killed him to stop him killing me. I know that. I was there. Grandma says that is all I have to do today. Tell the truth about what happened. The rest is up to the people on the jury. If they believe me, the judge will let Mum go and we can both go home. Although we haven't got a home to go to any more. The council have given it to someone else because we couldn't pay the rent with Mum in prison. If they don't believe me, Mum will have to stay in prison and I will have to carry on living with Grandma. She's been very nice to me, Grandma. But it is not the same as living with Mum.

I have been to see her in prison. Quite a few times now. She didn't want me to go at first. I don't know why, though

Grandma said she was worried it might be too upsetting for me. Grandma had to tell her in the end. That the thing that was really upsetting me was not seeing her at all.

The first time was the worst. Grandma took me on the bus. Three different buses, into Manchester then to Warrington and then to the prison, which is called Risley. It's a special prison for people who haven't been convicted of anything yet. Grandma says it isn't really a prison, it's a remand centre, but it looked like a prison to me. When the bus stopped outside, everyone looked at me as we got off. Grandma said to hold my head up high. That I had nothing to be ashamed of and that people ought to remember that you are innocent until proven guilty and to keep their silly comments to themselves.

We talked to a man in a security box first, then a warden came and opened a little gate in the big gate. She had a huge set of jangly keys on her belt. And every time I saw them or heard them jingle, all I could think about was the key to the kitchen door and how I had to get it out of Dad's pocket when he was lying there dead on the floor.

When we got inside we were searched and every time we went through one gate we had to wait for them to lock it before they could open the next one. By the time we got to the visiting room I felt like I was a prisoner.

Mum was sitting at a table in the far corner waiting for us. She looked thin and tired. She smiled when she saw me but it wasn't a proper smile, it was a sad one. I wanted to run up to her and give her a big hug but Grandma had already told me I wasn't allowed to do that or even to touch her. She'd said I could blow her a kiss but I didn't. I just stared and sort of smiled and tried very hard not to cry. Mum didn't talk about being in prison. She asked about school and Philip and Liverpool and stuff like that. I told her everything was fine. Though it wasn't; I was being picked on at school, Philip had a girlfriend (though he's dumped her now. Well, he says he dumped her, I think she dumped him) and Liverpool had lost 2–0 at home to Norwich in the league.

Grandma pats my knee again as a man in a funny wig and long black robes walks past, looking like something out of *Star Wars*.

'Not long now,' Grandma says.

I look up and nod, feeling the cement mixer in my stomach start churning again. My hands are cold and clammy, I sit on them to stop them shaking. The courtroom door opens and a woman in a black cloak holding a clipboard comes out.

'Daniel Brady,' she says. 'We're ready for you now.' She smiles at me as she says it. The same sort of smile that the teachers gave me when I first went back to school, a week after it all happened.

'You'll be fine,' says Grandma, patting me on my shoulder. 'I'll meet you back here when you've finished.' She's not allowed to sit next to me in the courtroom. She has to sit in a separate part for members of the public. Mum's not allowed to sit next to me either. She has to sit in a special place called the dock.

I follow the woman into the courtroom. It is silent inside, I see faces I don't know turn to watch me. I put my head down. All I can hear are my shoes squeaking on the floorboards. Grandma polished them specially for the occasion. She said it was important to look my best. That is why I am wearing my school uniform. I don't see why it matters what I am wearing. I thought all that mattered was that I told the truth.

The woman opens the little gate into the witness box, she gives me a bible and I have to put my hand on it and swear I am going to tell the truth. A bit like swearing on your mother's life that you didn't do something. It is only when I am finished that I look up properly. I see Mum straight away, standing in the dock across from me. She is biting her bottom lip and blinking a lot.

I look around again until I find Grandma. She is sitting with her red handbag on her knees. Clutching the handles so tightly her knuckles have gone white. I see some other people sitting in two long rows, mostly men and a few ladies. I think they must be the jury. I hear my name and realise a man is talking to me. I look up at who I guess must be the judge. He has one of the silly wigs on and a boil on the side of his nose. He looks a bit like I imagine God does. He talks like I think God would too, the sort of voice that you have to listen to. He is telling me to let him know if I need to take a break, that he understands how difficult this must be for me. I nod my head even though he is talking rubbish. He can't possibly know how I am feeling. He has no idea. None of them do.

Another man stands up and talks to me. He is wearing the funny robes and a wig too. He says his name is Mark and his job is to help me tell my story. I want to tell him it is not a story, it's the truth, but Grandma told me not to say anything unless I am asked a question.

I have to start by saying my name and address. My voice comes out sounding squeaky. I wish it wasn't so quiet in here. I wish everyone wasn't staring at me. Mark says I am doing well. He asks me to talk about the evening it all happened. Asks if I remember everything clearly. I give him the look Philip gives me when I say something stupid. He wants me to tell everyone what me and Mum were doing before Dad came home. I say we were eating cheese on toast in the kitchen and talking.

'And how did your mother seem?' he asks.

'Fine,' I say. I don't mention her being a bit sad about not getting a Valentine's card. She might not want people to know about that.

'And how did your father seem when he got home?'

'He was wobbly and his breath smelt. He'd been to the pub.'

'And what happened then?'

'He asked Mum for some money,' I say. 'But she said she didn't have any.'

'And how did your father react to that?'

'He got mad,' I say.

'What do you mean by that? Can you describe what he said and did?'

I look at Mum. I do not want to talk about it in front of her. I do not want to upset her. But I know I am going to have to. I know I must tell the truth. To help Mum. It all comes out in a bit of a rush. The stuff about Dad hitting Mum and me giving him the teapot of money to try to make him stop. Several times Mark has to ask me to slow down, to take my time. As I talk I see it all in my head. It is like describing what is happening on a video which someone else can't see. Sometimes he asks me to pause and rewind, to go over something again. I am OK until I get to the bit where Dad is hitting Mum's head on the counter, the bit where I think he is killing her. And then I go all shaky and my voice goes squeaky again. I look at Mum. She has gone all blurry. The judge asks if I would like to take a break. I shake my head. I want to get it over with. The lady who brought me in passes me a tissue and gives me a glass of water. I drink it even though I don't really like water. I know it would be rude to ask if they have any pop.

When my eyes clear I see that Mum and Grandma are crying too. Though they both try to smile at me when they see me looking at them. The judge asks if I am ready to carry on. I nod and Mark stands up again. I tell him about hitting Dad, about knocking him unconscious. I describe how I tried to get the key from his pocket but couldn't. How he got up again and grabbed the knife and said he was going to kill me. How Mum screamed and I jumped out the way and he fell down again. The court-room is silent as I talk. No one even whispers. Mark asks me to go on. I look at Mum. She is staring at me with sad eyes. I remember what Grandma told me. That the best way I can help Mum is to tell the truth. So I tell them. About Mum asking for the knife and me passing it to her and her kind of dancing with Dad before he fell back down again with the knife in his chest.

I look at Mum as I finish. She looks down at her feet. I wonder if I said something wrong. If I forgot a bit. Mark asks me how Mum seemed afterwards. I say she was sad and upset. And her head was bleeding. He asks me how I felt afterwards. I say relieved that it was all over but sad because I did not want Dad to die. He nods and shuffles some papers before thanking me and saying, 'That will be all.' I let out a big sigh. I want to go now. But another man in robes and a wig stands up. He says his name is Crispin. I think it's a silly name. He says he is going to ask me some more questions about what I have just talked about. That I might have to go over the same things again. He makes it sound a bit like redoing your homework because you have got it wrong. I clasp my hands together tightly.

'How much money would you say your mother had hidden in the teapot?'

'I don't know. Maybe about seventy or eighty pounds.'

'That's a lot of money, isn't it? What was it for?'

'She said it was her rainy day money.'

'And was she planning to use it to run away from your father?'

I stare at him. My eyebrows push further together. I don't know why he said that.

'No. She wasn't. It was for bills and stuff.'

'But she didn't tell your father about it?'

'No.'

'Did she often lie to your father?'

'Objection,' says Mark.

'Sustained,' says the judge before looking down and telling me I don't need to answer the question. I want to though. Because Crispin has called Mum a liar.

'She didn't lie. It was a secret. It's different,' I say.

'Had she ever talked to you about leaving your father?'

383

'No,' I say. 'I'd asked her about going to live with Grandma but she said it wasn't as simple as that.'

'I see,' says Crispin. 'Had your father ever threatened to kill your mother?'

'No,' I say.

'Not even on the day he died?'

'No. He didn't say it but she went all limp and floppy when he was hitting her and he didn't stop. Even when there was loads of blood.'

'And had your father ever hit you or struck you with any implement?'

'No,' I say.

'And in the kitchen, on the day your mother killed him. Did he hit you then?'

'No but he would have. If I hadn't jumped out of the way.'

Crispin nods. The sort of nod teachers do if they don't believe what you are saying.

'Did your mother make any attempt to help you get the kitchen door key out of your father's pocket when he was unconscious?'

'No, she couldn't get up off the floor.' I feel the tears pricking at the corners of my eye. I am determined that Crispin isn't going to make me cry.

'Did your mother make any attempt to escape from the house while your father was unconscious? Did she try the front door at all?'

'No, she was too poorly to do anything. Anyway, the front door doesn't open. Mum doesn't know where the key is.'

'And when your father fell down the second time, did

she make any effort to escape the house then? Or to shout for help?'

'No, I told you. She couldn't do anything.'

'But a few seconds later she stood up and, as you describe it, did a little dance with your father before stabbing him in the chest.'

I feel myself frown.

'Objection.' Mark is standing up, shaking his head. He is cross with Crispin like I am. For making it all sound wrong.

'Overruled,' says the judge.

Crispin is waiting for me to answer.

'It wasn't really a dance. It was just the way it looked because they were holding on to each other.'

'When your mother asked you to pass her the knife, you say your father was still lying on the floor.'

'Yes.'

'So he wasn't making any threat to you or her at that point?'

'No.'

'And how long would you say it was, between him falling on the floor the second time and your mother stabbing him?'

It's like having a test where they ask you questions you haven't revised for.

'I'm not sure. A minute or so, I guess.'

'Enough time to think clearly and calmly. To go upstairs or try to shout for help through the window.'

'We didn't have time to do anything. He would have come after us. You don't know what he was like.' The tears are trying to come again. I am blinking hard.

'And after your mother stabbed your father, did she make any attempt to help him, to see if she could save him?'

'No. He died straight away.'

'And did she make any attempt to raise the alarm? To shout for someone to call an ambulance.'

'No, she was too upset. And her head was still bleeding. That's why I had to look after her.'

Crispin does the nod again. He doesn't believe me. He has made it sound as if it was all our fault. I want to tell him about all the times Dad hit Mum, about her black eyes and bruises and the way she used to shake when he came home. About hiding in the wardrobe listening to her screams. But he hasn't asked about that. He hasn't asked the right questions.

'Thank you, Daniel,' says Crispin. 'No further questions.' He nods to the judge and sits down.

I look at Mum. She is shaking her head. I have messed it all up for her. I have done it wrong again.

Mark stands up again. He is going to get another go.

'Was this the first time your father had attacked your mother, Daniel?'

'No,' I say.

'How many times would you say he had attacked her?'

'A lot of times. Too many to count.'

'And how long had this been going on? How old were you when you first remember it happening.'

I thought for a moment. Trying to remember when it started.

'It's happened for as long as I can remember,' I said.

'And what sort of injuries did your mother have as a

result?' He was asking much better questions than Crispin had. I was pleased about that.

'She had black eyes and bruises on her face and her arms.'

'And did she ever strike your father at all? Did she hit him or use any sort of weapon against him?'

'No. Never,' I said. 'Not until the day she killed him.'

Mark paused for a moment and looked down. 'And what do you think your father would have done on the day in question? If your mother hadn't have stopped him.'

'He would have killed me,' I said. 'And then he would have killed her.'

'Thank you, Daniel. No further questions.'

The judge thanks me and says I can go now. I don't think I gave the right answers. I don't think I have helped Mum at all. Grandma is standing up to leave, her face is pale. The lady is opening the little gate. I step down out of the witness box and follow her to the door as quickly as I can, not daring to look back and see Mum's face. See how cross she is with me.

Grandma follows me outside into the corridor. She puts her hand on my shoulder and gives it a squeeze.

'You did really well,' she says.

I know she doesn't mean it because of the way she squeezed my shoulder.

'I messed up, didn't I?'

She shakes her head. 'You told the truth, Daniel. To every question they asked you. That was all you could do. I'm very proud of you. I'm sure your mother is too.'

I look down and scuff the toe of one of my shiny black shoes against the floor. I don't think Mum is proud of me.

I think she is still cross at me about the teapot. I think I have let her down again.

I am sitting in courtroom number two a week later. Not in the witness box this time. That is over. In the bit where the people watching sit. Grandma is sitting next to me, clutching her handbag again. The trial has ended now. The people on the jury have been deciding if Mum is guilty or not. And now they have said they have made their minds up. That is why we are here. Waiting for them to say if they believed us.

Mum is sitting over from me in her special little box. She is not looking at me. I think she is still mad at me for messing it all up. We stand up as the judge comes back in again. Me and Grandma sit back down but Mum has to stay standing. A man from the jury stands up. He has got silver hair and looks grumpy. The judge asks him if they have a verdict on the charge of murder. He says yes and goes and gives the judge a piece of paper. My hands have gone all slippery. My heart feels like it does when I have run down the wing really fast. The judge begins to speak.

'Elizabeth Brady, on the charge of murder, the jury finds you guilty.'

'No.' At first I think it is Mum's voice. Or maybe Grandma's. But then I see everyone looking at me and realise it was mine. Grandma's bony hands hug me to her. I bury my face in her coat as I hear Mum start to cry. And in my head I see her dancing with Dad again. Only this time they are really dancing. Happy dancing. Dad is smiling at her with his twinkly eyes. And Mum is doing the special smile, the one she did in the wedding photo.

'Your mother's going now, she's waving to you, Daniel,' says Grandma.

But I don't look up. I want to keep the picture I have in my head.

Twenty-two

I pulled open the door and walked into the newsroom, trying desperately to appear businesslike and professional and avoid giving any hint of the emotional maelstrom within.

Alfie had cried when I'd left him at Mum's this morning. First for me, which I'd been able to put down to him being clingy after the accident, and then for Dan, in what could only be described as a masterstroke of a delaying tactic in preventing me from going to work. I'd had to sit him down and go through it all over again, all the time trying not to show that I was missing Dan every bit as much as he was.

Richard looked up from his desk as I approached. It was strange seeing him in this context again. Having looked at him over a hospital bed for the best part of twenty-four hours last week. And spoken to him on the phone every day since. I wasn't sure if he was going to go back to his bastard boss act again now. If I should apologise for being five minutes late.

'Hi, Jo. How's Alfie?' Richard asked, his tone softer than the usual work voice. His eyes opting for the blue side of grey.

'He's OK, thanks. A bit clingy this morning. Didn't want me to go. But that's understandable.'

'Well, if you want to leave before the debriefing meeting tonight, that's fine by me.'

I stared at him, not used to such generosity of spirit. Wondering if we had entered a new era of Entente Cordiale.

'Thanks,' I said, smiling at him. 'I might take you up on that. It'll be a long day for him otherwise.' I glanced over at the reporters' desks, wondering whose seat I was sitting in today.

'Toby's off this week,' said Richard, reading my mind.

'Good,' I said. 'Given the preference of having to look at pictures of Formula One racing cars, supposedly amusing cricket anecdotes or a scantily clad Kate Moss stuck on my computer, I'll go with the cars.'

'Steady on, you'll be saying you like Jeremy Clarkson next,' said Richard.

I smiled and went to my seat, aware that people were looking at us, wondering if their eyes and ears had deceived them or we'd just shared a joke.

Laura put the phone down as soon as she saw me and came over to give me a hug.

'Hey, good to see you. How's Alfie doing? You must have really been through the mill.'

I struggled to hold back the tears as Laura held me. Realising that it was going to be like this all day. People enquiring about Alfie. Asking how we were doing. The concern was lovely but it did mean that my hope of being able to put it all out of my mind while I was at work was clearly misplaced.

'He's fine, thanks. We both are. Just a bit shaken, I guess,' I said, managing to hold it together as Andy and Simon kept their heads firmly down in case there was a display of female emotion in the workplace. 'It was pretty scary at the time but we were lucky really. It could have been so much worse.'

'Richard seemed really shaken when he came back,' said Laura.

'Did he? I think it hit him hard. We had a long talk in hospital. We both had to listen to a few home truths.'

'So have you two buried the hatchet then?'

'I wouldn't go that far,' I said, lowering my voice as I glanced over at the newsdesk. 'But I think it's safe to say we've embarked on some sort of Northern Ireland-style peace process. We still find it difficult to be in the same room without shouting at each other but we both recognise that it's not doing either of us any good and for Alfie's sake we've agreed to make more of an effort.'

'Good for you. And whatever you said to him seems to have worked. He hasn't been nearly such a bastard since he came back, you know.'

'Well, at least that's one good thing that's come out of it then.'

'And what about Dan?' Laura asked in a hushed voice. 'Richard said he was supposed to be looking after Alfie when it happened.'

I noted the 'supposed to' phrase used, sure it was a direct quote. I ushered Laura over to a quiet corner of the office near the coat stands.

'I got it all wrong. Turns out it wasn't Dan's fault at all.

It was a motorbike, not a pedal cycle that was coming towards them. I guess I was in a bit of a state, not really thinking straight. Which is why I told him to piss off.'

'Oh, Jo. You didn't?'

'Well, not in so many words but I did finish with him. And now he's gone AWOL from his moorings. One of his neighbours said he left the day after the accident. And gave no idea when he'd be back.'

Laura stared at me open mouthed. 'You poor thing. What a nightmare.'

'Don't feel sorry for me. Not this time. I brought it all on myself. Too ready to apportion blame. As usual.'

'So what are you going to do?'

'Nothing much I can do,' I said. 'Until I find him.'

'Well, if I can help at all. Or cover for you if you need some time.'

'Thanks,' I said. 'I'll let you know.'

I hadn't even made it back to my desk when Moira came out of the studio.

'Jo. How are you? How's the wee lad?'

I smiled at her and took a deep breath, preparing to begin the story again. And wondering if it might be easier all round if I got them to put it out on the lunchtime bulletin.

I was on my way to the editing suite later that morning to try to find thirty seconds of decent material from the disturbingly dull responses to the day's vox pop question of, 'Would a super casino be good for Manchester?' when I bumped into Tricia. Literally bumped into her, as she was coming out of the room I was going into.

'Sorry,' I said as I rubbed my arm (her shoulders were bonier than mine so I'd come off worse). 'I didn't know there was anyone in here.'

'No, my fault,' she said, 'I hadn't booked it out. I was just working on my first out and about piece. I'm still not happy with it and it's going out tonight.'

I nodded, unsure whether she was angling for some assistance, although I couldn't believe that I would be the one she'd ask. We stood there awkwardly for a second.

'How's Alfie?' she asked.

'He's OK, thanks. No lasting damage,' I said, giving my now well-rehearsed answer.

'It must have been horrible for you,' she said, her face unusually devoid of a smile.

'It was. Although considering what could have happened I think we got off lightly.'

'Richard says you were brilliant, staying with him for all that time.'

I shrugged. 'It's what any mum would do.' I realised as soon as I said it how insensitive it sounded, bearing in mind Tricia's situation. But as I wasn't supposed to know her situation, I couldn't really apologise.

'I think Richard's just easily impressed,' I said. 'Given that he's not cut out for fatherhood.'

'Who said he isn't?' asked Tricia.

'He did. Not that he needed to. I can certainly vouch for it. That's why he left me. He resented the way Alfie came between us. I'll say one thing for him, he's very honest to admit it. I expect a lot of guys feel that way but don't own up to it.'

'Maybe when he's a bit older he'll change his mind,' said Tricia.

'I doubt it. He's been with Alfie enough to know what hard work it is. And you know how he hates mess and clutter. I think he'll be happy with his iPod and Sky Plus. And you, of course.'

Tricia gave a hint of a blush and looked down at the floor. I wasn't sure if she'd twigged that I knew. But if she had, she wasn't saying anything.

'Anyway,' she said, stepping aside. 'I'd better leave this now and let you get on.'

'Thanks,' I said. 'Why don't you ask Richard to have a look at your piece?'

She shook her head. 'I don't want him to think I'm some sort of air-head. That I can't do anything without his help.' She looked down at her feet and twiddled her thumbs. The glamorous celebrity weather girl who oozed confidence onscreen was as insecure as the rest of us underneath.

'Look, if you want, I could run a quick eye over it now,' I said.

'Would you? I'd be very grateful. You're the only one I can rely on to be brutally honest.'

'There you are, then,' I said, smiling back at her. 'That's one good thing about working with your boyfriend's ex.'

It was lunchtime before I had a chance to slip into the library. I'd already tried Googling Dan again, with no luck. It was time for some good old-fashioned research. The archives at *Spotlight North West* were enormous. Row upon row of video tapes of every bulletin, every report that had ever been filmed. But it was the newspaper archives I was going to start with. Crammed full of articles snipped out of all the local papers in our patch and stuck to sheets of thick white paper. The files went back years; somewhere in there, much to my embarrassment, was a *Rochdale Observer* photograph of me winning an infant school Easter bonnet competition at the age of six. Richard had found it once and had promptly copied it and emailed it to everyone in the office.

I went straight to the cabinet marked 'B'. Quite what I was hoping to find I didn't know. Maybe a photograph taken at a festival where Dan had appeared, something from his time at the performing arts college. Anything that may shed some light, provide some clue, however small. I started flicking through the files, Bradbury, Bradley, Bradshaw, until I got to Brady. There was a Darren, a Dawn and a Derek but no Dan or Daniel. I sighed, disappointed to have drawn a blank so quickly. I carried on through the Brady section in case a file had been put back in the wrong order. The librarians were always complaining that none of us seemed to know our alphabet. I got as far as Edward and was about to stop when I saw the name on the next file. Elizabeth Brady. An alarm went off inside my head. One that must have been ticking away subconsciously without me making the necessary connection. That Dan's boat might not have been named after a film star at all. I took a deep breath and pulled the brown envelope from the cabinet. It was old and crumpled, ripped slightly at one side, and from the weight of it, it was clear that whoever Elizabeth Brady was, she'd warranted a sizeable number of column inches. I knelt down on the floor and tipped out the contents, which fell face down on to the carpet. I picked up the biggest one I could see from towards the back of the pile and unfolded the newspaper.

'Mum jailed for husband's murder' screamed the front-page headline under an unfamiliar and outdated *Manchester Evening News* masthead. Alongside it a photograph of a woman with long dark brown hair, high cheekbones and rabbit-caught-in-the-headlight eyes, photographed as she emerged from a police van, handcuffed to a female prison officer.

I shut my eyes and dropped my head to my chest. Suddenly not wanting Elizabeth Brady to be who I suspected she was. Part of me didn't want to read on, scared of what I might find. But having got so far, there was no going back. I had to know for certain. I looked up and started reading the story, the newspaper shaking in my hands: 'A Fairfield mother has been jailed for life for stabbing her husband to death in front of their 11-year-old son.'

'Please, no,' I whispered under my breath. My gaze shot up to the date at the top of the page: Wednesday, 7 December 1983. I did the maths quickly in my head. It was Dan, the boy was Dan. I was sure of it. That is what he'd seen. Why his eyes looked so haunted, so hurt. I bit my lip and read on, the words blurring as the tears began to well in my eyes. Each new detail winding me like a kick in the stomach. And the judge's words, about how Elizabeth couldn't claim it was self-defence because several minutes had elapsed between the last time she'd been assaulted and the moment she'd stabbed him. I reached the end of the court report feeling physically sick and with dozens of unanswered questions still whizzing around in my head. I shuffled frantically through the remaining cuttings, finding and reading the initial story of the murder in Gransmoor Road and each day's report of the trial in turn. The heartbreaking evidence of the unnamed son. And the testimony alleging that Elizabeth had been subjected to years of physical and mental abuse. Made by her mother. One Ruby Nenitescu of Fairfield Road, Fairfield. I scribbled the name and address down in my notebook. Praying it was the grandmother Dan had spent Christmas with. Relieved to have found something to go on but equally appalled at what I had discovered. I carried on reading, unbearably grim though it was. Desperate to build a picture in my head of exactly what had happened. Of what Dan was obviously still struggling to come to terms with. And, as I read, so many pieces of the puzzle fitted into place: his reaction to the violence on the train, his wariness of the media and his appalling memories of Valentine's Day, which must have made Alfie's accident and my subsequent reaction that much worse. By the time I'd finished I felt like the thirteenth member of the jury. That I'd listened to the evidence with them.

I rummaged through the pile of cuttings again for anything I had missed and found another front page, from a more recent newspaper. I opened up the article, wondering what there could be left for me to see.

'Battered Mum Walks Free' ran the headline above a photograph of a much older, weary-looking Elizabeth, smiling on the steps of the Appeal Court, hugging a young man, barely out of his teens. He had long hair and half of his face was buried against her head. But it was unmistakably Dan. A surge of elation ran through me. She'd got out. Dan had got his mother back. Albeit years later. I checked the date at the top of the page. More than eight years later, in fact. Eight years in which Dan had grown up without her. Lost years that they could never get back. My mind was racing back and forth, trying to piece it all together. Excited at the prospect that Nina might be right, that Dan might have gone home to his mother after all. I hurriedly picked up the rest of the cuttings and stuffed them back into the envelope before heading for the video tapes. My eyes frantically scanning the dates as I hurried along each aisle. Until at last I had it in my hand. The *Spotlight North West* evening bulletin of 16 April 1992. The day of the appeal.

I went straight to the editing suite, taking the first free room I came to and ramming the video into the machine. I sat with my hands clenched tightly in my lap as the opening credits rolled, surprised at how old fashioned they seemed. It was headline news, of course. The suave, silver-haired news anchor delivering straight to camera. 'A battered mum who stabbed her husband to death has been freed by the Appeal Court. Elizabeth Brady from Fairfield, who endured years of physical abuse at the hands of her husband, Michael, had her murder conviction reduced to manslaughter on the grounds of provocation. The appeal judge imposed a sentence of eight years, four months and nine days, the exact time she'd spent in prison. Which meant Elizabeth walked free from court to be greeted by her delighted family. Samantha Perkins reports.'

The reporter recounted Elizabeth's eight-year battle for

freedom; being refused leave to appeal and then having her first appeal thrown out. But I wasn't really listening. I was watching the film of Dan beaming proudly as he emerged from the court building. His arm round Elizabeth, who was blinking in the bright sunlight. Her eyes wide and staring, as if she couldn't quite believe that she was finally out. And on the other side of her, clutching her arm, was a short, elderly lady with white curly hair and dark circles under her eyes, who I took to be Ruby.

I sniffed loudly as I wiped the tears from my eyes.

'Jo? Are you OK?' The voice was Richard's. He was standing at the open door of the editing room. I had no idea how long he'd been there.

'I'm sorry,' I said, fishing in my trouser pocket for a tissue. 'That's Dan,' I said, pointing at the screen. 'His mum killed his dad when he was a kid. He was there. She did it to save his life and got put away for murder.'

Richard stared at the screen then back at me.

'Elizabeth Brady,' he said.

I frowned at him. Not understanding. The whole thing starting to seem surreal.

'It was while I was at uni,' he explained. Richard had studied law at Durham University. 'I remember the lecturer talking about her case. It was a landmark appeal which led to several other women being released. She was big news at the time.'

I shook my head. It felt as if everyone had known about it except me.

'Didn't Dan tell you?' asked Richard.

'No,' I said, trying to hide how upset I was that he hadn't

felt able to confide in me. 'He said his dad had knocked his mum about. But nothing about this. About what happened to them.'

'It doesn't change anything, Jo. I mean, I feel for the guy, for what he must have gone though. But the thing with Alfie, it was still his fault.'

'No it wasn't,' I said quickly. 'I've been waiting for a time to tell you. It was a motorbike on the towpath, a scooter-type thing. Alfie told me and Nina saw it on the day. Going so fast it could have killed someone.'

Richard blew out and ran his fingers through his hair.

'Shit,' he said. 'Have you spoken to him since you found out?'

'I tried to. I went round to apologise but his boat was gone. He left the day after the accident apparently. That's what I've been doing in the library. Trying to track down his family in case that's where he's gone. And this is what I find,' I said, gesturing towards the screen which I'd frozen on pause.

'Have you got an address or anything?' asked Richard, ignoring the fresh flow of tears and being practical and to the point as ever.

'They used to live in Gransmoor Road and his grand-mother lived in Fairfield Road. Both in Fairfield.'

'Stay there,' said Richard, disappearing out of the door and returning a few minutes later with a phone book and the Manchester *A-Z*. I flicked through the phone book; no one by the name of Brady in Gransmoor Road but predictably there was only one Nenitescu. With the initial 'R', at number 44 Fairfield Road.

'His grandmother's still there,' I said.

Richard handed me the *A-Z*, open on the right page. 'And look,' he said, pointing at a thick blue line running alongside Fairfield Road and following it back the next page to the city centre. 'The Rochdale Canal links with the Manchester and Ashton-under-Lyne Canal near Piccadilly Station.'

I looked up at him, suddenly filled with hope. Sure that was where Dan had gone.

'You can go there now if you want,' said Richard. 'I was going to send you on a court case this afternoon. But I can ask Laura to go instead.'

'Are you sure?' I said. It was the first decent job I'd been offered since my return but this couldn't wait.

'Go on, quick. Before I change my mind and revert to my obnoxious, arsehole boss status.'

I dabbed at my eyes with the tissue and grinned at him.

'Thank you,' I said. 'I owe you one. But you also owe me a decent story next week, remember.' I took the tape out of the machine and headed for the door.

'Jo,' said Richard. I stopped and turned back. 'Thank you. For whatever you said to Tricia this morning. And I hope you find him.'

Twenty-three

I parked my car round the corner from Fairfield Road in Gransmoor Road. Because I didn't want to risk Dan seeing it before I arrived. And because I wanted to see the street where he'd grown up. Where his father had died. I sat there staring out at the bleak surroundings. Less certain about everything than I was when I set out. Whether Dan was going to be there, whether the word 'sorry' was anywhere near adequate and whether my tirade at the hospital and what I'd discovered about his past meant that resuming our relationship was now out of the question. There was only way one to find out.

I got out of the car, slammed the door shut and started walking down the road. Most of the narrow terraced houses were boarded up now. But it was easy to imagine how it would have been when Dan lived here. The children running up and down the alleyways. Women standing on their front steps talking to their neighbours. Old men sitting in the open doorways in string vests, watching the world go by. So different from the safe, middle-class suburbia where Richard had been raised. I wondered which house Dan had lived in. Eyeing each boarded doorway suspiciously in case the scene of the killing lurked behind it.

I rounded the corner into Fairfield Road and started counting down the door numbers until I reached number forty-four. A red door in need of a fresh coat of paint. I paused only for a second before walking on. I was going to the canal first. To look for Dan's boat. There was no point even knocking at the house if it wasn't there.

I turned right and dropped down on to the towpath. The *Elizabeth* was moored up less than a hundred yards away, her red and yellow diamonds unmistakable against the murky grey water. I stopped and shut my eyes for a second. I'd found him. Nina was right. He had gone home. I took a moment to compose myself and walked on, my step faster and lighter now. As I neared the boat I could see the curtains were open. I peered in, conscious that I looked like one of the gawpers Dan had complained about. There were signs of life inside, a loaf of bread on the kitchen counter, a mug in the washing-up bowl. He was obviously sleeping on the boat rather than in Ruby's house. Maybe there wasn't room if his mum was there as well. Maybe he simply didn't like being on dry land. I walked up towards the front of the boat. Sinbad squeezed through the cat flap, leapt on to the towpath and ran up to greet me. Sniffing my boots as he rubbed around my ankles and peering about anxiously as if expecting Alfie to jump out at any moment. I bent down to stroke him. Pleased to see him too. Because it meant that Dan couldn't be far away.

'It's OK,' I whispered. 'Alfie's not here today. You're safe.' Sinbad leapt on to the top of the boat, miaowing at me. It was clear Dan wasn't on board. If he was, he'd have been out by now. I sighed and gazed out across the water.

I could either stay here and wait or try at the house. I started walking.

I went to the front door, even though I suspected it was one of those houses, like mine, where everyone usually used the back entrance. The wind whipped my hair over my face. I tucked it back firmly behind my ears and reached for the brass knocker. Two taps. That was all it needed. I heard footsteps approaching, a shuffling sound before the door opened to reveal an elderly woman I recognised instantly from the *Spotlight* report as Ruby. She was much older now, of course. The wrinkles carved deep into her face, which was more gaunt, less rounded than it had been previously. Her eyes sadder somehow. She was dressed in a pleated red skirt and white blouse with a red cardigan over the top. Clearly being of the generation who liked to look their best even when there was no particular reason to.

'Hello,' I said. 'I'm very sorry to bother you. I'm a friend of Dan's. I couldn't see him on the boat and I wondered if he was here.'

'Is it Jo?' she said, peering at me through her thick glasses.

I nodded.

'Come in, dear,' she said. 'I was hoping you'd find us.' She opened the door wider to let me in, smiling as she did so.

'Thank you,' I said, stepping inside, wondering what he'd told her about me. And whether Dan would seem equally pleased to see me. I followed her through the tiny hallway, noticing the framed photo of Elizabeth Taylor hanging from the dado rail, listening for sounds coming from the rest of the house, before she led me into the small living room, which smelt of furniture polish and was decorated in a delicate rose-patterned wallpaper. It was empty. So was the kitchen beyond.

'Dan's popped out to get some shopping for me,' she said, reading my mind. 'He shouldn't be too long. Have a seat. Can I get you anything to drink?'

'No, really, I'm fine. Thank you,' I said, perching on the edge of a worn two-seater settee with wooden arms. Ruby lowered herself into the armchair in the corner, her long bony fingers resting lightly on the floral-patterned arm protectors which were draped over the ends. We sat awkwardly for a moment. I suspected she, like me, wasn't sure where to begin.

'It's not bad news, is it?' she said. 'About your little boy?'

I shook my head. 'No, Alfie's OK, thanks. Out of hospital now. The doctor says he'll be fine.'

'Oh, I am glad,' said Ruby. 'Dan's been ever so worried about him. He blames himself, you know.'

'I'm afraid I was very hard on him,' I said, looking down at my clenched hands. 'I didn't give him a chance to explain what happened. But I know now. Alfie told me about the motorbike. I know that it wasn't Dan's fault. That's why I'm here. To say sorry.'

Ruby nodded slowly. 'You were upset,' she said. 'Your little boy was hurt. He'll understand that. How far a mother will go to protect her child.'

I looked up at her, understanding exactly what she meant and feeling compelled to come clean.

'I know about that as well,' I said quietly. 'About what

happened with his parents, I mean. I found the file at work. Though I could barely bring myself to read some of the reports.'

Ruby's eyes glistened as she gazed out of the window for a moment before turning back to me.

'He wanted to tell you,' she said. 'He simply didn't know how. He still finds it very difficult to talk about.'

'I'm not surprised,' I said. 'It must have been so awful for him. I can't begin to imagine.'

'It was truly horrible,' said Ruby. 'But sometimes I think it would help him to talk about it. So he could try to move on. It's already ruined most of his life. I don't want it to ruin what's . . .'

Ruby's voice trailed off at the sound of the back door opening, of footsteps across the kitchen lino. I looked up to see Dan standing in the doorway, staring at me, a bulging Tesco carrier bag in each hand. He looked at Ruby's face then back at mine. For a second I thought he was going to run out of the room.

'You've come to tell me bad news, haven't you? About Alfie.' His voice was full of dread. I stood up, shaking my head, desperate to reassure him.

'Alfie's fine,' I said. 'He's out of hospital, running around all over the place. Asking for you all the time.'

Dan leant his head against the door frame and screwed up his eyes.

'When I saw your face,' he said, 'I just thought . . .'

'I think you two need to talk,' said Ruby. 'Why don't you go down to the boat?'

Dan nodded. I followed him out of the kitchen, through

the backyard and round the corner. It was only as we reached the towpath that he turned to speak to me.

'So, Alfie's absolutely fine?'

'Yes, honestly. I tried to let you know. I left messages on your phone.'

'It's not working,' he said. 'Not since going in the canal. I haven't got round to getting a new one yet.'

I nodded and took Dan's outstretched hand as he helped me on to the boat. Savouring the touch of him, the smell of him. Trying to resist the temptation to throw my arms round him as soon as we were both on board. The tension eased slightly. We were back on familiar territory, albeit in a different location.

'Alfie told me about the motorbike,' I said. 'And Nina, she saw it too. I know it wasn't your fault. That's why I came. I wanted to say I'm sorry. And to thank you for saving Alfie's life.'

The hurt in Dan's eyes spilled over, a solitary tear rolling down his cheek.

'It all happened so quickly,' he said. 'One minute we were feeding the ducks under the bridge, the next thing I knew this thing was coming straight at us. I didn't have time to think about what to do. I just grabbed hold of Alfie and jumped in. When his head hit the trolley, I felt sick inside. I couldn't believe it. I wished it had been my head instead of his.'

'Did he cry or scream or anything?' I asked.

'No, he was out cold straight away. That was the worst thing, worse even than the blood, the fact that he didn't make a sound.'

'Did anyone else help you?'

'I managed to get him out of the water on my own and lay him down on the banking. Then the guy walking his dog whose phone I used gave me a handkerchief to hold against his head. But that was it really. It was such a relief when the ambulance arrived.'

'And then I turned up and started screaming at you,' I said, shaking my head.

Dan shrugged. 'He's your little boy. You had every right to.'

'When you said about the bike, I thought you meant a mountain bike. That's why I couldn't understand why you jumped in. But I should have let you explain properly. At least at the hospital.'

'I wanted so much to be there for you both,' said Dan, another tear following the trail of the first down his cheek. 'And all you did was push me away. I couldn't believe it when you said we were finished.'

'I know. I'm sorry. I guess I was in too much of a state to think straight. It was an awful thing to do. Something I wish I could undo.' I looked at Dan, hoping to see that he understood, that I was trying to turn the clock back. To start again.

'How long was it?' he asked. 'Before Alfie came round.'

'Not till that evening. Although we'd had the test results by then so at least we knew he was going to be OK. It was simply a matter of waiting. Do you know the first thing he said when he opened his eyes? "Balloon man Dan gone."'

'Sorry,' said Dan, managing a weak smile.

'No, it was great. Really pissed Richard off.'

Dan smiled again. A proper smile this time. 'And there's no lasting damage? To Alfie, I mean.'

'No. All the scan results came back negative. He's still pretty shaken up, mind. He freaked out on Saturday when a motorbike came past. That's how I found out. I went down to Mayroyd yesterday to see you. Except you weren't there, of course.'

Dan gazed out across the water, a frown spreading across his face.

'How did you find me?' he asked.

'I'm a journalist. It's what we do,' I replied with a shrug.

He went quiet for a moment.

'You know, don't you?' he said.

I shut my eyes and nodded. 'I'm so sorry.'

Dan swallowed hard and started fumbling with the lock on the boat doors. He pulled them open and went downstairs without a word. I stood for a second, unsure whether to leave him for a while. And then I remembered what Ruby had said. About it doing him good to talk. And followed him down the stairs.

Sinbad got up to greet me for the second time that afternoon, purring loudly as I bent to stroke him again. Dan walked over to the window. I decided to fill the silence.

'I found your mother's file in the archives at work. I've sat through a lot of horrible court cases in my time. But nothing's ever come close. And to know it was you, you were the boy who saw all of that . . .' I shook my head, unable to continue.

'It was all my fault,' said Dan, his voice shaky, still not turning round. 'I gave him the teapot, you see. Where

Mum kept her savings. I thought I was helping. I was trying to stop him hitting her. Only I made it so much worse.'

'You were eleven years old,' I said. 'How could you have known? You were only trying to help.'

'I should have listened to Mum. She tried to tell me not to do it.'

'And if you had he'd probably have found it anyway. And it would all still have happened. Or maybe it would have been even worse. Maybe you and your mum wouldn't be here today.'

Dan turned round, looking strangely at me. I realised I hadn't explained how much I knew.

'I watched our report of the day she was freed before I came here,' I said. 'I saw your face when she came out. How proud you were of her, how happy to have her back.'

Dan screwed his eyes tight shut again. Silence filled the boat. And filled me with unease. I stood waiting for him to say something.

'Mum died a year after she was released,' he said, opening his eyes to reveal two pools of tears. His words seared through me, turning me cold.

'I'm so sorry. I had no idea. Had she been ill in prison?'

Dan shook his head. 'She overdosed on antidepressants. It was accidental, we're sure of it. She'd never have done that on purpose. The coroner at the inquest agreed with us too. I think she was simply desperate to appear more cheerful. For my sake. That's why she took more than she should.'

I nodded. Wiping the tears from my own eyes. Desperate to touch him. To reconnect.

'Come here,' I said.

Dan stepped forward. I took another tentative step towards him. And a second later we were locked together. Our arms like scaffolding around our bodies, preventing us both from collapsing. Our heads buried against each other's shoulders, our skin connecting, soaking up each other's pain.

'I wanted to tell you,' said Dan. 'But I couldn't. Not without telling you everything. And I didn't want to frighten you away.'

'You've told me now,' I said, stroking his hair. 'And I'm still here. I'm not going anywhere. I just can't believe that she was snatched away from you like that. So soon after you'd got her back.'

Dan shook his head. 'I never really got her back,' he said. 'She died with Dad that day. Died inside at least. She never got over what happened. She still loved him, you see. Even though he had knocked every ounce of spirit out of her. She used to be so bright and beautiful, you know. But by the time she came out of prison she was a broken woman. It was like they'd taken the sunshine away and left only the shadows.'

'Didn't she get any help?' I asked.

'No. It's not like when they know people are going to be released. It all happened so quickly. There was no time to prepare for it. She went to court and they let her go. That was it. She used to sit on the sofa in Gran's house for hours on end, staring out of the window. I thought she might have that post-traumatic stress thing you hear about on the news. That's why I encouraged her to go to the doctor's.

But all they did was dole out antidepressants. And look what good that did.'

He pulled away and walked over to the window, staring out across the canal.

'What did you do?' I asked. 'After she died, I mean.'

'I threw myself into my work. Built up the business until I had enough money to buy the boat,' he said. 'She was in a bit of a state. I spent ages doing her up. Quite therapeutic really, I guess. Restoring something to its former glory.'

'And that's why you called her Elizabeth.'

'It was a way of keeping her memory alive. And being close to her.'

I looked at him questioningly.

'We scattered her ashes in there,' he explained, pointing out at the water. 'So she'd be free at last.'

I nodded, as the final piece of the jigsaw slotted into place.

'Nina was right then,' I said. Dan looked at me and frowned. 'She said you'd have gone home to your mother.'

'It was all too much,' he said. 'Being on Valentine's Day and everything. I thought you were going to lose Alfie. And then to lose you as well. I couldn't bear it and it was all my fault.'

'But it wasn't, was it?' I said. 'You saved his life. Like your mother saved yours. She'd have been very proud of you.'

He put his hands over his eyes, I suspected to hide the tears.

'And you haven't lost me at all. I want you back. If you'll have me, that is, after the way I treated you.'

Dan walked towards me and held my face, staring deep into my eyes.

'I need to know that you're not saying that because you feel sorry for me. All my life I've had people saying "poor Dan" and making allowances for me where they probably shouldn't have made them. I don't want it to be like that with you. That's one of the reasons why I didn't tell you.'

'I understand that. I fell in love with you before I knew any of this, remember. You made me laugh. Me and Alfie. And you knew all the words to "Dingle Dangle Scarecrow".'

Dan smiled, a tiny light flickering in the darkness of his eyes.

'Come back to Hebden,' I said. 'We miss you, me and Alfie.'

Dan sighed, I felt the warmth of his breath on my face.

'There's nothing I want more,' he said. 'But I'm not sure I'm ready for it yet. I can't seem to break free of it all. I thought when I met you it could be different. But it always catches up with me. Always spoils things. Stops me being happy.'

'Your mother wouldn't have wanted that,' I said. 'If you owe her one thing, anything, it's to be happy.'

'I know,' he said. 'And that's why I'm trying to do something about it. I'm still seeing the counsellor. He's even agreed to come out here, says it might be good for me to confront my demons head on.'

'Well, that's good.'

'It's a start, at least. Bad things happen in life, I know that. But I need to be strong enough to deal with them.

Instead of taking off like I did. The trouble is, I don't know how long that will take.'

I nodded, I didn't know either. All I did know was that I wanted him now more than ever before. That I didn't want to go back to how my life was before I'd met him.

'There's no pressure,' I said. 'No need to rush things. Whenever you're ready, we'll be there. Waiting for you.'

Dan nodded, stroking my face with the back of one finger before gently removing his hands.

'And if there's anything I can do to help in the meantime.'

'Thank you,' said Dan. 'But I think this one's down to me.'

I nodded, catching sight of the clock on the wall as I did so. I should be getting back to work.

'Look, I need to make a move,' I said.

'Thank you for coming,' said Dan. 'I've missed you so much.'

'Not as much as I have,' I said, kissing him softly on the lips before turning to leave. Climbing up the stairs and stepping over on to the banking. Glancing down briefly into the canal. No longer seeing Alfie's face under the surface. But Elizabeth's.

Twenty-four

'I did a wee.' Alfie beamed up at me as I came in from the kitchen. He was clearly so proud of his achievement that I managed to cover up my frustration that he'd chosen to go on the living-room carpet rather than the potty in the kitchen.

'That's OK, love,' I said. 'Let's get your wet clothes off. Maybe another time it might be fun to use your potty. Let's go and have a look at it, shall we?'

I peeled off Alfie's trousers and pants and he ran bare bottomed into the kitchen and pointed to the cheap, no-frills potty which had been sitting there unused for the past few days.

'Use potty,' he said. I looked down to discover he'd amassed a collection of half-eaten rice cakes in it. I counted to ten in my head.

'Potties aren't for food, sweetie,' I said, scooping them out and depositing them in the bin. 'They're for weeing in. Just let me know next time you need to go, OK?'

Alfie nodded. Though somehow I suspected it would be a long time before the potty was used for its correct purpose. I got a wet cloth and knelt down in the living room to start work on the carpet. Maybe I'd picked a bad time to start potty training. Alfie was a lot better than he had been. The physical scars were healing well and a month after the accident we could now walk along the towpath and under the bridge into town together without any mention of noisy bikes. But he was still noticeably clingier than he had been before and still woke in the night sometimes crying out for me. It worried me, of course. The fact that it was still troubling him on some deeper level. A level I couldn't seem to reach. I didn't want him having flashbacks about shopping trolleys. I had visions of him turning into a troubled teenager – the sort that goes around riding scooters along towpaths.

No doubt Dan's disappearance was a contributory factor as well. Alfie still asked about him, though mercifully no more than once a day now. He spoke about him as if he was some mythical creature he had once encountered. I suspected he was up there with Father Christmas in his head. And that one day he would question whether he had really existed at all.

I was starting to feel a little like that myself. I hadn't heard from Dan. No phone calls, no texts. And I knew his boat hadn't returned. Not that I was checking on some sort of compulsive, every-day level but I had stopped the car a few times when I was passing and made the odd detour or two.

I didn't think he'd come back now. The moment had passed. The longer it went on, the more likely it was he was thinking of the reasons not to. The chance that it wouldn't work. Rather than the possibility that it would. Maybe his demons were simply too terrible to overcome.

I was desperately upset about it but I didn't see much else

I could do. I'd told him there was no pressure. And I knew that me going back there would only add more pressure. It was like he'd said. This one was up to him.

I sighed and returned the cloth to the kitchen to find Alfie conducting some kind of experiment involving trying to shut his genitals in the freezer door (he'd long ago removed the child-proof freezer lock, discarding it with a look of utter contempt).

'Willy go cold,' he said, giggling. I shook my head as I struggled to keep a straight face. The joys of single parenthood came in the most unexpected places.

'Right,' I said, 'let's get you upstairs and get some dry clothes on.' I scooped him up in my arms and carried him up to our bedroom. My work suit was hanging up on the wardrobe. I'd ironed it especially. I was covering a court case tomorrow. Only some *Coronation Street* star up for drink driving but a court case none the less. Last week I'd interviewed one of the Manchester MPs about gun crime. The new single-mum-friendly Richard appeared to be here to last. I was still doing the 'And Finally' stories as well, of course. But I was starting to feel like a real reporter again, albeit a part-time one. And that was good enough for now.

I found Alfie a clean pair of *Bob the Builder* pants and the least crumpled pair of trousers on the pile and lifted him on to the bed to put them on. He wriggled about as usual, so much so that he ended up with both feet down the same trouser leg. He chuckled as he looked up at me. I blew a raspberry on his cheek and rolled on to the bed next to him, tickling him until he couldn't speak for laughing.

'Mummy loves you so much,' I said, kissing him on the

forehead. We made a good double act, me and Alfie. I was getting used to it now. There just being the two of us. All I had to do was convince myself again that I wouldn't want it any other way.

I got Alfie dressed properly, picked him up and lifted him on to my shoulders.

'Come on, then. Let's go and get some lunch ready,' I said.

'Balloon man Dan,' Alfie screamed excitedly.

'Yes, he used to do this with you, didn't he?' I said.

'Balloon man Dan's boat,' he yelled again, jumping up and down on my shoulders in exactly the same way he used to jump up and down in the buggy when he saw him. I turned to look out of the bedroom window we had just passed. A red and yellow harlequin boat was mooring up outside. A familiar-looking figure, his beanie hat pulled down over his ears, jumped down on to the banking, a coil of rope in his hands. The sense of wonder and delight spread up from my toes until it made every nerve in my body start to tingle.

I hammered on the window, unable to contain myself any longer. Alfie started hammering too. Dan turned and looked up, a huge grin spreading over his face as he caught sight of us, and waved.

'Come on,' I said, patting Alfie's legs, 'let's go and see him.' I lifted Alfie from my shoulders and hurried downstairs with him in my arms. Alfie banged on the kitchen door like he had the window as I grappled with the key. The second it was open, Alfie was digging me with his heels like a jockey urging his mount to go faster. We got to the towpath as Dan finished securing the second rope.

'Balloon man Dan home,' shouted Alfie. Dan stood up and strode towards us, his smile threatening to split his face in two. 'Big hug,' said Alfie Teletubby-style, as we collapsed into his arms.

We stood for a long time, our bodies pressed together, my hair blowing over all three of our faces, two of them soggy with tears, the third, the smallest one, beaming with unbridled glee.

'Wow, Alfie, you're looking great. And you've grown so much. Why, you're nearly as tall as me.'

Alfie's grin-o-meter went off the scale.

'Bob pants on,' he said, pointing at his crotch.

'Alfie's just started potty training,' I explained.

'Fantastic,' said Dan. 'I'll have to teach you how to make a Fireman Sam hose out of your willy.'

I laughed and put Alfie down for a moment, letting him cling to Dan's leg while I gave him a hug all of my own. With a mass of kisses thrown in.

'I expect you'd given up on me,' said Dan, stroking my face.

'Almost,' I said. 'Although I don't think Alfie had.'

'I just needed some more time,' he said.

'So why now?'

Dan stepped back and took my hand. 'Let me show you something,' he said. He led me down to the front of the boat. To where the name *Elizabeth* was scrolled in black paint. Except it wasn't there any more. There was a new name. *Jade.* I turned to frown at Dan, not understanding.

'I never had you down as a *Big Brother* fan,' I said.

Dan laughed. 'Think about our initials,' he said.

I read it again, out loud this time. 'Jo, Alfie, Dan.' I paused for a second. 'Is the E for Elizabeth?'

'No,' he said. 'It's for eternal. Because I'm finally putting my past behind me. To concentrate on my new family.'

'Thank you,' I said. 'I feel suitably honoured.'

'Good,' said Dan. 'It was cheaper to rename the boat than get a tattoo. And this way I get to keep my options open, of course. Should I ever meet J-Lo or some other hot woman whose name begins with J.'

I laughed, relieved we'd slipped back into the old banter.

'Oh, and you've both got an open invite for Sunday lunch at my gran's,' added Dan. 'She's desperate to meet Alfie.'

'Good,' I said. 'I'd like that. I was about to make lunch for us, actually. Are you staying?'

'It took me nearly four days to get here,' he said. 'Believe me, I'm not going anywhere for a long time.'

We started to walk back towards the house, Alfie holding a hand each.

'Oh, I nearly forgot,' Dan said. 'I've got you both a little present.' He ran back to the boat, disappeared inside and returned a few moments later with his hands behind his back. 'For you,' he said, handing a silver and purple balloon vacuum cleaner to a delighted Alfie. 'I figured the old one might need replacing. And for you,' he said, handing me a heart made out of red balloons. 'Because it's the only thing I have to give you.'

'Thank you,' I said with a smile. 'It's all I need.'

Acknowledgements

Warmest thanks to the following people: my fantastic editor Sherise Hobbs, for helping me to knock Jo and Dan into shape (and being very understanding about the whooping cough!); my previous editor Harriet Evans and all the team at Headline; my agent Anthony Goff for his expertise and support; everyone at David Higham Associates; Martyn Bedford of Literary Intelligence for yet another invaluable critique; Char, Liz, Terry, Katie, Bridget, Mandy and all the other members of the unofficial Hebden Bridge novel group for their helpful feedback; Anne, Leah and Peter for letting me snoop around on their canal boats; Winston for balloon-sculpting tips; Gill Hoyle of the Calderdale and Huddersfield NHS Foundation Trust, Marika Killilea and Al Day for their medical knowledge; Sue, for her insights into life as a single mum (and for doing such a great job of it); my friends and family for their ongoing support; my gorgeous son Rohan for asking me to do made-up stories all the time, haranguing people to 'buy Mummy's book' and for taking me to his Christmas party to meet the balloon man who gave me the original idea. And, most importantly, my long-suffering husband Ian, for putting up with everything that living with an author involves, for giving me the time and peace of mind to write by being such a great dad and for sometimes having to do his own made-up stories for Rohan (even if they do start badly, tail off a bit in the middle and the less said about the ending the better!).